Lady
MACBETH

Lady
MACBETH

A NOVEL

SUSAN FRASER KING

Crown Publishers New York

Copyright © 2008 by Susan Fraser King

All rights reserved.
Published in the United States by Crown Publishers, an imprint of the
Crown Publishing Group, a division of Random House, Inc., New York.
www.crownpublishing.com

CROWN is a trademark and the Crown colophon is a registered trademark of
Random House, Inc.

Library of Congress Cataloging-in-Publication Data
King, Susan.
Lady Macbeth : a novel / Susan Fraser King.—1st ed.
p. cm.
1. Gruoch, Queen, consort of Macbeth, King of Scotland—Fiction.
2. Macbeth, King of Scotland, 11th cent.—Fiction.
3. Queens—Scotland—Fiction.   I. Title.
PS3561.I4833L28   2008
813'.54—dc22   2007020757

ISBN 978-0-307-34174-7

Printed in the United States of America

Map by Richard L. Thompson

10 9 8 7 6 5 4 3 2 1

First Edition

Always for David

Machbet filius Finlach . . . et Gruoch filia Bodhe,

Rex et Regina Scotorum. . . .

(Macbeth son of Finlach . . . and Gruoch, daughter of Bodhe,

King and Queen of Scots. . . .)

—Cartularium of the Priory of Saint Andrews, 1049

ACKNOWLEDGMENTS

I AM DEEPLY grateful to many good friends for support, advice, and great patience, especially Julie Booth, Mary Jo Putney, Patricia Rice, Susan Scott, and Joanne Zaslow. Thanks are due also to Jeremy King (Shodan, Shorin Ryu), for staging the fights; Joshua King, M.D., for medical advice on battle wounds and poison control; Edward Furgol, Ph.D., for help in sorting out history and warfare; Dougie MacLean, for suggesting that Macbeth would just take a boat; and my family, including my husband, sons, Dad, Norma, and my sisters, for putting up with the M'beths for way too long.

Special thanks are due to Benjamin Hudson, Ph.D., for clarifying very complicated history, for suggesting a noble ending for a noble king, and for listening to my interpretations; thanks also are due my editor, Allison McCabe, for helping to shape a few bazillion words into a reasonable story; and my agent, Karen Solem, for belief, for patience, and for reminding me now and then to pull up my socks.

CELTIC SCOTLAND

11TH CENTURY

ORKNEY

CAITHNESS

SUTHERLAND

NORTH SEA

ROSS

Burghead

Dingwall •

Moray Firth

• Pitgaveny

Craig Phadraig • • Cawdor

Elgin

• • Inverness

MORAY

Loch Ness

• Crom Allt

BUCHAN

Lanfinnan •

Kincardine O'Neil •

SCOTLAND

Dunkeld •

• Glamis

BIRNAM WOOD

• Dunsinnan

ATHOLL

Scone •

Firth of Tay

Abernethy •

• St Andrews

FIFE

Loch Leven

Firth of Forth

Dun Edin •

LOTHIAN

• Berwick

• Carham

STRATHCLYDE

NORTHUMBERLAND

Durham •

IRELAND

CUMBRIA

ENGLAND

N

0   20   40

Scale of Miles

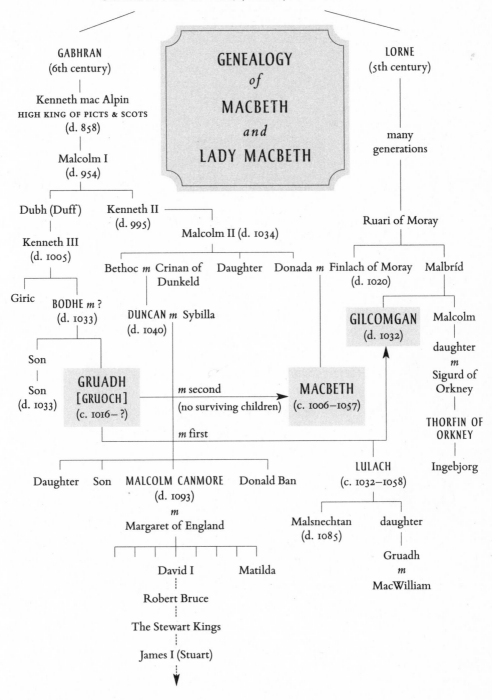

ERC OF DAL RIADA

GENERATIONS OF IRISH, PICTS, AND SCOTS

GENEALOGY
of
MACBETH
and
LADY MACBETH

GABHRAN
(6th century)

Kenneth mac Alpin
HIGH KING OF PICTS & SCOTS
(d. 858)

Malcolm I
(d. 954)

Dubh (Duff)   Kenneth II
(d. 995)

Kenneth III   Malcolm II (d. 1034)
(d. 1005)

Bethoc *m* Crinan of   Daughter   Donada *m* Finlach of Moray   Malbríd
Dunkeld   (d. 1020)

Giric   BODHE *m* ?
(d. 1033)

DUNCAN *m* Sybilla   GILCOMGAN   Malcolm
(d. 1040)   (d. 1032)
                                         daughter
                                         m
Son   Sigurd of
                                         Orkney

Son   GRUADH   *m* second   MACBETH
(d. 1033) [GRUOCH]   (no surviving children) (c. 1006–1057)   THORFIN OF
           (c. 1016– ?)   ORKNEY

                          m first   Ingebjorg

Daughter   Son   MALCOLM CANMORE   Donald Ban   LULACH
                 (d. 1093)   (c. 1032–1058)
                 m
                 Margaret of England   Malsnechtan   daughter
                                                   (d. 1085)

David I   Matilda   Gruadh
                                                            m
Robert Bruce   MacWilliam

The Stewart Kings

James I (Stuart)

LORNE
(5th century)

many
generations

Ruari of Moray

HISTORICAL NOTE

THIS NOVEL is based not on Shakespeare's brilliant drama about Macbeth and Lady Macbeth, but rather on the most accurate historical evidence available to date regarding the lives of these eleventh-century Scottish monarchs. The conclusions of historians and scholars have been interpreted through the filters of imagination and fiction. In particular, some recent scholarly theories regarding the warrior-king Macbeth and his elusive young queen have informed and inspired the story.

Prologue

S nowflakes dazzle against the evening sky and fall gentle around this stark tower. The false King of Scots expects us to trudge our ponies through that cold deep, so that I may tuck myself away in some Lowland monastery. Malcolm Canmore, he who murdered my husband and now calls himself king, would prefer I went even farther south into England, where they have priories just for women. There his allies would lock me away, as the Scots will not.

But my son is the true crowned king now. I am under the protection of his name, and the strength of my own. Had I agreed to marry Malcolm Canmore despite all, I would be honored now. Weeks ago, at the turn of the new year, he sent a messenger with a length of green silk, gold embroidered, and pots of spices and perfumes, with a request for my hand in marriage.

If power of that sort was what I craved, the gifts and request would have intrigued me. But I am a Celt and value honor more, and prefer Scottish wool to oriental silk. Coarse by comparison, our weavings have the honest strength and handsomeness of this land.

I wrote an answer with the very hand Malcolm wanted, though my Gaelic script is worse than my Latin. Only a few words were needed for a refusal. I sent the note and most of the gifts back, and kept the silk. My handmaid, Finella, likes it.

As for convents, I will send another message to the usurper Malcolm:

The Dowager Queen Gruadh, lately wife to King Macbeth whom you have slain, chooses to remain in her fortress.

A dare of sorts, and we shall see what he will do.

The winds howl—it is no wonder February is called the wolf month—and we sit, my companions and I, before the iron fire basket absorbing warmth and brightness. Dermot, my household bard, plays a melody on his harp. Shivering, I draw my cloak about my shoulders. Though I have lived scarce forty years and still burn with life, the chill riding the air this night is keen.

Servants draw curtains over shuttered windows that leak the cold, and then stoke the fire with peat and sweet applewood, branches saved from autumn. My little sons are gone to their peace—fair candles blown out too soon—and my husband is dead too. The endless evenings do need filling of late.

In shadows and firelight, two others sit with me listening to the harper's music, while surly Finella moves in and out of the room like a wraith. Bethoc, seated nearest me, is my cousin and the healing woman in my household; the monk Drostan sits apart from us, his shoulders hunched as he reads the pages of a small book. Both of them ran with me as youngsters. Given my temperament, perhaps only Celtic loyalty has kept them with me since.

Bethoc is a true friend, though at times she judges me harshly, and I her. The monk is one of the *Céli Dé,* or Culdees, those who allow priests to marry and Sabbath to be celebrated on Saturdays, among other rebellions that delight me. In much else, Rome has nagged the Scottish church to its knees.

Drostan, who has long known me, has a fine hand with a pen and hopes to write a chronicle about me. This would be an encomium, a book of praise, for his queen. I told him it was a silly notion.

Sparks fly and small flames leap. Truthfully, I am considering it.

I am granddaughter to a king and daughter to a prince, a wife twice over, a queen as well. I have fought with sword and bow, and struggled fierce to bear my babes into this world. I have loved deeply and hated deeply, too. I know embroidery and hawks and kingship, and more magic than I should admit. And I refuse to end my days in a convent. Now that is enough chronicle to suit me. Better to record the life of Mac bethad mac Finlach instead, the king who died near Lammas but six months past.

From what my advisors say, Malcolm Canmore—*ceann mór* in Gaelic, or big head, two words that suit him—will order his clerics to record Macbeth's life. Within those pages, they will seek to ruin his deeds and his name. My husband cannot fight for his reputation now. But I am here, and I know what is true.

An old woman, who crossed the threshold of life years ago, once peered into still water for a vision and told me that one day the world would immortalize me without understanding me. That will come after my lifetime. I do not care to be remembered, whether it is clear or sullied. Besides, if my life is not done, why memorialize it. I might yet choose a new husband; I could have children again, for my womb still ripens. I refuse to cross the threshold of age.

Perhaps I will take up my sword again, summon an army, and ride with my son to seek revenge, or weave a spell and undermine the usurper in some secret way. A few know my temperament and my wicked ways, my kindnesses, too: some do.

My memories are mine to keep. I fold my arms, satin and wool rustling, silver bracelets chiming. Bethoc looks up; Drostan, too. They exchange glances. When I need it, I can call bitterness around me like mail armor, every thought a knot of steel, shielding the tenderness I have learned to hide as daughter, mother, wife, and queen among warriors.

Snowflakes drift through a window, and a serving girl draws the shutters tight by reaching with a long stick. We will go nowhere for days. But the music sweetens the silence, and we have stocks of imported wine and spices, plenty of smoked meats and fish, and barrels of grain in the storerooms of this stout fortress. We have two Roman priests willing to save our backward Celtic souls with proper prayers, and among our warriors are a few Norman knights who came north to stand with Macbeth and remained as sword and shield.

We few in this room are a cluster of Celts gathered against a storm. The old Scotland fades into the new. I feel the threat blowing toward us like a great wind.

Some truths there are which must be said, and I wonder if I have that much courage in me.

I.

The generous king . . . will take sovereignty . . .
The red, tall, golden-haired one, he will be pleasant . . .
Scotland will be brimful west and east during the reign
of the furious red one . . .

—Eleventh-century *Prophecy of Berchán,* on Macbeth
(translated from Old Irish by Benjamin Hudson)

Chapter One

S carce nine the first time I was stolen away, I remember a wild and unthinking fright as I was snatched from my pony's back and dragged into the arms of one of the men who rode toward my father's escort party. We were heading north to watch our kinsman, King Malcolm, second of the name, hold an autumnal court on the moot hill at Scone. Proud of my shaggy garron and painted saddle, I insisted on riding alone in the length between my father, older brother Farquhar, and several of their retainers. Then horsemen emerged from a fringe of trees and came straight for us. As men shouted and horses reared, a warrior reached out and plucked me up like a poppet.

The memories of that day are vivid but disjointed. His furs smelled rancid and smoky; his whiskered chin was broad from my view beneath, trapped before him in the saddle; his fingers on the reins were grimy and powerful. I can recall the russet brown of his cloak, but I do not recall his name. I know it was never spoken in my hearing for years afterward.

Kicking, shrieking, twisting like an eel in the arms of that stranger, I managed to tear his dagger from his belt, slicing my thumb like a sausage. With no idea how to handle the thing, I meant to defend myself. A fierce urge insisted upon it.

He snatched the dagger back, but next I tore the large round brooch from his cloak, shredding the wool, and whipped it upward to jab it into his cheek. That slowed him. Swearing, he released me for an instant, and I lurched from the saddle, falling and breaking my arm in my thud to cold earth. Rolling by accident more than intent, I narrowly missed the forelegs of a horse as my kinsmen thundered past me.

Shouting then, and steel and iron clashed, and within minutes of yanking me from my pretty saddle, the man was dead, and two of his guard with him. My father and the others took them down with swift and ugly certainty.

Huddled beside the road on the frosted earth, I watched, arm aching, heart slamming, while men fought and died. Until then, I had never seen a skirmish, nor so much blood. I had heard steel ring against steel in the practice yard of our fortress in Fife, but I had never seen blade sink into flesh, nor heard the soft, surprised gasp as the soul abandons the body without warning. Since then, I have heard it too often.

I own that cloak pin still, good bronze and smooth jet, and I will never wear it. In the little casket with my jewels, its dusky gleam reminds me to stay strong and wary.

My brother, Farquhar, died of the wounds he took in my defense. I saw the angled sprawl of his body, though my father's men shielded me from the full sight. I remember, too, the taste of my salt tears, and my father's roar of grief echoing in the chill air.

Farquhar left a small son, Malcolm, and a pale wife with a grieving spirit, who soon returned to her Lowland family, leaving Malcolm to foster with Bodhe. My father found solace in the boy's presence, and he swore to discover who had plotted the attack that had nearly taken his daughter and had killed his son.

Through subtle inquiries, Bodhe learned that the men were sent by Crinan, the lay abbot of Dunkeld as well as mormaer—the Celtic equivalent to Saxon earl or Norse jarl—of Atholl. He was married to the king's eldest daughter. My father already loathed him as an arrogant fool, and now outright hated him. At the king's next judgment court, Bodhe accused Crinan of Atholl of plotting to abduct me to marry Crinan's son Duncan, a young warrior, and of cruelly killing Farquhar mac Bodhe. Denying all, Crinan claimed that Bodhe attacked his men without provocation, thereby inviting Farquhar's death himself.

The guilty party would have to pay *cro,* a customary penalty in recompense, a certain amount of livestock or other goods according to rank. While they awaited the king's decision, tensions were such that Bodhe and Crinan nearly came to blows, but for the king's housecarls who stood between them.

Justice stumbled on barren ground that day, for my father paid, as a prince, many cows each for Crinan's deceased men, some to their families and some to the king. Crinan basked in smug victory, keeping the fat coffers of his church at Dunkeld, and the continued favor of his royal father-in-law. The king, old Malcolm, showed no loyalty toward Bodhe and Farquhar, his own blood kin. My father never forgot it. Added to past offenses, the whole was fuel for fire.

Early on I learned why we despised Malcolm's faction of our kinsmen. Our kin group had endured the deaths of others, including Bodhe's father, King Kenneth, the third of the name. He had been murdered by then-young Malcolm, called the Destroyer, who took his cousin's throne.

My blood had even more merit once Bodhe had no other heir. Because I am descended in a direct line from Celtic kings, the purest royal blood courses through me and blushes my skin. I could prick a finger and it would be gold to some.

I am Gruadh inghean Bodhe mac Cineadh mhic Dubh—daughter of Bodhe son of Kenneth son of Duff. My grandfathers going back were kings of Scots, and I was born a princess of the house of Clan Gabhran that boasts Kenneth mac Alpin, the first king of Scots and Picts together. The line reaches back to the Picts who were native to this land, and the Scotti who came over from Ireland to settle as the Dalriadans in Argyll. We are proud of our heritage, and know the old names by heart: *son of, son of.*

My lineage combines the ancient royal branches of Scotland through my father, and through my mother, the proud line of the high kings of Ireland back to Niall of the Nine Hostages and beyond. Our old tree has many branches, some warring and some not, and divides along two main trunks, Clan Gabhran and Clan Lorne, descended from a single king, ages past.

Because a man could claim the throne of Scotland by marrying me, I was not safe. Nor were my kinsmen, come to that: if they were killed, one after another, our line would be eliminated at its heart, making room for others' ambitions. Such is the way of things when one's heritage is ancient, pure, and royal.

Little good did the blood of ancients do me. I was like a lark spiraling upward, unaware of the hawks above judging time and distance to the prize.

T HE SECOND time I was snatched off, I was walking the hills with my cousin Bethoc and Aella, my Saxon maidservant. I was a fortnight past thirteen, having been born in the last of July after the Feast of the Seven Sleepers. We were plucking wildflowers for Bethoc's mother, Mairi, a healer. She had sent us to search out club moss, yarrow, and heather—including the rare white sort if we found it—and we were dropping blossoms into the large basket that Aella lugged along. Finding club moss, we were careful to pick it with our right hands tucked through our left sleeves, so as not to taint the plant's healing power.

The summer sun was warm that day, and I was glad to be dressed simply in a tunic gown of lightweight blue-gray wool, a gauzy shift beneath, and plain leather shoes. Earlier my nurse, Maeve, had braided my hair out of the way into one fat plait, looping and securing it with a thong. Bethoc remarked that my hair's sheen, like bronze, looked like a fire beacon in sunlight, so that Maeve, who had kept close watch over me since my mother's death two years before, could see me from the walls of Abernethy, and be content in my whereabouts.

"Once I marry I will cover my head with a veil," I replied. "And Maeve will not be able to spot me when I go searching for heather and lavender."

"Those flowers, my mother says, will keep spies away," Bethoc said. "Maeve, too." We all laughed. My cousin Bethoc, daughter to my father's cousin and Fife born, knew our Celtic customs well. Aella was of Saxon birth, stolen away as a small girl and enslaved by the Irish, then rescued by Bodhe, who bought her in a Dublin market. She did not know Scottish traditions so well and was wary of them. But she knew the Saxon tongue and taught that to us, as we taught her the Gaelic.

Below the hills where we walked, men were busy far out in the golden spread of fields, taking in the hay; that morning, women had sained their cattle, putting a spell of protection around them with juniper smoke and tying fresh juniper to their tails. The Gaels have a *sian,* as is properly said, for every situation and every creature. No one had sained us that day as we went into the hills to search for blossoms among turf and rock.

Talking and laughing, not looking about as we should, we ran ahead and left my guard, Dugal, well behind. Bethoc, whose angelic fair-haired looks hid a talent for mischief, began a game of guessing how long it might take lazy, good-natured Dugal to catch up to us, following the torch of my hair in the sunlight.

Then men appeared over the rim of the hill. My constant guard was not with them. His head, however, was.

Bethoc screamed, Aella dropped the basket, and I stood transfixed in horror. Two more men surged out from behind a cluster of boulders and then we ran, but my friends were thrown roughly aside. One assailant grabbed me up while I dragged and struggled. Another took my feet, and we went over the hill with me slung between them like a whipping hammock.

Other men met us, all of them strangers to me. Someone bound me with ropes and swathed me in a blanket—a filthy thing, nipping with fleas—and put me on a horse to ride in front of a silent warrior. Over hours and near a day, I was moved from the horse to a cart that rumbled over rough terrain, and finally to a boat, gliding on lapping water. When the blanket was removed, night had descended, the air fresh and sea-damp. The men dipped oars over a distance through mist, and no one spoke to me. Among them I heard more Norse than Gaelic, and heard them speak of boats, oars, and the sea. Then I knew them for

Vikings: no Gael would name such things directly while on the water. I hoped the Norsemen would invite bad luck to themselves so that I could escape, but we reached shore safely.

Recalcitrant by nature, I refused to walk, but going limp earned me nothing. Thrown over a shoulder, I was carried. In all that time, I was not mistreated, but for being dragged about and frightened. They gave me a hard oatcake to eat and swallows of ale from a hide flask.

"I am a princess," I told them. "And Bodhe mac Kenneth mac Duff will come after you and kill you." Someone laughed.

We entered a long hall, larger even than my father's hall at Abernethy, though not near so fine. This compound was more like a farm than a fortress. The house had a sunken floor that ran the center length of the smoky, firelit room. Raised platforms along the walls to either side held benches where people sat eating and talking. Beds were fitted against the walls behind curtains, and in the shadows I saw men and women embracing in ways they might better have done in private. Other than guarded and curious glances, I was ignored by those present as my captors took me toward a far corner.

Someone tied my hands and feet with ropes and left me on a narrow bed behind a red curtain. Firelight spilled through the fabric, reddening all, including my temper. My bed niche was at the end of the room nearest the attached animal byre, and I heard the lowing of cows and the bleating of goats. Smelled them too, the odor leaking through cracks between the wall planking. My father's hillfort was a clean place, with a hall perched high on a center mound and separate buildings for animals, a byre for the cows, a stable for the horses, a smaller building for our hawks and falcons. We did not dwell with the beasts.

After a while, an elderly woman pushed aside the curtain to hold a wooden cup to my lips, grumbling something in Norse. I drank thirstily of some foamy dark ale, and then she went away.

Hands and feet tied, I lay on my back and kicked at the curtain and the wall, shouting and making noise deliberately. No one rushed to my aid. I whispered a charm for angelic protection: "*Mhiceil nam buadh, bi fein mi ro chul*"—Michael the victorious, be at my back. Finally I slept, curled and weepy, stirring only when the old woman returned.

She glared and grumbled as before, but brought food in clean wooden dishes. Freeing my hands and feet, she snarled a warning that was clear in any language, and left me a bucket in which to piss before yanking the red curtain shut.

The drink tasted of apples and spice, the porridge was soggy with onions, and I did not like the fish, wrapped in greasy parchment, but I ate a little. I glanced about in the reddish darkness of my enclosure wondering if I dared run while my limbs were free.

But the house was filled with Vikings, and I was not a fool. When the footsteps returned, I expected to see the old woman.

This time a man entered the sleeping space, long haired and bearded, broad and frightening in leather and furs. I backed into a corner as he sat on the straw-filled mattress and reached toward me. He smelled strongly of ale and wood smoke, and he smiled and touched my cheek gently. I stared at his braided brown hair, as fine and glossy as a girl's, his ruddy beard plaited into tips. Then he traced his fingers down over my chest. Horrified, I bucked like a colt. He grabbed my arm, and at the same time, fumbled under his tunic.

Though I tried to yank my arm back, he threw himself on me. His hands shoved at my garments, dragging them upward, terrifying me. The texture of sound beyond the curtain—voices, laughter, music— was loud. I shrieked but no one came to my aid, and my cries were muffled by the big man's shoulder smothering my face as I struggled against his hands. He was more concerned with his male member than his knife, for my fingers encountered the dagger hilt undeterred. I thrust the blade upward; aided by his own weight, the point sank through wool and flesh and took the breath out of him like the hiss of a kettle.

We rolled from the bed, knocking into the curtain, which was quickly ripped aside as others came toward us. Someone snatched me up and tossed me back onto the bed, and others pulled the man's tunic down and slid the knife out of him while he shrieked. Heart hammering, I scrambled backward into a corner. My assailant, his florid face gone pale, swore at me in Norse. He stood and made as if to cuff me, but lacking the strength, limped away with his comrades.

One man stood watching me. He was tall and lean, his long hair black, his eyes startlingly dark, like someone of Pictish descent. He had the crag-faced look of a vulture, or of the wizards I had heard about in stories, often described as black haired, ominous, and disagreeable in appearance. Judging by the company he kept and his style of dress, he was Viking, for he wore the long trousers and tunic in Norse style, with a red cloak fastened at the left shoulder by a silver brooch with twisted dragon heads in the design.

"What do you want?" I asked sullenly. "Why am I here?"

"Greetings, Bodhe's daughter. I am Thorfin Sigurdsson," he said in capable Gaelic, though moments ago he had spoken to the others in fast, fluent Norse. "We must talk later, you and I."

"My father will kill you first," I said.

"I think not." His dark eyes were frightening, and I resisted an urge to scuttle backward. "He and I will talk as well, when it suits me to do so."

I knew his name, though I had never met him until now. Thorfin Sigurdsson was a grandson of the Norwegian king, and his maternal grandfather was the great steward of Moray, the largest region in Scotland, its powerful mormaers near kings, though subject to Scotland's kings. This Thorfin was jarl of the Orkney Islands as well as Caithness, on our northern mainland. From the talk around my father's fireside, I knew he was both clever and brutal.

"If the grandson of kings will not defend a princess in his care," I said, "then he should go away and leave her to take care of herself." Alarmed by my own boldness, I yanked the blanket over my head. When I took it down, Thorfin was gone.

Soon the curtain opened again, and a young man entered, with Danegeld hair, pale gold, and water blue eyes. He reached out for me. This time I lurched off the mattress in fear, and felt my stomach turn inside out. Falling to my knees, I retched into the bucket.

"I will not harm you," he said, while I wiped my mouth in embarrassment. "My name is Ketill Brusisson. Thorfin Sigurdsson sent me to guard you." He, too, spoke good Gaelic with a trace of Norse accent.

Jarl Thorfin was his uncle, so my guard said. "Raven-Feeder, they call him, for his warrior skills," Ketill added proudly.

"That name does not augur well for my fate," I said.

He laughed, thinking it a jest.

The man whose lung I had punctured was called Harald Silkhair, Ketill said. A housecarl, or elite warrior, of the Orkney jarl, Harald was no brute, Ketill insisted, just a mead-drunk, grieving widower, and therefore not himself. The temptation of getting a son by a princess of the house of Alpin and Gabhran had apparently overwhelmed him.

"The Raven-Feeder will deal with Harald," Ketill told me. "Norse laws are strict regarding unmarried girls of high status. Abduction for marriage is one thing, drunken assault another."

I assured Ketill that my father would handle the matter succinctly once he arrived.

Ketill went on to explain that his uncle was a man of power and consequence, both among the Norse and on our own mainland. Thorfin had sent men to take me after Bodhe refused to grant me to him in marriage.

"A lesson and bargaining are in order," Ketill told me, "or Thorfin could just marry you and be done with it."

"If Thorfin thinks marriage to me will gain him the throne by virtue of my blood, he is wrong," I said haughtily. "No Viking could ever become King of Scots. Celtic warriors would never allow a Norseman to rule over them."

My guard shrugged. "Thorfin's father, Sigurd, once defeated the Scottish mormaer of Moray with only the protection of his raven banner, which they say has magical powers. Thorfin inherited his father's yellow banner and its spellcraft. He could win a war with that if he wants."

I wondered that Ketill could believe a bit of cloth could do that. "I am glad Bodhe refused Thorfin," I replied, "and I will remind your jarl of it when he comes back."

"You will see him next when you are escorted by boat over to Orkney."

I lifted my chin. "Thorfin should have better manners than to steal a princess, abandon her to danger, and force her to marry. His men ought to know better, too. But warriors descended from Vikings cannot help their bestial ways."

Ketill did not speak to me after that insult. He sat on the edge of my bed, hand on dagger hilt, and watched the company through a gap in the red curtain. After a while I lay back, exhausted, and slept.

Just before dawn, my father and other men of the kingdom of Fife entered that compound and put it to fire and sword, razing the place to the ground. I was pulled into Bodhe's arms, held safe against him, and within minutes we were riding away in the darkness. In the chaos of the fight, I did not see Ketill Brusisson again, and I could not tell if his body was one of those that lay on the earth behind our departing party.

FOLLOWING THE deaths of my brother and mother, Bodhe must have thought more closely about souls and their fates, and perhaps about my education, for he had invited an Anglo-Saxon priest to join our household. After my second abduction and bloody rescue, Father Anselm began to call me not the Princess Gruadh, but simply Hreowe, which sounded in his language a little like "rue" and meant "sorrow." That Saxon priest never could manage my given name, pronounced *Groo-ath*. His tongue was shaped not for the grace of the Gaelic, but for the clumsy sounds of the Sassenach language and the Latin he spouted daily. There was eloquence and truth in his name for me, though I did not want to admit it. And so I came to be known as Rue of the Sorrows.

After the second abduction, my father assured me that I need not fear any further attempts. As soon he could arrange it, I would be married off to a man of his choosing, for he sought both a protector for me and an unbreakable alliance for our Fife lineage.

One by one over the next year, I met his choices among the chieftains and lords of Scotland: mature, tough warriors all, most of them widowers with children, several with battle scars, few with a complete set of teeth. "Of course there are younger men to consider," Bodhe replied when I asked, "but some are married already. The rest cannot properly defend you and protect this heritage of ours."

While my father searched, I became determined never to be stolen away again, nor to cost the lives of others as the price of my defense. Not yet a woman, I had already wounded two men by my own hand, and had caused the deaths of good warriors, including my brother and my personal guard. So I set about to find a means to ensure my own safety.

Chapter Two

I found my father in the place where he kept his hawks, a sturdy
enclosed byre fitted with latticed windows and curtains to keep the
wind off the birds at night. That trapped the smells, too, and as I
entered I yanked the nearest curtain aside to let in more light and air.
My father's newest red-tailed hawk, perched on Bodhe's gloved fist,
jerked at my entrance. Soothing the bird's ruffled breast with a finger,
my father sent me a stern glance.

"Quiet, Rue," he said. "You know the birds startle easily. What is it?"

"I want to learn to fight." I planted myself before him, arms
folded and legs apart as if I were a tough-hearted boy instead of a girl
of fourteen.

He said nothing for a moment, stroking the bird's crop. "What sort
of fighting?" he asked in the calm tone he reserved for his birds.

"Blades," I said. "Bow and arrows, too, and hand combat. Whatever you will teach me."

A quick, sharp glance. "A princess of Scotland has no need of such
skills."

"Scathach was also a princess," I pointed out. "Scathach of the old
legends, who had a school for fighting on the Isle of Skye and taught
the heroes of the Fianna their skills—"

"I know the tale," he said curtly. "Those were older days. It is not your place to fight, but ours to defend you, if need be." He set the bird on a wooden perch.

"Had I known defense when the Vikings took me, many men might be alive today—and you would not have such enemies in Thorfin and his Orkney men."

"Even with skills, you could not stop several men determined to take you." He hooded the hawk. "Thorfin and I will come to truce again, as we have done before. Rue, your mother taught you needle arts and household managing, and the priest schools you in letters and prayers. One day you will be wife to a powerful lord, perhaps become a queen. Let that be enough. Leave swording to your kinsmen."

"If I cannot use weaponry," I persisted, "I will have to use the spellcrafts my mother taught me."

That was bold. My father's glance was keen. We rarely spoke much of my mother and never of her secret gifts, passed down through generations.

"Leave it," he repeated. "You will do well to serve your most important role as the only female in Scotland directly descended from Kenneth mac Alpin. You carry the blood of the Picts and the Irish high kings."

"Warriors all. I would be worthy."

"Your worth is already unique. Only you can make a future husband into a king by virtue of your hand in marriage, should that man ever bid for the throne."

"And so I should be strong, just as my mother told me before she died."

Bodhe looked away. The hawks and kestrels nearby fluttered and cheeped, their sensitive natures alert to any subtle change in air or mood about them, even when hooded.

"You are too young for some of the lessons you have had," my father murmured.

"I want swording lessons," I pleaded. "Otherwise, more men might be slain for my sake, like my guard, or my brother—"

"We will not speak of your brother!" Bodhe, big and gruff, with black hair beginning to silver, glowered. "And it is foolish to think that a blade in your hand could avert a war."

I nodded, silenced. My father still nursed anger and grief over the death of his only son, who had been a candidate for kingship by the old Celtic practice of alternating succession. Men would always fight dear over such rights. Disputes and violent solutions were part and parcel of our world.

The hawks stirred, fluttered, settled.

"I am your direct heir now," I reminded Bodhe. "I must be prepared, since you say I could be a queen one day, and my husband a king. So men will always argue over me, and more deaths will occur on my account." I drew breath. "If you will not teach me to fight, I will ask Fergus mac Donal, or Cormac, or Magnus, or Ruari . . ." I named warriors in my father's household.

Bodhe reached out and took up another bird, Sorcha, a small kestrel with a bent wing that never rested flat against her. She did not fly far, our Sorcha. My father stroked her breast. I realized he did not want me to fly far, either. Not yet. "You have a warrior spirit," he admitted, "for a gently raised daughter."

"Scathach of Skye," I reminded. "No one would have stolen her away."

He nodded once, just that. "Tomorrow, after morning prayers, go to the lower bailey where the men practice. I will tell Fergus to meet you."

Aɪʟꜱᴀ ᴏꜰ Argyll, my mother, daughter to a mormaer in a western Highland kingdom, was a wise woman by virtue of the teachings of her Irish mother and grandmother. Before she died the year I turned eleven, she taught me something of what she knew, whetting my appetite for more. She was still in her thirties when she passed into the next world, defeated in the birthing of her last child. Had she stayed with us longer, I might have learned to hold my temper and foster wisdom; might have been less impulsive and more gracious, with a finer hand for herbs and spells.

Ailsa carried about her the scents of heather and mountain air and the herbs with which she worked, her fingers green smelling at times, her skirts sometimes scattered with flower petals and small leaves. I would sit near her while she embroidered or played at her harp, and pick the small stems and bits caught in the weave of her apron. She favored greens and blues in her gowns; though green is said to be an unlucky color for women, it reflected the hue in her eyes. Under a veil, she wore her glorious hair in two long braids, and I loved to watch her loosen the bright russet plaits at night, her ivory comb turning it to spun silk.

My sister was a squalling scrap of a creature on the day she was born, black haired like our father and far too small. She lived for five days, long enough to outlive our mother by hours, long enough to weave her way into my heart. I held the baby and walked the floor with her while the women tended to Ailsa. My mother faded to pale silence, glistening with the fever sweat. Her eyes burned bright as green glass, her very soul rising there, for she was already turning to spirit. Years later, her voice still sounds in my dreams with her last words to me: *Be strong, my dear one, for what will come.*

Our priest baptized the child to protect her soul, and the midwives bathed her in warm milk and lifted her in their hands as they spoke charms against all manner of ills: fire, drowning, illness and injury, fairies, bewitchings, elf bolts, all conceivable harms. Bodhe named his new daughter Brigid to further protect her. Yet within days, Ailsa and tiny Brigid were buried together on a hill overlooking the sea, and I, who heard equally the catechism and Celtic tales, wondered if their souls would travel to heaven or Tír na n'Óg, the paradise beyond Ireland in the misty realm, which our bard spoke about.

The evening before the burial, my aunt Eva, who was married to an Irish king but had come to Fife to be at her sister's side, took me in her arms and let me weep against her shoulder.

"Now dry your tears and go to your mother," my aunt said, "and bring her the gifts she will need in her new life." She held out a small linen bag. "We will never say that your mother and sister are dead," she went on, "for they have only changed their form. Ailsa now takes her child with her on her journey. Such the Celts believe, and let it comfort you." Then she taught me a chant for the protection of the newly wandering soul.

We were standing in a corner of the great hall at the time. Father Anselm, our Anglo-Saxon priest, walked past. His hair, ringed around his tonsure, was thick and black and he was vain about it. His nose was sharp, his face was lined, and he had long ears that heard all. "Ailsa of Argyll is dead," he said bluntly, stopping, "and her soul needs our prayers, not trinkets, so that she may be forgiven by grace of God. Perhaps she need spend only a little time in purgatory before her soul is purified of sin."

"My mother will go straight to heaven on the strength of her character," I said. "Though she might prefer Tír na n'Óg, where she would not be judged." Even my aunt, who disliked priests, gasped at that.

Anselm narrowed his eyes. "She practiced pagan arts and taught her daughter that same insolence against God. You, lady"—he nodded to my aunt—"only encourage harmful beliefs in your niece. Take better care of her soul, and your own."

My aunt, a visitor and no authority in our household, said nothing. She only grabbed my hand and hurried me from the room. We passed Bodhe, seated silently by the fire, turned to stone by grief.

"That priest would make all Gaels into Sassenachs to save our souls, as if we are an ignorant people," Eva hissed. "But a princess of an ancient Celtic line has an absolute duty to honor the old traditions. Here," and she gave me the linen bag. Inside was my mother's spindle wrapped in the last thread she had spun, and steel needles from the Orient, stuck in a bit of half-embroidered cloth. A few brass strings from the harp she had played so sweetly were curled there too, tucked beside her ivory comb and two bracelets of braided silver. Tears rose in my eyes to see these familiar things.

Three natural crystals fell into my palm, and I tipped them back into the bag. The personal items would remind Ailsa's spirit of its time on earth, and the crystals would help her soul find its way home to heaven. Crystals are like tiny bits of heaven caught in the matter of the earth, and thus are guiding stars.

"This is for the child." Eva handed me a tiny straw doll bound with red thread. Meant to bring her luck as well as joy, it had a crystal tied around the neck.

Later, when at last I summoned the courage, and after the priest had recited the Office of the Dead, I went into the room where my mother lay on a cloth-draped bier. She seemed only asleep, her face beautiful, the skin drawn smooth over her bones. Finespun silk shrouded her, and coins rested upon her eyes. Her long-fingered hands, always so busy, were still and folded. The small bundle of her newborn lay tucked over her heart under the translucency that turned them both to ghostly, graceful forms.

I whispered part of the old chant that my aunt had taught me:

> *Tha mi sgith is mir air m'aineol*
> *Treoraich mi do thir nan aingheal*
> I am weary and I a stranger
> Lead me to the land of angels . . .

I left the bag beside their bodies, kissed my mother's hand, and sat near Bodhe, who kept a vigil there.

Though my mother had told me to be strong, after a while I let the tears slip down in silence. The dead can possess a peace that the living cannot always find, for we are left with our grief while they slip onward to paradise. Yet I found peace, that evening, in my mother's presence. It surrounded her like the light from the beeswax candles that encircled her bier.

EVEN BEFORE I spoke and walked unaided, I was a temperamental child, given to willfulness, so I was told, capable of outlasting most anyone in my insistence. Some might say that has not changed much. Then as now, I felt soothed by music, for my mother lullabied me with melodies on her harp, and with the old singsong charms of the Gaels and the Picts, whom the Irish called the Cruithne and the Romans called the Picti, or Picts, for their decorated bodies.

I carry a decoration myself, a symbol of blessing that my mother marked upon my skin when I was small. Time has faded it, but it will never wear off my shoulder completely, for Ailsa applied it with needles dipped in copper salts and woad to produce a dark blue-green. A barbaric custom in some eyes, pagan markings were banned by the Church three centuries before my lifetime. Celtic people are proud, poetic, and inherently stubborn; such signs are not uncommon even now, though rarely revealed.

A simple thing and beautiful, the three-spiral cluster I wear is the *triskele,* the symbol of Brigid, the ancient Celtic goddess of conception, childbirth, smithing, and creative endeavors, whom we must call Saint Bridget if we speak of her around priests. The triskele, whose three swirls represent the joyful spinning of the spirit as it creates art, craft, and life, has protective power.

The design on my shoulder is hidden beneath my shift and never seen unless I allow it. Now and then I mix the elements in a little copper dish until the color is just so, and rework the design into my skin using a needle and color-soaked thread. For a day or so after the application I am slightly ill, for there is a trace of poison in the necessary blend. When I feel the need for additional strength, I draw the sign in earth, water, frost, or air: three spirals, just so. The eloquent design holds blessings near, while keeping harm at bay.

Chapter Three

The clash of steel and iron or the thud of hardwood meeting in fierce blows, emanating from the practice yard, was a constant thread in the fabric of sound that encompassed our hillfort. Days at Abernethy were often bee busy, with Bodhe's men practicing at arms in the lower bailey, while farmers and locals, messengers, and warriors came and went on foot or horseback. Servants moved between keep, yards, and outbuildings tending to chores and errands; children ran, played, were scolded; chickens and geese wandered oblivious, dogs chased about, cats leaped and vanished. The goats did as they pleased, chewing through their gate at will.

Inside the keep, Dolina and her women supervised the household, stitched seams, chatted, and often went out for charitable visits, walking the hills looking for herbs, sometimes riding and hawking with the men. Outside, natural sounds added to the constant texture—the burble of water, the sweep of wind or rain, the sparkle of birdcalls. Bells rang from the high church tower in the glen, dividing the days. In the evenings, quiet enveloped Dun Abernethy. With each sunrise, the whirlabout of life began again.

At first, whenever I came to the practice yard, the men would ignore me, while the youths dispersed. They did not want to spar with a girl, especially their chief's daughter. Sessions spent awkwardly knocking wooden blades with Fergus mac Donal, a blacksmith and former retainer to my father, taught me basic moves and stances. I flinched and retreated from the oncoming blade so often that Fergus threatened to banish me from the yard for my own safety and his peace of mind.

His four sons—two older and two younger than I—tried to avoid me too, but their father would not have it; someone must practice with the girl, he told them. The sons of Fergus sent any willing substitutes, even my nephew. Eight years old and smitten with fighting and weaponry, Malcolm was like a clumsy puppy, but I had too much pride to spar with a child. Drostan mac Colum, another fostered son in my father's household and closest to my age, was my most constant friend. Each day after our lessons with Father Anselm, which Drostan enjoyed more than I did, he came to the lower bailey to spar with me. I suspect Fergus terrified him into it.

Side by side or facing off, Drostan and I learned how to hold the hilts of our wooden wasters with one hand or with two, how to lunge forward and sweep the blade down from overhead, how to thrust forward and up, knocking the breath—or the entrails, had the blades been real—from an opponent.

Fergus had helpers and apprentices in his forge, where weapons were repaired, shoes and harnesses made for horses, and implements made for farm and kitchen. One of them was Bodhe's other fostered son, Finn mac Nevin, a few years older than I. He sometimes came to the smithy door when I walked past on my way to the practice yard. Tall enough to bow his head under most lintels, he had the black hair and pink-stained cheeks that showed his Irish ancestry. His late father, I knew, had entrusted his son to Bodhe as fosterling and future warrior.

"She'll need no helmet with hair that thick," Finn said as I went by one morning, lugging my wooden sword and carrying a leather helmet and hauberk.

Redheaded Angus, one of the more annoying sons of Fergus, snorted agreement. "No headgear would fit her, true, nor would she be able to stand up if she wore an iron helm and a full coat of mail, with a steel sword in her hand. Fighting requires strength for more than just sword wielding."

"There are reasons females do not wear armor or carry weapons into battle." This from Ruari, the oldest mac Fergus. A warrior newly admitted to my father's household guard and proud of it, he generally ignored me.

Angus and Finn chuckled, while I glared at each of them and marched past. I deemed it wasted breath to explain about Scathach of Skye to them.

The training area was located on the northwest side of the lower bailey, where men practicing with weapons were within shouting distance of the western entrance to the compound. Dun Abernethy was a hillfort of good size, a double-ringed mound two hundred feet high, twice that across its long oval top. The base of the hill was surrounded by a high wooden palisade pierced by a gate that opened into the lower bailey, which held practice yards, an exercise ring for the horses, stables, smithy, a joinery, a granary, and byres for a few cattle and two oxen. Other outbuildings included a small metalworker's shop, where Fergus's wife and her brother crafted horse fittings, buckles, small necessary items, and some fine pieces of jewelry in silver, bronze, even gold when they had the metals to hand.

A long flight of wooden steps, precarious in places, led from the lower bailey and mound to the upper one, where a second barricade surrounded the high mound with its keep. Sections of the steps were suspended like bridges over ditches that ringed the whole, with removable ramps in case of attack. No enemy ever breached our fortress in my father's day, though a servant boy running on a cold, rainy night fell off one of the bridges and died in the rocky ditch below. I was very young at the time, and insisted on creeping on hands and knees on the ramps until Fergus took me by the hand to show me it was safe. Like any manned and stout fortress, Dun Abernethy had its hazards, and the possibility of attack fosters either a sense of fear or security in its residents.

Our keep was a tall wooden tower on a stone foundation, with turning stairs and several rooms. The ground level housed a garrison and storage rooms, and the upper floors contained the great hall and bedchambers fitted like boxes, small on large. My own little bedchamber was claimed from space within a thick outer wall. The keep windows had hinged shutters and glazing made from hides scraped thin and oiled to admit a glow of light. Among the outbuildings, those that held fire—two kitchens and a bakehouse—were set apart. We also had a brewery, a dairy for making butter and cheese, the falcon mews, coops for chickens and doves, a byre for our milch cows, and pens for the goats; we kept no pigs, which were disdained as a food source. Finally, we had modest housing for guests, servants, and the rest of my father's guard, a separate bathhouse, and four privies, two inside the keep and two more tucked at the back of the palisade, each with discreet drainage that emptied into a sluice at the back of the hillside.

ONLY FINN waited in the lower yard to act as my opponent one day. He thrust a long, thick wooden staff at me, which I took out of surprise more than willingness.

"I am here to learn swording." I glanced about for Fergus with the wasters, the wooden practice swords.

"You must learn other weapons too, in order to handle a sword competently. You will need to practice dancing steps as well. Fergus said I am to work with you."

"Fergus already showed me the dances." The stick was awkwardly long, and I felt rough slivers under the skin on my fingers. Lifting my free arm, I spread my fingers in the air as if I was a deer running from the hunter, for the dances originated in hunting and fighting, and I bounced from foot to foot. "I am also learning to dance over a shield, and Fergus taught me the *Ghille Chaluim*—the old dance over crossed swords to celebrate victory over an enemy." I leaped sideways, then front and back, shook my raised foot gracefully, light on my feet and grinning.

Finn scowled. "If you leaped crossed swords gory with your enemy's innards, you would not be jumping about like one of the *daoine sìth*, the fairy ilk. Dancing is a serious skill that can save lives on the battlefield. We must move quick and clever to avoid blows and strike well."

I made a jest of spinning about, then brandished the staff. "Come on, then."

Somber and serious, he tilted his wooden staff in both hands. "Hold your weapon like this, and place your feet just so."

I did, and when he came at me, I retreated quickly, tripping on my skirt. His arms and torso were heavily muscled: at eighteen, he was a big lad. I was tall for a girl, but slight and still growing, and uncertain in stance and strike. We went at it again, and my stick smacked him across the knuckles and flew clumsily from my hands, knocking him a quick black eye. A look like a bear crossed his face. I gasped, remorseful, but waited, aware that warriors do not coddle each other.

Finn tossed my stick to me and resumed the lesson. "If your opponent is on foot holding another staff, keep your hands well apart on the stick and strike forward with the heart of the wood," he said, demonstrating. "If he sits a horse, tilt one end of your pole and weave it between the animal's legs to trip it up and unseat the rider. When a horseman has a bladed weapon, sweep the pole at the front to cut down the horse."

"But I do not want to hurt a horse."

"What if it carried Thorfin or Harald Silkhair coming straight for you?"

I struck, swinging madly. Finn arched back to avoid me. We continued, and the blacksmith's apprentice proved a patient teacher. By the time the long, intense lesson was finished, I was coated in dust and sweat, but more adept with the staff.

Day and night I practiced with waster, staff, and shield, with footing and thrust and downsweep. I worked with whoever would face me, even Dull Andra, one of our grooms, whom I could usually coax to anything. Strong as an ox, he always let me win. Soon I smacked my wooden waster with swiftness and confidence against those wielded by the sons of Fergus. Their return blows jarred my wrists and arms, but only Aella and my nurse, Maeve, knew that at night I ached so that hot baths and a good rubbing with a pungent ointment of bog myrtle and lavender were needed. Maeve knew something of healing, and Aella very little, and more than once my cousin Mairi was fetched, bringing her little bag of simples, ointments, and herbs to treat my various knocks and bruises.

The months grew to a year, and soon I was quick and agile enough with weaponry and sparring that Fergus let me leave wasters—both wooden swords and daggers—for battered, blunt-edged swords and round targe shields pocked with use. Neither Fergus nor his sons trusted me with good steel or iron. Drostan teased me by saying that they remembered poor Harald's fate and did not want to share it.

As the only daughter and heiress of the lord, I had many duties, both domestic and scholarly. Dolina, my father's mistress, was adept in household crafts and concerns, and she supervised me in tasks like the making of cheese, beer, new wine, as well as tallow and beeswax candles. Often she sent me to assist like any servant, or took me to the storage rooms to assess supplies. I trailed after her at market fairs, where she frugally bargained and purchased necessities not produced at Abernethy, while I yearned for small luxuries.

Several hours each week, Drostan and I were obliged to sit with Father Anselm for reading, letters, languages, numbers, and history. I did not mind, except when Anselm went on about the greatness of the Saxons; he regarded Scots as half-wits in need of guidance. Drostan was a serious pupil, devouring whatever we were taught, while I was quick-witted but impatient, as in most things. Anselm regularly protested to Bodhe that girls did not merit so much education, but my father replied that it was Scottish custom to educate freely, including females, and prevailed.

Often I watched from the yard or a window as Bodhe and his men, including his fostered sons, rode away from the fortress. They left to patrol the perimeters of Bodhe's lands in Fife, sometimes dealing with raiders, bands of cattle thieves, or renegade Vikings who swept in along Fife's coastland. Bodhe was a powerful mormaer who held his lands with a keen sword and force of will. Few dared cross him.

Sometimes my father appeared in the practice yard, arms folded, to watch me in my sessions. Though he said little, neither criticism nor praise, one day he smiled.

"Perhaps we should call you Rue of the Sword, eh?" he teased.

On the fifteenth anniversary of my birth, he gave me the fine sword that is still in my keeping, its blade engraved with Brigid's triskele, the triple spiral.

That gift told me much.

FINN WAS the first to kiss me, one day when we were sweaty and dusted after a hard hour of training—axe and shield, that day, it was. I followed him to the smithy when he went to repair the blade of my axe, which I had split in my enthusiasm, hitting wild into a rock instead of the wooden teaching post used for the chopping strokes. I stood close to watch as he handled the steel blade, which he had crafted himself.

His hands fascinated me—deft and nicely shaped, moving with sure and wonderful skill. I watched as he heated the blade to glowing and hammered it back to evenness, then slid the heated tong into a new wooden handle to bind the whole together with leather. And I wondered, suddenly, what those hands might feel like upon my body.

He set the blade aside to cool, and I realized he had similar thoughts, for when I glanced up he was watching me, eyes dipping to my breasts and back up, which felt to me like an invitation. Though I did not know quite what to do, I was willing and curious. Possibly I kissed him first. It would not have been outside my nature. Whoever moved first, the other understood; lips touched, hands found. Breathless and silent, we tugged at clothing and found a dark corner in which to lean, and while the smithy forge crackled, we quickly added to the heat in that snug stone house. We met in secret a few times more, as if a lodestone drew us together, and though I urged in my eagerness, he held back. Both of us knew that marriage between me and a foster brother, even one unrelated by blood and descended from great warriors, would be all but impossible.

Still, we learned each other delicious lessons.

Then one day Finn said we must not, we must never, and he grew cool toward me. Perhaps Fergus had approached him, or even Bodhe, but likely he realized our risk himself. We continued sword and staff lessons, and while I nursed my thundery heart and watched him with eyes like a moon calf, he remained distant and polite. He broke my heart, the first to do that, and while I remembered it for a long time, I think he quickly forgot.

Chapter Four

On a March morning, when the damp air promised rain and spring, my life turned and changed. "Rue!" Drostan came toward me. "Fergus said you are to muck out the stalls today. He sent me to find you, before he and some others rode out with your father."

"Where did they go?"

"Probably hunting. Bodhe had hawk and hounds to him, and others carried bows and spears. Come on, then. I will help you in the stable."

We walked down the hill, Drostan and I, of a height and in step. Taking up a rake that leaned by the stable door, I entered the coolness of the building, while Drostan snatched up a hoe. Mucking more earnestly than competently, we made some progress. I was glad to be wearing an old dun-colored tunic and leather cuarans on my feet. Raking out the stalls was preferable, I thought, to sitting sedately in the hall embroidering hems, listening to my father's mistress and her maidservant gossip about people they knew and I did not.

The sky was clouding over by the time the riders returned. Hearing shouts and the creak of the wooden gates, Drostan and I ran out of the stable to see Bodhe and the others riding inside. The men had been hunting, I saw immediately—two red deer, on the thin side after a long winter, were slumped over the back of a riderless horse, and a brace of hares hung from Bodhe's saddle. My father saw me, frowned without greeting, handed his hawk to a groom, and dismounted. As his comrades dismounted around him, I noticed that Finn, Ruari, and Fergus did not glance toward me, and I sensed an odd tension. Then I saw that several strangers had returned with our men.

Nine or a dozen of them were housecarls, helmeted and silent as they dismounted and stood aside. The six largest men were fearsome, looking like a Viking war band. The other strangers appeared to be noble Scotsmen in their prime, with fine gear and proud bearing. Two banners flapped on upright spear shafts, one blue and scattered with silver stars, the other yellow with a design of a black raven. I knew the raven symbol was favored by the Orkney Vikings.

One man wore a leather hauberk and a brass-trimmed helmet, and when he lifted it away to reveal his black hair, my heart seemed to drop into my stomach.

"Raven-Feeder," I muttered.

Drostan nodded in silence.

Bodhe spoke with his guests, all of whom wore mail coifs and hauberks over tunics and trews. Clearly I could not come forward as my father's daughter to extend a courteous welcome—not with a mucking rake in my hand, and fouled shoes. No wonder Bodhe had frowned at me. I leaned toward Drostan. "Who are those men? Besides Jarl Thorfin."

"The tall golden one, I do not know. The shortest one is the mormaer of Moray, Gilcomgan mac Malbríd. His man carries the blue banner with silver stars." Drostan generally knew such things, for he paid avid attention to any talk between my father and his warriors. "The leaders of Moray are more like kings than mormaers, and those stars have been their insigne since ancient times. The Picts of Moray painted themselves all over with blue stars and moons and suchlike before they went to war."

"Is Moray the one who was fined with his brother in punishment for their uncle's death several years ago?"

"He is. The brother is dead now, and Gilcomgan claimed leadership over his younger cousin Macbeth, whose father they had killed. The dispute continues to this day, so I heard. Thorfin of Orkney did not bring a war band, just a few housecarls. I wonder why he is here—he rarely sets foot on this part of the mainland, though he has kin among the Moray lords."

My hand tightened on the rake. "Why is Bodhe hosting all these men?" Drostan shrugged. We watched as Bodhe escorted the men up to the keep. "I hope my father does not think to wed me to one of *them*," I said.

"Not the Raven-Feeder, for certain," Drostan said. "Your father may truce with him, but would never give you to him. A Viking alliance might be useful, but such a marriage could help them gain a foothold in Scotland."

Fat droplets of rain fell as we returned to the stalls to resume our work. Soon Aella came running with the message that Bodhe wanted me to appear in the great hall, clean and presentable. I ignored her, raking up another patch of filthy straw, dragging it outside to add to the pile that Dull Andra was now loading into a wheelbarrow to haul away to the outfields.

Aella repeated her message. I remained at my task, unwilling to meet the men Bodhe had invited. She shrugged and left the stable, and Drostan set aside his rake and headed for the keep as well. I mucked more straw, knowing that Bodhe would be angry if I delayed too long. But I did not want to share a table with Vikings.

Finally I went out into the drizzle, just as shouts sounded from beyond the palisade. Two sentries ran forward to open the gates for more riders. Pounding rain turned the yard to mud as the leader dismounted quickly, his men doing the same. Cormac, our head sentry, stepped forward.

"Welcome to Dun Abernethy, Mac bethad mac Finlach," he said.

Macbeth. I knew that name. Bodhe had been a close comrade of Macbeth's father and had befriended the son, too. Fostered by his grandfather, the king, Macbeth had grown into a fierce warlord, and now it seemed everyone had heard the name. His reputation as a young general and an elite guard for King Malcolm, along with the tragedy of his youth, was widely known.

He was also a cousin to Gilcomgan and Thorfin Raven-Feeder both. And they were inside our house. I scowled, wondering.

Noticing me through sheeting rain, Macbeth extended his hand with his horse's lead. "Here, you," he called. "Take the horse."

A tall man, perhaps only ten years older than I, he wore mail from neck to knee, with a broadsword slung at his belt. Bare of a helmet, his hair was dark gold in the rain, braided some, and he wore his reddish mustache long in Viking fashion.

"Take the horse and lead him to the stable!" he shouted through the downpour.

For the sake of the animal, I came forward and took the lead. The warhorse stepped forward obediently, a grand beast, reddish gloss over taut muscle, black mane braided with silver beads. The glorious creature was not to blame for his master's behavior.

Cormac saw me and began to speak, but I shook my head to stop him from revealing my name. Tugging on the rein, I turned, and the horse followed willingly.

I led the bay inside the stable to a freshly cleaned stall, and directed Dull Andra to bring oats and an apple and to care for the animal. Then I ran for the keep, sopping wet, aware I had lingered far too long.

As I passed the curtained doorway where my father and the others sat in the great hall, I could see the men gathered at the long table in the glow of the fire, with several of our best candles lit against the gloom. Dolina never wasted beeswax. These men were important indeed. Seated at the table, Dolina ordered a servant to bring the good French wine, while Bodhe inquired sharply if his daughter had been found yet. The others discussed the provinces of northern Scotland: Caithness, coveted by Vikings, and powerful Moray. King Malcolm's name bounced from lip to lip as well.

Dripping and muck stained, I could not enter the room, though I was curious to know what brought these men together, some of whom were better kept apart. Running to my bedchamber, accessed by steps in a shadowy corner, I flung off my dirty garments and ransacked the wooden chest beside my bed for a clean tunic, undergown, and slippers. Wriggling into a bleached linen shift, I dropped over that a blue tunic gown embroidered at hem and sleeves, one of Dolina's castoffs remade for me as I grew. My nurse, Maeve, opened the door.

"Hurry," she said, "your father is asking for you!"

She combed out the snarled, damp mass of my hair, rebraided it with yellow ribbons, and set a brow band woven of colored yarns over it. I pulled on stockings and impatiently shoved my feet into slippers. Even as I left the room, Maeve still fussed over me, tucking a square of embroidered cloth into my sleeve.

I heard shouting as I approached the great hall. Men were arguing, and fiercely. As I slipped through the curtained doorway, I saw Macbeth rise from his seat, and the sudden flash of a sword showed in his hand. The whip of good steel sounded as another sword was drawn, for the mormaer of Moray was on his feet as well.

Chapter Five

Macbeth was a boy standing on a hill in sunshine when I saw him first, on the day we watched the king make a judgment for a heinous murder. Clinging to my mother's hand, for I was very young, I watched the proceeding without fully understanding the grand spectacle of warriors, priests, and a red-cloaked king gathered on the flat-topped judgment hill at Sgian, called Scone. The year was that of Our Lord 1020, and the summer morning was already hot.

Royal judicial hearings occurred regularly in Scotland, either at the royal center at Scone, or while the king rode progress through the land, visiting his regional leaders; the courts were usually timed to coincide with local fairs and cattle markets. The proceedings could show a king at his best, powerful but fair, and provided entertainment as well. That day, a crowd of men, women, and children clustered around the base of the hill.

Like the other mormaers, my father owed loyalty to King Malcolm, his close cousin through their relationship to my grandfather, the third King Kenneth. The Celtic line of succession confuses some, for it is not the vertical handing down of primogeniture favored by Saxons and other cultures. Significant Celtic titles and property descend in zigzag or even lateral fashion, from uncle to nephew, brother to brother, cousin to cousin, and so on, according to many factors. Ideally this distributes rights among the branches of a lineage, rather than limiting the power to one chain of descent, and it acknowledges matrilineal lines as well. The Celts have long relied on this system, a merging of Pictish and Irish practices, but it can engender bloody disagreement and murder among kin. Some men are ever hungry for power and overestimate their place in the order of things.

Standing between my mother and my knee-woman that day, I thought mostly about ribbons and sweet cakes, for my mother had promised to take me to the fair afterward. Waiting, I gaped up at the king's great fortress of Dunsinnan on its high hill, and then down at the wide River Tay, whose waters swept out to the firth and the North Sea. Breezes off the river relieved the day's baking heat, gulls reeled and cried overhead, and the bronze bell rang out from the tower beside the church when some Celtic monk climbed to the top to strike the notes with an iron bar.

Finn and Drostan were with us, too, small boys jumping up for a better view of the mound. My father stood on the mound near King Malcolm, and between them stood a boy whose hair shone gold in the sunlight as he looked around with a keen gaze. Here was the wronged party, people said around us, the son of a murdered lord.

"Mac bethad mac Finlach is your cousin removed, Gruadh," my mother told me, speaking also to Finn and Drostan. "He is here to accuse his cousins—his father's nephews—of slaying his father, Finlach, who was mormaer of Moray, a large province, very significant for its resources, its seacoast, its trade," she went on. "Now the boy is orphaned, for his mother is gone, too, nor does he have an inheritance. He is not yet fourteen, his majority, but King Malcolm is his grandfather and will foster and defend him."

The king's guard formed a half circle near them, and across the mound came Celtic priests in white robes embroidered with elaborate crosses, their tonsures shaved ear to ear in the way of the Culdees. Two carried a large silver cross between them, and another held a brass reliquary. As they walked they sang chants, and people bowed their heads. Behind the priests came guards escorting two men, the offending brothers of Moray, both dressed in fine robes. Mature, robust warriors, they were of an age with my father. The bearded one was announced as Malcolm mac Malbríd; the younger brother, Gilcomgan, had brown hair, a square face, a drooping mustache. As they knelt before the king, my mother turned to Maeve, my knee-woman.

"Macbeth's first cousins are old enough to be his father," she whispered.

"The men of Moray have married so often, there are multiple generations between brothers and cousins," Maeve replied. "They made Viking marriages, too. One of them married a daughter off to Sigurd, the fat prince of Norway."

My mother raised her brows. "Did he?"

"And got a son, a dark whelp like no Viking I ever saw. He is standing just there. When his parents died, he and his Irish grandmother came to live in Moray under the protection of his kinsmen." Maeve gestured toward a thin black-haired boy at the other side of the crowd. "Thorfin is his name, and a fierce warrior he will be."

A cleric stepped forward to read out the accusation, and King Malcolm asked the brothers to explain why they had killed Finlach of Moray. The brothers had never denied the murder of their uncle, just the reason for it.

"We disputed the inheritance," Malcolm mac Malbríd said. "By Celtic custom, the stewardship of Moray should have come to our side next. Finlach never trusted us, shaping his own son to be warlord in his place. Our uncle could have had us murdered."

"You acted on fear and suspicion," Malcolm growled, "and nothing more solid."

"When our uncle met us crossing the moorland between Elgin and Forres, his men drew blades," Gilcomgan explained. "Solid enough. We engaged in a skirmish."

"Finlach died fighting," the elder brother said. "He died well."

"By whose hand?" The king sat forward. "Who showed their blade first?"

"Finlach planned treachery. We had to save ourselves," Gilcomgan replied, evasive.

"Liar," the boy said, his husky youth's voice ringing clear. "My father distrusted you, but meant you no harm. Speaking ill of him here does not polish your black deed."

My father stepped forward then to address the brothers from Moray. "How do you know that your uncle plotted to harm you?"

"We had word from Orkney men," Gilcomgan said.

"Not surprising," Maeve murmured to Ailsa. "The Norse have a strong interest in who rules Moray, since they have holdings nearby in Caithness, and Orkney is but miles over the sea from the Moray coastline. They intermarry, but some Vikings would rather undermine Moray power. My Einar always said so." Her late husband had been a Dane, a warrior turned Scottish farmer. Maeve seemed to know all there was to know about the Northmen.

The king's cleric called a Moray man who swore that Finlach had died fairly in the skirmish; then one of Finlach's own housecarls came forward to declare the murder one of cold blood, which would require a more severe penalty. King Malcolm leaned often to confer with my father and the bishop and priest who stood with them.

"I wish to speak," Macbeth said then.

The king turned in surprise and nodded.

The boy stepped forward, his hair lifting in the wind, his feet firm and shoulders squared. "Before my birth," he said, "my father took his army north to Skitten to face troops led by Sigurd, jarl of Orkney. As protection from the wild Moray men, Sigurd carried a banner sewn by his Irish mother, an image of a raven, stitched by the magical arts she knew."

He had the innate skill and subtle command of a natural storyteller. The crowd was silent as he spoke, his voice calm yet strong. "Sigurd sent a Norseman to wave the raven banner, and Finlach sent his own man to slay Sigurd's bannerman. Three times this happened. Later my father withdrew his troops for the sake of peace and truce, but he met the threat of the Norsemen fearlessly and with honor. His courage that day was legendary. Would such a man bother to plot against two nephews who coveted his title?"

Macbeth paused. "If Finlach had intended to kill his nephews," he continued, "they would be dead now, and forgotten for their pettiness. Instead, my father is gone, ambushed unaware. Treachery killed Finlach mac Ruari of Moray. Nothing less."

Gasps sounded around us, admiration and agreement. My mother pulled me close and pressed a hand to her heart. Macbeth stepped back, and the king leaned sideways once more to speak to his advisors, who bent close.

We waited.

Scotland's laws, based on ancient Irish codes and Roman law, do not condone murder. But deaths by dispute are common in a society ruled by steel-games. A king who battles and murders his way to the throne cannot honorably condemn others for doing the same. If all offenders were executed for such deeds, judged as mortal sins by the tenets of the Church, who then would be left to defend the land? Ancient tradition allowed a King of Scots, as well as his mormaers and thanes, who dispense justice at lesser levels, to demand penalties and fines according to a man's rank and the severity of the offense. Death by battle, death by cold blood, and the crime of blood drawn without death—all have assigned fees and had best be paid.

"Malcolm mac Malbríd, since you now call yourself Moray," the king said, "you shall pay a mormaer's fine. Seven score and ten cows for the death of Finlach mac Ruari, or thirty-three ounces of gold, shall be paid by you and divided, two-thirds for the keeping of the young son of Finlach, the rest to the crown."

Murmurs wafted through the crowd. The fee was the largest possible. Some whispered it was too much; others said it was not enough to compensate for the death of such a man.

"To be delivered by Martinmas, according to the instructions my cleric will give you," the king went on. "In addition, Finlach's nephews shall forfeit properties to young Macbeth to compensate for his losses. The title will remain with you, Malcolm mac Malbríd," the king droned. "If you are fierce enough to kill Finlach the Mighty, then you are strong enough to hold the province of Moray."

"That is not justice," my mother murmured. "The boy deserves more than that for what he has suffered."

On the hill, Finlach's nephews looked displeased but bowed to the king.

Maeve leaned toward Ailsa. "King Malcolm is crafty," she muttered. "Moray needs a strong warlord, and one indebted to the crown is even better. Those two will do whatever the king wants now. Finlach's son is too young to avenge his father, and can do nothing."

"For now." Ailsa drew me close. "Once he is a warrior, he will fight for Moray."

"Whoever holds that province," Maeve said, "holds the greater share of Scotland. The king is not stupid. A tight rein over Moray will expand his own power."

"May God punish you both according to His laws for this crime," the king continued. "May your priests assign penances of the spirit—"

Even as his royal grandfather spoke, young Macbeth turned on his heel and walked away.

As he left the mound, a warrior in the crowd began to knock sword hilt on shield in a rhythm. One sword and shield after another, the beat spread. Such a gesture of respect was reserved for great men and kings. The pounding felt like a heartbeat, a thunder of support for the boy whose composure, and rightful cause, had been noted.

Chapter Six

Fingers clutching the curtain, I now watched as Macbeth and his cousin Gilcomgan faced each other, swords lifted and menacing. Bodhe and others stood, stools knocking over, wine spilling from cups to pool on the tabletop. Dolina kept her seat, a hand over her mouth. Our two hounds beside the fire barked loudly.

"Now!" Macbeth shouted. "We will do this now!"

"Here or in a field, you shall not see the sun tomorrow," Gilcomgan growled. Shorter than Macbeth by a head, he was built for power. He lifted his sword with clear intent in his eyes, but Macbeth lashed out first. Swords struck, rang sharp, while Maeve gasped and pulled me back.

Bodhe roared for them to stop, while another of the guests leaped forward to separate them. But the swordsmen moved out of reach, blades beating together heavily. A bench tipped and fell, and my father's mistress shrieked, running for the safety of a corner. The men gathered in a circle around the two opponents, so that I could not see what was happening in the center of the room.

Pushing through the curtain, I hurried forward. Bodhe glowered and gestured for me to retreat, then turned his back to join the circle of spectators. Swords slamming, blows heavy enough to chip steel or split a man's body, the two cousins edged dangerously near the fire basket bolted in the center of the room, coals and peat blazing hot inside iron bars high as my shoulder.

Macbeth lunged and struck Gilcomgan's forearm, but the chain mail sleeve held. Fergus, my swordmaster, appeared beside me. "Watch from here," he warned. "And pay attention. Macbeth has skill, and as a sword pupil, you will learn something."

"I am learning that men can be fools," I snapped, "to fight so near fire and womenfolk. What is this about?"

Fergus shrugged. "One insulted the other. Hatred burns hot between these two."

"I know. What sparked it here?"

"The king intends to appoint his eldest grandson, Duncan mac Crinan, as his heir and successor. You know a king can decide his *tánaise* from among his close kinsmen. Many do not approve his choice, and there is unrest over it."

"Is that why these men came to Dun Abernethy?"

"They meet to talk secretly here, knowing that Bodhe mac Kenneth has the first right to be named tanist by succession law. There are other worthy candidates as well."

"Macbeth is also a grandson of King Malcolm, so he too could be named tanist. Why Duncan over him? He cannot be a better warrior than Macbeth." Even I had heard of the latter's skill.

I could see that Macbeth was more than skilled, he was agile and remarkably at ease, while Gilcomgan had begun to sweat and fume like a bull. "Look there," Fergus admired. "If Macbeth had Moray, he would be a brilliant warlord, and a true strength against the Norse threat. Yet if he were to turn his eye southward, *he* would be the threat. Old Malcolm sees that. Likely it is why he chose Duncan, who is competent, but more important, agrees with his grandfather in all things. Even after death, the old king can keep hold over Scotland through his line and his laws."

One of the swordsmen knocked over a stool, and the other leaped over it. "So these two argue not only Moray, but who should be king," I said.

"That could be. Gilcomgan provoked Macbeth by saying that since

Macbeth has lost two kingdoms now—Moray and Scotland—he should seek the kingdom of heaven instead." Fergus shrugged. "Meaning, he wants to see Macbeth either dead or a monk. But Macbeth is no monkish sort. Gilcomgan had best watch his back."

"Whatever their dispute, there should be no threats within my father's walls." I watched Macbeth beat Gilcomgan toward the fire basket and away again.

"True," Fergus agreed. "But it makes an interesting dinner."

The fighters sidestepped in a rapid, wary circle, and Gilcomgan stumbled. Men guffawed, cheered, raising their drinking horns. The clang of swords rang on.

Frowning, I considered the argument; aside from the murder of a father, there was still cause enough for a blood feud. Scotland's royalty has two main branches on its great trunk: the old houses of Lorne and Gabhran. Macbeth and Gilcomgan were both of Lorne, while Bodhe and I were descended of Gabhran. The flowers and thorns on those branches—warlords and warriors and the women who bred more of them—had vied for various regions, and for the throne itself, for generations. Now old Malcolm thought to change this with the foreign concept of linear descent, so that kings would drop, one after another, from his own tree.

"Enough!" Bodhe plowed into the fray. "Kill each other outside if you will, but not in my house!" Ignoring his host's demand, Gilcomgan thrust forward. Macbeth leaned away, but the edge of the blade caught him along the jaw, a long slice in the skin.

"Blood drawn," Fergus muttered. "Gilcomgan should pay recompense in cattle. That is, if Macbeth can get his cousin to the court hill again."

Blood dripped along Macbeth's jaw, but he drove back with heavy blows, steel on steel. One of them would be killed, I thought. I clenched my fists, felt my stomach wrench. Then Macbeth slammed his blade against his opponent's arm so hard that the mail links split, and flesh erupted red beneath. Men cheered at the strike taken. Bodhe shook his head, furious but resigned.

"It is all sport to them," someone said beside me. "The steel-game, as they say."

I looked up to see the tall blond Norseman beside me. He seemed familiar as he glanced toward me. "You have seen such strife before in a hall, lady. Been the cause of it yourself."

I frowned. "Ketill?"

A little smile, a bow of the head, showed fine and humble manners. Ketill Brusisson, Thorfin's nephew, had once shown me kindness, but after the ugly events in that hall and my father's attack, I did not know if he was a friend. "That night," I said hesitantly, "I wondered if you had been hurt or killed in the raid. I am glad to see you here, and well. Were you injured?"

He shrugged. "I was hurt, and it healed. You were not responsible for the attack. Besides, it is done and in the past. Peace and restitution have been made."

The crowd shuffled backward as the opponents spun. "Jesu, they may well kill each other." Ketill touched my arm. "Lady, you must move back."

I gathered my skirts just as Gilcomgan leaped backward. His foot caught my long hem as I turned, and Ketill snatched at my elbow. I stumbled into others who stood nearby, and for a moment I was caught in a thicket of tall men, all shoulders, bumping arms, shifting feet.

"That is enough!" Bodhe roared, pushing through the crowd to take my arm. "Take care near my daughter, for love of God!"

The cousins lowered their swords, both men exhausted and breathing hard. Blood seeped from the cut on Macbeth's jaw. Gilcomgan clutched at the wound on his forearm, fingers staining red. He looked at me, his squarish face flushed, brow sweaty. "This girl is your daughter?"

"She is," Bodhe said, hand gripping my shoulder.

Chest still heaving, Gilcomgan bowed courteously, which seemed more than odd given the moment. "Lady Gruadh."

I lifted my chin. "Moray," I murmured. A host of sharp comments poured through my mind. My father's hand, squeezing my shoulder, kept me to my manners.

"Lady." Macbeth murmured a greeting as well. A trail of blood stained the neckcloth tucked beneath his mail coif. If he recognized me from the encounter in the rainy yard he gave no sign. "I ask your pardon for disturbing the peace of your home."

Gilcomgan echoed an apology. Dolina swept forward then, all gliding skirts and soft murmurs, and a serving girl followed with a bowl of water and clean cloths tucked under her arm. My father's mistress—I rarely thought of her as his wife—dipped a cloth in the water and pressed it against Gilcomgan's wound.

"We must get you out of this armor," she said. "This gash needs stitching. I can do that here." Like many women in charge of households, Dolina was innately practical and could stitch a wound as neatly as any curtain hem.

Gilcomgan nodded, glanced at Bodhe and then me, and turned to follow his hostess. Ketill moved quietly away, and around the room, the men drifted back to their seats. Someone called for fresh rounds of wine and ale, and as they settled there was some laughter, the sheepish sort. A servant began to refill the drinking horns to sloshing full.

I turned to my father with a sudden inkling. "Have you decided on Moray for me? I will not marry that one. He is a murderer."

"Your memory is longer than it should be," Bodhe said.

Macbeth watched us. "You speak of Gilcomgan?"

He was pressing his fingers to the cut on his jaw now. I pulled the little embroidered square from my sleeve and handed it to him. "You need stitching, too. Lady Dolina will see to it, go ask her."

He ignored me, though he tucked the cloth against his chin as he turned to address my father. "Do you plan to give your daughter to my Moray cousin?"

"No matter, for I refuse," I said. "He is a troublemaker, and too old."

"Age and refusal are not conditions for a wedding," Bodhe said brusquely. "He holds a great province and is a widower. His grown sons are dead, lost in Viking raids. Moray needs new sons."

"The eldest died in skirmish with my men," Macbeth supplied quietly. "The blood grudge between Gilcomgan and me will descend to our sons, do we live to have them."

Bodhe grunted. "You have always been a direct and honest man."

"If you two feud so, why did you come here to join this meeting?" I asked.

"Sometimes it is necessary to meet at the same table with one's enemies in order to gain peace elsewhere," Macbeth replied. He gave me a quick and cold glance. I knew he wanted me gone, so he could have words with Bodhe over their opposing views.

"I would not marry your Moray cousin or you, if it came to it," I said, annoyed. "Men intent on destroying each other cannot make very good husbands."

"I am married. Bodhe——"

"Pardon her. Finding a man worthy of my daughter's lineage is not easy," my father said. "A man willing to tolerate that temper will be harder still. Rue," he said, "you will marry my choice, or enjoy a convent. You have had too much freedom as it is."

I gasped, stung to be so chastised in the presence of another.

"An alliance with my cousin is not wise, Bodhe," Macbeth said. "Take warning. Do not yoke your daughter, and therefore Fife, to him."

"Not everyone bears the depth of your grudge," Bodhe said.

"You should," Macbeth growled. "Friend to Finlach, you should. There are other marriage alliances which would benefit Fife and your line. My cousin Thorfin has a half-brother and nephews——"

"I will not send my daughter into that Norse kin group. Strange things are said of the Raven-Feeder, besides."

Macbeth gave a bitter laugh. "True, it may not be wise to give a Viking a foothold in Fife, so close to the royal center at Scone."

I glanced at the mormaer of Moray, who now sat divested of his hauberk and tunic, bare chested in the firelight while Dolina fussed over him. He was thick and muscular and middle-aged. "Father, please tell me—have you made an agreement with Gilcomgan?" Beside me, Macbeth glared at Bodhe, too. We were odd allies for that moment.

Bodhe sighed. "The betrothal will be soon, once the banns are shown."

"Then you are a fool," Macbeth growled, and spun away, still pressing my cloth against his jaw. He left the hall, shoving through the curtain.

My father spoke first. "We cannot delay your betrothal any longer, Rue. Men are uncertain what will happen, given the king's choice for tanist. This is the best match for you now."

"Best for *you*," I hissed, "not me! What do you want from this alliance? Do you think to help Gilcomgan challenge the king?"

"Quiet," he said. "We will have none of this from you." He looked toward a man who now approached us, leather hauberk creaking, face lean and cruel, framed by black, partly braided hair.

"Lady Gruadh," he said pleasantly. "I am Thorfin Sigurdsson. We have met."

"How unfortunate that we do so again," I said.

"Gruadh," Bodhe warned. "Jarl Thorfin and I have made our peace. He has declared himself an ally of the kingdom of Fife now."

"He made no peace with me. I suppose now he will send Harald Silkhair for our housecarl." I turned away.

"Harald is dead," Thorfin responded smoothly.

My fingers clutched among my skirts. *A Dhia,* had the man expired of the wound I gave him? "How—"

"I beheaded him," Thorfin said. "With my own blade. For your sake." He inclined his head, then turned to address my father as if nothing much had occurred.

Chapter Seven

The night air was cool and misted as I slipped out of the keep while others slept. Against my chest I clutched a square of dark silk wrapped around a few things: a small brass bowl, three candle stubs, a stone with a hole worn through. What I wanted was some hint of my future, but with my mother gone and her sister, my aunt, living in Ireland, I had no one to do quick divination that night. Bethoc's mother, Mairi, had good knowledge, but she lived in the hills, and I had neither time nor means to go there. My betrothal to the brutish Moray leader was set for morning, and such a marriage, to my thinking, could not bode well. So I set out to determine the omens for myself. Half knowledge carries its own risks, among them foolishness.

Two sentinels approached me in the yard, but let me go when I told them that there was a sick bird in the mews who needed my attention. They watched me: Bodhe's men knew there was a touch of wildness in me that could not be trusted. Near the byre where the birds were kept, I saw Ruari, the eldest son of Fergus mac Donal. He fell into step beside me, though I hissed at him to leave me be.

"Off to some secret assignation? *Tcha*," he teased, "and you about to be betrothed."

"I am only going to the birdhouse. The falcon master is gone trapping new birds, and I worry about the little kestrel." Sometimes a small untruth is like oil for a key.

"Sorcha? You do have a hand for soothing the birds. I will come with you."

"You will not," I snapped. "I want to be alone, this last night of my freedom."

"Well then," he said, stopping, "do not think to go outside the walls."

Without reply, I ran for the byre and went inside. Surrounded by the cheeps and flutters of hooded birds on perches, I paused to think. My original plan to skirt past the mews and slip out the postern gate in the back wall was useless, thanks to Ruari. Casting a charm in here would disturb the birds, sensitive creatures with a nature of air and fire.

Two feathers molted downward, and I caught them: a pinion from a goshawk, and a downy feather from Sorcha, whose wings did not carry her far. I considered them as omens, for such was my mood, so to me they signified flight, from the byre and from the marriage. Wrapping the feathers in the silk, I dropped to my belly and slid beneath a gap in the back wall, where some boards were loose. I ran through shadows and slipped into the kitchen house. Before dawn, Cook and his assistants would arrive to begin a breakfast of oatcakes and sausages, and start kettles of soup, but for now, it was deserted. With iron tongs, I retrieved a glowing coal from the hearth and dropped it into a small iron bucket. I bolted again, avoiding sentries, and headed for the postern gate.

The hinges creaked as I went through. Inching along a narrow ledge of rock with the tall wooden stockade at my back and a hundred-foot drop beneath me in the darkness, I did not falter, having taken this route in childhood games. Reaching the slope that fronted the fortress, I headed toward a wooded area to seek out a familiar glade of oak and birch. A burn trickled over stones, and mist dropped thick through the treetops as I sank to my knees in a sheltered space between the trees.

I opened the silk and set my treasures on a flat-topped rock, then filled the bowl with water from the burn and lit the candle stubs from the coal in the bucket. The little stone, with its natural hole worn by time, was a precious thing which I had found in a box of my mother's possessions. Looking through that special stone, she had once explained to me, would reveal what could not be seen with the human eye. I placed it on my square of silk, with the candles and water bowl arranged around it. Walking *deiseil,* left to right in the direction of the sun's turning, I went around the rock three times, my feet crushing bracken in the quiet. Then I knelt to breathe in a slow pattern that eased my spirit, and softly murmured a chant that my mother had used often, an appeal for protection to the good Brigid.

Though I knew some rituals and chants, I did not comprehend how the forms applied or quite what they could yield. Later I would learn that the trappings of magic are less essential than genuine understanding. Alone that night, unskilled but determined, I meant to force a little magic to my will.

The glade was misty, cool, eerily silent. I closed my eyes and chanted again. My mother had trained me to remember charms and songs with a trick used by bards: sometimes I would lie in a dark room with a cloth over my eyes and a fist-sized stone resting on my stomach, and recite chants. The darkness focused thought, and the feel of the stone kept the mind from wandering. Bards claim that crystals and other stones can hold words within them, and thus are aids to the memory. By the time my mother died, chants, charms, and songs were tucked inside my head like rolls of parchment in a box.

Again I circled the rock where my silk and things were spread and the candles flickered. As I spoke another chant to invoke help and protection, its rhythm calmed me, deepened my breath and my resolve.

> *No fire shall burn me*
> *Nor wind cool me*
> *Nor water drown me*
> *Nor stone fell me . . .*

I knelt, gazed at a candle flame, then looked into the bowl of water. My mother had warned me to be strong. I wanted to know why. What had she seen of my future?

"Show me what will come," I whispered, and waved my hands over the water in the bowl. I had seen my mother do that over water, over fire, over ailing children, even animals and plants; soon they would flourish again. "I would see what life holds for me."

The water reflected candlelight, and the blur of my own face: blue eyes, wide and dark in moonlight; pale cheeks, hair like a sheen of bronze. Nothing more appeared.

"Before dawn is done this day," I whispered fervently, "before the sun rises full, I ask that my future reveal itself to me."

The water rippled in wind, creating delicate circlets of gold in the candle flames. No vision. Did I have no future? Would I perish in child-birth? I murmured words to stave off that fear: "*Cuidich mi a Bhride*"—Help me, O Brigid. Again I waved my hand over the bowl, like the moon passing over the earth, then took up the stone with the hole and held it up to peer through it. In the darkness, I saw only trees, the glim-mer of dawn.

Behind me came the sudden sound of heavy footsteps crashing through the undergrowth. Quickly I blew out the candles and leaped to my feet.

"Lady Gruadh!" Ruari's voice.

Torchlight flickered, and I glimpsed men among the trees. Hastily I dumped the water, tied my treasures back in the silk, and turned to wait. Within moments, Ruari entered the clearing, behind Finn and Drostan, who held the torch.

"Gruadh," Ruari said sternly. "You are to return with us."

I lifted my chin. "I came out for some night air. Go on. I will be along directly."

"Now." Ruari beckoned. "Before your father discovers you are gone."

Finn, never one for wasting time, took my elbow. "Come along, girl."

"No need to drag me," I said, shaking him off. "Do you think I would run away?"

"Perhaps," Finn said. "Given the betrothal this morning, and your discontent clear to those who know you."

"Better she runs or fights, rather than casts spells," Drostan said, glancing around. The smell of candle smoke still lingered in the little glade.

I sent him a glare. "If you had the knack of such things, you'd do so too," I hissed.

"You do not have the knack," he replied, "which is worrisome."

I yanked free of Finn's grip. "Oh, leave off," I said irritably. Gathering my skirts, stuffing the silk-wrapped package into the little bucket, I moved ahead of them.

We climbed the hill toward the fortress under a tarnished silver sky. Daylight would bring my betrothal hour, I thought, and as the gate opened, I walked past the sentries into the shadowy yard. Men were already moving about attending to tasks; a cow lowed somewhere, a cock made a nuisance of himself in the upper bailey. The fog dissolved and the sun crested pink over the eastern hills as I walked through the yard ahead of Ruari, Drostan, and Finn.

Macbeth mac Finlach strode toward the gate, his path nearly crossing mine, and the dawn light seemed to halo his head with gold. He met my gaze in silence and went past. Behind him, Thorfin and Ketill paused, bathed in shadow. Behind me, my friends went still; nothing moved. For a moment, the space between breaths, the world altered somehow, dreamlike and strange.

The men formed a circle around me, friends and enemies both. Ahead, on the earth of the practice yard, two swords lay crossed and ready, shining blades reflecting the glow of the sunrise. Nearby, horses stood, gleaming and grand, ready to be ridden, while overhead, two eagles winged toward the mountains, and a raven settled on a gatepost. Moon and stars were still visible in the sky, and the sunrise flowed over the hilltops like a spill of blood, the sun in its midst like a golden wafer.

Quick as it came, the strangeness lifted and the ordinary world returned. Men moved, spoke. Dogs barked. I breathed.

Macbeth walked past, shoving his helmet over his hair, shutting out the light of that gold. He turned to speak to Thorfin and Ketill, and the three strode toward the waiting horses. Ruari walked toward the sentries and Finn headed for the smithy, where the smell of charcoal fires wafted. Drostan said he was for the keep and breakfast, and asked me to go with him. Macbeth and the Northmen rode through the open gates, and a young groom ran forward, whistling, to pick up the crossed swords and toss them to two men ready for morning practice.

And I stood stunned.

I had asked to see an omen of my future by break of dawn. Now I realized that the signs had appeared as a dazzling weave made of ordinary threads. I knew some of the elements—ravens were death and warning, eagles pride and pairing, horses freedom; the swords might be conflict or war, and the circle of warriors around me could have been a sign of protection, or the men in my future.

We Celts are taught to watch for omens all around, in nature and numbers and objects. There are heaven-sent signs, they say, in birds and clouds, in patterns of leaf and stone, a fire's flicker, the sheen on water, even the etchings on a soup bone. My mother had been gifted with the Sight that brings spontaneous visions, so common among the Gaels that we call it *Da Shealladh,* the gift of two sights. A great-grandmother on Bodhe's side had been a *taibhsear,* a seer, from whom others sought advice.

Until that moment, I had not known that I, too, had a hint of that talent.

Hearing my name called, I looked up to see my father and Dolina standing at the top of the hill, waiting. I hurried up to meet them.

AFTER BREAKFAST and morning prayers, I was attended and dressed by Aella and my knee-woman. Together they scrubbed, tugged, combed, decorated, and smoothed over me until they were satisfied. My dress was of dark green, regarded as unlucky for a bride and a betrothal, but it was my mother's best gown and I loved it, and made my stubborn choice. Under it I wore a lightweight gown of creamy wool with hems embroidered in golden threads, and I folded back the green sleeves to show the handiwork of the undergown. Over all, Maeve tied low around my hips a long belt of linen stitched with a bright interlaced design. My hair was plaited with yellow silk ribbons, and upon my brow Aella set a thin fillet of silver studded with a crystal drop, another of Ailsa's special things.

Aella pinched my cheeks until they hurt, and Maeve rubbed an ointment of almond oil and crushed berries over my lips. Dolina arrived to look me over, her eye keen for crooked hems and loose threads. Once I passed that scrutiny, the women escorted me to the great hall, Maeve whispering that I looked like the queen of the fairy ilk.

I did not care how well I looked. Had we gowned, painted, and oiled me up for a beheading, it would have felt the same to me.

My father waited by the blazing fire basket along with Father Anselm and Gilcomgan mac Malbríd. My nephew, young Malcolm mac Farquhar, stood with Finn and Drostan, who as Bodhe's fosterlings were included in the family gathering. My women and a few servants who were kin to us also joined us. Dolina took her place beside Bodhe, looking proud as a puffed-up hen in her russet gown. And I, taller than my bridegroom and slim compared to his bulk, I felt like a green tree beside a boulder.

Gilcomgan and I acknowledged each other politely. Father Anselm droned on about the banns posted on the doors of the church in the village of Abernethy, spoke a prayer of binding and betrothal over us, and we repeated vows. My groom's fingers were rough but damp, as if he was nervous. My hand was cold and still. The priest appeared smug and satisfied. He would soon be rid of Bodhe's daughter, his least favorite sheep in the Abernethy fold. Tears stung my eyes, but I would not show them.

Bodhe congratulated us at the conclusion of the ceremony, Father Anselm offered useless words of wisdom, Dolina smiled, and my almost groom clutched damply at my hand. I could guess his thoughts. A betrothal is near enough to a marriage that the groom may have his will of the bride before the marriage ceremony takes place. But I was determined that my groom would wait upon my will, and get no sweet concord of me.

. . .

THAT NIGHT's sleep was a fitful jumble of dark dreams where I was drowning and woke entangled in the bed linens. Dressing by moonlight, catching up a cloak, I slipped past Aella, who slept in a little bed built into the wall. I wanted to walk off the miasma of the nightmares. Downstairs, I saw Bodhe in the great hall by the fireside, alone but for our dogs, who lolled and slept at his feet. He sat in his carved high-backed chair, slouched and thoughtful, and as I approached, clutching my plaid cloak around my shoulders, he turned, more expectant than surprised. Neither of us could sleep. Sinking to the floor at his feet, I petted our great, gentle wolfhound. I looked up at my silent father.

"Two months from now, I will not be here to pet this dog," I said, ruffling the gray mop between the wolfhound's ears. "I will be in Moray."

Bodhe sighed. "It is a fine province and will be a good place to live," he said. "It stretches from the eastern sea as far west as Argyll, and it is filled with mountains and green glens, lochs and seacoast. Moray is a rich place, with cattle and silver and fish for trading. It has beauty and wealth and wonders, its people are clever, its warriors strong and proud. This is all a kingdom could offer. And the well-being of Moray is essential to the whole of Scotland."

"I do not need a geography lesson. I need the truth."

"The truth is in what Moray offers," he said. "Every mormaer of that region has an ancient right to be called *Rí a Moreb,* king of Moray. His wife can be called *ban-rí,* queen. Just now, Gilcomgan and King Malcolm support one another. But if the *Rí a Moreb* ever summoned men to revolt, the strength of that army would be such that the mormaer of Moray could himself be king over all Scotland."

"And marriage to me could ensure that for Gilcomgan. Or for our son," I added.

"Clearly you understand. So what is on your mind?"

"It seems to me," I said, "that in all this, Bodhe mac Kenneth stands to become father to a queen, and close to a king's ear. There is power in this for you and our kin. But why this through me, when you never made a bid for the throne yourself, despite the worth of your own claim?"

He sucked in a breath, paused. "Power is a swift and changeable beast," he said low, "ridden by determined men . . . who will fight dire and dirty for the reins. I will join the ride this way, when I have kept out of it before."

"Ah. With my brother gone, it falls to me, this obligation."

"Now you have it," Bodhe said. "Moray is key to power in Scotland."

"His cousin Macbeth has a better claim. The king is his grandfather."

"That one has no land under him now. He is married, besides," Bodhe replied. "You were too young to wed when he looked about for a wife, and he does not hold the province. Though I would not be surprised if he will try someday. He is a strong and capable warrior, and already has had a direct hand in driving the Vikings from the shores of his uncle's coastal lands in Buchan, and has negotiated truces with the Orkneyings. He helped mend the dispute between Thorfin Sigurdsson and myself."

I huffed, disliking any mention of that name.

"If Macbeth gains power as a warlord, as many expect from him, it would be worthwhile to consider a match between you two. Wives can be set aside, and widows are often made."

I stared. "That is hateful scheming!"

"Strategy," he corrected, "not scheming. Our lineage has the most honorable claim to the throne of Scotland, yet Malcolm the king would shut us out. My son could have been . . . well, that is done. As for me," he said, "I will never make a bid. Old Malcolm would have me killed within a day of the very thought. My bold young grandson is a boy yet. But you!" He looked hard at me. "Even carrying the blood of Celtic kings, you cannot rule alone. You need a strong and ambitious husband."

"Our blood needs one," I corrected bitterly. "Crinan of Atholl tried to have me stolen once, to marry Duncan—who now stands to be king one day. You should have let them take me." Suddenly I wished I had not said it, for my brother had died in my defense.

Bodhe narrowed his eyes. "Old Malcolm wants to keep the king-ship in his bloodline. Duncan will name his own son as his tanist, and so it goes. We dispute that."

I nodded. "Straight descent is not the Celtic way."

"Exactly. Our branch, not theirs, must rightfully supply the next king of Scots."

Chapter Eight

Spring rains began, so persistent that we kept to our fireside more than usual. Dolina, Maeve, Aella, and I met daily in the hall, where there was light, warmth, and room to spread fabrics and stitch my wedding linens. Easily bored with hemming, I took up a piece I had started long before, determined now to finish it. Of bleached linen over an ell long and less in width, the panel was worked in a frame on a stand, and later would be sewn to a curtain for practical use. The knotwork border had cost me months of time, and too many finger jabs to count. I was proud of the design, the center space filled with figures and objects copied from carved Pictish stones found in the fields of Fife; I had roamed outside sketching the old carvings of warriors, animals, birds. I stitched the piece using thin, bright woolen yarns—brown, black, blue, and red—some skeins of which my mother had spun. So her hand was in my needlework panel, too. Once I lived in Moray, these things would remind me of home.

Day after day, seated in the hall with my wool basket and needlework, I listened to Dolina, or overheard some of the conversation of the men who often gathered with Bodhe at the other end of the chamber. They discussed matters that affected Fife and Scotland itself. I knew that a mormaer's wife must be aware of such issues, and the wider scope of the world beyond her household.

Messengers came and went, too, and one day after two had gone back and forth, Bodhe summoned his housecarls into the great hall. "King Cnut of England and Denmark is marching northward with an army," he announced. "The word came from Neill, mormaer of Angus. He reports Cnut has already sent his ships into the North Sea and could cross into Scotland from the south as well. He is set to make trouble unless he and King Malcolm can agree on borders and rights."

I gasped, listening. As our neighbor to the south, England was often our enemy as well. There was a tradition of tensions, truces, and the back-and-forth movement of regions. The Saxons were the wolves at the southern gates of Scotland, while the seaborne Vikings were the dragons and ravens to our east and west.

"I will send word to Neill of Angus that I will join him and other mormaers to meet with the king at Dunsinnan to discuss the threat of Cnut at our border," Bodhe said. Though he and old Malcolm had only a cold peace between them, Bodhe did what he must for the sake of Fife and Scotland.

"We will advocate a show of peace with King Cnut," Bodhe told his men that day. "Who rides with me to Dunsinnan?"

Several men stood, among them Ruari and his brothers.

In the silence of my needle plying, I listened and learned, and waited out the weeks.

WHEN DOLINA and her wedding preparations became too much to bear, I begged my father to allow me to visit Bethoc and Mairi in the hills for a few days. My time in the practice yard no longer provided escape, for Dolina was newly concerned for the state of my soul; she had been talking to Father Anselm, and now feared that a taint of heresy could interfere with the wedding arrangements, since a woman using weaponry was frowned upon by Rome. The Celts had no quibble with such things, given their long, proud history of warrior women, and Bodhe argued that my future status might require such trappings and gear.

Nonetheless, to be safe with the pope more than God, I was banned from going to the yard. Father Anselm, whose face always had slyness in its angles, seemed pleased with his little victory. Since I still spent a few hours a week studying letters and maths with the priest, I asked to study Greek during my extra time, and Bodhe thought it a good idea. So I learned *alpha, beta, gamma, delta* with uncommon fervor because it seemed to annoy Father Anselm. Drostan, working with us, genuinely savored the material.

Bodhe readily agreed that I should visit my cousins, and assigned an escort to take me over the hills to their home. My guards were Ruari, Bethoc's older brother Lachlann, and Dubh mac Dubh, a cousin on my father's side; he was a skilled fighter among my father's elite housecarls, and a pun on his name, essentially Black mac Black, suited his sullenness and his Pictish coloring. We all set out on garrons, slapping at the midges as we rode over sunny slopes.

Bethoc was one of my closest friends, as well as kin to me. Her father had been thane of a small region in Fife until his death, and Mairi, her mother, a dark and lovely woman, was one of Bodhe's many cousins descended of Duff. Bethoc's brother Lachlann, one of our youngest housecarls, would make a good thane one day. Until then, Mairi managed the small thanage and her thriving practice as herb woman and healer. I loved visiting their hillside home. After my mother's death, what more I learned of herbs, divination, and the warmth of kin and friendship were acquired beside the central hearth in that snug little house.

Bodhe had sent me away certain that my cousins would exert a calming influence over me. What he did not realize was that Mairi taught me new charms and chants, and would sometimes divine for me. On the day I arrived, over a supper of stewed vegetables with a trace of mutton, and thick, salted oatcakes, I told Bethoc and her mother of the strange, slowed moment at Dun Abernethy when I had seen the men, the swords, the horses and birds all under a rising crimson sun.

"I knew the Sight would show in you someday." Mairi smiled, and leaned forward. "Often the meaning of the omens we see is not clear until later. If we knew too much about the future, we might be afraid to step from our houses. Do not fret—the signs you saw speak of Scotland's future even more than your own."

"Scotland?" I blinked. "Because of the warriors and symbols of warfare?"

"Perhaps they will be Rue's husbands in future," Bethoc said. "Well, not all of them," she amended when I gaped at her.

Mairi took my hands in hers and closed her eyes. "Two husbands," she said. "Three, if you so choose. Like most women, you will have a share of happiness and measures of sorrow. Unlike most, you will have . . . power." She let go of my fingers. "You can draw strength from within yourself, like water from a well. Your mother gave you the sign of the good Brigid on your shoulder," she went on, touching my upper sleeve, which covered the symbol. "Call upon that protection whenever you need it."

My mother had told me to be strong, too. I stared at my cousin. Mairi knew how to divine using rune stones, but I had not seen her simply close her eyes and have a knowing such as that. "Husbands? I did not see Gilcomgan in my vision," I answered.

"There is a new moon on the day you return to Abernethy," Bethoc said, and looked at her mother. "The ancient tradition on new-moon night might help Rue."

Mairi nodded. "Good fortune can come from kissing the person next to you when you see the black sky of the new moon, so it is believed. And a kiss can reveal truths." She watched the lazy rise of the fire's smoke. "Remember that, if the chance should arrive."

Mairi taught me chants I had not heard before, and she taught me more about potions, herbs, and their uses. She also renewed the color in the little triple spiral on my shoulder, letting me rest late the next morning. When my escort arrived on the day of the new moon, I returned to Abernethy with a basket of little clay pots and vials of potions, ointments, and infusions for those at Abernethy who had asked for her treatments and medicines.

Later, when it was dark, I left the keep and went to the bailey, intent on my mission.

The sound of hammering on iron lured me toward the smithy, with the blazing forge at its center. Finn had a pink flush in his cheeks from standing near the fire, and a sheen of sweat on his arms and chest where the tunic gapped open under a leather apron. When he walked over to me, wiping his sooty hands on his apron, I paused in the doorway and looked up at the sky, which held no light but for stars. "New moon," I said, feeling awkward. Rising on my toes, I kissed him. His lips under mine were surprised, then he caught my waist and returned a kiss that asked for more.

"What do you have in mind with this?" he asked, laughing.

"Just the luck of the new moon," I answered. He pulled me toward him for a proper kiss, long and lush, as we had shared before. "That should bring us both luck," he murmured, and let me go. "But with you about to be married, we cannot—"

"I ask only for your friendship." Then I walked away, knees wobbly.

Near the gate, I saw Ruari, his chain mail gleaming under torchlight. Though not tall, he was strongly built, with a sober demeanor. He scowled. "Go inside, it is late."

"I came out to honor the custom of the new moon," I answered, "for luck."

"What custom?" he asked, like a mouse to the trap.

"This," I said, and leaned fast to kiss him lightly.

"What!" He pulled back. "You will get no luck that way. Be off with you." But he touched my cheek gently. "Go into the keep," he said, then turned to walk away.

When I entered the keep, there sat another of my new-moon quarry in the great hall. Seated in a corner, Drostan was playing a game of chess by himself, moving both dark and light pieces. My father and some of his carls occupied benches near the central fire basket, talking quietly and passing a bladder of wine between them. Some held the bladder high to send gleaming spouts of liquid into their mouths. I drew aside the curtain, meaning to go toward Drostan.

"Lady Gruadh." Macbeth appeared in the shadows behind me. "I would like a word with you. Will you walk a little with me?"

"Sir," I said, startled, "I did not know you were here."

"Only arrived this evening." Macbeth led me outside, and we walked through the bailey toward where a garden and orchard flourished near the back wall. All was greening up, filling and fragrant, and the apple trees formed a sweet, thick overhead canopy of blossoms as we moved along the path.

"Watch your step, it is dark as a grave tonight," Macbeth said.

"A dark moon brings new beginnings, and good fortune," I ventured.

"Does it? We should have brought a torch," he said.

I stopped, uncertain in his company. Macbeth had an air about him like a shield wall. I faced him. "What do you wish to discuss with me?"

"If you think to marry my cousin," he said bluntly, "understand something first."

"If? We will be wed by late summer. Gilcomgan's fortress at Elgin is far north, and my father does not trust the weather in the mountain passes, for it sometimes—"

"I know," he said. "I know every inch of Moray, and its seasons and weather."

"Of course, you were born there." How had I forgotten?

"Born to a good woman, raised by a great man, and cast out by traitors. I brought you out here to warn you against Moray's mormaer." He stood very close, and I realized he had been drinking, the odor strong on his breath. No doubt he had been at my father's fire with the rest.

"I know you despise Gilcomgan. Do you plan a skirmish to ruin my wedding?"

"If you marry him," he said low, "you will never be safe. He is hated by many."

"Including you. I am warned. Good night." I began to step past him.

He took my arm. "Refuse the marriage. The match is unwise for you, for Fife."

"It is wise and prudent to join Fife and Moray." I mustered pride, though I, too, had protested my father's decision, as Macbeth well knew.

"Would be, if Moray had a fit leader." He did not release me, though I yanked my arm in his grip. "Know the risks, then."

I stood with him in that dark orchard patch, the smell of apple blossoms and green and earth surrounding us, and felt something strange shimmer through me. I leaned forward, close enough to kiss him.

"What is this?" he murmured, and drew me toward him to touch his mouth to mine, lightly at first—then not. The kiss was unlike any I had ever felt. This was deep, dark, strong stuff—the fiery taste of *uisge beatha,* the water of life, when one has tasted only wine. I curved even closer.

He pulled back, stepped away. "Moray," he said, "has a fool's luck."

I felt the fool, sucking for breath, caught out by my own silly game. "Good night," I gasped, and moved past him.

"One more word of advice, Lady Gruadh," he murmured. "If you would kiss for luck under a new moon, choose carefully. Luck can open the door to fate."

I did not turn, but continued to walk. His footsteps took an opposite direction.

MY FATHER brought me a gift, wrapped in his cloak: a slender hauberk shaped of boiled leather and a helmet of brass trimmed in silver. "You will ride with my party to witness a pledge between kings," he said simply. "It is time you saw more of the world, now that you will be wife to a leader."

Surprised, I listened while he explained that King Cnut of England and Denmark had agreed to meet with King Malcolm for a show of mutual homage at their shared border. I knew it was an honor to be included in Bodhe's party for such a momentous event. Dolina had not known of Bodhe's intention to give me war gear. Later, she had stiff words with him over it: first sword training and now armor. I heard them argue, and my father elaborated my own point—that it was an old, proud Celtic custom and befitted my new status.

And so I rode with Bodhe's host under the lion banner of Fife, black on red silk.

Chapter Nine

The place where the kings would meet was far south of our land of Fife, along the shared border between Lothian, recently claimed for Scotland, and Saxon Northumbria. We were to gather in considerable numbers from the four corners of Scotland in a glittering show of strength. "Malcolm will not submit to Cnut, for the Scottish kings are not vassals to the English king," Bodhe explained as we collected in the hall the morning of our departure. "If Cnut decides he wants obeisance, there could be war. We will be courteous but safe—our men will be fully armed."

Old Malcolm, for all his faults and cruelties over decades of kingship, was a clever ruler who knew when to flatter, when to pander, where and when to attack in order to protect his kingdom and his line. Cnut, they said, was a strong king, both fair and tough. His queen, Emma, called Aelfgifa in England, was of Norman and Viking descent, and so the Saxons had the advantage of the combined might of Vikings and Normans behind them, so long as those groups all remained at peace, a challenge at best.

Once, I heard, Cnut took his court to the coast and planted his chair in the surge and spray of an incoming tide. He lifted his arms to the sea and called out for it to stop. Of course it did not, and the tall, bearded Dane was soon soaked to the skin, and before long dragged his chair back. His enemies said it was an arrogant attempt to command the ocean to cease. Others, his supporters and those of a wise turn of mind, pointed out that Cnut showed that he could not, indeed, stop the tide. Not even the most powerful king could master nature, God's own domain.

Hundreds of years before Cnut, one of my royal Pictish ancestors invited several kings and subkings to the edge of the northern sea and set a row of chairs in the sloshing tide. The wooden seats of the others washed out from under them, but his own was made of waxed feathers and lightweight wood. The king's chair buoyed up and became a boat, so that he sailed to a nearby promontory and climbed up, standing aloft to show his might. We Celts were the first to think of that trick, and bested the very sea.

A bright phalanx rode out of Dun Abernethy's gates that morning, steel sparkling, hooves pounding. At the center of the group, I rode a white mare, not my usual garron, and wore my armored gear over the gown of dark green, with my sword buckled at my hip. A woman traveling among males needs a female companion, and Aella came along, glad for a glimpse of the southland, being of Saxon birth. Bethoc came, too, anxious for adventure, and we kept one another company. Our close escort consisted of Ruari mac Fergus and two of his brothers, red-headed Angus and fair young Conn.

We took boats to carry people, horses, and gear, and to shorten our trip, we docked at the port of Berwick for a day, and then sailed along the River Tweed a little ways to come closer to our destination. Then we set to riding. Having never been so far south before, I felt excited as we rode closer to the borderland between Scotland and England.

In the afternoon I looked up toward the ridge of a hill and saw a stand of tall pikes thrusting up like slender trees. The point of each carried a decapitated head, black and gruesome, pitch-soaked to preserve them a long while, until they decayed to skulls.

I gaped upward at what was left of those hideous faces, the scraggly hair and sagging jaws, the eyes horrible hollows. Some of those evil pikes bore body parts—ghastly arms with curled hands, a leg with groin still attached, a single booted foot.

Aella gasped, near to retching, and hid her eyes with her hand. Bethoc looked away. But I stared, horrified and transfixed, even when Ruari and Conn drew their horses alongside to urge us onward. I remembered that my guard and my only brother had been beheaded but, thank the saints, never piked.

I would not shrink from the grim display. Someday I might have to show toughness for such things, even if I quailed within. As wife to Scotland's most powerful mormaer, it was in my interest to understand the ways of men and warfare. My own life might turn on that knowledge one day.

"Who were they?" I asked Ruari.

He shrugged. "Probably the victims of some raid or battle over territory. Perhaps they were Saxons killed by Scots . . . or Scotsmen slaughtered and piked by Northumbrians. Not recently, though. They have been there a long time."

I caught my breath, dismayed to realize that these might be Scotsmen. "What will happen to them . . . now?"

"Eventually they will fall to the ground, and some local farmer will bury them."

"They had families," I said. "Loved ones who would want to give them decent wakes and burials, and pay for Masses to be said for their souls for a year or more."

"That may never happen. Come ahead," he urged.

We traveled onward through a vista of sweeping meadows and hills, the sky blue over all, the earth generous and lovely. Yet the vision on the hill had touched the bright day with darkness. Ruari still rode beside me and glanced at me.

"If they believed war would bring them a good death, Rue," he said, "then it did."

I nodded, and sent a little blessing backward on a whisper for their ghosts to hear.

We spent the night at the home of a thane, many of us crammed into the beds and pallets in his house, while the housecarls slept outside in the animal byres or rolled in sturdy woolen plaids over heather for a bed. Scotsmen needed no elaborate tents such as southerners might require, I heard them say.

Journeying farther south the next day, we reached the place where the meeting of kings would take place, near an old monastery with a small church dedicated to Saint Cuthbert. The parties of English and Scots convened on a broad moorland gone golden in the sunlight. Bodhe and the other mormaers were to join our king in the center area, though Gilcomgan was not in attendance, having been delayed by raiders harrying Moray's coastland. Curious to see the proceedings, I guided my mount toward the front for a better view, but Bodhe turned.

"Stay with your guard," he said sternly, "in case of unrest. She is in your keeping," he told my escort. Ruari, Angus, and Conn led me farther back again.

Priests and monks stepped forward in rows like a small army, the Celtic monks robed in white, the Saxons in brown and black. Preceded by bishops, each party carried large enameled and jeweled crosses and reliquaries containing the bones of saints, including good Saint Cuthbert, who was asked to intercede for the Saxons and their Danish king. We Scots appealed to the saints Columba and Fillan. Led in prayers, we were then blessed, the lot of us.

At last the two kings rode forward with their immediate retinues to meet on the flat of the meadow. Behind them stood rows of helmeted guards carrying round shields and tall spears, some of them horsed. Cnut was a huge figure, bearded and cloaked; the glint of gold on his nasal helm, made in the Danish style with eye holes, lent him further fierceness. King Malcolm was resplendent in an iron helmet trimmed in bright brass, and his red cloak was edged in feathers, such as the old Celtic tales boast of for their kings.

The kings presented their accompanying lords. With Cnut rode Siward, Earl of Northumberland, and others. Malcolm introduced Bodhe, and then Duncan, who was called king of Cumberland and Strathclyde, as well as tanist. He was a young man, stocky and plain featured, in a gleaming mail hauberk, his helmet bedecked with feathers. Beside him was his father and Bodhe's old enemy, Crinan of Atholl, whose elaborate leather hauberk and red cloak made him look more boastful than any king. Two more were with them, the tall, red-haired Imergi, king of the Western Isles, and the last man to be introduced, whose shield bearer carried the banner of Moray, silver stars on blue.

At first I thought Gilcomgan had arrived late. The man wore a cloak of dark red, and his mount was a beautiful bay horse, with silver beads threaded in its mane and tail; I recognized the bay. When the warrior removed his helmet in courtesy before the two kings, his hair spilled out like gold.

"Mac bethad mac Finlach, *Rí a Moreb*." Malcolm's gruff voice carried far.

I gasped and looked at Ruari. "He is not king of Moray!"

"The king must have ordered Macbeth to take Gilcomgan's place. The province of Moray is too significant to go unrepresented on this occasion."

"King Cnut would not know the real Moray from a shepherd," Angus observed.

"Still, it is not right." I clenched the reins, and my horse stirred.

Ruari took my bridle. "Calm down, Rue. It means nothing outside the ceremony."

"The claim to Moray is like a gnawed bone between those cousins," Conn mac Fergus said. "The king could be stating his preference with this introduction."

I nodded. "This is an insult and threat to Gilcomgan. King Malcolm is conniving. When my betrothed learns about this—"

"Do not send word to him," Ruari warned. "It is not your place."

"He will find out, nonetheless. The monks here will record this event and list the attendants in their annals. Word will spread. Gilcomgan will know."

"The matter is between him and Macbeth," Ruari said.

Remembering Macbeth's warning to me, I sat silent. As the kings made pledges regarding their shared border—without a statement of obeisance, pleasing the Scots if not the Saxons—I nursed resentment. That day sparked the first loyalty I ever felt for the region of Moray. Macbeth was a usurper. I would see it no other way.

I glanced around at the spectacular view of the hills and glens of both Scotland and northern England, rolling hills and lush meadows that made cattle fat and sheep content, and caused men to lust after claiming the territory. Father Anselm once told me about a long stone wall south of Lothian, which Hadrian the Roman leader built to hem in the Picts and Scots. Little good it did, for those early people were persistent defenders of their lands. After a while the frustrated Romans built a second wall, farther north, to keep the wild Picts from attacking them. The Scots like to boast that the conquering Romans left Britain shortly after that.

"I wonder why," I mused to Ruari, who leaned to listen, "men cannot just let old Hadrian's wall define their borders, and have done with disputes. Let the Saxons stay south of the wall, and the Scots north, so we would all have peace."

"Why let ancient Romans decide our boundaries, when men can fight for new borderlines and gain more land?"

I remembered the sight of heads on pikes, and souls lost. "Why indeed," I said bitterly, "does death become an ordinary price, when dominion is at stake?"

"Consider what is best for Scotland and its Scots. Then you will understand."

I did, and nodded. From my father and the lessons all around me, I knew it was essential to defend and nurture Scotland. I saw in count-less ways, significant and trivial, how we valued not only kin and kin groups, but the beautiful land that supported us.

We turned our attention back to the ceremony.

THAT EVENING many of us gathered to stay the night at a Lothian house belonging to one of Malcolm's thanes. Others stayed at a monastery, and many of the Saxon party set up tents in a meadow. The house was long and roomy and could accommodate dozens of guests at table, fewer in beds. As one of the few females in the party, I was given a large box bed to share with Aella, Bethoc, and the thane's daughter.

At the celebration, we dined on thick broths, roasted meats, and vegetables made savory with salt and fresh herbs. Musicians sat in a corner of the hall, playing tunes on harp and drum, and I tapped my foot and nodded my head to the music. An inept juggler dropped his bright ribbands and balls of stuffed leather, and went chasing after them while we laughed heartily. The food, music, and entertainment were all excellent, and the imported wine made my head spin.

Most interesting was a Breton *conteur* supplied by King Cnut, who had also sent tuns of wine to entertain the Scots staying with the Lothian thane. The bard plucked the strings of his harp and began a new poem, one he composed on the spot in honor of the day. The group listened eagerly, applauding or stamping their feet to show approval. After describing the meeting of the kings in flattering terms, the bard mentioned each notable man present, including "dark-browed Bodhe, strong of heart," and "the fierce red giant of the Isles," upon which Imergi bowed while others laughed.

Next the bard spoke of "the warrior from the north with hair like the sun, the son of life." We are fond of puns in our land, and this bit of cleverness was met with applause, for the bard made up his rhyme in a blend of Saxon and Gaelic. All knew he meant Macbeth, whose name in Gaelic is *mac bethad,* son of life.

"Bodhe's fire-haired daughter, with eyes like stars, a voice like a lark," he said.

Sitting straighter, flushing to the roots of my hair, I heard him speak of the princess who would soon be small queen, as some call it, of Moray, with her grace and her swan-necked beauty. I ducked my head while people clapped and looked toward me.

Beside me, Ruari laughed. "Grace! The bard never saw the swan-neck take down her opponent in the practice yard!" Nearby, Angus and Conn chortled. "Though we will never dispute the beauty." Ruari lifted his cup to me and drank. So did others around us, and thankfully the bard moved on in his poem.

"Ruari mac Fergus," I said low, "if you are sodden, do not guard me this night."

He set down his cup. "If you ever need true guarding rather than nursemaiding, I will be there, Lady Gruadh." He glanced at me for a moment—sincere, he was, not the least drunk—then turned to speak to Angus.

After that, I conversed a little with Lady Sybilla, wife of Duncan mac Crinan and daughter of Siward, earl of Northumberland. She was sturdy and fair, and seemed weary, having not slept the night before, as her two small sons had head colds. The toddler was Malcolm for his royal grandfather, the infant Donald Bán, a word meaning pale or fair. We spoke of the evening's entertainment, and Sybilla eased my embarrassment at being named in the bard's poem. She admired the handiwork on my undergown, cream wool edged in Dolina's fine stitchery, intertwined vines in many colors. When Lady Sybilla left to sit with her children, she embraced me like a friend. She was a warmhearted woman, despite being both Saxon and Danish.

Later, I saw my father seated at a small game table with Macbeth. If Bodhe had not beckoned me over, I would have kept my distance. They played chess, and I watched them for a few moments. My father made an ill-thought move and jeopardized a key piece, which Macbeth snatched up.

"Perhaps my daughter should advise me in this next move. She can hardly do worse." Bodhe shook his head. "The French wine is telling upon me."

What game was this, besides chess? He held his wine well, and his game could be saved.

"If you prefer, let the lady take your place," Macbeth said. "I would be honored."

The wine was telling on me, too, for I agreed, though my chess skill was modest. Macbeth stood, Bodhe, too, and my father drew out his chair of wicker and wood for me, then walked away to greet another man who had hailed him.

Seated, I glanced at the board, then at Macbeth. In the firelit glow, his strong-cut features bespoke some Norse blood, as did his deep-set eyes and tall build. Two slender braids mingled in his hair; I wondered if his wife or a mistress had done that. Along his right cheek, a faint scar slanted toward his mouth and mustache. I glanced away when he looked at me.

Studying the board, I saw my principal pieces, and a few ways to defend territory, royalty, and men. Each stocky little piece had been carved from small blocks and incised with minute details, including embroidered robes and chain mail, wide eyes and solemn expressions, even wicker chairs much like the one that supported me.

"This is a fine set," I commented. "My father has one with pieces carved of oak and walnut, though not so well crafted as this. Is it ivory?"

Macbeth nodded. "Walrus tusks and teeth. I own one similar to this."

"At your home in . . . Moray?" I said carefully.

"I have property along that border, where my wife and I make our home."

"Is your wife from Moray, then?"

"Orkney," he answered succinctly.

So he had solid Viking connections with his cousin Jarl Thorfin through a wife. Why did Bodhe want us to sit and talk in this cordial arrangement, if I was already betrothed? I did not see the point. "You also stay with the king. I hear he fostered you." I tilted my blocky little king with a finger.

"As one of his men, I am often with his court. Lady, your move."

I lifted the pawn, a warrior carved with helmet and shield. My game pieces were cream colored, with a little ink rubbed into the grooves to bring out the details. Macbeth's chessmen were stained dark red.

He tapped his fingers, watching me. Seeing my best chance, I shifted the pawn to capture his bishop. Macbeth cocked an eyebrow in silence, reached forward to slide a rook from the back row, taking a spot between my queen and bishop. His single move threatened both my pieces. I had not seen it coming.

I frowned. If I moved one out of danger, the other would be taken. Leaning forward, my braid looping over my shoulder, I perused the board. Then I took his offending rook with my queen. Sliding her into place, snatching up the defeated piece, I looked up at Macbeth.

He inclined his head graciously, hovering his fingers over the board. His hands were large, agile, rough. He touched a reddened horseman that sat between one of my men and a bishop, then snatched up my queen and set her aside. "Beware, lady," he murmured. "Sometimes an unassuming warrior can move swiftly to possess a queen."

"Boldly said for one who plays with walrus teeth."

"Just so." He sounded amused. "Lady Rue, I hear they call you for a byname, rather than Gruadh, your formal name, is that so? Odd to use a Saxon word for a princess of the Gaels. Are you called so for the herb?"

"Hreowe," I said, gazing at the board. "Rue . . . of the Sorrows."

He lifted a brow. "For the old Irish tale of Deirdriu and the Three Sorrows?"

"A Saxon priest gave me the name when I was young."

"Gruadh," he murmured. My name sounded different in his care, *Groo-ath,* said softly. "There is an old tale about another of that name. Gruaidh Ghrian-sholus, the lady of the sunbright cheek. Cu Chulainn, the great hero of the Fianna, fell in love with her."

"What girl did Cu Chulainn not fall in love with, I would like to know," I muttered.

He laughed. "Gruadh suits you. No lady so lovely should bear a sorrowful name."

Wary, I glanced up. "And your name? Macbeth is not commonly heard. In fact, today I heard some Saxon call you 'that king with the outlandish name.'"

"The name is strange to non-Gaels. They think it is a patronymic when it is not. My parents lost the infants born before me, and though I was born early, I survived. They baptized me 'son of life' in gratitude, and with hopes for my future."

"Better to be named for life than sorrow."

"Life and sorrow," he said, "often go hand in hand."

"Too often, they do." I returned my attention to the board, and he sat back.

Soon the abduction of my queen crippled my campaign. "Care for your king," Macbeth warned, with proper manners. I saw the danger and slid a warrior along to protect. But Macbeth's king aced my own stout little fellow, who had no defense left.

"Why were you announced as Moray at the border homage?" I asked bluntly.

"Your beloved was not there, and it was important for Moray to be seen."

"That title is not yours to claim under any circumstance."

"Some would disagree." He shrugged. "Will we have another game?"

"We will not," I said haughtily, and rose to my feet. He stood as well.

"Lady Gruadh," he said. "Beware, when you go to Moray. Tell your guard to watch you close, each day." He nodded toward Ruari, who waited nearby.

I frowned. "Another warning? I understand your grievance, sir," I replied. "But it is yours alone to bear. Do not burden me with it."

"Tell him, or I will myself," Macbeth repeated. "Lady." He inclined his head, and I turned away without reply.

Ruari had witnessed my defeat at chess, but gave no sign he had overheard. He held out a hand to escort me, and we crossed the room together. I told him nothing.

THE NEXT morning, we gathered outside the nearest church to witness the final homage ceremony. Malcolm and Cnut would meet again, and Duncan's eldest son, another Malcolm, would be presented to the Saxon king. At one point, King Malcolm himself carried his great-grandson and held him out to King Cnut. The prince, at two years old a sturdy handful, set up a lusty caterwauling, so that both men looked annoyed. Still, the message was clear: young Malcolm mac Duncan of Scotland had made a symbolic homage to the ruler of England.

And it was clear to those watching that in making his great-grandson pledge to England, old Malcolm was declaring that his line, grandson to son, would be kings hereafter. I saw Bodhe, Macbeth, and several others looking grim. Few applauded.

The child's mother, Lady Sybilla, stepped forward to take her boy from her father-by-law. I was among the retinue of women who walked with her, and she turned to give the squalling child to me. He struggled to get down, and I set him on his feet, taking his hand. He pulled me along rather like a ram dragging its shepherd. Others were amused, but I felt a strange sense, like a weight on my shoulders, on my soul.

And then, with a shudder, I knew it for an omen of the future—myself, and all of us gathered that day were linked to this moment as if by the tug of a heavy chain. That quick symbolic pledging between a fussy child and two old warrior-kings held some meaning, but I did not yet know what.

Chapter Ten

Nearly everything in Dun Abernethy was oiled, polished, scrubbed, and repaired as we readied for the wedding. Dolina thrived on the whole business, creating a daily, sometimes hourly, flurry. She oversaw the brewing and baking for the wedding feast, and commanded servants like a *dux bellorum,* so that they ran to do her bidding.

In the kitchen, she stirred pots and tasted new dishes, and in the hall she had two seamstresses, along with Aella and myself, stitching at a lunatic pace. She made sure our dogs were bathed weekly in bog myrtle to discourage fleas, so much that they slouched away when they saw her coming. In every room in the keep, but for the garrison on the ground floor, she was little short of a terror. Bodhe and I avoided her as much as possible.

Weeks earlier she had dragged me off to a weekend fair to buy lengths of silk and linen, and we all worked tirelessly to stitch the cut fabrics into gowns, chemises, veils, and bedclothes. These were packed into a wooden chest with dried lavender and bogbean, ready to be carted to my new home in Moray.

Then, on a drizzly May morning, I was wed to Gilcomgan in the way of the Roman Church, with vows repeated and blessings intoned on the rain-swept porch of the parish church, rather than inside. Only a true queen could be married within the walls of a bishop's church. Truly I had wanted a Celtic wedding, with ancient poems and heartfelt vows spoken over the eternity of water and flame, with hands and arms entwined to symbolize infinity. I did not smile, not when I received a cool, bristly kiss from my groom, nor when my father whispered that I looked as beautiful as my mother had on the day of their marriage. We entered the church to kneel in repentance for sins we had not committed but apparently would. And then we were done.

I sat through the supper, the music and dancing afterward, feigning happiness. My bridegroom said little to me, but enjoyed himself otherwise, laughing and raising his cup to the company gathered in our hall.

Late that night, when we were led to our bed in a guest building, we were followed by a raucous band of merrymakers—those who could still walk, for Bodhe had supplied French wine and Danish mead, and a heady batch of Dolina's own birch leaf wine. Accompanying us to the bedchamber, the guests played small pipes and drums, clapped and sang and otherwise made a good deal of noise. Gilcomgan, who had to wait until his bride was ready, was carried off by his own men. They are not called "wild Moray men" for nothing. I had never seen males who could drink more or shout louder.

Dolina and my women undressed me, my stepmother clucking over every detail, insisting on flower petals in the floor rushes—bluebells and primroses—and beeswax candles burning on the iron-spiked candleholders. She sprinkled the essence of sweet myrtle inside and outside the curtained bed, knotted red threads on the bedposts, and draped a leafy rowan branch over the doorsill, all for protection from evil spirits and the mischievous fairy ilk.

Maeve made me drink a draught of wine laced with an infusion of willow and chamomile to dull discomfort, and *sceach,* or hawthorn, to stir my body. Then my women rubbed me all over with an ointment of sweet myrtle and lavender, and tucked me into bed, naked, shoulders and arms outside the covers, hair combed out in a fiery stream.

Shortly afterward, my father and several others—all men, by tradition—came in to kiss me good night, one after the other. I could not look at any of them.

Finally Gilcomgan stumbled in, fair intoxicated. Crouching, he jumped onto the bed, for tradition demands the groom leap like a salmon swimming upriver to find its mate. The bed almost collapsed, our laughing friends withdrew, and we were alone.

He was not unkind or brutish. Rather, he was a fast rutter, inconsiderate and unskilled, a solid and heavily muscled man with ham hands and a soggy kiss. Our first encounter was over in moments, leaving me astonished to be so handled, and bleeding slightly. The spots on the linen pleased him to no end, for he judged it evidence that I, too, had enjoyed our encounter.

Past dawn, he startled me awake, and I shoved him away in a panic, scrambling out of reach. He sat up, naked and groggy, and I gave him such a lashing of words that he blinked at me and stammered an apology.

It was a start.

THE DAY before I left Abernethy for Gilcomgan's northern home, my nurse, Maeve, remarked on my paleness and the circles beneath my eyes, and wondered if I had already conceived a child. I reminded her snappishly that the days were rainy, and I never thrived in damp weather. I would not admit my dread of leaving home for remote Moray.

I went to my father's bard, Luag, who was already an old man then, and asked him what he could tell me of my new home. He was stooped and white haired, but his voice was strong and his memory keen. He took up his brass-strung harp to help him remember, and he closed his eyes and began to recite a long list of kings and warriors going back to the Picts who inhabited the northern lands before the Scotti, who were Irish invaders, came eastward to conquer and settle Scotland. He, too, said that Moray was an enormous land, stretching east to west, a fertile land of mountains, moors, lochs, and beaches. Most important, Luag assured me, civilization and not just hillside savagery would await me. I would be a contented lady, he promised.

That day, Drostan sought me out to tell me that he, too, was leaving

Dun Abernethy. He would not ride north with the Fife men assigned to Moray, but would join the monastic community on an island in Loch Leven in central Fife. That peaceful isle, which I had visited with Bodhe, was dedicated to Saint Servanus, an Irish monk who helped bring Christianity to Scotland. The monastery was kept by the Céli Dé, the "servants of God" or the Culdees, and kept Celtic ways despite Rome's ongoing dispute with some of their rules and practices. Among the greatest treasures at Saint Serf's, other than sheer peace, were the books in their small library.

"They have copies of the works of Saint Adomnan, who wrote a life of the holy Saint Columba, and recorded the ancient laws of Ireland," Drostan said. "And they own a book of laws written in Adomnan's own hand. I will learn a great deal there, and may be allowed to copy the works of Adomnan myself one day, in their scriptorium."

He seemed excited, and his path was not altogether surprising, for as a boy he had come to Abernethy from a monastery that had burned down. The abbot, my mother's cousin, had sent the child to Bodhe for safety.

Learning that Drostan would leave made my heart plummet. Yet I smiled and wished him well, and hid my sadness.

When my bridegroom and I left Fife, we took with us a caravan of men and horses, with Aella and Maeve on garron ponies, and servants guiding three carts packed with my belongings and some household goods. As part of the bride gift, Bodhe had given Gilcomgan the service of twenty housecarls, including three of the sons of Fergus, because they were my friends. My father added two dozen horses, three fine hawks, and ninety-nine cattle, a particular number believed to bring good fortune. And I had the gray wolfhound, Cu, as comfort and companion.

Even with so much of home with me, as we lumbered away, I could not bear to look back.

WE CAME to the fortress at Elgin, a ringed citadel on a windswept hill, and we came to an odd peace, Gilcomgan and I. He liked the way we warmed a bed together, and other than a hunt, a fine vat of wine, and skirmishing with raiders or Norsemen, the man needed little to content him. Bed warming became tolerable for me, with glimmers of pleasure. We had moments of laughter, even of understanding. After a while I grew fond of him as a fireside companion in the evenings when he was at home in Dun Elgin.

He kept a scant household and a tight purse, so that we had no household bard, nor even a harper to entertain and soothe us, but for itinerant bards who came to the gates now and then. They were welcomed for the news they brought as much as their music. Yet Gilcomgan himself was surprising good company. His comments regarding the wars and grievances and feuds in Scotland were insightful, and he had a long memory and long experience. He also had a gift for mimicry. His imitations of old King Malcolm and Thorfin the grim Raven-Feeder were sharp and amusing, and his recountings of the old Irish tales, which were already dear and familiar to me, were excellently done.

Aella and Maeve, along with Angus, Conn, their youngest brother Brendan mac Fergus, and others, would gather round the bright hearth to listen as my husband recounted battles he had seen and tales he had heard, and spoke of leaders he knew. We all laughed and applauded and looked forward to evenings when my husband was home and in a mood for stories after supper, for he was often away with his retainers for hunting, or to visit his thanes or patrol the borders and coasts of Moray.

I came to believe that Gilcomgan should have been a bard. He might have found contentment, and a comfortable old age, along that path.

I even half forgot that my husband had taken part in the murder of his own uncle. He never spoke of it, nor did I tell him that I had witnessed the king's justice in that matter. Yet at times I saw a cold brute in him like a flash of lightning. I came to understand that killing is a necessary and grim consequence in a warrior's life. Sometimes it must be done.

· · ·

So THE first months of my marriage passed with the seasons. For luck we placed rowan branches over the doorways and left them there through autumn, replacing them in winter with juniper and pine swags for that cleansing aroma. Lavender from the kitchen gardens was scattered everywhere underfoot for its fragrance, with long dried stems tied and placed near the entrance gates to protect against enemies. We sat with our mending and embroidery, and Maeve taught me to spin yarn on the distaff. I taught Aella what reading I knew with the help of my little gospel book, with its brightly painted images and carefully scribed words, a precious thing I had inherited from my mother.

At Elgin, I was not daughter but wife, with household concerns to oversee. Now and then Angus and Conn would cross swords with me in the yard when my husband was away, but Gilcomgan disliked me to handle swords. "I want sons of you," he told me one day, "not wounds." We laughed a little, but I knew the seriousness beneath his jest.

Most of the time I was ensconced within Elgin's thick walls, venturing out little enough and with a close guard, my company limited for the most part to my two women. My husband frequently visited other fortresses in his province, but hated the fuss of moving households for a season. While I visited a few of the closer forts with him, we always returned to Elgin when possible. Though Lady of Moray, I did not feel so. Most people of the region, with its wide expanse and remote corners, knew my name, but few saw me.

With the help of Maeve, Aella, and the serving women, I learned the ways of running a household on the rules of scarcity that Gilcomgan set: our candles were of tallow, not expensive beeswax, even though tallow burned faster and had a rancid odor. Nor did we spend more than necessary on linens, dishware, or spices, though good imported wines were an exception. I was expected to keep tight account of the larder stock, although during the winter's cold, I sent sacks of oats and root vegetables to the local tenants, knowing that some of them suffered dearly in their wattle-walled homes.

Nearly a year into our marriage, I did not come into my flowers, as some women call their courses. I was with child at last. And if all went well, just past the turn of the new year, I would fulfill my responsibility and produce a son or daughter for the house of Moray.

Filled with a little spark of new life, I cherished the future at last. Other than some early sickness, I was very well, and grew lush and content. I began to hope that the pattern of sorrows would vanish at last for Lady Rue, and joy would be her name.

II.

A falcon, towering in her pride of place . . .

—*Macbeth,* act 2, scene 4

Chapter Eleven

"Rise up, lady," my nurse whispered, shaking me. "You must wake—oh, hurry!"

Seven months gone with child and groggy from it, I woke feeling as if I swam upward through peaty water. Then I realized that the other side of the bed was empty and cold. My husband had not returned in the night from his patrol. Suddenly alert, I swung my feet over the side of the down-filled mattress and stood as Maeve draped a robe over my shoulders, the fur lining silky and warm in the chill.

"What is it?" I wrapped the robe over my swollen belly. The child tumbled within, its foot finding my bladder. I winced.

"A messenger came knocking at the gates. He was sent by the thane of Banchorrie, who warns us to leave soon. Men are approaching Elgin."

Puzzled, I hastened toward the curtained doorway that led to the latrine. If the child kicked any harder, he would kick himself clear out, I thought.

When I came back, Maeve was rummaging through the large wooden chest that had belonged to my mother, carved with interlaced birds painted red and yellow. I poured a cup of water from an earthen pitcher. Wine, even watered, no longer agreed with my childbearing body, and I had taken to drinking boiled water infused with herbs, or heated milk with a little honey. "Why would he send such a message? I do not know the thane of Banchorrie, though my father does."

"No matter—if your husband's enemies are coming, we cannot dawdle!" Maeve snatched up a tunic gown the color of midnight, an underdress of linen, stockings with ribbon garters, and thrust the bundle at me. Shivering, I dropped the fur robe to dress, settling the garments around my distorted shape.

"Likely it is only the thane of Rothes on his way here again, to complain that his herds are lighter because his neighbors are all thieves," I murmured, stifling a tug of concern. "Whoever they are, I will send them away."

"The child within you has addled your brainpan, I swear it! You have an unnatural calm about you these days. We will all die here if you do not hurry!" Maeve paced, looking out the narrow window.

"And you talk nonsense." I drew a breath, for my back ached suddenly, sharply. Smoothing the long plaits of my hair, I took up a veil of loose-woven linen and set it in place with a band of braided yarns. If men were indeed coming to the hall, even to gripe about missing cows, I must appear the capable lady of Elgin and Moray.

"Listen to me," Maeve insisted. "It is Mac bethad mac Finlach who rides for your gate with a host of men at his back! Banchorrie's messenger warns us to *flee*!"

I looked up quickly. "Macbeth?"

"And he has reason to hate your husband," Maeve pointed out. "Whatever brings him to Elgin, it is a matter for warriors, not women, and so we must leave quickly."

"I am not going anywhere."

"I have seen a fighting spirit in you like a hot lick of fire," my nurse said, "but this is not the time for it. With Macbeth riding here in the dead of a cold night, and your husband not at home . . ." She gave me a hard stare.

Awkwardly, I stuck my foot into one of my leather slippers, foregoing hose for the sake of speed. "This is my home, and I am great with child. *Oof,*" I added, stretching my foot toward the next shoe, "and I resent being ousted from my bed. I shall tell these men so—Macbeth, too—if they are so rude as to knock on our gates."

Maeve knelt to tug up my slippers. "A woman will not dissuade men intent on mayhem."

"Then let the edge of my blade turn them away." I walked to another chest, which contained linens and the sheathed weapon my father had given me. I had not practiced for months, and it would be neither easy nor wise to swing a blade, when I could not even see my feet. My balance was all wrong.

"You cannot mean to bring that," Maeve said.

Unable to belt the sword, I carried it with me to the door. *Dear God, where was Gilcomgan?* "I am in charge of Elgin just now. Come ahead. Where is the messenger?"

"Eating oatcakes and butter in the kitchen."

"Desperate indeed." I stepped out into the dank corridor.

"Watch yourself on the steps," Maeve warned. "You are big as an ox."

THROUGH SMALL arrow-slit windows in the walls, the cold midnight wind blew, and I heard a heavy pounding at the gate. Down the steps we went, I as cautious as an ox on stairs should be. When we reached the landing and the heavy outer door, we took another downward course to reach the yard.

Here the thudding was loud, and torchlight flickered beyond the palisade walls. I hastened toward the main gate, clumsy and increasingly alarmed. The sentinel, Angus mac Fergus, waited with staff and sword in his hands, several housecarls with him. Gilcomgan had ridden out with fifty men on patrol, leaving these few to guard the gates, the keep, and his wife. Usually he was more cautious.

The gate, stout oak and iron, trembled with the next volley of slams, as men shouted to be let into Moray's tower. Glancing around, I saw others running toward me through the darkness, one of them old Aedh, Gilcomgan's head groomsman, cloak and tunic flapping about his bony legs. With him was the messenger, a lanky boy with dark hair and flushed cheeks. "Lady Gruadh! I am Donal, sent by Constantine of Banchorrie."

"Tell me what this is about, Donal." The hammering at the gate continued.

"Men sent by the king are on their way here. The son of Finlach leads them."

"Apparently they are here now, and impatient to be admitted."

A shattering slam sounded then, and I jumped. My child within leaped. Setting a hand to my belly, I hastened toward the entrance, still carrying my sword. Angus tried to bar my way, but I gave him a searing glance and marched forward. Behind me, throughout the bailey yard, more men came running.

On that November night past Martinmas, we had no more than twenty men in all to defend the gates. Anxious but hiding it, I peeked through a crack between the massive doors and saw torchlight and shadows, and the shapes of armored men. "Who are you, and what do you want?" I called.

"We seek entrance into Moray's tower," a man answered.

I knew that voice. A shiver went through me, followed by a sear of anger. "Moray himself is not at home. Be gone from here."

"I am Mac bethad mac Finlach, and known to the lady of this keep. Tell Lady Gruadh that I seek conference with her."

"She will not admit men who behave like wild boars. Be gone from here."

Silence. Then the creak of leather and the sound of steel sliding clean from more than one sheath. "Let us in, Lady Gruadh." He stood very close on the other side of the thick wooden barrier. "Or this gate comes down."

"Say your business from where you are."

"I bring a message from your husband. Lady," he said, sounding grim and weary, "extend us hospitality."

Celtic tradition demanded that I do so, even to enemies of the house. "I will not."

"Well enough." He gave an order behind him.

Angus took my arm and moved me forcibly back. I shook him off, raised my sword high, and shifted to stand where I would be seen immediately if the doors gave way. "Wait," I told my husband's men— my men. "Do nothing yet."

I could easily have ordered them to open the gate. *Let Macbeth work hard at this,* I thought. *Let him sweat and curse and know the barrier of Moray strong about me.*

The pounding came in earnest, the sound of a ramming log and splitting wood. "Angus," I called. "Stand back, lift your bows. Load them, and I will stand here." He nodded. I knew my men would protect me, and I gambled that our unwanted guests would spare me for my gender and condition, and the precious blood that ran through both me and my child.

Soon the oak cracked, split, gave. I held the sword upright, edge outward, and widened my stance. The wooden bar splintered and fell at my feet, and I danced backward as it bounced, thinking of the babe, wondering then if I had gone lunatic. My fingers shook on the sword grip as the gates swung open, and men filled the gap like a gruesome beast, glowing in torchlight and spiny with spears. I stood my ground.

"Lady," Macbeth said, eyes gleaming beneath the helmet, jaw square, unforgiving. "What welcome is this?"

"Be gone from my house." I kept my sword upright. Behind me, Angus and the others raised their bows, arrows nocked.

Macbeth flicked his hand, and the men behind him lifted their bows too, wicked arrow points aimed at us. My faithful few and I did not waver. I was breathing so hard it hurt. "Be gone, son of Finlach," I rasped, sword blade bisecting my view of him.

He gestured toward my men. "Is this all the guard your husband left you?"

"All I required, until you brought your brutes here."

"I warned you that you would need a guard here in Moray. Put down your sword," he said, impatient. "It is not seemly for a woman to be warlike, especially one in your state. I came here only to speak with you, not to harm you."

"So your manner of knocking proves." The sword was heavy, my back ached. "Get out."

Macbeth sighed, half turned, then lashed out and took my sword edge in his gauntlet. He wrenched the weapon away from me. Stumbling, I fell to my knees, so off balance that I tilted, but caught myself and rolled to my side to protect my child.

Chaos. Angus and the others let loose their arrows, and the Elgin few came forward with swords, spears, axes. When I reached for my discarded sword, Macbeth kicked it out of the way, then grabbed me under the arms and dragged me backward to the foot of the palisade. As he strode away, I saw a few men stumble and fall, and heard him shout orders to bring in the horses, secure the gates, move the dead out of the way.

On hands and knees, I crawled forward. Macbeth strode toward me again. "Foolish woman!" he growled. "Do you want to kill your babe? Stay by the wall!"

Subsiding against the wooden barricade, I looked up at him. "What do you want here? You bring no word from my husband—he would never trust you."

"I carry his last words to you," he answered. "He is dead."

My blood went cold. "Dead? You killed him—"

"Not I. He burned, he and his men, in the tower at Burghead. They are gone."

All of them? I stared. "It is not so."

"It is." Beyond us, I saw his men dragging a few Elgin men—I could not see whom—slowly, so slowly, heels tracking in the dust.

"What message did my husband give you?" I could not comprehend what he told me—it could not be, any of this.

"He was brought out before he died," he said. "We spoke. He asked me to watch over you and the child."

I would have thought a murderer would look away from his victim's widow. Not this one. "Why did you do this?" I burst out. "So you could be Moray?"

"I was always Moray." His voice was quiet as death.

Chapter Twelve

I did not go willingly, near dawn, when I was walked out of Elgin fortress and down the hill. The mere fact of my belly intimidated my guards, who hesitated to lay hands on me, until a giant of a man, black bearded and wearing chain mail, lifted me up in his hulking arms and carried me to the yard of the church. Steady, he was, and silent. He set me down and stood back.

"Giric, bring her here," Macbeth called. "This will be done under holy sanction," he continued, taking my arm in a hard grip as I mounted the step with Giric the giant.

"Married hastily with a war band for witness is no good omen," I said. "And you are married already." That was no deterrent to some Vikings, but I thought it should be for him.

"I am free for this," he replied, "as are you."

He and Giric kept me fast between them—as if I could flee, weighed by grief and exhaustion, and the needs of my child within. Moments later the parish priest arrived, having been dragged from his bed to first bless the dead inside the fortress and then marry a murderer to his victim's widow.

Fog lingered eerily in that early hour. Dawn is one of the time-between-times, as the Gaels say, and it seemed a poor omen to pledge sacred marriage at that mystical hour in so dishonorable a way. Up the hill, I could see the glow of moving torches, as more men entered Elgin's gates. I shivered. Macbeth, I knew, awaited men who would bring the shrouded bodies of Gilcomgan and his slain warriors to Elgin for burial.

Of our men, Aedh the old groom and a housecarl had perished. Among the wounded were Brendan and Angus mac Fergus. Though Angus had taken a sore wound to the head, he was on his feet, but Brendan's fate, after a deep cut to the thigh, was unknown as yet.

I faced Macbeth, exhausted and angry. "I would prefer to be wed in the old Celtic way, with charms and blessings. And I have the right to choose my next husband myself, now that you have killed the good one I had."

"The old Celtic way, is it." He took my arm to walk with me, turning so that we circled round the priest, who stared as if we were mad. Three times we did this, moving sunwise left to right, in ancient blessing tradition.

"There is your charm." Then he pointed toward the hills, where the sun was a pink-gold wafer through the mist. "And there is your omen. Father, go on."

The priest began to intone the Latin, and though I answered terse and unwilling, the union was pronounced. Barely widowed, I was wed again. I glared at the priest, who kept the parish at Elgin. He must have felt ashamed, for he looked away from me.

"The priest is not to blame. I will send a portion in thanks, Father," Macbeth said.

A chiding, after murder and a marriage, did not set well with me. I gathered my skirts and headed back up the long slope toward Elgin's palisade and open gates. Though breathless and clumsy, I did not stop until I reached the gate, then paused, dizzy, pressing a hand to my belly. When Aella rushed toward me, we embraced, and I smoothed her hair, seeing that she was pale and quivering. "Did they touch you?"

She shook her head. Still, I could see she was frightened; temper flaring, I walked over to confront Macbeth. "The laws designed by the holy monk Adomnan, set down by his hand three hundred years past,"

I said in hissing fury, "state that the women and children of the Gaels must be treated fairly and morally, without violence of any kind."

"Excellent. The lady knows her letters and her laws."

"I do. And I know you have broken the laws of the land in more than one way."

"Lady Gruadh, I did only what was necessary to claim Moray back again. Mungo," he said, calling one of his retainers, a man roughened by time, age, and lack of washing. "Take the lady to her chamber and see she stays within."

"First I will see to my household." Linking arms with Aella, I climbed the steps to the keep, the guard following. The door was closed, but a sharp glance toward Macbeth's housecarl opened it fast enough.

In the great hall, the peats burned too low, not yet stirred and stacked for morning. Sniffling, Aella set to the task, and I helped. Maeve entered with cups, a jug of ale, and a wrapped cheese for the men. Finding me there, she made me eat for the sake of my child.

Macbeth entered then, steps heavy on the floorboards, and poured a cup of ale for himself. I would not do it for him. "Lady Gruadh," he said, "you will depart Elgin later today. Have your maidservant pack whatever you need. You will be taken to safety."

I faced him. "I will stay. My child will be born here, as befits a child of Moray."

"As you wish," he murmured, and drained the contents of the cup.

RAIN POURED down the day Gilcomgan and many of his men were buried on a grassy slope beside Kineddar churchyard. A mason provided a headstone for my husband, a chunk of honey sandstone carved like a small thatched-roof house to identify his eternal home in the earth. The priest asked heaven to bring peace to their souls.

Refusing to keep to my chamber, I went with Aella and Maeve to our accustomed place in the great hall, some cushioned benches beneath a window at one end of the room. There I took up my stitchery again, abandoned when life was sweet enough for no complaint. The rhythmic movements of the sewing, the bright colors, and the feel of the wool helped me to calm my mind. Feeling numb, I sat sewing and silent, waiting to heal.

And I waited for my father and the men of Fife to avenge my treatment. Soon Bodhe would hear of this, I told myself. He would stir blood feud against my usurper husband on behalf of my dead one. I wanted vengeance, neither the first nor last time I felt that craving. A wild urge in the Celtic blood, passed down the generations, demands justice at any cost. I felt it stirring within.

At night, I tossed alone in my bed, weeping for my lost husband and my child's lost future. Aella and Maeve slept on pallets by the door in case Macbeth tried to breach it in the night. He never did.

"The man should fear for his very soul," Maeve whispered to me one day. "To wed the widow of a slain enemy is old tradition, and he had that right. But to burn his cousin alive and bed that one's pregnant widow . . . ah, that guarantees hellish damnation."

I had no doubt Macbeth knew that already.

A week passed, another, as I waited for the men of Fife to come for payment in kind. Then we saw the king's host riding for Elgin, with the lion banner, red rampant on yellow, fluttering in the wind before them.

Chapter Thirteen

Horsemen streamed through the gates in grand style, shields bright and spearpoints glinting, the king in a billowing red cloak. Malcolm remained mounted while Macbeth and others came forward to meet them. Unnoticed, I crossed the yard too, stopping to watch, hands crossed high on my belly. I hoped Malcolm the Destroyer had come to mow down my second husband with justice's sword. *Now, now for revenge.*

The king exchanged words with Macbeth, then dismounted; though elderly, he was robust and disdained assistance. The two leaders went toward the keep, while our grooms caught the reins of the horses, and other lads ran to fetch ale for the king's men.

So reprimand was not to be immediate. Very well. I waddled after Macbeth and the king. A warrior, gray bearded, ran to give me his hand on the steps.

"Thank you," I said. "Your name?"

"Constantine mac Artair of Banchorrie." His manners were good, his smile warm. Despite my mood, I liked him, and recognized his name.

"Banchorrie! I owe you thanks. You sent a warning on that night . . ."

"I did what had to be done. It was not right to—" He paused. "Lady Gruadh, Macbeth is my nephew, so I hope you will allow me to offer an uncle's goodwill and advice now and then."

Grateful for an unexpected ally, I nodded. He escorted me to the great hall, and we entered together, though neither of us had been invited. Turning, Macbeth glowered.

The king grunted. "Banchorrie," he said. "Lady."

Unsmiling, I bowed my head. At the long oaken table, a maidservant set down a clay jug of red wine. I quietly dismissed her. A few drinking horns lay on the table, and I chose three large horns banded in engraved brass, filling one after the other to their brims and handing them to Macbeth, his uncle, and the king. A full drinking horn cannot be set down, so once accepted, the drink goes in the man.

Luckily, I had no poison to hand. Only Banchorrie would have been safe.

"Welcome to Dun Elgin, Malcolm mac Cineadh." I had been raised well and knew how to greet, how to serve wine with flattery where needed. In Scotland, our manners are forthright; nobility and even kings may be addressed by name, or called by the name of their property. The Franks and Byzantines, I hear, indulge their kings with great fussiness; the Saxons as well.

Malcolm grunted some dismissive reply. He was well over seventy, an astonishing age for a warrior-king. Somehow he had survived every battle, attack, and hate arrow aimed at him.

"I would offer better hospitality, sir, but for the recent death of my husband, Gilcomgan mac Malbríd," I then said.

Malcolm murmured flat sympathies, then raised his horn to drink.

"Have you word of my father?" I asked.

"Gone to Dublin for trading," the king rumbled, clearly uninterested in a troubled widow. But I would not serve wine and withdraw. Not that day.

My wool basket sat on the table. I handled the yarns, fingers sinking into the colored strands, the textures soft, soothing. I swallowed tears, having looked forward to some word from my father, even from such a source as dreadful old Malcolm.

"Lady," Macbeth said. "The king and I have matters to discuss. Let my uncle escort you—"

"I am interested in some of those matters." A woman heavy with child can claim the privileges of the very young and very old, and do what she wills. Lifting a linen cap I had embroidered for my babe, I picked up scissors and nonchalantly trimmed threads. *Snip, snip.*

After Constantine took his leave, Macbeth frowned at me, then joined the king in quiet discussion. Their voices, however, carried well. "So she is alive," the king said.

"Lady Gruadh was not with her husband at the time of the fire, Grandfather," Macbeth said. "Gilcomgan and his men were in the old tower at Burghead."

"Burghead," Malcolm snapped. "Not Elgin? I sent men here—"

"We intercepted them. The deed was done, and as your general, sir, I decided the men need not ride on to Elgin." He held his drinking horn with a white-knuckled grip.

I picked up a woolen skein. "So you rode to Burghead to kill the mormaer and marry the widow before she could even bury her husband." I hoped to stir the king to outrage.

"Marriage!" Malcolm bellowed. "You married that one?"

He jabbed a finger toward me. It was not the response I had expected.

"I did, as the victor." Macbeth's manner was unwavering. "The widowed Lady of Moray is about to bear a child. She needs protecting."

"Ah, the lion takes the wolf's cub into his den." Malcolm sipped from the drinking horn, watching his grandson.

Macbeth shrugged. "The child is my kin and cousin."

Lifting a handful of yarn, I looked up. "This marriage was ill done and should not stand. I refuse it, and appeal to king's justice."

Malcolm wiggled the fingers that held his drinking horn. "Justice was done when Gilcomgan was taken down. Send her away," he told Macbeth.

To him, I was an insignificant creature—a woman, worse, a pregnant one, my womb so full there was nothing left to feed the brain. But if I bore a son, he might someday become a threat to his father's murderers, as Macbeth had done. That could place my child in serious danger. Watching them, I felt a shudder of alarm.

"I gave you Moray," the king told Macbeth. "The girl and her pup hinder you."

His words cut through me like a blade. *I gave you Moray.*

Macbeth glanced toward me, then away; I sensed wariness and quick thought. "It is done," he told his grandfather. "The province is mine."

The king shrugged, as if no blood had spilled, no lives sundered. "Good. With Duncan as tanist and you installed here, my grandsons own near all of Scotland."

"With Duncan for a king, his son after him, and so on," Macbeth said low, "the line of Malcolm will hold Scotland's throne. Such is not the way of the Gaels."

"So you disagree now that you have Moray, and Bodhe's daughter?" Malcolm laughed bitterly. "Age has not made me foolish. Know this—my line must continue into generations for the good of Scotland. The old Celtic ways have lost their purpose. There is much dispute over titles and land these days, and the arguments weaken us from within. My line will end the question of kingship and descent, at least."

"What happens after your death is not your choice," Macbeth replied.

"Did you wed the heiress of the alternate line to power your own claim? Give me homage for Moray, here and now. Loyalty," he roared. "I demand it! By God, my line and Scotland will stand whole after me!"

"You have my loyalty." Macbeth spoke flatly. Though his gaze never flickered, by the door, his housecarls straightened, alert.

"I will call upon it," his grandfather replied. "Never doubt it."

I gave you Moray. Together they had conspired to kill Gilcomgan and wrest Moray from him. Macbeth had overtaken my future, and my child's, out of his own ambition and desire for revenge. My fingers let go the clutched yarn, red strands unraveling like blood to pool on the floor. I turned to leave, to suppress my anger, as Bodhe might have done. But I was not my father.

Swords sparked bright against the wall, where a few of them leaned, unused. One of them was my own. I snatched it up and turned back to face the men. "Upon this sword, which Bodhe gave to me," I said, "I swear to protect my child from all your cold scheming. Listen to me," I said through my teeth when Macbeth stepped forward. "No more of Bodhe's blood shall suffer for your ambitions!"

They stood still, king, husband, and housecarls. An oath made on a blade was a fierce thing and never taken lightly. I wanted them to understand that I was not helpless, no pawn to stand by while their plans destroyed my father's proud line. Wild Celtic blood ran strong in me, a legacy of warriors, warrior queens, and sword oaths. It was not the wisest thing I have done; it was something foolish, something brave. For a moment, we all stared at one another.

Then they moved. Footsteps, angry words, drinking horns set aside to spill out. A hand flashed out to jerk the hilt from my hand. Macbeth took my shoulder and stepped me toward the door, where his housecarls took my arms.

"Jesu," Malcolm growled. "That is a madwoman!"

"It is her grief," I heard Macbeth answer, as I was led away. "She is no threat."

THAT NIGHT I wept until my belly ached. Maeve and Aella said little, only sitting by. A woman, especially a lady and virtual queen in her husband's land, must not give in to the impulsive fires of the heart and baser instincts. She should be exemplary in all matters, dignified and saintlike, charitable and forgiving. I had not been, but refused to apologize.

My oath was sincere and would stand. Somehow, I meant to protect my own.

The king and his men finally left Elgin, and I left my bedchamber, wiser about treachery and more cautious about ambitious warlords. Macbeth did not mention my outburst and allowed me freedom within Elgin and its environs, provided I had a guard at all times.

A FORTNIGHT AFTER my disgrace, when I had grown so big that walking sometimes left me breathless, a group of men rode through the gates. I was in the yard and gasped with relief to see the banner of Fife at last: a stylized lion in black, sewn on a red field. My father was not there, but Finn led the men. As I came forward, they looked surprised, but I was much changed. Then they waved in greeting, and Finn dismounted. "Lady Rue," he said. "You look . . . healthy."

"Kind of you," I said. "What word from my father? Did you come to fetch me?"

"We are here with Fife's bride gift to Macbeth—thirty men and horses in tribute."

"Tribute! Bodhe *approves*?"

"He does, and is glad you are safe at Elgin," Finn said. "He sends fond greetings and regrets that he cannot come north, but looks forward to news of a healthy grandson."

Swallowing bitter disappointment, I smiled, grateful after all to see friends from Fife. I glanced past Finn. "Did you bring Bethoc, or her mother? I will need them soon."

He frowned. "We did not know your need was so . . . imminent."

"No matter. Welcome to Elgin. Come into the hall."

In the hall, I served them myself with handsome cups molded of Moray silver, filled with the imported red wine that came through Moray harbors from France and Flanders. I did my best to show as much grace as I could muster.

Macbeth approved my decorum. I know, for he watched me and nodded.

P EACE AND acceptance were not pretty threads in my wool basket that winter. I realized that I was alone in my resentment and anger. Others readily accepted Macbeth as the new mormaer, soon calling him Moray when they addressed him. He spent hours in discussion with his men, like a king with his council. I do not know where he slept that season— it was not with me. He was often not at Elgin, engaged in hunting and riding patrol, or visiting the local thanes, tenants, and farmers, those who had once given loyalty to Gilcomgan and now seamlessly gave their support to his cousin. He set a sizable guard in place at Elgin, yet no dissenters or enemies appeared. From what I heard, Macbeth had strong support in Moray before he ever moved to take Elgin. He had worked toward it, my Fife men told me, for years.

Left to the company of my women, my embroidery, and my sorrowful thoughts, I was resentful and irritable. Unsure of my status, I felt equally widow, nonwife, lady, prisoner, and soon mother to a fatherless child.

One day Maeve pulled me aside. "Find some peace for yourself," she said. "This grief and torment will poison your babe."

That night I sought out Elgin's little wooden chapel, intending to pray for serenity and forgiveness. When I pushed open the door, I saw that Macbeth was already there, on his knees before the altar. He wore only a simple long shirt and trews, and for a moment I did not know him. His head was bowed, glinting dark gold in the light of candles. I saw him cover his face, and then he prostrated himself on the worn planks of the floor like a suffering pilgrim.

Faith is a private thing to my thinking, and here I witnessed an intimate side of the man. He appeared contrite, even tormented. I guessed at his sin, the murder of his first cousin Gilcomgan. By the teachings of the Church, it could blacken his soul and affect him for all eternity come Judgment Day, if not expunged.

Backing away, I closed the door. I felt a stir of sympathy for a man who felt such clear anguish within himself. When I wanted to hate him most, I could not. By inches and breaths, my resentments faded, much as I strived to stoke them.

Chapter Fourteen

Bitter air and a chill gray sky heralded snow when I sought out my husband, who had just returned from a day's hunting. In the time since the king had departed Dun Elgin, I had scarcely spoken to Macbeth, but now I found him in Elgin's small stone mews, setting a goshawk on its perch and unwrapping the jesses to wind them round the post. When he held out his hand to the groom for the bird's hood, I was the one handed it to him. He took it without a flicker of surprise.

"Kei does not like the hood," I said. "He must be coaxed with a bit of meat."

"He was fed well before our hunt to make sure he would not cover the prey for himself. He cannot be hungry yet." When he began to hood it, the bird bated, falling back from the perch, fluttering its wings wildly. Macbeth and I waited, for there was no other remedy. When the bird tired of its protest, Macbeth righted it again.

"He is temperamental, as goshawks can be," I said, "and expects a treat when he takes the hood. Else he will bate."

"We all like some reward for our cooperation," Macbeth murmured.

I took the little hood from him and stepped forward to whisper to Kei and stroke his breast. Choosing a tidbit from some scraps of fresh meat from a leather bag filled daily, I fed the bird. When I dropped the hood over his head, he took it calmly. "My father allowed me the freedom of his hawks and his mews. I have missed hawking these months." Resting a hand on my high-curved belly, I made my point.

"So you came here to visit the birds? I know you are not keen for my company." He set his hawking glove on a hook with others by the door. "Or do you have something to say?"

"What happened to the wife you had?" I asked. "It is not why I came here, but the mystery concerns me. Did you set her aside so that you could be free to wed Moray's widow? As your new wife, should I take warning?"

"She died last summer," he said, "birthing a stillborn son."

I gasped. "Forgive me." Sympathy washed through me, for I cherished my own unborn child and felt trepidation about the birth to come. "God's mercy on her soul. Who was she?"

"Gudrun was her name. A niece of the king of Norway." He went to the door, put a hand to its iron ring. "Was there anything else, Lady Gruadh?"

"There is. I want to send some men southward to Fife."

"To send word to your father for a rescue?"

"Why bother? He sides with you, no matter that you killed my husband."

"Ugly things happen in war. Spare yourself fretting over it, for the sake of your well-being and that of your child. Shall we go?" He opened the door to a chill wind.

Snowflakes blew about as we walked through the yard, and early twilight cast the world in blue and silver. I shivered. "I need to send some riders south to Fife."

He nodded. "With what message?"

"Angus and Conn mac Fergus will take their brother home— Brendan is recovered enough to travel. And they will fetch my cousins Mairi and Bethoc, who are healers and midwives. Soon I will require their skills."

"A local woman can be summoned quickly when necessary. There is the old herb wife who lives in the glen, who helped the injured men a few weeks ago—"

"I cannot trust anyone in Moray . . . with this birth."

"Because your fortress is filled with enemies?"

"Because I can entrust my child's life only to my own kin."

"Do you think I would order harm to your child because of his lineage?" The words were sharp, angry. "Lady, you do not know me."

Childbirth had taken his wife and son. I should have weighed that before speaking. "Not you. The king and others might regard a child of Bodhe's blood as a threat."

"Be assured, you are both safe in my keeping. Your men may ride south, but there is no guarantee of their prompt return." He looked up to the sky, where soft white flakes swirled. "The mountains passes to the south are already filling with snow, and here we have more. In winter, there is no easy way in or out of Moray. How immediate is your need?"

"My nurse says I have to the kalends of January, two weeks more, before I should count the days."

"Are you sure you have so long? Very well. The men will depart at first light. If they do not return before your need arises, there are other midwives."

I was silent, frowning, my mind set on having Bethoc and Mairi with me.

"All will be well," he said. "Do not worry."

I glanced up at him. "You are no diviner."

"True, but the omens seem good."

I gave a skeptical laugh. "Snow and dread weather?"

"A fresh blanket of snow," he murmured, "covers all that is dark and bleak, and heralds a new beginning. Dread weather, they say, can take the ill luck off of us, and sweep it away in the clouds." We reached the steps to the keep. "And it is nearing Christmas, when we feel a brightening of spirits." He held out a hand to assist me.

I turned and climbed the steps alone.

THE TIGHTENING of my belly awoke me three days later. Resting, it clenched again, and repeated. Carefully I rose and relieved myself in the

privy, then padded out of the room. Aella and Maeve slept on pallets in
a corner; I did not wake them. Down the few steps I went to the level
of the great hall, stopping now and then as the muscle of my womb
grew taut. Uncertain what to expect, not yet sure my time had come,
I did not want to wake Maeve, who would be an anxious whirlwind. I
craved peace before the storm.

The sensations were strong but brief and not constant, and I was
able to leave the keep for the yard, thinking a short walk might bring
comfort. I nodded to the guards as I went. When one asked me if all
was well, he heard my assurance that it was.

In the kitchen building, the cook was early to work, already baking
oatcakes and chopping vegetables for soup, while two girls cut up
plucked fowls to add to the stock. The sight made me suddenly ill. But
I made myself nibble half a buttery bannock and sip some hot vegetable
broth from a ladle, then made my way back to the keep through the
pale dawn light.

At the steps, I felt a strong tightening and paused, setting my hand
upon the wall.

"Lady Gruadh?" A man's voice in the darkness. I turned to see
Constantine of Banchorrie. "Is it now?"

"Soon." I felt a new tensing within. "I hoped my midwife would
be here by now."

"If it comes to a race, your child will win." His hands steadied me
up the stairs, and I was grateful for a solid friend in time of need. Sometimes there is nothing so comforting as that. "My wife has had seven
children," he said.

I sighed. "Even though a man, you know more about the process
than I."

"It is not a man's domain, surely, though sometimes even a man is
called upon to assist. Women are practical creatures, after all, and will
ask for help where it is available. A man's strength can be useful. I have
served as birth chair more than once."

"I have heard of the tradition. Well, if need be, I can send for Banchorrie."

"He will answer if you do. Easy, now." We entered the keep and passed the great hall, where the curtain had been pulled aside. Macbeth was there, and turned to see us.

"What is it?" my husband asked. "Gruadh?" He came closer, scrutinized me. "I will send someone to fetch the local wise wife."

"Do not," I said. "Leave me be with this." A fierce tightening grabbed me, and I pressed a hand to the wall. When the demand upon my body lessened, I straightened and stepped away from both of them. "My women will tend to me."

In the bedchamber, Aella and Maeve were already awake and quickly set to fretting over me. Frightened to my core, I would not show it.

All that day I endured without progress, though Maeve assured me that the birthing would take time and that we must have patience with the phases. I walked the floor, rested in the bed, clung to the posts, and alternately thanked and snarled at my women. Throughout, they were my saviors, rubbing my back and feet, changing my gowns and linens, warming me with blankets or cooling me with damp cloths, depending on my mood. When the waters that cushioned the babe burst from me, and the force of my pulsing womb grew even more intense, I hoped the birth would soon be over. Son or daughter, I craved to see and hold my child.

As night approached, I flagged and faded, putting forth exhausting effort for little advance. The hours wore through the night and into the next day, and I slid down my mountain of courage and grew petty and petulant in its shadow.

Her usual brassiness gone, Maeve turned warmer and loving. She taught me a chant that we recited together, she hoarse, me breathless:

> *Help me in my unburdening,*
> *Assist me, gentle Brigid,*
> *The babe to bring from the bone,*
> *Help me now, dear Brigid . . .*

All through the second day I paced, leaning against my women, sometimes taking to my knees or to my bed. I napped a little, ate nothing, sipped water or the herbal concoctions they gave me. Maeve insisted that we must send for the local midwife, but I refused. Obstinate, unclear in my thinking, fearful of outsiders, I trusted only my own.

"My cousins will come," I said, "they will be here soon."

Aella went to the window repeatedly at my bidding, and even out to the battlements to look, though Maeve said it was a foolish waste of time. My nurse sent her out again to the storerooms for dried lavender, which Maeve sprinkled about the floor and rubbed into my palms to help ease my distress.

Now and then I heard male voices beyond the door, Macbeth and his uncle, too, murmuring in low tones when Maeve went out to speak with them. She came back each time pleading with me to allow them to send for assistance.

"Macbeth is very concerned," she said. "His first wife—"

"Do not say it," Aella and I said in unison.

Still I refused a stranger's help. Maeve insisted that she was a knee-woman, not a womb-woman, as the Gaels call midwives. "Mine is to hold the child, cleanse it, sing to it," she said. "Mine is not to deliver the mother!"

Late on the second day, exhausted and irritable, I could hardly bear to be touched. I was reduced to groaning, panting, sweating, subject to fierce urges to grunt. That encouraged Maeve, who said my passage was opening. But the urge faded, stranding me in a limbo of pain and weariness.

Maeve did what she could to relieve my suffering. She rubbed me with ointments and made me sip hot infusions of raspberry leaves saved from summer, with basil and chamomile added. Sending Aella to fetch two rods of cold-forged iron from the smithy, she placed one under the bed and another before the door to keep away the fairies, who might try to steal the newborn. After draping red threads over the head of the bed, she unbraided my hair, then untied every knot in the room, even to the thongs at the neck of her own tunic and Aella's, too. She also placed a reed basket with oatcakes and cheese outside the door, again to satisfy the fairies and distract them from coming in to snatch away the child.

Putting a burning peat in a dish, she carried it round the bed and the room, sunwise left to right, with a melodious chant that soothed my spirit. She sent Aella out to run the peat coal all around the keep, and to tell the sentinels to open and unbolt all the doors in the compound. Nothing should be sealed, to enable the mother to deliver with better ease.

"The *daoine sìth* will not have this child," I heard Maeve mutter to Aella.

Soon the pains were relentless, yet still the birth did not advance. Maeve sat by me, shaking her head. She, too, looked exhausted.

"You will see your mother sooner than you want," she said harshly, "in the next world when you cross over, for your stubborn nature is your enemy just now. Trust me, and your husband, too. We will not let harm come to you!"

"I must be strong," I panted, "my mother told me to be strong."

"She did not tell you to be stupid," Maeve snapped.

"Rue, your babe is turned wrong, and Maeve is not sure we can coax it round for a proper birth," Aella told me, stroking my damp hair. I panted, shook my head.

When a knock came again at the door, Aella went to answer it, returning in a moment. "Moray himself has gone to fetch a womb wife," she told Maeve.

"Then he has more sense than his lady," my nurse said.

Teeth clenched, I was unable to protest as the crashing waves began anew. "*Cuidich mi a Bhride.*" I began to fear I might die.

Later—who knows how long, I had lost the grasp of hours—the door opened and a woman entered. She was young and dark haired, lovely. In my sweaty, bloated state, her cool hand on my brow felt like an angel's touch. Removing her cloak and pushing up her sleeves, she questioned Maeve, who sounded relieved to answer. The woman bathed my head and hands with a wet cloth.

"My dear," she said, "how you must be suffering. I am Catriona of Kinlossie. Let me help." Her eyes were gray and calm, and I nodded. Then she slid her hands beneath the bedcovers, fingers lightweight and slim as they rounded over my pulsing, turgid belly.

Dipping her fingers in oil, she slipped them inside me, quick and gentle, though I was stunned by such contact. She pushed, tugged, and I cried out, and did again when she enlisted Maeve to shift me to my hands and knees, rump exposed, while they rocked me between them; then more oil, more startling touch, and much murmuring between the women. But if this Catriona could pull my infant out of me and save us both, I did not care if she trussed me like a fowl.

Asking for water, Catriona took the clay dish that Aella fetched, and reached into the seam pocket of her skirt. She withdrew coins, rings—I saw the gleam of silver, gold. She stirred these in the water with a finger, murmuring an invocation.

> *Grace over her, grace under her,*
> *Grace of graces surround her,*
> *No peril shall befall her . . .*

Another traditional appeal to Brigid, whose sign I bore on my shoulder, was a comfort to me. I gripped at the bedclothes while Catriona chanted over the water, gold and silver chinking. She held the bowl to my lips. "Sip," she said, and I did. Bathing my face in the water, she set the bowl aside.

"Why the coins?" Aella asked.

"To brighten her spirit and give her courage and will," Catriona answered. "Coins will ransom the child from whatever forces would prevent the birth. Now we wait."

How long we did so, I cannot say—I thrashed, moaned, nearly a lost soul. The womb wife gently prodded my belly again. I began to shudder, wanting to push with all my being.

"Good," Catriona said. "I will call in Macbeth or Banchorrie to serve as a birthing chair. They both stand ready. You are too weak to—"

"Only my women," I gasped. "And you."

Another spasm caught me fast and hard. When it faded, the women lifted me together until I was upright, nearly squatting. Catriona kneaded my belly to shift my child further, and I lowed like a damnable cow, not caring, wanting only salvation for my babe, and myself. Then the child tumbled like a great fish inside of me, and a grinding urge overtook me. The women made a chair for me of arms and shoulders, and I entered the heart of the whirlwind.

"Push, love," Catriona said, "push . . . good, now breathe . . ."

I did, and again, straining to my soul, and within moments, felt a great, slick shudder as my child slipped out of me, with another push, and safe into waiting hands.

"A son," Catriona said, half laughing, "oh, a beautiful one!" She tipped him downward, then held him up for me: a tiny creature, a wavering cry. Maeve took him to swaddle him, and Catriona led me through the last cleansing push before she and Aella laid me back against the pillows.

Catriona handed the swaddled babe into my arms. His face, miniature and puckered, seemed perfect to me, and I laughed; the pain, though it still hurt, did not matter so much now. Through stinging tears I gazed at him and tumbled headlong into love. Catriona bent forward. My tiny son gripped her finger, and we laughed.

Maeve opened the door and admitted Macbeth, who came toward us, looking weary and shadowed about the eyes. Catriona stood back. As he gazed down at the child, the corner of his mouth lifted in a smile, just where the scar puckered the skin. I had never seen him smile like that, gentle and genuine, and it was surprising fine. As I recalled his lost wife and child, my tender, overwrought heart nearly burst. I drew the blanket down so that he could better see my son.

"He does not look much like his father," he murmured, "but is more the image of his mother, and blessed he is for that."

"Hush," Maeve said. "It is poor luck to speak of a handsome child, for the fairies will become interested!"

Gazing at my son, I saw the resemblance, as if heaven had turned a mirror to my face and made it small, perfect, fragile. He was fair indeed, and he was all to me in the world, my dearling, my son.

"Fought hard and well," Macbeth said, and touched the child's head, then mine, smoothing my hair where it curled, damp, upon my brow. Nodding to the women, he left.

Catriona gave me a strengthening infusion of thyme and honey to sip, and then I rested a little, watching while Aella sanctioned the birth by waving a candle flame three times over the bed where I lay holding my child, my arms and legs still shaking, and my heart so glad after so long with worry and fear. Maeve, taking her right as knee-woman, carried my son sunwise around the room while murmuring a charm meant to spin a whorl of protection against all harmful influences. She held my swaddled son high, his mewling cry heartrending to hear, and passed him over a smoking peat coal in a dish, then over water in a bowl, calling upon dear Brigid to watch over him in all matters, all his life.

Unwrapping him, she splashed drops of water over his brow and chest, and he gasped and startled his arms and legs. Then his knee-woman sang what is known among the Gaels as the sweetest music that can ever be heard on earth:

> *A little wave for body, a little wave for speech,*
> *A little wave for health, a little wave for luck,*
> *A little wave for courage . . .*
> *And nine small waves for grace*

Even in her crusty voice, the melody was lovely, and when Catriona and Aella joined in harmonies, the song took on the eloquence of angels.

Chapter Fifteen

"Lulach," Maeve commented, "is a name for a milch cow."

"It is an uncommon name for a son," I agreed, "but I have heard it said in the long list of my father's ancestors. There was a Lulach in Bodhe's line who is remembered as a fine warrior, and so it seems fitting for this one."

"You could name him Gilcomgan," Macbeth murmured. He stood looking down at the child in my arms on a morning when I sat in the great hall with my women and my newborn. He reached out as if to touch the child's head, then paused and did not.

"It is Norse custom to name a newborn son for his deceased father," I said. "We are not Vikings here. Besides, that name would remind me of too much. He deserves a unique name."

"A cow?" Maeve would not let it go.

"Cattle are our best wealth," I said. "And he is my fortune. All I have," I whispered, tucking a finger under his chin while he yawned. "My Lulach."

"As my cousin, he is of Clan Lorne on his father's side," Macbeth said. "He should bear a name from that heritage."

"Lulach mac Gilcomgan," I replied. Macbeth only nodded.

Tucking my child close, I decided to someday tell Lulach only the best of his father: a strong warrior with a gift for storytelling. In the land of the Gaels, those qualities do much to recommend a man, so his memory in Lulach's keeping would be honorable.

WITH CHRISTMAS upon us, we did not feel its full cheer at Elgin, though the child brought deep joy to me and mine, and juniper boughs and prayers sweetened the air for the rest. Catriona stayed at Elgin for a little while, helping me with the child while she waited out the blustery weather before returning north to Kinlossie. Grateful to her, I was glad for her company as well, and came to admire her knowledge and natural poise. She and Maeve helped me look after my son, and Catriona encouraged me to nurse Lulach myself, though Maeve insisted that was not done by highborn ladies. Knowing he would be safe in my arms, I could not give my child over to the special care of another.

Catriona herself was a widow, left with a two-year-old child; her husband, gone a year, had been a Moray thane, cousin to both Gilcomgan and Macbeth. One of her brothers had perished with my first husband, and so she and I found ties of kinship as well as circumstance. She was intelligent in her observations, and often we sat talking without care for time. I learned much from her, and was pleased she seemed so much at home at Dun Elgin. I offered to find her a house close to Elgin, but she refused quietly.

WE HAD done without a bard at Elgin due to Gilcomgan's ability, and soon Macbeth invited his personal bard to Elgin, a Moray man called Dermot mac Conall, for harping and storytelling. The position of a *seanchaidh* in a warlord's household is so exalted that these men—sometimes women, to be fair—are given a high place at their patron's table, and at councils, too, where their opinions are respected. To the Celts, the *seanchaidhean* are the keepers of the old wisdom, the ancient tales and songs essential to the heart of our culture. I enjoyed Dermot's harp playing and well-spoken tales, but missed Gilcomgan in that, and did not converse with the bard.

So when Macbeth came to the hall one day to tell me that Dermot wished to speak with both of us, I was surprised and nodded, so that a housecarl left to fetch the bard.

"The baptism is tomorrow," Macbeth said as we waited. "I wonder, after the holy droplets give the child heavenly protection, will his mother mark him in the pagan way, as she herself is marked?"

He must have seen the small blue spiral on my shoulder the day of the birth. "I may, or may not," I murmured, patting Lulach's small back as he slept on my shoulder.

"That practice was outlawed by the Church long ago as savage. I am surprised you wear one. Though it is a pretty thing."

I glanced away, unsure yet which way his thoughts went with regard to Celtic practices. "My mother gave it to me. She saw no conflict between Celtic traditions and her Christian faith, though Rome disagrees. She had an independent spirit, and made her own decisions."

"Like her daughter."

"I suppose I learned a little fire of the heart at her knee."

"A little!" His laugh was deep and pleasant. "Lady Gruadh, you were born with more than enough fire. About births"—he glanced toward the door, where a single housecarl stood guard—"that is why the bard wishes to confer with us today. Dermot mac Conall is also a *fathach*—a prophet who relies upon the stars for wisdom. On the day of your son's birth, I asked him to look at the heavens and map out the stars."

I blinked. "He practices *naladoracht,* the divination of the clouds and stars?"

He nodded. "So you know of such things."

"My mother practiced a little divination." I would not tell him that I had an interest in such matters myself. Not yet. "Only bards with long years of training have the esoteric knowledge required for star mapping. I am impressed that Dermot does. Indeed, let us hear what your wizard has to say."

"This is my baptismal gift for your son." Macbeth bent close. "And we need never to mention it to the priests," he added. His eyes twinkled, and I smiled unbidden at our shared secret. For a moment, I liked him very well.

"Dermot mac Conall was in your father's court. Did he map your birth stars, too?"

"Not he, but another bard did so, an itinerant who came to my father's hall to tell tales and divine omens when asked."

"What was predicted for you? That you will be king one day, or that you will desire it?" The words slipped out impulsively in the amicable moment.

He shrugged, dismissing, or ignoring, the implication. "I was born under the sign of An Corran, the sickle, on the eighth day of August."

"An omen in the heavens said to govern those who are strong leaders, and often admired." I smiled. "I was born under An Corran as well, late in July."

"We have something in common after all."

"So you are both children of the harvest," the bard said, "and of the sun."

I glanced past Macbeth. The man who walked toward us was broad and toughly built, more like a warrior than mystic or bard. He had unkempt brown hair, greenish eyes, and a crooked and toothy smile that tempted me to smile in return. I did so.

"Dermot mac Conall," I said, "greetings."

"Lady Gruadh, and Moray, greetings to you this fine day." He bowed a little, grandeur in every part of him. "I have a report of the *reithes grian*, the wheel of the sun, for your fine new son."

"Please, tell us." I sat straighter, and Lulach stirred and began to whimper and thrash. I handed him to Aella, who gave him her little finger to suck.

Dermot raised spread fingers, looking upward. "I sat upon a hill the evening of the child's birth and watched the sky—luckily it was clear for the son of Macbeth—"

"Stepson," I said quickly.

"When Macbeth's man came to tell me that the birth had occurred, I drew the map of stars into the earth with a stick, so that I could study the wheel's alignment. I saw fine auspices for him."

"He will thrive?" I asked eagerly. A prophecy of health was indeed good news.

"To manhood, so the stars showed that night," Dermot said. "Sun, moon, stars will align in harmonious ways for twenty years, so goes the wheel of stars at his birth." Still he looked upward, recalling what he had seen. Such men never write down what they know, unlike monks dedicated to quill and ink, but keep records in the old way, through memory.

"He is born under Pócan, the goat," he went on, "in the season of our Lord's birth. He will be stubborn and serious, and his stars are such that they add a lightness of spirit to his nature. He will be a good man, and brave. Train him well, Macbeth," Dermot said, "train him with weapons and with wisdom, for he will be a king."

"King!" I looked at Macbeth, who frowned, alert. Lulach began to cry, and Aella stood as if to take him away, but I calmed him. I wanted my son to be present for this, though he could not comprehend it.

"Indeed, for this is indicated by his *tuismea,* the map that the heavens made for him alone. A king's power was shown to me, before clouds obscured the rest of his future. I believe you hold a king in your arms, dear lady."

"Tell me more," I said. "You said harmony for twenty years. What then?"

"That is all I know. Later, your son himself can ask me to look at the rest."

I noticed the quick glance that passed between the bard and Macbeth. "The rest?" I asked quickly, as a thought occurred to me. "What else do you cast by the sun and stars, Dermot mac Conall? Besides star maps of a life at the time of a birth?"

"There are many uses for divining stars and clouds," he said.

"I have heard that some who practice the art of *naladoracht* can also divine the clouds by daylight, or map the night sky for other auspicious times . . . such as when the moment is right for a king or a warlord to be crowned, or to attack an enemy," I said. "Have you ever done that?"

"I sometimes did so for Macbeth's father, and saw an early end to his life. I warned him, but he rode out against my advice on his last day. I have advised Macbeth often in the years since."

"Did you map out the stars and advise Macbeth when to ride into Moray?"

"He did not," Macbeth said quickly. "You go too far, lady."

"Have you predicted that my husband will be king one day, given the right time and circumstances?"

"Gruadh," my husband warned, low. I watched the bard. I had to know if this issue was keen between them, if Dermot was another conspirator in my household.

"A man like Macbeth does not need such assistance, Lady Gruadh," Dermot said. "When he was born, another *fathach* mapped an auspicious placement of sun, moon, and stars. His destiny is one of greatness, without doubt, and his stars showed that he would be a king one day." He glanced at Macbeth.

"He is *Rí a Moreb,*" I pointed out. "King enough."

"He is, and can become the most powerful warlord in Scotland, but for the High King," Dermot replied smoothly. "Should he have a greater destiny, Macbeth himself will determine that. He has an instinct for key action and makes his own decisions, his own fortune. Macbeth will not rely only on a star map, though lesser men with great ambition might do so. But he wisely listens to such advice," he added.

I glanced at Macbeth. "So you put store for yourself in divination and omens?"

"I do not discount them," he answered.

In my arms, the babe began to squall loudly in the rhythmic, piteous cry of newborns. Standing, I faced the men. "Dermot mac Conall, will you give me your word that you did not assist with the overthrow of Moray in any way?"

"Believe me, lady, I did not." He met my gaze simply, openly. I trusted him.

"Very well." I paused. "I have a touch of the Sight myself, inherited from my mother and grandmother. Once I had a vision that hinted at Scotland's future, and Scotland's kings." Although I had never fully understood the strange vision I had seen at Abernethy before my betrothal, I now felt it had to do with Macbeth even more than me; Macbeth and Scotland.

"What vision?" Macbeth demanded. "You prophesy?"

"It is merely *Da Shealladh,* the two sights, and common enough among Scots. I saw a crownlike light about your head once, and other symbols around you," I said, thinking of that day in my father's bailey. "Make of it what you will. King Mac bethad . . . or perhaps Saint Mac bethad," I added with a little edge to my tone.

"I would be informed if you have such visions again," he said, glaring.

Smiling, I thanked Dermot for the star work and walked past the men, with the babe wailing on my shoulder and Aella hastening in my wake. Now I had new leverage: I knew Macbeth put his trust in portents and omens, and he believed I had knowledge of such things myself.

A BLUSTERY WIND swept my Fife friends through Elgin's gates at last. We had not expected them to return before spring, but Angus and Conn brought Bethoc northward quick as they could, along with two female serving girls, distant Fife kin, who then joined our growing household. I was glad beyond measure to see any and all of them, especially my dear friend, and they were relieved to find me safely delivered of a healthy child.

Angus said that Bodhe was traveling again, this time southward. Dolina had sent a message to express her good wishes, written in Father Anselm's pristine script, and she also sent a packhorse laden with gifts, including sacks of almonds and honeyed, spiced hazelnuts; Dolina knew I had a taste for sweets. She also sent a tun of her birch wine to celebrate the child's birth, as well as a length of blue-dyed linen, a hooded cloak for me of brown wool trimmed with wolf fur, and leather boots lined in lamb's wool. Wrapped in the cloak were embroidered garments for the child. Recognizing her hand in the delicate stitchery, I felt the warmth of gratitude and a sharp longing for home.

We gathered by the fire that evening to enjoy good company, while I wiggled my toes luxuriously inside my warm boots. Supper was a thick soup of winter vegetables from the storage barrels, with more salted beef than usual added to give it heart. Cook prepared sweetmeats from the nuts and honey Dolina had sent, and I ate more than my share, perhaps because the treat reminded me of Fife, and home. We had a thick brose, too, of oats and cream with a touch of Danish aqua vitae from Elgin's stores to warm our bellies.

After news and conversation, Macbeth questioned the sons of Fergus about matters to the south of Moray: where was the king now, what was the outcome of the coastal raids to the south, what was said of the recent changes in Moray? Then we settled back to listen to Dermot mac Conall tell a story of the birth of the ancient hero, Cu Chulainn. My spirits were bolstered: I had my child, who was my delight, and now friends and familiarity surrounding me. Even my grudge toward Macbeth had lessened some, though resentments lingered.

CATRIONA OF Kinlossie was eager to return home to her small son, waiting in the care of his aunt, now that the weather had improved enough for travel. My women and I had grown fond of her, though sometimes I sensed an odd tension from Bethoc, who grew silent when Catriona joined us to talk and do handcrafts. She favored yarn making over stitchery, and had acquired a basket of dyed wools from a farmer's wife. With dexterous fingers on spindle and distaff, she spun tufts of wool into silken strands while Aella rolled the newly made yarns into small, perfect balls of color. On other days, she went to the kitchens or to a little hut near the kitchens where the herbs were dried and kept, and she prepared medicines, usually boiled infusions or ointments with oils. Bethoc, trained in the same by her mother, showed some interest in learning what Catriona knew.

"You will not remain a widow for long, lovely and kind as you are," Maeve told Catriona one day, after the young womb wife gave us all hot herbal possets to help the winter coughs that some of us had. For Maeve, whose cough was worst, she brought an aromatic ointment, which could be applied in a hot pack on the chest at night.

In answer, Catriona laughed, a sparkling sound in the winter gloom. "The kinsman who took over my husband's thanage of Kinlossie has asked for my hand," she admitted. "He gave me a little house on the property so that my son and I still have a home there. But so far I have refused him." She did not say why. Knowing she had loved her husband, I nodded in sympathy.

When she left, we all wept a bit and waved as the escort guided her through the gates. But I saw Bethoc's face, chin set, eyes hooded, before she turned away.

LULACH'S NAMING ceremony was held at Kineddar church, where his murdered father had been buried. I did not attend, as custom kept the mother home until her churching day a month after the birth. Later I heard how my son slept sweetly, startling only when the priest drizzled water on his brow. His godmother, my cousin Bethoc, knew that a silent child could have bad luck in life, so she gave him a good pinch.

Afterward we had a modest midday feast at Elgin, although I kept apart, being not yet welcome to share in communal meals. After the child had been ceremonially passed over the fire three times in his basket, the household went back to their daily tasks. Maeve tucked Lulach in his cradle in the brazier-heated nook where I sat with spindle and distaff. This was not a task wellborn ladies generally did, but I enjoyed the rhythm and simplicity of spinning dyed wool clusters into yarns, and I was not prideful about my position. When Maeve asked if she could speak with me in private, I nodded, surprised.

"I held the babe on our way to the church," she began, "with Constantine of Banchorrie and Macbeth riding with me, for the importance of my charge. We fell behind the rest of the party, and Macbeth took us a different way for caution's sake."

I nodded. "The forest route is longer but safer."

"We saw an old woman tending a bonfire there. Wild, she looked, with face and hands smudged. I thought her an elvish one, popped up from the wood, or a madwoman."

"Una, the charcoal burner's wife. She and her family hold the rights to that land. She is an odd one. Her son perished with Gilcomgan at Burghead," I added softly.

"When she saw us, she came at us, waving her arms like a *ban-sìth* and reciting luck charms for the child. Well and good, until she began to prophesy."

I raised my eyebrows at that. "What did she say?"

"The child born at Elgin would one day wear a gold crown on his head."

I gasped, remembering Dermot's star map. "What more?"

"She spoke more charms and waved smoke toward us, and then said that Lulach could be protected by magical help. She gave me this for him"—Maeve took a small stone from her pocket—"and said he should always carry this with him when he travels beyond Moray."

The stone was a bit of quartz the color of peaty water. It felt cool and smooth in my palm. I tucked it into a seam pocket. "Go on."

"The old madwoman told Macbeth that no soil he stood upon, Moray or Scotland, would change his fate. No charm would prevent his destiny, for his path would lead him to a crowning. Una said Macbeth would be remembered into the ages, long after his son."

"Lulach is not his son," I insisted. Would Macbeth someday have a son who would be mine as well? As for Macbeth and a crowning, I dared not think upon that either. Not yet.

"We continued on our way, and Banchorrie said the woman was a lunatic and even a witch. Macbeth lingered to give her a coin in honor of the christening." She bent forward. "He spoke with her alone before joining us again."

Intrigued, I leaned in, too. "What more did the woman tell him?"

"He did not say. But he has strong ambition, that one. You yourself are the pathway for his goals, if you do not see it already."

"Is that your own prophecy?" I teased to lighten the mood. Others had come into the hall, including Macbeth. I angled away, as did

Maeve, and we put our heads together as if fascinated with the yarn spooling from my distaff.

"It is what many of us see," Maeve whispered. "I have even heard it mentioned among his housecarls. The son of Finlach would take the throne if he could. The mormaership increases his power, and marriage to you strengthens his blood claim."

"The king is his grandfather, and Moray was his father's region."

"But his lineage is not so fine as yours," she persisted. "His intentions went beyond Moray when he wed you. He could have sent you away, or ordered some harm to come to you and your child, so that no son would live to avenge the father someday. He did not."

"It is tradition to wed a victim's widow, and he had no heart for killing a woman with child." But the edge in my voice did not quell Maeve, intent on her thoughts.

"Listen to me. I feel this deep in my bones, especially after hearing the old woman's prophecy. Someday you will be queen," she finished in an intense whisper.

I glanced around, shook my head. "Queen of this region. Just because he married me and might someday aspire to—" I stopped. "We will not discuss this."

She sat back, looking satisfied. "So you do see it!"

"I am not blind," I said quietly. "But I will not wish for it myself. Too many lives would be lost if he tried to take the throne. I cannot wish for death and destruction."

"Macbeth is cautious and will wait until his time comes. Else he would not survive long, nor would you and Lulach. Rumors are dangerous enough—"

"Maeve," I warned. "Stop."

She shrugged. "I tell you, Moray is too small for such a man as that one."

Glancing the length of the hall, I saw my husband conversing with his housecarls. Macbeth stood tall, taller than most, and I saw, not for the first time, a kingliness in his bearing and in the sharp glance that missed nothing around him. Whether or not he aimed for it, he was suited to the role. I myself had seen a crowning of light around him.

Maeve and the charcoal burner's wife were not alone in their intuitions. I spun the distaff in my hand, aware that in Fife and elsewhere, a low thunder of discontent still rumbled over Malcolm's choice of Duncan as tanist. Macbeth's takeover in Moray, and a marriage that joined his name to Bodhe's line, was more than coincidental.

Step by step, he was advancing his cause. By nature and character, he possessed the wit and will to fulfill any claim, even a royal one. Those dissatisfied with old Malcolm and Duncan would gladly follow such a man, if and when he made a bid for something greater.

Queen. Suddenly it seemed plausible.

Chapter Sixteen

Icy blasts froze most of Scotland that winter, and as we heard later, England as well. At Dun Elgin, we gathered close to the fire baskets and corner braziers on any excuse, and went to bed with the early darkness to burrow like moles beneath furs and blankets with heated stones at our feet. Sometimes I took Lulach from his cradle to sleep beside me, afraid he might die of cold in the night. Aella and Bethoc crawled under the covers with us as well, for the bed was generous enough for a large warrior and his wife, and not used for that purpose.

If my female friends wondered when I would open my bed to my husband, they did not say so. I rarely saw Macbeth without his guard—they stayed with him at every turn, seated by the fire on cold evenings, riding out on hunts and patrols, training in the yard or in the hall itself in poor weather. When we met, we were distant but polite.

Throughout, my son showed a sweet nature and was a source of joy. My own temperament softened, for although in my heart I nursed lingering grief and anger, physically I nursed my child, and the lush, drowsy sense of goodwill that came with that had me yearning for peace, even forgiveness.

"It is the mothering instinct," Maeve told me one day. "Women are peace weavers by nature, in their marriages, in their homes. Keep hold of it," she added in her acerbic way, "for your temper needs it."

Accepting my circumstances and my marriage would bring me more peace of mind and benefit those around me. Still, letting go of resentments came hard to me that winter. Uncertain as yet of the situation at Elgin, I took the little quartz stone that the charcoal burner's wife had sent for my child, and I sewed it into the hem of the blanket that I wrapped him in most often. And I resolved to ask Finn to use his smithing skills and make a cage of silver for it, either as a brooch or a chain, for my son to wear. If it would help keep him safe against future threats, so be it.

O NE DAY when the sun shone enough to melt the snows a little, Constantine mac Artair and his dozen carls left Elgin to cross the mountain passes southeast to Banchorrie. He came to the hall to bid us farewell, and invited us to visit his hillfort, east of the River Dee. Excited by the prospect of travel, I smiled and laughed with Constantine, whom I considered a friend. Macbeth was somber and silent, and I sensed a loneliness about him like a gray pall. I wondered if he was disappointed to see his uncle and mentor leave.

"We will make a progress around Moray in warmer weather," Macbeth said then, "but we can stop at Banchorrie when we cross the mountains to head south."

"Fife, and Abernethy?" I brightened at the thought of seeing kin and friends.

"North and west, to the remote fastnesses of Moray, to visit with those people and their thanes, and to hold moot courts and run patrol where it is needed. We should be seen," he added.

We? Gilcomgan had not been seen that far and wide, and had not often taken me with him locally. Macbeth, I reluctantly began to realize, was a different sort of mormaer.

Snow fell yet again, sifting deep around our palisade. Nearly every day, when it was possible, Macbeth and his carls rode out. One day I brooked enough courage to approach him. "If we are stranded by the snows," I said, "then so are your enemies, and you can dispense with your war patrols. All of Moray is conquered between Macbeth and the weather."

"We ride out to look after tenants and livestock who need help in this hard and dangerous winter," he corrected me, "not to burn and destroy."

Not long after, he and his guards helped a farmer drag back the frozen carcasses of four cows that had wandered away from their winter byre. Another day, Macbeth, Giric, and Angus rescued two boys who had fallen through the ice while fishing to help feed their families. The men brought the lads back to Dun Elgin, where we warmed and fed them, and gave them supplies to take home. Seeing my husband exhausted, stiff, and sore after his efforts, I regretted my criticism of his patrols.

Often he and his men helped at Elgin, and beyond in the villages, with various tasks—repairing roofs collapsed under snow, clearing ice from frozen wells, searching for scattered livestock, and delivering provisions from Elgin's own stores. We all suffered, in fortress or bothy, that long winter, and we all tried to help one another. Hearing of deaths and tragedies, I would hold my son close, grateful for him, for small comforts, for friends around me.

In those white, frozen weeks, I saw the generous lord in my husband more than the warlord. He shared from Elgin's storage rooms to fill the larder cupboards of tenants in the hills and glens, and did not begrudge the baskets I sent out. Had we been reduced to scraping bones for meat and boiling thin gruels ourselves, he would have counted it fair.

"When I took Moray," he told me, "I accepted its responsibilities as well. In my boyhood, I knew many of these people, and the older ones knew my father and grandfather. Now it comes to me to protect them in their need, just as the men of Moray will answer my summons in time of war."

"If it ever comes to that." But I knew inevitably, someday, it would.

At odd moments, he watched me intently, silently, and a yearning flickered through me. I was lonely. I had a husband. Yet a breach existed between us due to my grievances and his distant nature. He never came to me at night, and that remained a relief to me. Yet I began to wonder when he would, and I pondered accepting him.

"I am thinking your husband is a good man," Maeve remarked one day. "You would do well to remember that a queen cannot make a prince without a king's help."

"Wretch," I told her. "Since I am no queen, it is not a concern."

The weeks were long and miserable, the light dim from morning until dusk, the smoke from oil lamps and the sweetish smell of burning peat a constant in every room. Cold seeped through the thickest walls, and icy dampness leaked through cracks despite shutters and heavy curtains. Sometimes I wore nearly every garment I owned, and my little son was wrapped so thoroughly, as my women and I cuddled and carried him about, that all we saw of him was two blinking indigo eyes and a pink button nose. I ordered the servants to tack stretched, oiled skins over all the window openings. This helped against drafts, but we could not look out, and inevitably someone would peel back the parchment to peer outside. Usually this was Bethoc, who hated confinement as much as I did.

"Some churches and fortresses beyond the island of Britain," she told us when she looked out one frozen morning, "have windows of framed glass, painted with bright color. Sunlight turns the glass to ruby, sapphire, emerald, and crystal. I have heard, too, that hillforts there are magnificent hilltop citadels constructed entirely of stone, a structure called a *castellum* or castle."

"How do you know?" Aella asked.

"Father Anselm told me," Bethoc answered. "Imagine such sunshine and beauty."

I listened with interest. In Scotland, some churches were of stone, and some farmhouses had drystone walls, though most were wattle packed with mud and lime, topped by thatch. Even our largest fortresses were of wood, with fieldstone foundations.

"A stone citadel, or a church with jeweled windows, would awe eyes and soul," I said, hoping to see such marvels someday.

On days when the world outside was frozen and tree limbs wore glassy sleeves, we would sit before our fires sipping hot soup from bowls and heated spiced wine in cups, and listen to music or to stories by grace of Dermot the bard, who was winter-bound with us. The thick ice on the lochan below the fortress hill would sometimes crack loudly, the sharp sound making us all jump, and then we would laugh.

"That was the Old Cailleach's belch," Dermot told us, speaking of the legendary crone said to live inside the mountains. "She holds spring hostage in the person of the beautiful Brigid herself, so that the earth has little sunshine and no flowers. The Old Cailleach likes to keep the world in perpetual winter to suit her ill mood. But Brigid will break free," he said. "It is her nature to escape, and the Old Cailleach's nature to capture her, over and over, and so it goes."

Dermot had many stories, for a bard must know at least one new tale for each day in the year. He composed his own poems and tales as well, somehow keeping all those verses in his head; I suspected he used memory tricks, such as the stone on the belly, on days when he kept to his own chamber.

Finally the cold eased and afternoon sunshine began to melt the snow. Like Brigid escaping the old hag's gray mountain, we left our fortress with a sense of relief to have survived such a winter. We opened the windows and the servants took up the old, dirty rushes from the floors, sweeping them into piles to be carried out and burned. The floorboards were scrubbed, fresh rushes brought in, and sacks of early flowers—snowdrops and crocuses—scattered on the floors, mixed with evergreen needles for the clean scents we craved. Fire baskets and braziers were swept clean, and peat bricks stacked in concentric rings to be lit anew.

The air was so tantalizing that I felt near drunk from its hints of flowers, sunlight, and breezes. I ached to get away. "Aella, if you please, find Angus mac Fergus," I said one day, "and ask him to have horses saddled and ready. Tell him I want to ride out, and he can accompany me." She nodded and ran outside. "Maeve, please watch Lulach for the afternoon. I will not be gone long, and he can take thin porridge if he is hungry."

"Only Angus? As Lady of Moray and Bodhe's daughter," Maeve reminded me, "you require an armed escort and a lady when you travel outside. Take Bethoc, too."

My Fife cousin eagerly agreed, and we went to fetch outdoor cloaks and heavier shoes, mine the brown cloak and sturdy leather brogans sent by Dolina.

Within an hour, careening seagulls overhead showed us that we were within a league of the long eastern coastline where Moray met the North Sea. Angus and Séan, another of Macbeth's retainers, had brought a pair of hawks to fly—the birds had suffered the winter as well—and so we released them, rode hard after them, whistled them back, and went at it again. The birds followed the sweet spring winds, and so did we.

The seashore was four or five leagues from Dun Elgin, and as we rode, the moorland changed to water meadows leading to a march of sandhills. The gray sea moved like silk in the distance, and we glimpsed the dolphins that frequent Moray's coastline. Séan said that to sight them so early in spring was a sign of good luck.

Curious and delighted, I wanted to ride toward the sandy swath of beach. While Bethoc and Séan lagged to call the birds back to the glove, Angus came after me like a grumbling nursemaid.

"Do you worry I will break my neck after so long away from riding?" I asked.

"I worry about pirates and raiders, and you the small queen of Moray," he said. "We can go north another league or two, where there is a cove to explore. Your handmaid wants to find flowers or some such." His sour expression made it clear that escorting ladies to pick flowers did not suit his status as one of Macbeth's elite housecarls.

"If Bethoc wants that, we will do it," I said, and off we went. We rode farther, gulls scattering like pale ash as our hawks arrowed through the sky. Bethoc's instinct for finding herbs was sound, and she dismounted to examine some plants she wanted. Séan stopped to help her, but I rode past, Angus following. I craved to see the ocean.

Dismounting, I walked along the beach, where the sea spilled into rocky pools and the air was saturated damp. I stood tall on a perch of rock, gazing out at the water. Angus, in his disagreeable mood, told me to get down, come back.

"Look! The dolphins!" I pointed, then noticed that the dolphins were following a long, curving shape gliding over the waves. A Viking ship. Two.

I gasped and Angus pulled me back to duck behind some rocks. He put his hand to his dagger and motioned for me to keep quiet and still.

Both boats had curving spiral prows, rather than the carved heads that marked them as warboats. As we watched, the smaller of the two vessels beached swiftly, and four men leaped out, splashing through the surf to reach the sand, their boots and leggings soaked. They wore helmets, trews and tunics, leather hauberks under cloaks, and weapons at their belts.

On the water, the remaining crew sat like cut shapes against the pearl gray sky. The larger was many oared, and the smaller, a birlinn with ten pairs of oars, was a swift and agile boat suited to slipping in and out of coves and bays, more useful for travel than merchanting or warring. Useful for spying and raiding, as well, I knew.

Silently, Angus and I watched, and he sent me a grim glance. Behind us, I hoped that Bethoc and Séan had seen and were well hidden. The Vikings waited on the beach, and one stood apart, wind whipping at his cloak. His black braided hair was visible under his helmet: Thorfin Sigurdsson, prince and Raven-Feeder.

"What in the devil's name does that one want here," Angus muttered.

I wondered too. Soon we saw four men riding over the beach from another direction, horse hooves making neat tracks in the wet sand. Their leader wore a green cloak pinned at the shoulder. I knew that fur-lined green cloak, and so I gasped.

My husband dismounted and walked forward, two of his men on foot with him, the others remaining with the horses. One housecarl carried a brass-trimmed wooden box of some weight on his shoulder. The Vikings and Moray men met near the water's edge.

"Why are they here?" I whispered fiercely. "What do you know of this?"

Angus shook his head. "Thorfin and Macbeth are close cousins and no doubt have trading and merchant ventures in common." He did not sound convincing.

"This has more to do with politics than trade," I said. "Thorfin holds the Orkneys, and the northernmost part of mainland Scotland in Caithness, too, along with some Western Isles. Perhaps he means to offer Viking strength should Macbeth want more than Moray."

Angus cast me a sharp look. "What do you know of such things?"

"I sit and stitch, I listen and watch. And I am not stupid."

In answer, Angus rolled his eyes. Then we saw two of Thorfin's Vikings approach Macbeth and his retainers. One reached out to accept the wooden box from Macbeth's man. Words were exchanged, grew louder. Swords were drawn then, and I cried out, so that Angus clapped a calloused hand over my mouth.

Within seconds, Macbeth slashed the throat of the man holding the box. Arching, the man died in an instant, blood soaking the sand. The others rushed forward, shouting, more swords drawn, more men engaged. My heart slammed in panic.

"Stop!" Thorfin bellowed in Norse, then Gaelic. The warriors halted, swords tipped down, and Macbeth approached Thorfin to argue bitterly, with hard and violent gestures. Then Macbeth thrust his bloody sword into the sand, a final gesture of some kind. One of the Vikings picked up the wooden box while the other grabbed their fallen comrade to drag him through the sand toward the waiting boat. Men splashed forward to help, but did not come ashore to continue the fight.

"*A Dhia,*" I moaned when Angus released me. "Oh God! He slew that man in cold blood!"

"Macbeth had no choice," Angus said. "Did you not see it coming? The Vikings would have slaughtered them and taken their gold. He showed the Orkney thugs that they cannot cheat the new leader of Moray."

"You are proud of what we just saw?" I gaped at him. "You approve of murder?"

"Were you a true warrior, rather than a woman keen to play with swords, you would understand," Angus replied. "The Vikings are not so bothered by that man's death as you. Sent him to the trolls—that is what the Norsemen call it. Now hush, or we will be sent to the trolls ourselves, for being foolish enough to be caught here. We should not have come this way—"

"Whatever you know of this meeting, tell me," I said, low and insistent. "Now."

He hesitated, sighed. "Listen, then. Many believe that if Duncan becomes king after Malcolm, things will go ill for Scotland. As you yourself said, lady—those two warlords, Orkney and Moray, may have to act as allies to prevent the worst."

"Allies against Duncan?" Beyond, on the crescent of beach within the rocky cove, I saw Macbeth and Thorfin walking, speaking as if in concordance, or collusion. I hated the sight of it—yet realized, with a cold chill, that it might be necessary.

"Duncan is not the warrior those two are," Angus said. "Our enemies, Saxon and Viking, sense this. Under Duncan's rule, Scotland could fare poorly and sink in a stew of war. They plot, those two. They scheme. Come ahead now—we must leave this place."

"Go find the others and come back. I will stay here. Go!" Any son of Fergus knew no good came of arguing with me. Angus left, hissing at me to keep out of sight.

Leaning against the rock, I watched the two leaders, still deep in discussion. Then they approached the birlinn, which floated in shallow water. At a signal from Macbeth, one of his own housecarls lifted a sack from a horse's saddle and carried it to the boat, wading through water, followed by Thorfin himself, who climbed easily into the low vessel. Swiftly, the oarsmen skimmed the boat backward in the water to join the waiting longboat. Macbeth walked back to the waiting horses, and he and his housecarls mounted to leave.

Behind me, Angus returned, softly hooting for me to come away. But I had seen murder done and a bribe paid, and I was angry. My husband had been secretive and cruel, and I would know why. Stepping out onto the beach, I walked over the sand openly, boldly, head high.

Macbeth saw me immediately and turned his horse, halting, folding his hands on the pommel as he waited. The wind blew back my cloak, whipped my gown against my legs as I came toward him. The Vikings on the water might see me, but I did not care, fueled by a searing and righteous anger. I would not be left ignorant while the man who had wed me for my lineage besmirched it with his deeds.

"Lady," he said as I came closer. If he was astonished, he did not show it.

"You killed that man." I stood before him in the blowing wind.

"Then you saw more than you should have."

"A good thing I did. I am Lady of Moray, and was before you came here. I would know what you do, and how you deal."

"No differently than other warlords, and better than some." He glanced toward the rocks and dunes. "Who is with you?"

"Angus. What did you give Thorfin? They say Vikings have a taste for gold, since their own lands yield only silver."

"Some of them have a taste for treachery, too. A man does well to watch his back. Tell Angus to fetch you home again."

"You paid a bribe to the Orkneyings." I faced him, while the breezes played with my veil and skirts, snapping the fabric. "Why? Did it come out of Moray's treasury?" In a small room at Elgin, Gilcomgan had kept more than one chest of gold and silver coin locked away, with other valuables, for a treasury.

"Go back to Elgin and leave this be." He pulled the reins to turn his horse's head, but I stepped into his path. He drew up.

"Not until I know your true business here."

He sighed, looked about, then back again. "Very well. My men and I came this way to look at the Burghead tower, which must be rebuilt," he answered. "Over the last few days, I spoke to tenants, found carpenters and a mason, and saw to other details."

"A shame you burned the tower, so that it could not be properly manned to watch for Viking raiders," I said bitterly. "But you solved that today with a bribe and a sword."

"You have a serpent's tongue at times," he said. "You would know the truth? Then listen well. Good men and good villages have long paid the Vikings to keep them away. If I pay my cousin of Orkney a tribute to buy peace for this coastline, it is gold well placed and none of your concern."

"If my husband bribes and then murders our Viking neighbors, it is my concern!"

"Was it your business before? The tribute paid today was one Gilcomgan promised Thorfin's man months ago," he said bluntly. "Thorfin came with him to discuss the matter. Had I refused, they might have murdered me. Instead, now the Vikings know how the new Moray will deal. That greedy fellow, a threat to me and mine, is dead. And Thorfin and I will agree to new terms, which may include further tributes to keep Moray's coastline safe."

Stunned, I gathered my wits. "Gilcomgan never mentioned any arrangement with Vikings. And Thorfin is your cousin. Kinship is better shown through loyalty, not tribute or outright treachery. I know it is often the way of things among warriors, but it seems to me—"

"I hear," Macbeth said, "that wives of other mormaers, even kings, stay at home where they are safe, and keep mute about steel-games unless asked for their opinion."

"I am none of that cloth."

"So I am learning. Penance comes in various ways. Angus!" he shouted, making it impossible for Angus to continue hiding. "Fetch the lady, and take her back to Elgin!"

When my escort appeared on the sand dune, Macbeth pressed knees to horse and cantered through the surf's edge to join his men at the other end of the beach.

Walking through dry sand to meet my friends, having witnessed my husband do cold murder, I yet felt a stirring admiration for him as a capable warlord. That day, as at other times, he had demonstrated uncompromising will, as well as physical ability and courage. He revealed a strong sense of what was right and what was not, and what was possible between those points—and he took steps to achieve it.

Whether or not he knew it, I considered myself his capable equal, not a subservient wife. Raised by a warlord in a nest of warriors, I would not be regarded as significant in my small household circle, only to be dismissed beyond its boundaries.

That day, I resolved to stay aware of any matter that might affect my kin, my son, or the great tree of my descent. For the sake of kin and heritage, I could not afford to submit, but rather must keep apace however I could.

Chapter Seventeen

Ale must be brewed new each month in a large household, linens washed and aired, and clothing washed and patched as well; floors must be swept clean, rushes replaced, wicker furniture repaired, for it does not hold up to heavy armor and sizable men. There were tables to scrub, fires to be laid, baking to be done, day in, day out, in endless rhythm. Household matters had never been my strength, despite Dolina's best efforts, but now I did not exclude myself from the work to be done.

With improved weather, the kitchen lads and grooms were sent out to fish the rivers and burns, and tenants sent sea catch to our fortress as well, so that we had fish to salt, dry, and pack into barrels. Our winter supplies of dried beef and mutton had diminished, and the livestock were not fat enough to be slaughtered for meat. Stored fruits and root vegetables were in fair supply, along with a few sacks of oats and barley. We ate soups and fish stews often, with plenty of oatcakes. Highland fields do not produce wheat, and we did not bake rising breads as was done in England and elsewhere; imported wheat was dear and did not travel well. Each year, the miller paid a certain amount to Elgin in multure, or meal rent, for the keep of his lands and mill. I took account of the oats and barley grain used over the winter, and calculated the amount needed when the miller had grain to grind later in summer.

Macbeth ordered frequent patrols and rode out to visit his other fortresses in vast Moray, though he had no opponents in the region and had made arrangements with the Vikings for a while. Men arrived at Elgin with gifts and offers of support, while others brought their grievances to be settled by the mormaer's judgment. Some came to see Macbeth and take his measure for themselves, then report back to their clachans and thanages. Thanes and retainers who held their lands of the mormaer also came to meet with Macbeth. I knew some of them already, and though they congratulated me for my son, little was said of my widowing.

No one said how unfair, how wrong. Not a one. The former lord was gone, and his vanquisher was esteemed as warlord in his place, and as a high general, or *dux bellorum,* to the king. The people of Moray were pleased to have a strong defender with powerful connections, so the means of his succession did not matter.

Some days, when I climbed the battlement steps or walked into the hills with my women and my guard, I would stop at vantage points where the view extended for miles. On bright days, looking east to the sea, I glimpsed tiny dots that were ships. Longboats might mean raiders and danger, but wide merchant ships meant prosperity, with goods to be traded in Moray's eastern harbors. Westward lay the Highland mountain fastnesses, and to the south, the great dark mountains between Moray and Fife. Gazing that way, I would think of Bodhe, and home, and feel a sharp longing.

MACBETH, STOPPING to speak to me of a household matter one day, reached out to touch Lulach's blanketed foot. The infant gurgled and grinned. We laughed together—how could we not—and Macbeth looked at me. His gaze was not that of a warlord, but of a man who yearned. Uncertain suddenly, I turned back to folding some cloths. After a moment I heard his brisk departing footsteps over the floor planks.

Late that night, a knock sounded on my bedchamber door, and I called out a welcome, expecting to see Aella returning with more toweling, for I had just stepped out of a hipbath in front of the brazier. Seeing Macbeth opening the door, I gasped and snatched a linen sheet close around me, my hair falling in wet loops over my shoulders, dark red in the firelight. "I thought it was Aella," I said, flustered.

"I sent her away." He closed the door. "We have a matter to settle between us." Coming close, he touched my shoulder. "You needed time to recover after the child," he said, tracing a finger along my jaw. "And I have waited." He bent his head, and I allowed him to kiss me, the touch surprisingly tender, tasting of the wine he had been drinking.

I bowed my head, resting it against him, and felt his heartbeat pound against mine. Breath, and breath, and another—we waited, both of us. Something shifted in me, altered subtly, a willingness, almost a forgiveness. He must have sensed that, for he lifted me and brought me in two or three strides to the bed and laid me down, himself as well.

Silent, we were, courteous more than passionate, though we fit sweet as glove to hand, a tenderness with more promise than either dared take just then. For that night, it was more than enough. I breathed quiet as he drew back, adjusted his tunic, pulled the coverlet over me, and quietly bid good night, a touch of loneliness in it.

"Rue." At the door, he paused in the darkness. "I did kill him."

I knew. "Why tell me so now?"

"I want you to know the truth." He stood with head bowed, and I remembered the sight of him prostrate in the little chapel, when he had thought himself alone.

"Early that day, we met in skirmish, my forces and Gilcomgan's. We pursued them north to Burghead," he went on. "By my command, my men set fire to the wooden tower, intending to smoke them out and finish the fight on solid ground. They should have escaped—but it went wrong and they did not. What I wanted was honorable revenge," he said. "I did not intend to burn those men like souls in hell."

"Malcolm sent you there?"

"We conferred," he said. "We agreed."

Shuddering, I drew my body into a curl under the covers, and did not answer.

"Kin is the strongest bond," he said then. "Even when murder is done, those ties do not break. Ever afterward, we must live with our deeds. Good night," he added softly, opened the door, and left.

THOUGH CATRIONA had gone home as soon as the weather allowed, by May she returned again, summoned to attend the birthing of a child for the wife of Mungo mac Calum, Macbeth's cousin and close retainer, whom she had known for years. This time Catriona brought her flaxen-haired son, Anselan, with her. We enjoyed his impish disposition, and he made us all laugh with but a glance or a grimace. His mother clearly doted on him, too.

I warmly welcomed her to Elgin and into my household circle for that fortnight. Yet again I sensed a tension between Catriona and Bethoc. My cousin took pride in her midwifery skills, and had assisted at two births since coming to Elgin, yet Catriona, being a friend, had been asked to attend Mungo's wife at her time. I knew Bethoc regretted missing Lulach's birth; she had mentioned her jealousy toward Catriona for having that privilege. "A strong bond forms between a woman and her midwife," Bethoc told me once, "especially when lives have been scooped from the brink." I could not deny it.

One warm day we sat on benches in the garden with our children, beneath the pear trees in full bud. Aella played with Anselan on the grass while Maeve scolded them both, and Catriona was spinning yarn. Bethoc sat apart and studied a small book of gospels I owned; she did not read, but enjoyed the little painted images. On my shoulder, Lulach drooled on a fistful of my veiling, and I asked Catriona how she had come to midwife me at Elgin, something I had not thought to ask in detail before.

"Macbeth appeared on my doorstep before sundown," she replied, "and asked me to return with him to Elgin. He would not even sit for supper, which was in the kettle."

I rubbed my son's back. "But how did Macbeth know to fetch you, rather than the local midwife?" I asked, confused. "He had only recently come to Moray."

"Do not forget that your husband was born at Elgin and spent his boyhood in Moray. He knows this place, and its people, very well."

"I am aware," I murmured.

"Mac bethad," she said, using the name in a familiar way, "has many friends in Moray, and many hope he will bid for kingship. He has much support and faith here." A note in her voice, pride and more, made me glance up.

"Lady Gruadh knows this about her husband," Bethoc said. "I thought you were but an acquaintance, Lady Catriona." As widow to a thane, the midwife was called such.

"We were children together at Elgin, so I have known him all my life. My father held lands of his father, and rode as his retainer. My family was often here, and my brothers and I ran with Macbeth when we were small. He is very like his father," she went on. "Finlach was a fine warlord, and though the son was deprived of his father since the age of twelve, the lessons and guidance in boyhood were strong."

Macbeth had told me almost nothing of his father, let alone his mother. I was curious to hear more. "What was he like then? What of his parents?"

"His mother was the youngest daughter of King Malcolm," she said, "fair and quiet, is all I remember of her. She died when her son was a child. Finlach was a tall man, Viking through his mother, a warrior to his bones. Their son was determined," she continued, "yet somber. He was devoted to dogs and horses, and even when small, he would watch the men in the practice yards for hours, until his father allowed him to join them with a helmet and wooden sword. He often sat beside his father, listening, absorbing what was said among the housecarls, and Finlach did not send him away. In most of our children's games, we looked to Macbeth's lead. Early on, he had a quality about him that found the loyalty in others."

I nodded, comprehending, having seen in the man what she described in the boy.

Catriona smiled, her charm irresistible. Maeve and Aella smiled, too, though Bethoc looked a tad sour. And I felt a sudden loneliness, as if Catriona belonged here with more right, though I was lady of Elgin and Moray.

"Macbeth could never become king," Bethoc said then, "unless he began a war."

Catriona shrugged. "Swords speak the last word."

"What the Church teaches us about mercy and morals seems of no consequence when men will murder their own kin for land and title," Aella said, and Bethoc nodded.

"Men," Catriona said, "understand life and death differently than women. Ours is to give birth, life, and comfort. We cannot bring ourselves to take life, knowing its struggle and value."

Somehow this saintly show of opinion irritated me. "If I had to kill to save a life, mine or my son's," I said, "I would do it."

"Rue is trained at arms," Bethoc said proudly.

"Lady Gruadh has a stiffer backbone than I do," Catriona said. "It is my work to bring life into this world. My heart is far too tender to destroy it."

"That is not my intent," I defended. "The lady of a powerful region must have a martial spirit as well as a virtuous one. I would not hesitate to put on armor and take up a sword, if such was needed for the good of all."

"You will never have need. Macbeth is a good mormaer for this land," she said.

I felt a disagreeable urge to contradict. "His actions in coming here killed many."

"He told me that he had no other choice," Catriona responded. The others were silent, looking from one of us to the other.

He told her? I felt a frisson of jealousy, even warning. "Men commit acts in war that they would not otherwise do, and they must accept much, true. Yet widows feel the brunt of the spear, too, in their grieving and altered lives."

Calm, impervious, she nodded. "When my husband died, I cast no blame. Lady Gruadh, you will learn, with one warrior husband gone and another quickly in his stead, this is the way of it for women. It is our role to accept and support. We are the coals of the hearth fire. They are the flames."

"I would rather be the flame than the coal," I snapped. When she only smiled, I bristled further. "I do not see how you can forgive wrongful deaths so easily."

Tipping her head, she regarded me. "I do not see how you cannot."

Perhaps, in that moment, I should have sensed the serpent in the garden.

Later, when Catriona and Anselan set out for home accompanied by an escort of our men, I waved and smiled, though this time I was not so sad to bid her farewell.

Sweet weather and more flowers lured me, and I sometimes left my babe with my knee-woman, now his, to go hill walking with Aella and Bethoc as we used to do. Our guard was usually eight or ten men, and we ventured only a few leagues at most. Just to walk those sunwarmed slopes, filling baskets with blossoms and plants, was good for soul and body. Bethoc had us all searching for certain plants, and we happily complied.

Soon after she had arrived, Bethoc took over a small outbuilding near the kitchens for her increasing stock of herbs and plants. I would meet her there to hang plants for drying, grind petals and stems and blend them with oils. Bethoc, who had learned much from her mother, tutored me, and we filled the shelves of the wattle hut with small pots and vials of simples, potions, and infusions for healing purposes. In that snug place, laughing with my cousin and smelling the greeny fragrances and picking seed bits from my skirts, I thought often of my mother, Ailsa, and hoped she would be pleased with me.

Summer warmed into true heat, and sometimes at supper, while Dermot played or sang, I would sit quiet and watch Macbeth. When he met my glances I knew that he, too, felt the certain spark and fire between us, acknowledged but once. I longed to invite him to my bed. Yet pride was my backbone then, and to willingly invite him, to abandon my established position as the truculent young woman, would be to sacrifice the essential element that held me together. Without my prickling pride for a cloak, I would be bare, and the vulnerable heart of me would be exposed.

I meant to be strong. Just that.

Our only priest at Dun Elgin was the wizened old fellow who had been bullied into performing my marriage. We saw him infrequently, due to the demands of his widely scattered parish. Sometimes we heard Mass only once in months, so we were left on our own, as is often the way in remote Scotland, to make our own appeals and pacts with God. We did our best to keep our souls safe.

Among us all, Maeve was the most pious, I think. She prayed daily in the chapel, and often paused during the day to murmur and bless. She had a pocket gospel, a small jet cross, and prayer beads with her at all times. I owned a little book of psalms and a gospel, too, and though I was not the most devout, I found solace in quiet prayer and comfort in my little illuminated religious texts. Most days, though, I was occupied with the care of my household and my child. Lulach was the light of my world, and so I left the contemplation of the greater *lux mundi* to others, and never felt a lack of priests, or guidance, or God.

Dun Elgin's chapel boasted its own reliquary. A Pictish saint had left behind a toe bone that was treated with such reverence it might have dropped from the foot of the very Lord. Housed in a silver and brass box, this marvel accompanied Moray's mormaer when judgment courts were held on moot hills, or when Moray men went to battle. Even the smallest bone of a saint will lend luck and blessings to those who tote it about.

Leagues to the east, there sat a larger church and a Celtic monastery. Arguing rose now and then over installing a bishop there, to add status to Moray. As mormaer, Macbeth—not the Church—had the power to appoint a bishop for his region. The priests, aware of his relationship to the king, vied for Macbeth's attention, and so we received gifts of furs, wines, even offers of blessings and Masses for his soul to secure him a better seat in Heaven.

Macbeth considered the matter carefully, talking it over with his preferred advisors. One day, he asked me what I thought of this matter of a Moray bishop.

"If the people of Moray would benefit from a bishop's guidance," I said, "and if you know a devout man of Celtic blood who will think of Moray souls before himself, then send for him. If not, then wait, and let it be God's matter, not Moray's, to solve."

"I should add you to my council," he said.

"You already did. The night you seized Moray and took me to wife, you took on my opinions and advice henceforth." As I walked away, I heard him laugh quietly.

I did not want his affectionate tolerance. Mine was the bloodline, mine the right, more than his own but for virtue of my anatomy. I would not be shut out of matters that would affect home, kin, land, or future.

WHEN MACBETH and his men rode off for a few days to visit a thane in the north, Finn and Angus invited me to join them for hunting and hawking, as it was time to stock the cooking pots again. Off we went, riding north and west, where we had some luck early on: a few birds for the pot and two hares brought down by the hawks, and a buck, arrow shot by Angus. That meat would stretch to soups for a while. I was good with hawks and had a hand for bow and arrow, and though I had not practiced for a time, my natural aim was true. That day I hit a hare, but disliked the deed and missed the next one by intent. My friends teased me, saying motherhood had softened me.

"Let the hawks take the hares," I said. "I do not care for killing."

They laughed, and by afternoon we looked for rest before returning. Angus said we were closer to Kinlossie than Elgin, so I sent him to ask a farmer where to find Catriona, and we went in that direction. I thought to ask her for some simples and potions, and I hoped to ease the tension of her last visit, desiring no rift between us.

The day was clear and warm, the far hills blue and peaked. We rode the horses only so far as the sloping terrain would permit, and then dismounted. Intending to ask for hospitality first, Finn and I left the horses and hawks with Angus and the guards. Always cautious where raiders and caterans might lurk, he carried a sword and I retained my bow.

Nestled at the foot of the next slope, the house was roofed in heather thatch weighted with ropes and stones over wattle walls on a stone foundation. Whitewashed, neat, it looked a cozy place. A ribbon of smoke wafted upward, a goat bleated in the yard, chickens scurried. There was a little garden and a few blossoming apple trees. A horse was tied in the side yard, a bay with black mane and tail, a handsome creature, munching grasses.

Heart thumping, dread growing, I started down the hill.

"Come back, Rue," Finn said. "We will send a man for your simples later."

I did not answer. My husband was alone with Catriona—that horse had been there long enough to content himself on grass.

Finn snatched at my arm. "Rue," he said, "do not go farther."

I turned on him. "Does everyone know, but for his wife?"

"Listen," he said firmly. "This is no time for you to confront your husband about anything. Wait, and resolve it later."

I yanked free my bow, snatching an arrow and launching it before I could think. The point struck the center plank of the door, embedded, quivered.

"*Jesu!*" Finn grabbed the bow from me. "You will not do murder over this!"

The door opened, and my husband stepped outside, wearing a loose tunic over trews and no hauberk, his dagger grabbed up in his hand. He glanced around, then up at the hillside. He saw me; I felt it like a blow. As he tore the arrow loose, Catriona appeared behind him in the shadowy gap of the door. Her lovely face was flushed, her hair mussed. She rested a hand on his shoulder, spoke to him. He shook his head, and they both stepped back. The door closed.

I whirled and walked away, Finn behind me.

· · ·

Hours passed while I paced my room and fumed, unwilling to admit my own role in the creation of the dilemma. My mutterings shocked Aella, who had tender ears. She took the babe, who was fussy, and escaped my wrath. I began to pack to return to Fife, tearing things out of the wooden chest in the room, cramming them into a leather satchel. Bethoc came to help, efficient and perversely pleased, I think, that I would return to Fife, for she could go, too; she had only stayed at Elgin out of loyalty and love.

Rain drummed on the walls when Aella came back, and I nursed my child, which quieted me. "Find Angus," I told Aella, "and order an escort for our journey. We are leaving Elgin and Moray, all of us."

"You will travel nowhere," Macbeth said then. I turned to see him in the doorway. "Go," he told my women, letting them out of the room and closing the door. "Your behavior ill suits the lady of Moray."

"Yet the mormaer does as he pleases," I said, "even fetching his whore to deliver his wife of a child."

He strode toward me, and I stood my ground. His hair and the leather shoulders of his hauberk were damp and he smelled of horses and rain; he had come straight from the yard. "She is no whore."

"Murderer's mistress, then. Keep her if you want. I am going home."

"I can keep you here no matter your will," he pointed out. "Rome gives me that right, as do the Irish laws, barring physical harm. Your father's sympathies are with me. Bodhe will send you back if you go to Fife against my wishes."

"Only because Fife needs Moray for an ally," I said, stuffing more items into my satchel. Furious, I felt trapped and wild with it, and lobbed a shoe at him. I looked about for something more to throw, any weapon to hand. But he snatched at my arm.

"You conspire and bargain with my personal enemy in the Raven-Feeder," I seethed, "you bring your mistress into my home to befriend me—and my son has no father, which I lay directly at your feet!"

Releasing my arm, he stood so close that my back checked against the wall, and I could only glare at him. "Your son has a father in me," he said fiercely. "I owe that to him. To you. We will have our own children, and your anger over this will pass."

I shoved past him. "You will get no son on me. Go to your whore for that."

"Catriona and I have known each other since childhood." He stepped in front of me, his large size and sheer presence intimidating. "We were not suited for marriage, but for friendship. We each married another, were each widowed. The affection remains, always will. I make no apology—we have sometimes sought comfort in the other."

My breath heaved. "You take no comfort from me, who is your wife now."

"You offer none," he murmured.

"Nor you me. All I ask is loyalty."

"I can tell her it will not continue," he said.

"If you can cast aside a mistress so quickly, what then of a wife?"

"What of your loyalty to me? You have a keen mind, a good heart, but at times your words have the hone of a Norse blade."

"So my words drive you elsewhere?"

"I have never quailed from a blade. But I want a welcome in my own hall, and from my wife."

Holding back tears, I looked away. "I will not be shamed by my husband seeking another woman's body, when he does not seek mine."

So long a moment passed that I thought he might leave. "I will not set you aside, for it undoes one purpose of this marriage union. However, you can return to Fife, if you must. For now."

He strode for the door as if it were decided. Though he was angry, too, he had control, unlike myself, who breathed like a bellows, fast and deep, and wanted to hurl words, objects. Yet I had to master my temper, as he had done, and stay. Obligation to my kin group demanded that I remain with Moray's new mormaer, who had no equal among other warlords. Fate had set me in this situation, after all.

I frowned, for he left something unsaid. "What purpose do you see in this union?"

One hand on the door, he turned back. "Together we can tap the power of your legacy and mine," he said quietly, "and take Scotland under our rule."

There. He said outright what I, and others, suspected. I straightened my shoulders. This, then, was what Bodhe wanted, and what generations of my kin deserved in their honor. "A thing like that turns on loyalty," I said, "or falters for lack of it."

He nodded. "It does."

"Well enough," I said, watching him. An agreement of sorts.

"So be it. Your loyalty would be like gold, I think." Then he pulled at the door ring and was gone.

Within the week, he came to me in dark of night, and we were silent and careful with each other, as if we coaxed and protected the spark of a need-fire between us, a fire made new and not taken from an old ember. Soon after, he returned to me another night, and another. A bond began to form that had not been there before, something tender, something forged.

Soon enough we took to sharing a bed, having found a shaky peace. I did not ask if he kept his mistress—I did not want to know—nor did we speak of any plans that might take us beyond the curtained bed, the walled fortress, into the larger world.

In JULY, when the purple fairy flowers were abundant—those blooms and stems so helpful to the heart, and dangerous, too—Bethoc and I went out into the hills to gather them carefully, avoiding their poison, so that she could have a store of that potent medicine if necessary, particularly for complaints of the elderly. I knew she gave some to Maeve now and then. Later we joined a crowd to watch Macbeth dispense justice on a court hill near Elgin. Hearing word of the upcoming court, people traveled from all over the region to bring various grievances for airing.

At the opening of the judgment court, his retainers announced Macbeth's entrance with a rhythmic beating of swords against shields that reminded me of the first time I saw him, standing on a moot hill as a boy to accuse his father's murderers. Now he walked to his seat, a tall and strong warlord, a respected man, the growing hope of many.

Several Culdees followed, holding the reliquary from Elgin's chapel. The priest whom Macbeth had appointed bishop in Moray was there, too, a learned man of old Celtic lineage, who had proven his worth to my husband and his warrior council in meetings over the summer. Macbeth took his formal chair as others echoed the pounding rhythm with clapping hands or thumping boots to make a noise of welcome for him.

Watching, I felt drawn, too, as if we were lending not just our hands, but our wills as well, so that we might all make a great noise in Scotland someday.

Chapter Eighteen

Three ravens, black and gloss, perched on a high standing stone as our escort party rode past Lanfinnan and southward to attend a summer wedding. I shuddered to see them there. Beside me, Macbeth glanced up, grim and quick, and our escort was quiet as we filed past—just the creak and jangle of harnesses and carts, the thud of hooves, the wing flutters of the hawks, meant for a wedding gift, traveling caged in a cart.

Stark and ominous, those birds watched intently from their stony perches. A dreadful omen, I knew. The only thing blacker than a raven, goes the adage, is death.

Brechin, our destination, was a bishopric with a round stone tower beside the church. Some eager cleric rang the old iron bell in the tower as we rode past on our way to the fortress belonging to Neill, mormaer of the region of Angus. The wedding was between his son and Constantine mac Artair's daughter, but we arrived days before the event for a meeting between Macbeth and the other thanes and mormaers whose lands sat shoulder to shoulder like sentinels between Fife and Moray.

Bodhe was expected, too. I had not seen him since marrying Gilcomgan, and I looked forward to his arrival. Two years earlier, I had left Fife a bride, in heart still a child. Now I was a woman grown, wiser for the lessons life had heaped upon me harsh and quick. And I had a son to show my father. Lulach was plump and pretty, with Gilcomgan's fair sturdiness, Bodhe's eyes, Ailsa's smile. He was a calm child, and a joy to tote about.

Bodhe and Dolina arrived with young Malcolm, my late brother's son, and we greeted each other warmly, though a stiff politeness hindered Bodhe and me at first. For so long I had felt betrayed, yet that vanished when Bodhe took his grandson into his arms. Dolina, who had no child of her own, was thrilled with Lulach, who had a devoted knee-woman in her for the time we were there. And my nephew Malcolm, grown dark haired and tall, was proud of his new sword and hauberk, and that he was permitted to ride with Bodhe's young housecarls. My heart gave a tug to see him, so much like the father he had not known, and with so much life in him and before him. I imagined seeing Lulach like that one day, too, and my heart filled as I had rarely felt before, for him and all my beloved kin, so few and dear.

WHEN NEILL of Angus took some of his guests hawking and hunting the day following our arrival, I went too. We gloved, chose our birds, and rode out with lures and sacks of meat bits in case the birds needed rewarding. The birds had been fed first, to be uninterested in eating what they caught, and would return easily to the fist when whistled down. Macbeth carried a large red-tailed hawk on his wrist, one of a pair, and Bodhe had the other. I chose a small kestrel with a cream-colored breast, her gray wings lightly speckled. She was delicate and lovely.

We dismounted. Bodhe sent his bird after a lark high in the air, walking over the tufted ground to whistle him back again, followed by a ghillie on foot who would retrieve any catch. Seeing my father alone, I went toward him, carrying the pretty kestrel on my left wrist. Long experience told me that Bodhe would be calm and approachable around the birds, and I desired to speak with him.

His bird was already on the ground now, covering its prey with spread wings, and Bodhe sent his ghillie there as I joined him. We watched the lad distract the bird with a lure, then snatch up the prey in a sack, running back to the larger group to add it to the lot. Bodhe called back the big redtail with a confident offer of his wrist.

"A nice kestrel," he said, looking at my falcon. "Did you know that Sorcha died?"

I had not, and felt a twinge of sadness for that gentle bird. "We shall all miss her."

"True. You look well. And you have not lost your skill with the birds."

"Did you think childbearing and a forced marriage would addle my brain?"

He scowled. "Well, then, we are alone here. Say what you came to say."

Lifting my arm, I cast off my kestrel, who flew high and fast. We strode after it, staying apart from the group. "Macbeth and the king conspired to kill Gilcomgan."

"Rue, it is a regret, your widowing," Bodhe sympathized. "But do not blame your new husband overmuch. Sometimes killing must be done to protect life and kin, the good of others, and the very future."

"You made no protest to the second marriage, or to my treatment."

"A father does not arrange marriage for a widowed daughter. Macbeth had the right. I knew you would not be harmed," he added.

"Perhaps you knew about their scheme and went to Ireland to stay out of it."

"I do not conspire to kill kinsmen," he said curtly. "But I was not surprised by it."

"I know you would rather I had married Macbeth two years ago."

"Had he not been wed already, and had he been more than a thane, that would have happened. No matter, now it is accomplished." He sounded satisfied.

I felt disgust. "Why did you marry me off to Gilcomgan if you suspected he might not last long with such an enemy?"

"I wanted you removed to a safe place. Moray was the best choice."

Narrowing my eyes, I realized more. "You gambled that I would become Moray's widow—so that when Macbeth took his right there, he would take me in marriage."

"Fate lent a hand," he answered. "He was free of his wife, and you were . . . well, now you are just where I wanted you, even when you were small."

My bird landed high in a tree overhead, watching me. To keep her from tasting too much freedom, I raised my arm. She sailed down to land lightly on my wrist.

"Macbeth means to be king," I said, for we were alone on the sweep of land.

He nodded. He clearly knew. "Most of the leaders will support his bid. You will be queen someday, as I hoped." Bodhe moved ahead, gauntleted hand lifted high, his bird looking about, keen, restless. I caught up and we walked in silence, while our birds took stock of the air, and we of our own thoughts.

"So if support for Macbeth is growing . . . Duncan mac Crinan should watch his back," I finally said.

"Some would think it. Go, you!" He cast off his hawk, who had become restless when some birds flew overhead. Bodhe turned to me. "You have a fine son and a new husband. Put your thoughts there, and leave these other matters be. Time and God will unfold what will come. We can determine nothing here and now."

"I am small queen of Moray, and no hearth wife to be kept out of men's matters. I want all the truth." My kestrel stirred too, ready to be off, and I released her. She arrowed high, a beautiful sight in the clear blue overhead.

Bodhe sighed. "Then listen. Word is that King Malcolm wanted Gilcomgan killed, and sent Macbeth to see it done. Macbeth in Moray clears the way for Duncan in the south. Malcolm believes Macbeth has enough challenge now, with such a vast region to oversee—preventing cattle raids, keeping open trading ports, and the constant need to keep Vikings in check."

"My husband has that well in hand already, and he is ranging about looking for more to do. Now tell me what you truly think, not just what you have heard."

"I think Macbeth is the best guardian that Moray, and therefore Scotland, could have against the Norse threat. I am convinced he would be the better king for Scotland. Whether or not that comes about is largely left to him."

I nodded. "Malcolm has arranged all the way he wants it, with Macbeth in Moray, Thorfin in Orkney and Caithness, and all the rest for Duncan. Nothing will change unless Macbeth makes a move, which he cannot do without a great force of men at his back."

"He will not do so with his grandfather alive." Bodhe raised his fist for his hawk.

"Ah." All the pieces came together. "He waits for Duncan."

Bodhe smiled. "We will make a queen of you yet. There is something more you must know, Rue. Macbeth saved you that night."

"Not so. He broke down Elgin's gates—"

"Hear me. Macbeth asked his uncle to warn you to leave, once he suspected the king's full intention. He did not trust your life to Malcolm's keeping."

While I stood stunned, my father whistled out, and the redtail swooped down to his fist. My own kestrel circled high, and I waited until Bodhe lowered his wrist with his bird. A trained raptor is still wild within, and makes its own choices; but they will come to the highest perch, and to certain comfort and reward. As I stretched my arm upward, my kestrel saw no better choice and came swiftly down to me. I wrapped the jesses around my gloved fingers. The little bells on the bird's ankles chimed softly.

Still thoughtful, I walked with my father toward the rest of the hunting party. Just before we reached the others, Bodhe halted to look at me. "When next you go to Mass," he said, "I want you to say an extra prayer while you are there."

"Of course. I will attend the service before the wedding to pray for the bride and groom. If you will not be there then, I will light a candle for them in your name."

"Dolina will do that," he said with a wave of his hand. "You must make an appeal for the sake of those who share your bloodline."

A fillip of fear stirred. "Why?"

"Pray for us," he said. "We are not long for this world."

· · ·

THE WEDDING itself was a delightful thing, from the first blessings and vows on the porch of the little church, to the sweet faces of the bride and groom, and to the feast and celebration that lasted three days. On the first night, the male guests carried the groom into the bridal chamber and tossed him on the bed amid guffaws to join his bride. In the morning, blushing and happy, they walked through the nearest villages to scatter silver coins and distribute gifts of sweets. There were games, too, horseback races and foot sprints, and a great chasing about of lads and a much-battered leather ball through the very streets of the village. The last day saw another feast and a huge evening bonfire, with dancing, too, until the last mead-drunk fool was left leaping about alone while his friends lay dozing on the ground. When dawn finally came, his friends dragged the lone dancer away to home, and the wedding feast was done.

Then Bodhe and young Malcolm and their party rode back to Fife, and we turned north for Moray, and autumn.

SAFE IN my Elgin bed with my husband asleep beside me, I dreamed a harsh and vivid tapestry of images: men fighting hand to hand, faces close and fierce, spears and swords wicked and dangerous, lashing out, gore spattering, throats slit. I stood in the midst of this, a pale wisp dressed in white but for my hair like a sheen of fire. As I walked through the frenzy, they parted for me and did not strike. My husband was there—the first, the second.

I moved over moors and hills, then over a seastrand. Looking out, I saw a ship so large it suited only a dream. Its clinker-built sides were painted red and black, its oars were manned by a thousand men, and the curled prow became at its peak a dragon's head. But the head was alive, mouth opening to spew flame and smoke, and the ship itself was alive, too, breathing hard, claws coming up to clutch, oars lifting like wings. The ship-monster beached itself, groaning and spitting fire, and the men spilled out, silver swords gleaming, to spread thick over the white sands of Moray.

That was to the north. I turned toward the south and saw more hordes spilling over the hills. Beside me on the beach, suddenly, was Macbeth. He alone saw me standing there.

"He must be stopped," he said. "This cannot continue, for the sake of all."

"Who must be stopped?"

"He who comes after," he said. "There."

Turning again, I saw men in pale tunics, features blurred by shrouds. Two of them came closer: old Malcolm and Duncan. The others behind them were shadowed.

I woke on a half scream, and knew in the pit of my gut that the Sight had come to me through the dream. Once old Malcolm died, Scotland would know chaos and defeat, and something must be done to stop it.

Macbeth woke to ask what was wrong, and I told him what I had seen, while he circled an arm around my shoulders, listening. When I leaned in, wanting some comfort, instead he rose from the bed and left the room. I think he paced the hall and did not sleep again that night.

WATCHING AN impromptu footrace in the lower bailey one day, I applauded with the others, but soon we all heard shouts from the barricade. A single rider was approaching Elgin at a furious pace. I ran with Macbeth to see Ruari mac Fergus ride through the gate and dismount from a slick, exhausted horse. My heart turned to see him, and I knew something was very wrong.

"Bodhe mac Kenneth is killed," Ruari rasped out, "and young Malcolm mac Farquhar with him. My father is dead as well, killed in defense of his mormaer."

A terrible quaking overtook my limbs, and my chest felt bound tightly. Yet when Macbeth touched a hand to my arm, and when Aella appeared to urge me away, I stood rooted. "What happened?"

"We were ambushed by a group, ten at least," he answered. "At first we took them for raiders, but we could not see—just at dawn, it was, in a narrow glen as we set out on a morning's hunt. We fought, and they fled. And Bodhe and Malcolm were killed," he said bluntly. "My father was slain first. He put himself in front of them. Others were sore wounded."

I stood motionless, enduring the heavy shock of it, and did not speak—could not.

Ruari wiped his face with the back of his fist. "By their armor and weapons, they were elite guards and had to be sent by a man of note."

I gasped at that, then saw Ruari press his hand over a bloody bandage wrapped around his arm. "You are injured!" I said, finding my voice.

"A sword cut. Minor enough."

"It needs tending." I was grateful to focus on that. "Bethoc will see to it."

"Come inside," Macbeth said. "You risked your own life in that fight, and rode near fifty leagues to reach us. That will not be forgotten. We are in your debt."

"Very much, Ruari—" Unable to speak further, I touched his hand. We could not seem to look at each other. "Aella," I said, making my voice firm, "go inside and tell the servants that Ruari is to have whatever he needs. Send a lad to find the cook, and ask Maeve to open the linen chests and order the servants to prepare a bath and a fresh bed. And find his brothers, Angus and Conn."

She nodded and ran, and when Macbeth led Ruari toward the keep, I went too, but more slowly. My legs shook, and a leaden feeling weighed in me. Bodhe, the others . . .

One thought rang clear through my grief and shock. My father had tried to warn me, asked me to pray for our lineage. Now both he and his oldest grandson were gone.

Inside the keep, I ran up the wooden steps toward my bedchamber. At the turn in the landing, I sobbed out and fell to my knees. Macbeth found me there, but I brushed away his offer of a hand. He waited, but was not one to coddle or offer solicitous comfort. "My father's bloodline," I said, my voice a rasp, "is now rendered to a trickle.

Those men were sent by the king to do that hideous deed. Tell me if I am wrong."

He did not reply. We both knew the likely truth.

Guiding me inside the bedchamber, he knelt to stoke a fire in the low-burning brazier, though with the late summer warmth, it was not needed. I looked through the window at gray thunderclouds overhanging the hills. Though it burned in me for release, I refused to cry. Anger was mine; rage would strengthen me.

When he turned to leave, I stretched out a hand. Just that, and he remained. His grief and outrage, I think, matched my own, and in his company, later his embrace, I felt safe and shored up for a few hours.

By dawn, I wanted revenge. It seethed in me like the start of a fever.

WE RODE hard and fast to Fife in a great body of grim men and sharp spears, with the blue banner of Moray riding high before us. None stopped us along the way, and we scarcely halted but to change horses past the mountains. The pace suited me, and I would not ask for slower. The bodies of my kinsmen lay cold, and I could not be there fast enough.

"Flowers will grow rich on the moor where his blood soaked the soil, and all will remember him," Maeve said at Abernethy, as we helped to shroud Bodhe. I set the gold coins upon his eyes with trembling fingers. My husband would not allow me into the room where young Malcolm lay, until the men had cleaned the boy's body themselves and set the head to the neck in a clean seam. We tended the body of dear old Fergus, too. His kinswomen, the mother and aunts of his sons, bathed and dressed him, and I helped, for he had been my mentor and friend, and had given his life attempting to save my father and nephew. Now the two old comrades would move on to the shining life, with young Malcolm safe between them.

I wept in secret, tears spent for all that was lost, then bathed my face and straightened my gown and veil, and went cool and calm to face the others. Throughout those days, I felt myself hardening within. Only that held me upright, at times.

Dolina wept and faltered, and Bethoc and Mairi dosed her with herbs and strong spirits until she could stand without trembling, speak without sobbing. Father Anselm said the Office of the Dead and offered blessings, and said little else. He was deeply affected; the aging Saxon had long been Bodhe's house priest and had full right to mourn alongside us. I wondered what would become of Anselm, for he had never kept a parish. I knew I should invite him to Elgin, but I could not bring myself to it, having not forgotten the bitterness of Father Anselm and his dislike of Celts and women, and me in particular.

"Let him remain at Abernethy," Macbeth told me. "You will inherit Fife, as Bodhe's own and only. Ask him to stay, and he will be glad of it."

At dawn before the funeral, as Anselm finished leading our morning prayers, I noticed how much he had aged, his shoulders bowed and his dark hair grayed, and his sly glance now red-rimmed on Bodhe's behalf. When he left the hall, I walked with him. "My father always respected you," I said.

"And I him," he replied. "We met on the battlefield at Carham. I was a young priest, wounded in Malcolm's attack on that town and taken prisoner by the Scots. Your father," he said, peering at me, "had me carried to Fife and nursed to health. In return he asked me to be his house priest. He wanted to know the wider world than Scotland, appreciated the Saxon viewpoint, and I had souls to mold for the Lord's work. We did not always agree, but we each learned from the other."

"I never knew. My father never said."

"Bodhe did not speak of his good deeds. He was a generous man in spirit and in actions. Honor his humility by emulating him, rather than fostering your pride and preening your female independence. Give yourself to God and His wishes for you."

Often Anselm's way of improving me was to disapprove. "My father was a great man, I agree. As his daughter and heiress, I thank you for your service to him and his household. You will always have a home at Abernethy so long as it is my decision. I will go back to Moray," I said. "We are not a match, you and I."

"Not so much," he said. "But there is a good deal of Bodhe in you. Be glad of it."

MY FATHER'S kinsmen and comrades came from Fife and elsewhere, linked distant or close in the blood, all incensed by the deaths. Among Celtic stock, loyalty is all, and many who came to Abernethy offered strength and sword to me and to Macbeth, too. I was darkly pleased: revenge was rife in the air.

Grieving Dolina needed careful handling, and my women and I, including Mairi, sat with her hour after hour. Lulach was a blessing then, his gentle weight and warmth in my arms a comfort, as were his sticky kisses and gurgling laughs in the midst of sorrow. The men clustered in groups, and some mentioned vengeance in quiet voices. King Malcolm's name was on every mind, if not often said aloud. I met more than one meaningful glance, and if a discussion grew passionate concerning who and what to consider in retribution, Macbeth would note my keen interest and escort me from the room.

"Tell me what is being said," I urged at night, when he crawled into my old bed at Abernethy, which we shared despite its size. I did not want to be alone, which he seemed to know. "I want to be part of the revenge."

"Leave it be, Rue," he answered firmly.

ONE COUSIN who arrived at Dun Abernethy was Dubh mac Dubh, whom I had not seen since I had gone to Moray. The one we called Black Duff was now a retainer in King Malcolm's household. Silence fell when this Duff entered a room, lest he carry word back to the old king. But he came to honor Bodhe, genuinely meant, and asked me if I would stay in Fife now that I stood to inherit Bodhe's properties.

"I do not know," I said. "My husband and I have yet to discuss our plans."

"You should more properly discuss them with the king," Duff suggested.

I murmured and took my leave, then found Macbeth. "Black Duff," he said in answer to my question, "is known to be Malcolm's man, and he supports Duncan mac Crinan and his father as well. He married a niece of Crinan last year, and now holds property in Atholl."

"Which means," I replied, "we should take care near him."

"We shall make a queen of you yet," he answered. Bodhe, too, had once said so.

Old Luag, my father's bard, spoke a tribute to the three dead that evening. Standing by the fire basket, he recited the lists of names that stretched from the Pictish kings down to Bodhe and his son and two grandsons, my Lulach being the last of that proud line. As the old bard uttered the final names, tears slid down his cheeks. I wept deep for all of them, my son as well. Now I knew Lulach would never be safe, never in his life, until the aging king and all his supporters were gone.

In the small hours before the burial, unable to sleep, I stood alone in the great hall, rocking my son on my shoulder, having taken him from Maeve to let her rest.

"Rue." A voice, quiet and dear to me, sounded in the shadows. I turned.

Drostan stood there, his black hair long but shaven across the forehead, ear to ear, in the manner of the Culdees. He came toward me, taller now, broad of shoulder, a man and a monk in white tunic and brown cloak, not the boy I had known. Much had changed for both of us.

"Bodhe—" I began.

"I know." Then he opened his arms, and I stepped into them, tears in my eyes.

Soon he was admiring Lulach, and together they made me laugh a little. Drostan asked after my husband, and I told him about one, then the other. He seemed to know much of my tale already, though he had been shut away in the monastery.

"We keep a chronicle of yearly events, my teacher and his students,

I among them," he said. "We hear much, even on our isle. Lords send their messengers with news when something of note happens. The upkeep of the annals is very important," he added.

He was shocked and sad over Bodhe's death, and grateful that the prior of Saint Serf's had allowed him to go to Abernethy, knowing he would hear details of the deaths for the annals' scribes. I was glad of it. Let them record old Malcolm's evil deed forever.

THE WEATHER was drear and rain for the funeral, and the wailing woman, hired to sing and moan over the hills to the churchyard, threw herself so much into her work that her shrieks tautened everyone's nerves. I wanted all of it done, the mourning over so revenge could begin. The wooden coffins were set into the ground—earlier, earth and salt had been laid upon the chests of the dead as a symbol of earthly past and heavenly future—and then clods of soil were dropped over them. Sandstone markers in the hogbacked shape of thatched houses were set down to mark the graves.

Unable to watch, I turned away.

We started back over the hills. I walked with Dolina, accompanied by our women, a mournful cluster in our long dark cloaks and veils. Looking up at the crest of a hill, I saw a row of men on horses lined up like chess pawns, stiff and silent as they watched our somber procession. The leader urged his horse forward slowly, an older man with him. Behind them came a dozen or more housecarls. In the misty air, the creak of metal rings and leather trappings was eerie and loud.

"Duncan," Macbeth murmured behind me. Recognizing the king's tanist, I left Dolina, and my husband and I approached the horsemen. I must have looked like a ghost of the shadowlands myself that day, in a brown tunic and cloak of black and brown weave, the hood pulled high. A veil of translucent gray silk, a sad gift from Dolina, hid my features.

"Greetings, Lady Gruadh, Macbeth. Please accept our condolences," Duncan said. "We ask pardon for arriving late. The king sends his regrets as well, detained this day."

I started to reply, but Macbeth set a hand to my elbow, not trusting me, I think. Crinan of Atholl, the lay abbot of Dunkeld, repeated brusque sympathies. I had not seen either man since the border homage between Cnut and old Malcolm. Now I hoped my silence and mourning status made them uncomfortable.

"Heinous, these deaths," Duncan said. "If we hear news, we will send word."

"Then speak to our grandfather about it," Macbeth said curtly.

"The king had no part in this," Crinan replied, somber as stone.

"Malcolm's lethal grudge against Bodhe and that line is commonly known. Bodhe himself warned his daughter"—here Macbeth touched my arm—"to beware the king's intentions toward him and his kin."

"King Malcolm was at Dunsinnan all that day," Duncan said. "He did not ride out to cut down one of his close cousins. Anyone should take care who implies otherwise."

"His men were seen near there that day," Macbeth said.

"I have not heard that," Duncan murmured, while his father looked on in silence. They affirmed nothing, and so denied nothing, in my estimation. "Likely caterans hoping to steal Fife horses or cattle."

"None were taken," Macbeth said, "but we heard the men wore very fine armor."

"We are aware of the old feud, but Malcolm meant him no harm. Bodhe was no threat," Crinan replied. "Duncan is tanist, and Bodhe never disputed that."

"My father respected peace. He understood its usefulness, until he was betrayed," I said, and once again my husband pressed my arm.

"Lady Gruadh, I promise you," Duncan told me, "the old feud between your father and Malcolm will not continue once I am king."

"I will hold you to that vow, should you ever become king." My qualification was bold. "May God hold you to that promise as well, since we speak on consecrated church ground—and in the presence of an abbot."

For what it was worth. Crinan was lay abbot of Dunkeld, though most said he was more concerned with his income from lands held by that church than with the welfare of the souls on that land. But my remark must have reminded Crinan of his obligation.

"May God rest their souls," he intoned, flicking his fingers in a blessing motion.

"Once I am head of Fife," I told Duncan, "be assured that my men will never forget the death of their leader. But I will bid for peace before warring."

"Leader in Fife? You?" Duncan glanced at his father.

"Lady Gruadh is Bodhe's only surviving offspring," Macbeth said, "and so will take her place as Lady of Fife. I hear that his thanes and retainers will not object."

"Ah," Duncan said, "because you are her husband."

Macbeth inclined his head. "I will support her in whatever way she requires."

"A woman cannot be mormaer in Fife," Crinan said. "A thane of a small property, perhaps, but not a great steward—the region is too crucial. The King of Scots will have to decide the matter. Fife is a wealthy province, and its seacoast is open to trading ships and Viking raids alike. Malcolm will consider the greater good and likely rescind her title, if not her inheritance."

I felt rising indignity at Crinan's presumption and was glad for the screen of my veil. Holding my arm, Macbeth stepped backward with me.

"This is not the place to discuss that issue," he said. "We are here to honor the three good men who were slain. Farewell, sirs. Our procession is anxious to move on." Behind us, the mourners waited along the earthen track that led back to Dun Abernethy.

"Lady. And Macbeth," Duncan murmured, then turned his horse's head. His father nodded and followed, and the lot of them, lords and silent carls, disappeared over the hillside. My husband and I turned in the cold misty rain to join the others.

That evening, we went to Abernethy's chapel again to hear the chants and prayers intoned by the priests in mellow tones, the first night of the blessings and appeals to be said daily for a year to honor the departed souls. But they could not comfort me. Instead, later and alone, I sought the seclusion of the garden in Bodhe's great keep, and turned to the ways of the Gaels. Under the cold stars, I walked three times round, then stood to sing an ancient song.

> *Sleep you, sleep, and away with sorrow,*
> *Sleep you, sleep, in the peace of all peace. . . .*

A little solace only. Had I been a son to Bodhe, revenge would have been mine quick. As his daughter, I had to wait upon others.

"No one is strong enough in men and arms, or foolhardy enough, to seek vengeance against the high king," Finn said, a week past the funeral, while we still lingered at Abernethy. After dark, Macbeth and a few men gathered in a corner of the great hall, with a guard at the door and only myself to pour the red wine and new ale, so that no servants need be present. I, too, had a share of wine. That night I needed bolstering.

"Revenge cannot be satisfied without men to pay the price," Angus said.

"Only Malcolm had reason to take down Bodhe of Fife," said Constantine, who had just joined us. "The king's men are an extension of his own sword arm. In my mind, there is no doubt who ordered the deaths. Ruari was there. He can say best."

Seated across from me, Ruari swirled ale in his wooden cup for a moment. "They had no standard, the attackers, but wore expensive mail. They carried fine weapons of Viking and Saxon make. A shepherd saw them riding past when he went out with his flocks before dawn. He said they looked like the ghosts of the Fianna come riding through the mist, so determined and powerful were they. I saw them, and believe they were king's men. But no faces were visible, with the helmets and the half darkness."

"What of Duncan or Crinan?" Finn asked. "They could have sent them. The attack was near Atholl lands. Both have reason to sever the Fife branch from the tree."

"Duncan can be a fool, and he does whatsoever his father and grandfather tell him," Macbeth said. "But a fool, particularly a selfish one in line for the throne, cannot be trusted."

"And we do not know for certain," Ruari said. "Not yet."

"We cannot shrug and say we do not know who—and thus do nothing," Angus said.

"True, but the risks are very great if we act. Be warned," Constantine advised.

I leaned forward. "Whoever sent those men out, you can be certain Malcolm knew of it. We waste time here—a week has passed, and more. There must be some kind of justice and recompense for these deaths!"

"Justice will be brought," Macbeth said low.

"When?" I asked, splaying my hands, slim fingered and beringed, on the table. Such feminine hands for such hard masculine thoughts. The urge sprang in me like a dark wolf within. I did not like it, but fed it nonetheless. *It is the way of things,* Bodhe would have said. "When will you avenge my kinsmen? Tomorrow? A year from now?"

"It would be a bloody matter, this, if it were pursued," Macbeth replied.

"I am full aware of the price," I answered, low and fervent. Though a deep twist in my belly warned me to slow, to think, I continued. "This was my father, and my nephew—your father died, too," I said, glancing at Ruari and Angus. "We cannot rest until payment comes to bear. In matters like this, many act quick, and have done."

"Revenge is best done when the matter is clear, but this is not," Macbeth said. "And the king is my grandfather. Such a deed would be abhorrent. It is not done."

"It *is* done," I pointed out bitterly. "Just not spoken of."

"*I* will not do it," he murmured, staring back at me.

"Yet you promise justice!" We could have been the only two in that room, for we glared intently, both fierce and stubborn, neither willing to give way. I wanted him to shout, order his men to ride. And I could scarcely breathe for the weight in my heart.

"If one of Bodhe's bloodline held the throne someday," my husband then said, "it would be a far more lasting revenge than bloodshed now."

"Lulach?" I waved a hand. "He cannot defend his lineage for a score of years!"

"You," he said. "As rightful queen and claimant."

For a moment no one spoke, yet I sensed a silent clarity of agreement at that table. Macbeth was bold and farseeing, cautious, too. He trusted the few men gathered there, or he never would have spoken those thoughts aloud.

In my agitation, I had overlooked the key: my right to sit the throne beside Macbeth was true vengeance. But his plan required a patience I did not have then.

"Dreams will not avenge my kinsmen," I said. "These killings require blue-steel payment, and quick." Knowing full well what I suggested, I felt nearly ill once the words were out.

Steel-games. Not yet twenty, I had seen too much of them already. I knew how swiftly the balance could change, knew that lives and kingdoms might pivot and fall, or triumph, upon crisscrossing blades. Now I urged the men around me toward more of the same.

Chapter Nineteen

O ur small party returned to Moray in late August after the Lammas harvest, when the hills were ragged gold under blue skies. We had lingered in Fife long enough to see our friend Finn married in a ceremony of muted joy after the deaths of the Fife men. The bride, whom I had met but once or twice, was the granddaughter of Luag, Bodhe's bard. She had a sweet hand herself for the harp, and had played the tunes of sorrow for Bodhe's wake. Macbeth granted Finn a parcel of land at Pitgaveny, near Elgin, with rental income from tenanted lands, making him a thane in return for the smithing that Finn would do for the mormaer of Moray. He would also remain Macbeth's retainer as needed. Watching the groom with his blond bride, she of sturdy build and gentle character, I felt an abiding if bittersweet affection for my friend. I knew that Finn would be content.

Once at Elgin, though my heart still grieved, my concerns were needed elsewhere. Macbeth decided to transfer our household from Moray's center to the northeast, where he held an old fortress. Craig Phadraig was solidly built on a hill not far from the firth at Inverness, with stunning views to the west of Highland mountains and to the east, the sea. Northward, the lights in the sky blazed and danced at night.

"A warlord who intends to warn away his enemies," Macbeth said as our entourage advanced noisily over the hills, "should not travel about with puppies and children."

"On the contrary, sir," I answered, feeling a rare instant of saucy contentment, "let your enemies beware, for you not only show your strength, but rally the people to you with the humble appeal of your escort train."

He smiled, then urged his horse ahead. We did not speak again until we reached Inverness through a downpour that soaked our train and made us all long to be indoors.

Moving a household is common enough for titled and landed men: keeping to one place in a vast region limits the sword arm of authority, protection, and justice. Though thanes act for the greater lord and report back to him, if left to their own, the outermost regions can go to wildness, with raiding and thievery and men of small, mean power. Macbeth's presence in the north would benefit upper Moray and discourage enemies from sweeping into that area.

Housecarls and servants remained at Elgin to keep its fires alive and its defenses intact, as was the case with Moray's other properties. The rest of us lumbered north with our caravan of furnishings, bedding, plate, chests of clothing, and all the miscellanea of home, from the chess games, leather balls, and harps, to the hawks and falcons in cages, and a few of our cats and dogs. Had we possessed good windows, we would have wrapped and taken them, too. I longed for beautiful glass inserts such as existed in other places, rather than oiled parchments.

Secure in our hilltop fort, we caught the mountain breezes on their way to the changeable sea. Whenever I saw the golden fields and heather-purple hills, all within sight of mountains and firth, I felt protected, insulated from both mourning and dread.

Within the first weeks there, a messenger arrived with word from King Malcolm, a terse letter informing Macbeth that the king had appointed a new mormaer for Fife. "For the safety and sake of the region," Macbeth read, while I paced anxiously, "Bodhe's cousin Dubh mac Dubh has been named to watch over Fife."

"Duff! His loyalties lie where he gains most benefit," I said.

"Within the triumvirate of Malcolm, Duncan, and Crinan, my cousin apparently prospers."

"He does play king's man well," Macbeth agreed.

"His blood is diluted with Saxon. He should not have Fife." I snatched the letter to scrutinize it, taking longer than my husband, whose reading skills were the finer. "The king acknowledges Lady Gruadh's lineage and grants her deed and income from lands within Fife—" I looked up. "He grants me the holding of lands beside Loch Leven."

"You will have a portion of the yearly revenues, and you may donate, divide, and bequeath the property as you wish. The lands are no longer under the rulership of Fife, nor are they held by the Church," Macbeth said.

"Saint Serf's monastery is on the island in that loch, where Drostan is of that brethren. Still, I will not be wooed by the king's gift. He strips me of my inheritance and rights, and thinks to placate me with this."

"Considering that he may remember sword-wielding Lady Gruadh all too well," Macbeth said, "it is an unexpected compensation."

"Should I be grateful? He garners favor with you, not me. Malcolm expects you to handle Fife lands for me, benefit from their income, and feel suitably loyal to him."

"The lands are yours to manage, not mine."

"Then I would like to send Angus south to oversee the building of a home on that parcel for Dolina," I decided quickly. "She has nowhere to go with Duff at Abernethy."

He nodded as if satisfied, and went off to talk with Angus. Unhappy with the king's decision, I was yet glad to possess a small part of beloved Fife, grateful to have a reason to visit there still and a place to stay when I did. Never again would I feel welcome at Dun Abernethy, a hard blow to follow the deaths of my kinsmen.

"THE THREE sons of Tuirenn," Dermot said to those of us clustered in the hall on a cool but lovely evening, with the windows thrown open wide to autumn breezes and a view of the stars, "went voyaging to find items to pay the fine for killing the great warrior Cian—who, it could be said, invited his own death when he used magic to turn himself into a pig, which only infuriated the sons of Tuirenn into pursuing him. So the god Lugh, Cian's son, burdened the brothers with an impossible death fine, a list of magical objects to steal."

We listened, hushed and avid, to the familiar story; Lulach in my lap was quiet as well. The *seanchaidh* had joined us at Inverness, and we welcomed his stories. The tale of the sons of Tuirenn was among my favorites, one of the Three Sorrowful Tales out of Ireland.

"Brian and his brothers found most of the wondrous magical objects they owed Lugh," Dermot continued, after detailing the long sea voyage of the three brothers, "but they lacked the magical cooking-spit of the women of Fincara, an island sunk beneath the sea long ago. A Druid gave the brothers the secret to traveling there, and they sailed to the spot where Fincara lay in Land-Under-Waves.

"His brothers hesitated, but Brian donned the druid's gift of a water-hauberk and a helmet of crystal, and sank into the sea. He swam down and down until he found the island, the fortress, and the women of Fincara. They sat in a huge hall, thrice fifty of them, each working part of an embroidered cloth. Chatting and singing, the women did not notice as Brian crossed the room.

"He snatched the iron spit and moved toward the door, but the women stood and turned, and in their hands held not needles, but bejeweled swords. 'Hold, son of Tuirenn!' one of the women called, and Brian had to stop. She was a *bana-ghaisgeach,* a warrior woman, as were her sisters, and not to be dismissed. 'The smallest among us could best you if she wished,' their leader said, 'but you braved the dangers of sea and sworded women. We honor that boldness, and you may take our cooking-spit with you.' Brian thanked them and left, swimming upward to find his brothers waiting in the boat."

I listened, thoughtful over the plight of those women, trapped underwater forever. The next day, when rain kept us indoors, I sat by a window with my women, our needles sliding in and through fabric, pulling bright streams of color. We chatted as we worked, and, looking out at the deluge, spoke of the women of Fincara.

"You have the training of a *bana-ghaisgeach,*" Bethoc said to me, "and so you are part of the old tradition of warlike Celtic women. If you ever fell into the sea, I think you would swim off to Fincara with a sword in your hand!"

They all laughed, and I shrugged. "True, women of the Gaels took swords in the early generations, even before the Scotti came here from Ireland. The old legends are filled with such women—the great Irish queen, Macha, and Princess Scathach of Skye, who trained warriors in her fighting school, and also her sister Aoife, who bested Cu Chulainn and bore his son."

"Huh, then he bested her," Maeve muttered to Bethoc, who laughed.

"And Boudicca, in my land, defeated the Roman army," Aella pointed out.

I nodded. "Celtic women have fought beside their men since before the names of kings were remembered. And even though Rome forbids Gaelic women to fight, it is rightful enough according to our customs."

"They forbid with good reason," Maeve said, bouncing Lulach on her lap. "Women have enough to do and should not have to go out and fight men's battles, too."

We all smiled at that. "The Irish laws protect women, and we are better for it," Bethoc said. "I do not want to fight, though long ago they say women pledged service alongside the men."

"The eyes of the Church cannot easily see beyond the mountains of the Gaels," I said, "where warlike behavior in a woman is not sinful heresy, and is sometimes even necessary." And I remembered my early vows—as a girl taking up a sword to defend herself, as a woman swearing on a sword to defend her own. Another facet of my obligation to my long legacy came clear: if others were so set on eliminating my line, and I and Lulach the last of it, then I would be steadfast as any warrior.

On a warm, misty morning, I went down to the lower bailey with the sword my father had given me, and walked onto the practice field. Surprised, the sons of Fergus, Angus and Conn, questioned me. I told them that I was restless and wanted air and exercise. So I began to hone my wishes, keen and dark, with every blow in those weekly sessions. More than once, I went to my husband to ask if there was news from the south.

"King Malcolm," he said, "thrives."

If he plotted revenge, or knew who did, he did not tell me.

Soon I dreamed again of a battle spread over a bloody heath, of men dying at my feet while I walked past like a wraith. Macbeth was there, too, facing an opponent whose back was to me. The clash of steel was horrid to hear, and I woke before I could see him hurt, or worse. Though I did not tell my husband of this nightmare, I carried a leaden fear in me that one day those dream visions would come about.

MACBETH RODE out many days to trace pith and perimeter of his northern territory, earning the trust of those people by sending men and goods to aid them with building, farming, or herding, and holding justice courts when needed. Showing a steady hand and head and a glimpse of heart now and then, he earned their loyalty like a merchant earns gold.

Most of my hours were spent with my child, surrounded by my women, tending to the household. I kept a firm, kind manner with servants and grooms, and took in Macbeth's Moray kin for servants when possible, by accepted custom. I counted the food stocks and wine myself, and went to market fairs with the cook and a few servants.

Only when I had a free hour did I go to the training yard. With his uncommon reserve and his instinct to let be where no harm existed, my husband rarely mentioned my practice. If he came to the yard for his own skill work and found me there, he would stand by to watch, then move on. I think he knew what brought me there.

Daily I prayed, finding a little solace in quietude and piety, and when a priest was available, I took confession, as did we all. But I never offered up the supposed heresy of my sword training for prayerful cleansing, nor did I mention my abiding desire for revenge. God Himself knew, I reasoned, and would either smite me or allow me some part of satisfaction.

. . .

LIKE BIRDS, we went southward as winter approached. Once the mountain passes filled with snow and ice, we would be trapped in the central bowl of Moray, and Elgin was a strong citadel. Inverness had brought needed respite, and wild, tender moments with my husband in our bed. I hoped we would start life within me again, but each month I met disappointment.

"Your weapons practice and your desire for vengeance," Maeve told me one day, "are hardening you, dulling the bed of your womb. How can you expect to conceive a child when you feed yourself on spite and anger? Those are poisons for the body."

She made me think, I admit, and she made me wonder. But I did not stop, not then. Perhaps I should have listened more closely to her acerbic wisdom.

Before Martinmas, I sent a message to Duff at Abernethy to request my father's hawks. A bold move, but I trusted no one to keep them as well as Bodhe had done. A fortnight later, I was surprised when riders arrived with cages on carts, bringing several birds surly from the journey and sore in need of exercise. A few of Bodhe's dogs accompanied the men, too, running much of the way beside the horses. Lean and fit, those hounds, and so affectionate and long of memory that I had sloppy kisses from them so soon as I came to the gate. Pleased to see that Ruari mac Fergus had led the small escort, I welcomed and thanked him.

"I will not stay at Abernethy under your cousin, lady, though I am a Fife man," he told me, then turned to Macbeth. "If possible, I would be honored to join your service, sir."

"Excellent," my husband said. "I have need of another good man among my elite guard." And so Ruari joined us, where I had always felt he belonged.

By the time the northern winds blew down from the mountains and the chill settled in Moray, we had acquired a new priest at Elgin. Father Osgar was both a Gael and a Culdee, and had spent years in

Rome and among the Saxons, so he was a cunning counselor for Macbeth, who wanted to know more about views and ways in other lands. He and Osgar sat up late many nights, debating Rome and its tenets, and the need for better harmony between the Celtic and Roman churches. Father Osgar left me be unless I approached him for confession and counsel.

"Your wish for vengeance is sinful," he told me one day after confession, when we walked a little. "But it is understandable. Let prayer and faith heal you."

"I cannot give it up," I said. "I am not yet done with this."

"Give it up or keep it close," he answered, "but know that until you find some peace in your heart, I will pray on your behalf. Grief is sometimes like a sharp-toothed demon that gets hold of our hearts. But its grip weakens with time, and one day you will be free of it."

"Then I will wait," I said, and as Osgar nodded, I thought of the tongue-lashing I would have had from Anselm for the same. Instead I had understanding and patience, and a priest who would generously pray for me. To me, that was revelation greater than any gospel verse.

THE GREAT hall was draped in fresh juniper for luck at Christmas, and the fire baskets and braziers blazed with fragrant pine, hazel, and applewood, rather than the usual peat. We attended Mass at the little chapel in the glen and returned uphill through drifting, magical snowflakes. Gifts were not often exchanged, but I had embroidered a shirt and overtunic for Macbeth, and he gave me a new mare, an Irish-bred white beauty with a silver mane and a gentle temperament. I called her *Solus*, or light.

Later, as we sat with Frankish wine in cups of thick glass, Lulach jumped so much in Maeve's lap that she set him down. He clung to her, staring around at us, his eyes a heartbreaking clear blue: Bodhe's eyes, he had, and Gilcomgan's stocky fairness, so that I could never forget my first husband. Then, surprising us all, Lulach took his first steps, a wobbly effort. Crying out with delight, I opened my arms to catch him, but he turned away to be caught up by the strong hands of his stepfather.

We laughed, and among all my memories, that day remains dear.

Bʏ Sᴀɪɴᴛ Brigid's February feast, I knew for certain that I carried new life within me. For a while I kept it to myself, smiling and silent, and when my women, even my husband, asked my thoughts—I may have looked smug as a cat at the cream—I shrugged. But my women washed my linens, and soon enough realized that I had not been in flowers for two months.

Kneeling more often to my prayers, reading in my small gospels and psalter, I whispered incantations to beloved Brigid, whom I always remembered in my devotions. Touching the woad sign on my shoulder, in need of a refreshing that would wait, I resolved to do my best in all ways. I desperately wanted a healthy new child.

With a break in the ice—that winter was not so bad as others— Macbeth rode out with his retainers to visit thanages along the coast; they were gone three weeks. He was planning a progress when spring came, a time when a lord or king travels around his lands, staying at one household after another. Expecting a child could affect my role in those plans, and I decided to tell Macbeth sooner rather than later.

The discussion was not necessary after all. One night I went to bed with indigestion and an aching back, and by the next day no longer carried a child. Bethoc, Aella, and Maeve, who saw me through those awful hours with tender care, were blinking back tears.

Not I. Cold as stone, I, bearing the devastation in silence.

When Macbeth returned, he saw his wife practicing in the bailey again, fiercely so. I said no word to him of my travail. All seemed as before, but for a bitterness growing in me like a hard kernel nut, the sort that turns to gall.

Chapter Twenty

Elgin's gates opened on a dewy spring morning, and we filed out in a broad ribbon of riders and carts. Behind us were packhorses laden with bundles, two-wheeled carts pulled by tough garrons, and a cart for Lulach's cot and necessaries. Our escort consisted of eighty horsed and armed men, several grooms, along with Aella, Bethoc, and my son. A host of retainers under Ruari and Finn would stay behind to keep watch over Elgin and the local properties. Mungo and Giric led the full guard that rode with us.

I insisted on bringing Lulach on our first official progress around Moray, and Macbeth agreed, wanting us to be seen with him to prove that peace and security existed in the house of Moray. He also wanted to avoid the appearance of a war band.

Yearly progresses enabled a king or mormaer to keep contact with far-flung tenants who see to the lord's wide lands, tend his herds of cattle and sheep, and fight his enemies at various borders. Hospitality is extended at each stop, so food and shelter are abundant, and judgment courts can be held to decide local disputes and fines. A circuit of a province can take weeks, even months, and Moray was an immense region.

Setting out, we passed the forested area where the old charcoal burner's wife had spewed strange prophecies to Macbeth on the day of Lulach's christening. The smell of burning was strong as we came closer, and the air stung with smoke and ash. Macbeth did not slow, and as I rode between him and Giric, his giant housecarl, I glanced toward the wooded area. "That old woman cast the future for you, I heard," I said to Macbeth.

He shrugged. "If her words prove true, she is a prophetess. If false, just a witch."

"You know the rumor that your cousin Thorfin of Orkney is a wizard. Some say he means you, and others, harm."

"I do not fear that." He glanced at me. "Thorfin may look wizardly, but he favors blunt words and direct action, and would have little patience with divining. But he no doubt considers all warnings. His grandmother, Enya, has much knowledge, I grant that. Having met her myself, I can understand why she is said to be a powerful witch."

"Grandmother? Where is she now?"

"She has a home in northern Moray on a land parcel that belonged to Thorfin's Moray grandfather, my cousin. Enya was an Irish princess when she wed Sigurd of Orkney. Supposedly she cast spells of victory for him, including a spell on that raven banner. The Vikings claimed it was why my father Finlach never vanquished Sigurd."

"Did she foretell your future? Will it prove prophecy or witchcraft?" I teased.

"Speaking of it might undo the magic," he said, and smiled, so that I did not know what he believed.

That evening we took shelter at the home of a farmer-thane whose sons had been warriors under Gilcomgan. We enjoyed generous hospitality in his comfortable house, built long and spacious in the Nordic style. His wife and daughters cooked kettles of fish and barley to accommodate all of us, and no small feat that was.

Macbeth had brought gifts to bestow on our hosts throughout the progress: furs, lengths of plaid wool woven by Moray women, daggers and silver buckles and brooches worked by Moray smiths. He gave these people a silver brooch and otter pelts, and we set off again.

Reaching Cawdor next, we were welcomed by the thane, Macbeth's cousin, who treated us to a feast that night. Cawdor properly belonged to the mormaer, but was so large that a thane oversaw it. Seated in that hall, I learned more of Macbeth's family, for Murdoch had been retainer to Finlach, and his wife knew the lady as well.

"Donada was her name. She did not live past Macbeth's fifth year," the thane's wife confided to me as we sat to supper at her board, "but, oh, she loved her son well, and was a good lady, minded her prayers and charitable deeds, and was quick to smile. Macbeth takes his coloring from her, golden like the sunlight she was," she added.

"Loyal and solid as a rooted oak was Finlach," Murdoch told Macbeth after the servants had ladled a thick beef broth into wooden bowls for us. "I fought beside him on the promontory at Tarbat, on the day he sent Fat Sigurd and his ships back to Orkney." He lifted his bowl and slurped his broth, then used his dagger to spear some roasted, salted vegetables on the wooden trencher in front of him. "That was the day Sigurd carried a magical banner, but he did not defeat Moray. The contest ended in a draw, so perhaps the raven saved his life."

"The raven banner, black on yellow?" I asked. "Thorfin Sigurdsson carries that insigne now. So it is magical?"

"Huh," Murdoch said. "Thorfin often carries the thing about, though such magic is not to be ill-treated. He hopes all will quail before the sign of the raven and the presence of the Vikings. But we do not," he added casually. "If they come here with their mischief, we would not hesitate to fight."

"The Vikings have not been troublesome along the coast lately," Macbeth said, leaning back as a servant came by to place thick, steaming slabs of meat, reddish and juicy, on our trenchers.

"They no longer raid as they did in my grandfather's time," Cawdor's thane answered, "but they still visit our coast too often for my comfort. No one along Moray's coast or its northern borders trusts a Viking sort."

Macbeth nodded and I met his gaze, remembering the gold he had paid Thorfin to keep raiders off the Moray coasts. I did not know how long that payment would endure, or what other agreement Macbeth and Thorfin had made.

Talk turned to battles fought by Finlach and the men of Moray. With the glories of the past on their minds, I wondered if the men planned to follow Macbeth too. Would they do so if he made a dangerous bid for the throne, or would they draw a line in the earth of Moray and not cross it to march south?

Soon the thane's wife took me away from the men's discussion, and she admired Lulach while we sat with our handmaidens. She had a cough, that lady, which I remarked upon, once even patting her on the back, for she seemed overtaken.

"It used to be worse than this, I tell you," she said, when she caught her breath. "There is a healing woman who lives not far from here. She doses me with honey and bitter herbs, nettle and cherry, too, which has improved me a bit. It is from sitting too close to the fire, she tells me, and bids me keep away from the smoke, drink watered wine, and eat stewed apples. The remedies have helped."

"Those are good cures," Bethoc said.

The woman nodded. "Catriona, she is called, of Kinlossie. Macbeth knows her well. Sometimes she visits when he comes here."

"Ah." I kept smiling. Beside me, I saw Bethoc and Aella exchange glances.

Cuddling Lulach on her lap, the thane's wife summoned her daughter to bring her five young sons, all handsome boys. "They will faithfully serve the son of Finlach one day," their grandmother announced proudly. "And his lady."

I greeted them and hoped to myself that they would all survive, for I felt sure that any man serving under Macbeth would eventually face battle, and not on Moray soil. As the mother led her young ones away, I took my own little one into my arms.

Approval gathered for Macbeth like a wave all around us as we continued our progress. From Cawdor in the northeast, we circled north and westward in a broad circle that would eventually take us back to Elgin. Everywhere we stopped, thanes and housecarls, farmers and tenants, men and youths alike declared their admiration and loyalty. While I knew that many Moray men would be willing to watch Macbeth's back, I was astounded at the breadth of his following.

Though it was not meant for my attention, I noticed that at each place we visited, men approached Macbeth to mention the number of men each could offer to serve under him, should they be needed. Hundreds, soon thousands were willing to be counted in his service. Warlords need armed men at their backs to defend the borders and reaches of the land, but regional leaders who can summon armies can pursue destinies beyond patrolling borders or taking down raiders. They can topple kings.

Gilcomgan had never inspired such feeling. I now saw how much the people had resented my first husband. Macbeth's father had been widely respected, and his unjust death, fourteen years earlier, had never been forgotten. The murdering nephews had never redeemed themselves in Moray eyes.

"You knew all along," I said to Macbeth one morning as we rode northward. "The people expected you to claim Moray again. They have been waiting for years."

"I have had the support of good men," he agreed, watching the far hills and wide blue sky. "They loved my father and want me to avenge him."

"You took Moray fiercely, but for more reason than your father's murder."

"Moray was mine, and I took it back. But this region is only part of Scotland."

"When did you begin to think beyond vengeance, and beyond Moray's borders?"

"I was scarce big enough to hold a wooden sword when my father told me that I should be a king one day, that I had it in me. My mother was a princess of Scotland, my grandfather a king, my father the most powerful mormaer in Scotland. And then he was gone," he went on, "and I was left to deal on my own. To my thinking, revenge is not yet satisfied for Finlach of Moray."

"If we were to gain rod and crown," I said low, so that none should hear but he, "we could satisfy our heritage and avenge our two fathers, all at once."

"Just so." He cast me a look that was sharp and clear.

I felt a chill. "You led me deliberately to share your plan, from the first."

"In part," he admitted, "for I knew the worth in your blood, and saw the worth of your nature. But I could never have planned as well as fate has done. It has twinned our motives now. Your father and mine are gone, and they deserve this. Our branches, Gabhran and Lorne, deserve this."

"And the ancient Celtic blood of the whole of Scotland—it, too, needs this."

"It does." He smiled, and we rode on in silence. My head whirled with thought, but he seemed calm, certain, as ever.

Soon we arrived at a property near Inverness, where my husband would hold a moot court for those within reach of that place. The thane came striding out of his gates, his home a wooden fortress behind a high stockade on a flat-topped hill. Behind him came his wife with a bronze-trimmed horn filled with wine to greet the mormaer and his lady, and their train of weary travelers.

That excellent feast was one of many such as we moved around the province in those weeks. Meeting so many thanes and their wives that I sometimes jumbled the names, I did my best to smile, nod, speak courteously. Everywhere, we were offered wine in the best cups, polished oak or precious glass. At night we sat at long tables beside blazing fire baskets or central hearths in smoke-filled rooms, and dined on beef, mutton, or fish—chicken being so ordinary it was near enough an insult and not offered—and we lingered by the light of good candles and new torches to hear bards sing Macbeth's praises, accompanied on well-tuned harps.

Conversation brimmed on many topics, and many dared mention the king's tanist and the unrest felt throughout Scotland over it. But word had spread of the king's feud with the line of Duff through Bodhe, and because I was of that blood, silence often fell if my father's name arose.

MORAY'S UPPER fringe shares a border with the province of Ross, and that mormaer, a friend to both Norsemen and Scots, knew Macbeth from boyhood and was glad to offer us a night's hospitality at his fortress at Dingwall, just north of Inverness. Macbeth knew the importance of gaining favor not just in Moray, but around its perimeters.

"Some say I owe my fealty to the Norsemen," Eric of Ross told us after a good supper, "and some say to Moray, and the Scots." He grinned, a strong and jovial man. "But I will balance them both, like this"—he raised two sloshing drinking horns high—"and so with caution, I enjoy the bounty of both." He tilted his head back to splash two streams of ale into his mouth at once. Much of the male company guffawed and stamped their feet, and we women smiled at the display.

Shaking his head in wry amusement, Macbeth chose a single, large drinking horn and held it out for a serving girl to fill. Raising it high, he tipped it to gush the gleaming wine into his mouth, swallowing quickly and efficiently.

"And look, Moray shall have it all!" Eric of Ross said, snorting with laughter.

In our bedchamber at Dingwall, Macbeth confided to me that he had been born there, perhaps in that very bed, when his parents had visited Ross. He had arrived early, he said, August rather than October, and had survived—earning him the name Mac bethad, Son of Life. His mother had stayed there with him until he was stronger. His first few months had been spent frail and then thriving, and perhaps that had shaped his character—the struggle for, then the vibrant claiming of life. I hoped the same would hold true for his ambitions.

We lingered at Dingwall, for Lulach had a sniffling cold, and it was a good place for all of us to rest, large and comfortable. After an evening meal, the bard would rise from his seat beside the mormaer of Ross, and cross to a stool by the hearth. He held up the silver branch that signified his status and training. This was a slender many-armed twig, painted silvery and hung with clear crystals and small silver bells, so that it chimed as he shook it. At that traditional entry of the *seanchaidh,* we all grew quiet. He took his brass-strung harp from its leather sack, set it on his lap, and began a melody that would lead to a story. One night he told some of the oldest Irish tales, and when he was done, still we wanted more, for he was a bard of easy power, like some kings.

"Deirdre," he said, "fell in love with the eldest of the fine sons of Usnach, the most beautiful of them, called Naisi." *Nay-shuh,* he pronounced it, like a breath of poetry. He spoke of how Deirdre was hidden from the world because her father feared a prophecy; how she saw no man before she set her gaze upon the fair, strong son of Usnach; how she fell in love with Naisi. "Once, due to her wild nature," the bard said, "she grabbed him by the ear while he was playing ball with his friends, and smacked him in the head and demanded, so boldly, 'I want you, why have you not yet taken me?'"

We all laughed, and some glanced around at others, I at my own husband.

Deirdre and the three brothers fled from Ireland and the king's wrath, settling in the remote Highlands of Scotland, where she and Naisi planned to be together forever, living in a little glen of stirring beauty, in peace and contentment. The bard recited Deirdre's own words—which I already knew by heart—describing the glen she loved so, its beautiful hawks and proud white swans, its playful otters and abundant fruits and harvests, and its serene vista.

I felt a bond with her tale, which was sometimes called Deirdriu of the Sorrows, and I was Rue of the same, and because she and I were so alike in some ways.

As always at the story's end, I blinked back tears when her beloved was killed, and she flung herself from a rumbling chariot to follow him in death. The tale was tragic, but filled with joy and great love, too, a tale of life drunk deep and tasted full in the days when legend and magic intertwined, and feelings ran swift and wild as river currents.

"We Celts and Gaels no longer have that freedom," I said to Macbeth later, in the darkness of the curtained bed we shared that night. I liked to turn stories round in my thinking and find the meaning in them, savoring it like all the pith of an apple. "No one can live like Deirdre and her Naisi nowadays."

"Thanking the Lord for it, too," he said. "A savage time, that."

"The Celts of Scotland have hardly abandoned brutality," I pointed out.

"We do what we must, when need arises," he answered. "But the

Scots and Gaels have moved on from those days, with more civil customs. When the Celts were taken under the wing of the Church, they left many of their heathen ways behind, gaining wisdom from faith, and learning the ways of the larger world."

"Well and good, so long as we stay Celts," I muttered, "and do not become Roman, or English, or Viking instead. I fear that the Scottish Celts will lose the old wildness, the old ways, for there is much that is good and beautiful in that."

"I do not want to see that lost either."

"If ever we do become king and queen," I whispered, "we will save it, we two."

He was silent for a moment. "Perhaps so. But be thankful you do not live in those old days, Rue. Remember," he said, turning to sleep, "Deirdre of the Sorrows came to great grief."

W E SAILED from Ross through the firth back to the mainland at Inverness in a sleek longship, borrowed from Eric of Ross, which held our escort party, while a wide knorr, a merchant ship, brought the horses, retainers, and our baggage and gear. In crisp, clear weather, I stood in the stern relishing the feel of the salt wind on my face. At Inverness, our boats entered the mouth of a long loch and sailed southwest along its length. Then we docked and took to our horses again to resume our cavalcade, having saved time and distance on our journey.

Stopped at the crest of a hill at sunset, I admired the view to the west, where the sun dropped like a red-gold flame between the black shoulders of the hills marching into infinity, all of it mirrored in that long, dark loch.

"*A Dhia,*" I breathed, as Macbeth stood beside me. "Dear God, it is beautiful."

"Beyond measure," he agreed. "The loch is called Ness—we follow it westward to reach our next destination. Here," he said, and reached into the leather pouch buckled at his belt to take out a leather sheath as long as his outstretched hand. "This is for you."

Surprised, I removed a slim dagger, called *biodag* in the Gaelic, and sometimes *sgian,* knife. Of gleaming steel, it had a needlelike point with a bone handle stained black, a plain and fierce tool. I hefted it in my grip, turning it a few times to learn its balance and weight, as Fergus had once taught me. I glanced up at Macbeth.

"This land is lovely indeed," he said, "and dangerous. Keep that with you."

I slipped the dagger into my belt. He moved ahead with his guard, sending a retainer back to ride with my women and me, with Lulach in a cart beside us. We rode under a wide lavender sky, for full darkness is rare in a Highland summer.

"They say a sea monster dwells in that loch," Giric told us, as we craned our necks to look at the dark, rippling water. "The holy Columba himself once crossed the loch in a boat and encountered that very beast. It rose up in the water about to devour him and his comrade, a terrified young monk." Giric crossed himself, and Aella gave a little cry, putting her hand to her mouth.

Secretly I wished for a sight of that sea dragon, but only ducks arrowed through the water. That night we stayed with a thane of humble abode, and ate fish and oatcakes, for it was Friday and we could have no meat by the rules of our faith. From there we followed a chain of lochs and rivers toward Argyll, the land of my mother's kin group. Though we did not cross Moray's border, word of our caravan traveled quickly, and my uncles and cousins, including the current mormaer of Argyll, came to visit us there.

I had not seen my mother's kinsmen since childhood, yet they looked familiar to me, with features cut like my own and resembling my mother. We shared hair color, too, copper and bronze bright. I missed Ailsa; Bodhe, too, with a fresh tug of the heart. My Argyll kinsmen gathered to confer with Macbeth, meeting for so long that my women and I took Lulach and went to sleep, all in one bed, exhausted by the weeks of travel.

My Argyll kinsmen promised Macbeth three thousand men and more, should he ever require them, and we bid them farewell. Attending Mass on that cool morning, we gathered in a simple thatched-roof church that reasonably fit only a dozen worshippers at a time. The rest of our party, along with local people, crowded outside to hear the priest speak the liturgy first in Gaelic, then Latin. Like most northern parishes, that community followed the Celtic laws of faith. It was a Saturday, the Gaelic Sabbath, and after the sermon the people returned to their chores and work if they chose—here was a place where the stern finger of the Roman Church could not tap and correct.

Macbeth left coins and a silver bowl for the parish, and the priest promised to dedicate a year of Masses for the mormaer's soul. My husband asked him to say the prayers for Moray, and all Scotland, instead.

At last we turned our cavalcade eastward for Elgin, and home.

Chapter Twenty-One

Days onward, as we cut southeast over the hills to home, we heard shouts from the front of our party. The earthen track was so narrow that we had divided into two groups, with plenty of guard for each. At the alarm, Macbeth launched forward on the bay horse, calling for men to follow, and when the riders pounded past me, I looked around in a panic. My little son, napping in a basket, was riding with Aella in a two-wheeled cart, surrounded by servants on foot and retainers on horses. I turned my own horse, white Solus, to go there.

"Keep back!" Giric shouted. Maneuvering his horse to block me, he tore his sword from its sheath, for men were pouring through the trees to surround our train.

A fearsome and crude lot, they looked like thieves or raiders, holding spears, axes, swords, and round shields, and wearing tunics and plaid cloaks, in the style of native Gaels from remote areas. Grimacing, roaring, they descended the hill to rush toward us. Macbeth's warriors engaged with the attackers, blades flashing and slamming together, horses rearing, men leaping to the ground. I heard my son wail, and the sound tore at me. Anxious to reach his cart, I edged Solus that way just as two men came toward me. Giric whirled again, sweeping his sword downward, catching one man at the shoulder, but the second man grabbed at my skirts, pulling me from my horse to drag me through the fracas. Solus stumbled away, and I kicked and twisted, but could not break free. The man had nearly reached the fringe of trees at the side of the track when I yanked the dagger from my belt and lashed at him, nicking him in the thigh. Roaring, he lunged, and then I flicked the dagger upward as he came downward.

Blood everywhere, and then his grip loosened and I scrambled free, while he collapsed, mouth agape, brown eyes gone flat. *Ach Dhia*. I knew then that he was dead by my hand. Crawling away beneath horse's hooves and men's legs, I headed toward the cart where my child rode. When a man on horseback stepped by and snatched me by the arm, I cried out, struggling.

"Only me," Giric growled, "come up!" He lifted me behind him, and I held on as he took us toward the cart. I sheathed the dagger and jumped down into the little vehicle alongside Aella, who had flung herself over Lulach's basket. Macbeth's guards circled us as the struggle went on. Then I realized that the raiders were trying to reach the cart where we sat, protected by the flank of housecarls. My son screamed piteously, and I took him into my arms and reached out for Aella, all of us huddling close.

Finally the shouting and the clash faded, and I lifted my head. I saw Macbeth walking slowly, leading his horse by the reins, wiping the back of his hand over his mouth, his fingers still gripping a dagger. I sobbed out, so grateful to see him alive. Handing my son to Aella, I climbed out of the cart and started toward my husband. One of our men held Solus's bridle—she was unharmed as well. Picking up my skirts, I began to run through the jumble of men and horses.

"Rue," Macbeth said as I came near. Handing the bay's reins to the man who had care of Solus, he caught my arm with an outstretched hand. "Thank heaven. The child?"

"Safe. Were any in the front group harmed? Bethoc and Angus are there—"

"All is well. She is tending to the wounded. How did you fare?"

"Your men fought fiercely around us. A man nearly snatched me, but I had the *sgian* you gave me, and used it to free myself." As I spoke, some of our men carried bodies into a wooded area, while others took charge of the wounded thieves who remained, tying their wrists behind them.

"Five are now in our custody," Macbeth said. "The others vanished into the hills."

"Who were they?"

He glanced around as his guards capably brought order back to our train, for which I silently blessed them. "We will not know until the captives are questioned. Judging from this location, where Atholl meets Moray in a tail of land, I would guess they were Atholl men."

"Crinan sent them? Why would he do that?"

"Bodhe's line," he said grimly, looking down at me, "still exists."

I caught my breath. "Perhaps Malcolm sent them."

"The king, Crinan, Duncan—one is the same as the other in the desire to end Bodhe's line, I suspect. But you are safe," he said. "I will keep you and Lulach safe."

I was silent, surveying the wreckage of our caravan. Men righted an overturned cart, lifted scattered bundles into it, while Aella sat in the other cart holding Lulach, who no longer cried. He looked about, too.

"He is so young to see this," I said.

"You cannot shield your son from the world into which he has been born."

I nodded. "I killed a man."

"Did you?" He sighed. "So did I. Two. Three."

"It was horrible," I said, recalling the thrust and give, the scrape of blade on bone, the blood that followed.

"It is," he agreed wearily.

"I need confession, a penance. We must find a priest to clear our souls of these deeds today." Suddenly it converged on me, what I had done, and my lip quivered. I felt desperate for absolution—not from the fear of sin so much as the weight of remorse.

"You do not need priest or penance. Forgive yourself and be done with it. In battle there is no time for penance before the next man steps up ready to take your life if he can. Battle killings are defensible even within the Church. Otherwise, they would have precious few converts among warriors and warlords."

"But how have you managed, facing this . . . more than once?"

"Let it go." He rested his fingers over mine. "Just that. I am glad you are so strong a girl." Then he walked away, calling to his men.

I returned to my son, who reached out for me, and I held him close as we resumed our journey. Behind us, some of Macbeth's men led the few prisoners they had taken. Soon we delivered them into the keeping of the thane of the next glen. Later we heard that nothing had been learned from the prisoners. Two had died of their wounds, and the others, refusing to talk or repent, had been hanged.

Soon after the skirmish, we came to a little hillside chapel, and I knelt in confession before the local priest, a surly man of local heritage. When I murmured of the killing I had done in defense of myself and my son, he absolved me of it with a wave of his hand and a few prayers to be said. He did not seem much bothered by my confession, and I wondered at how faith and violence could exist as near bedfellows, one allowing room for the other.

Finally we returned to Elgin in an autumn chill, with the trees gone amber, the heather pink upon the hills, and wild hawks soaring in clear skies. I had not felt such a sense of relief and homecoming since I had lived at Abernethy.

I swore not to travel again. Macbeth laughed. "That vow is not easily kept by a mormaer's wife, and false vows are wicked sinful. Though a little wickedness has its place now and then," he added.

FORDING a burn a few weeks later, Macbeth was thrown when his horse slipped. Mungo arrived with the news, and I insisted on returning with him when he said Macbeth lay in a tenant's house but a few miles over the hills. Bethoc came as well, and we walked there together, accompanied by a few guards, for a hill walk of even eight or ten miles is not so much to a Gael.

Inside the thatched farmhouse, I greeted the wife and looked around a dim interior lit by the glow of a floor hearth, the air rich with peat smoke. Macbeth sat in a chair by the table, resting his arm on a cushion. Catriona stood beside him.

I sucked in a quick breath. Behind me, Bethoc seemed to freeze. Macbeth looked up and lifted a hand in silent greeting. A bandage was wrapped across his forehead, and his eye was bruised. I moved forward.

"I am well," he said before I could speak. Even injured and weary, his voice was quietly commanding. Catriona stood silently by. I did not look at her, though I keenly remembered the day I had plugged her door with an arrow.

"How did this happen?" I asked. Macbeth explained that the horse had slipped on some frozen ground. He was more concerned for his horse than himself, but the bay was uninjured.

"Lady Gruadh, your husband will be fine," Catriona said, sounding formal.

I nodded. My civilized behavior was important, I knew, though I wanted to banish her from the farmer's house. "I brought Bethoc to help. I did not expect . . . anyone else."

"Giric rode for Catriona," Macbeth said. "She was staying not far from here."

"I am helping a woman who recently gave birth," she explained, hands folded, head high. What she thought, I could not tell—she had that much natural grace and calm about her. Certainly Macbeth might have visited her, since he knew she was nearby. I did not know if they continued their assignations, though he had promised otherwise.

"What of your injuries?" I asked him.

"A broken rib, some bruises." He waved a hand in dismissal. "All will heal."

"Come back to Elgin with us, and give these good tenants their home in peace again," I said. "Can you ride?"

"I can," he said. "Share my saddle if you think I need a nursemaid."

"I walked here and will walk home. I cannot travel by horseback for a while." My heart thumped loud in my ears, and I spoke impulsively. "I am with child."

Not meaning to reveal it so soon, I felt a strong urge to claim my territory.

Macbeth looked stunned. Behind me, Bethoc was silent—she had already guessed. Catriona smiled. "Lady, my congratulations," she said.

My husband took my hand, pressed my fingers in a quick grip, and stood slowly, refusing help. We thanked the farmer and his wife, and I went outside with Bethoc first, while Catriona came outside to wait for Angus, who had offered to see her safely home.

She came toward me. "Lady Gruadh," she said, "I am happy for your news. If I can help in some way—"

"Thank you. Bethoc will be my womb-woman," I answered.

"She is very young," Catriona said, as if Bethoc were not standing there. "Is she experienced with troublesome deliveries, as you had before?"

"I am very well trained," Bethoc said.

Catriona turned to her. "Should you want for anything, herbs or simples, or advice, come to me quickly, or send someone. I will come at any hour, any day."

"Why would you do that?" I spoke low and wary.

"Your husband wants a son of you," she said. "That I know."

"Ah," I said, and turned away, biting my lip to stifle a curt reply. Within moments she departed with Angus. The rift between us felt even greater, somehow, than before.

Macbeth rested a few days, and I made sure he stayed tightly bandaged, though he complained that he could neither breathe nor ride, and was not enfeebled.

"Let me treat you like an old man in this," I told him, "and you will be one."

He smiled. I knew he was pleased with my news, but I could not shake a fear that some ill might befall us. The sense was pervasive.

I DREAMED THAT I rode in a boat alone, with the oars in my hands. Far away, I saw a longboat, a dragon warship, newly painted, sails billowed, a magnificent thing. Macbeth stood in the prow. With him were two handsome young men. They sailed fast for the west, the setting sun an amber light upon their faces, each of them with hair like golden silk, blown back. Their profiles were alike, sculpted clean and strong. In my dream state, I knew that the young men were our sons, tall and grown. Strangely, Lulach was not there.

Calling out, I rowed faster, but could not get close enough to reach them. Macbeth tossed a long rope back toward me, hemp slithering through water, and I grabbed it to tie it on, but the knot loosed and slipped. When I looked up, the dragon ship was far ahead, already vanishing into the red light of the setting sun. I woke to darkness.

ALL SAINTS' Eve was upon us—or *Samhain,* as the Gaels call it—a time when the translucent veil that separates this world and the next, like the caul sac of a child, is exceedingly thin. Spirits may slip back and forth between worlds then, and pranks may be played by both humans and otherworldly beings. Divinations are often sought out, for the mood of those days enhances prophecies and dreams. Perhaps that was why my dream of Macbeth and our sons sailing westward in a ship was so vivid and somewhat disturbing.

At darkness, Bethoc and Aella and some others from Dun Elgin left the fortress to walk out and see some of the merriment—bonfires would be lit, and young people would run from one house or village to the next playing tricks, begging for cakes in return for a song or a spell to keep the dark spirits away. I went with them, for Macbeth was away again on a patrol, and I craved some freedom and enjoyment. Wherever I went, a full guard went, and so we all set out on foot for the glen.

A group of boys came past us leading a mule and singing songs, banging on iron kettles, and ringing small bronze bells. Their faces were painted, and they wore black cloaks and shouted that the best sweetcakes were to be had at the far end of the glen, at the home of the blacksmith. We laughed, for those were baked by Lilias, Finn's new wife. With word going around about her delicious cakes, she would be kept busy making more to appease the wandering "spirits" that night.

Bethoc and Aella pulled me along, their goal the home of the weaver, where an old woman was to divine futures for those who came to visit that night. Aella carried a basket of nuts and apples from Elgin's orchards, for apples were said to be the fruit the spirits like best. Inside the weaver's house, a bright hearth fire and oil lamps illuminated the place, their glow visible from afar. The crowd was considerable when we women entered; my guard stayed out in the yard.

Recognizing me, the weaver's wife came forward with cups of spiced ale, and we gave her our basket. Most of the visitors were girls and women, and they, too, greeted me, alternating shy and bold. I knew some of their names, not all, though they knew me. They insisted that we come closer to the fire, and the weaver's wife led us to a pine table spread with platters of cakes, fruit, and jugs of ale. Standing close to the fire was an old woman, tall but stooped, her hair caught back in a dark kerchief.

"The Old Cailleach has come down from the mountain tonight just to foretell our futures," the weaver's wife said. Carrying on the ruse was part of the fun, for the Old Cailleach was the hag-queen who lived in the high mountains and captured Brigid each winter. The old woman looked up and fixed a hard stare on me.

"The charcoal burner's wife," Bethoc whispered.

I greeted Una, the old woman, and watched as she divined for three girls clustered near her. She had a bowl of eggs and three bowls of water brought to her. Each girl cracked an egg, dropping only the white of it into the water. As it spread, we all leaned forward to see what design it took, for the patterns would form an omen of a husband. The charcoal burner's wife held up her hand.

"A husband for you within a twelvemonth," she told the first girl. "He will come from north of the glen. And one for you in a few months' time," she told the second. "My advice is to hurry, before your wedding gown is an ill fit for the babe under it." Several of the girls tittered, while the hapless questioner blushed.

"You have had one husband already, and lost him to war," she told the third, peering at that egg tracing. "A second may never come to you." The young woman paled and stepped back. "Visit me at Beltane and break an egg then, and we will see if it changes," she added, not unkindly.

The weaver's wife pushed Bethoc and Aella forward, and the old woman gave them eggs to break. "For you, a fine man, tall as an oak," she told Aella, "but for your dark-haired friend, I see none for now."

Aella thanked the old woman, and Bethoc looked stunned. Boldly, she took another egg and cracked it again. The charcoal burner's wife shrugged and looked at the floating mass. "A score of years," she said, "you will wait on the will of your lady"—here she pointed at me— "and once she finds contentment, for that will be a time coming, you may find a husband of your own."

Once I found contentment? I wanted to ask what she meant, but kept silent. Old Una stretched her arm toward me, her fingers grimy with charcoal dust. "Come, Lady of Moray. We will talk, you and I. You came here to see me, to talk of what weighs upon your heart."

A chill went through me, and the women went quiet. This night was for merriment, but Una had not pleased all with her egg readings, and had turned the mood somber when she spoke darkly. Seeing the weaver's wife frown, I shook my head.

"I have a husband already, and am quite content. I will not set my man aside just yet," I said in a light tone, and some laughed. "Go on with your divining, please. I do not wish to interrupt." The old woman beckoned to the next girl who awaited her future.

The weaver's wife took me aside to ply me with her best ale and show me her husband's weavings, handsome patterns of good cloth. I asked her to send a few lengths to the fortress and promised to pay her generously for them.

As we said our farewells, the charcoal burner's wife came to me and clutched my arm, asking to speak with me outside alone. I went with her, and we moved a little distance away in the glow of a bonfire. Similar fires all over the hillsides glittered like yellow stars in the darkness.

My guards and my women waited in the yard, where laughter erupted when a few girls came outside to toss their shoes high up, trying to clear the thatched rooftop of the house, then running to see where the shoes landed. Whatever direction the shoe pointed, from there would a husband or lover come. Shoes that landed sole upward indicated no marriage, so the tradition went. Bethoc refused to play the game, while Aella launched her shoe high, showing such spirit in the effort that Angus and my other guards laughed and cheered her.

"You came here hoping to speak to me," the charcoal wife stated.

I shook my head, but she persisted. Seeing keen intelligence in her eyes, I took a chance. "Do you know much of dream reading?" I asked.

"Some and a good deal, depending on the dreamer and the dream. Tell me yours."

I told her of my eerie vision of a longboat and sunset, of husband and sons, and how I could not reach them as they sailed west.

"That way lies the land of Tír na n'Óg, where the dead go to find paradise." She stared into the bonfire. "Your mother resides there now, and . . . your father and other kin. A brother," she said, "and a tiny sister."

I caught my breath. My parents and kinsmen she could have heard about, but she would not know of a sister gone just days old. "Go on," I said.

"When we sail west in dreams, or loved ones do so, then death is beckoning."

"We will all die someday. I do not fear that. The when of it is more my concern, and . . . who these sons were. Can you tell me about them?" I waited, breathless.

"They will go to the west, and paradise there," she said, "but not all together."

I set a hand to my belly, not yet bulging, though ripe. "I will birth sons, then, to be warriors." This was what I wanted most to know.

"Your husband Macbeth will be remembered among the greatest of his ilk, the kings of Scotland," she said. "One of your sons will be a warrior. Not the others."

"Others," I repeated, pleased. "Monks, then, or abbots? Bards, perhaps."

"They will not be," she murmured slowly, eyes very dark, "warriors."

A shiver slipped down my spine. "What, then?" Suddenly, I felt afraid, unsure if her talents—for such she had, and no doubt—were of the light or the dark. I feared she spoke only of dead sons, not thriving. Perhaps she pretended soothsaying and was only an entertainer with a good grasp of egg-white omens, and the rest of what she said all bluster, mist, and nonsense. Or perhaps she wanted gifts and patronage from the mormaer's wife, and so tried to tantalize me with a little mystery. I would not fall for it.

She peered at me, leaning so close that I could smell charcoal smoke on her clothing and garlic on her breath. Taking my hand in hers, she pressed her palm to mine and closed her eyes.

"Husbands three," she said, nodding to herself. "Six times you will nurture the seed of a great warrior within your womb. Six times, and more than that, you will reap heartbreak." She opened her eyes, like twin coals. "Strength itself will nurture in you and be born there. It is not an easy path."

"I do not understand—" Yet I feared that I did.

"Carry this warning to your husband. I have told him the same, but tell him again from me. Beware the son of the warrior whose spilled blood will make him a king."

I stared. Her cloak, when she turned, was a swirl of utter blackness, so that I stepped back for fear the portal to the other side, open that night, might overtake me.

I DID NOT repeat her message to Macbeth.

Only Bethoc knew, for I confided in her later. "Nonsense," she told me. "Old Una has malicious intent. Her son was killed by Macbeth and his men. Do not consult her again. She did not tell me the truth, either. Not to be married! Of course I will. Aella before me, timid as she is?" She rolled her eyes.

Either Una told falsehoods, or spoke truths neither Bethoc nor I wanted to hear. Upset that I had trusted a madwoman with a grudge against my husband, annoyed that I had let her frighten me, I resolved to forget her bitter prophecies. I plucked out the little crystal stone, which she had given Lulach at his christening, from the hem of his blanket where I had set it. The next morning, All Saints' Day, Bethoc and I left Dun Elgin in a misty dawn and walked to a remote field. Angus stood bewildered, waiting, while Bethoc and I dug up a clod of earth and buried the stone.

"Put a rock over it," Bethoc said, "to render it harmless forever. What if the old hag put a poison magic on it, or a black spell? You have had bad fortune since that thing came into your house. Though your son has been well and safe from harm," she added. "Still, one never knows. The old haggy thing wants you to fear your own future."

I set a large rock over the crystal's grave, and murmured a request to all the saints, especially holy Brigid and Columba, to watch over my son, my kin, my own, and those to come. Before I left, I traced the triple spiral in the air over the large rock, and Bethoc spit on the ground.

"There," she said. "Neither of us will seek out ill-willed prophecy again."

Macbeth and I and several others were sharing a plain supper on a frosty evening in late November when a young groom ran into the hall, the door curtain flapping behind him.

"Riders," he said breathlessly, pointing toward a window. "The sentinels say men are coming with the lion banner of the king!"

Leaving oatcakes scattered and soup cooling in bowls, we ran outside, our breaths small clouds as we went toward the gate. I could not imagine why King Malcolm would come this far north without notice, but the reason could not be pleasant.

The messenger rode through the gate with a half dozen warriors behind him. He handed Macbeth a rolled parchment and dismounted. "Sir, Duncan mac Crinan sends this word to you."

Opening it, Macbeth read silently, while the sun fell behind the mountains in a blaze of red and purple, and a dark chill gathered. He looked up from the page.

"King Malcolm is dead. He was killed in ambush near Glamis."

"God rest his soul," I murmured instinctively, though I felt the shock of the news. "And Duncan?"

"Is now king." He handed the page to me. I scanned the Latin while Macbeth spoke with the messenger, whose men now stood in the yard looking weary and grim.

"You are welcome to our hospitality," I told them, and after Bethoc led them to the hall for ale and soup, I turned to Macbeth. "What more have you learned?"

"Malcolm was cut down near his royal fortress at Glamis." That place lay between Fife and Moray, in the region called Angus.

"Who did this?" I asked anxiously, while we began to walk toward the keep.

"He had any number of enemies, Rue," he said. "As with Bodhe, we may never know. The funeral and Duncan's crowning at Scone will both take place later in the week. Duncan will expect me to accompany my grandfather's body westward to the Isle of Iona, where the royal kings of Scots are buried. You need not come along," he added. "No need for you to travel unduly, and you had a rightful grudge against Malcolm."

I felt a wash of remorse. An old man, not just a king, not just an enemy, had been unfairly slain. And, as Lady of Moray, I should be above base grievance in public. "I will go to Scone with you."

He nodded. "Very well. We can take a longship from the coast and sail into the firth and up the Tay to Scone. It will save time, and save you the burden of riding."

My women and I packed what was necessary, and next day we departed with a band of fifty men, with Bethoc for my companion, while Aella and Maeve kept Lulach at home. A ship waited at the harbor, for one or more were always ready for the mormaer. We heard a report of a cluster of longships sighted beyond the coast, floating, watching.

"Thorfin," Macbeth said, as we stood beside the mast gazing at the expanse of gray sea beyond the firth. From there, we could not see those ships, but the captain of our boat confirmed that they had been sighted since morning. "Thorfin has been quiet for a time," Macbeth said, "but now that the old, battle-scarred lion of Alba is gone, the Vikings will be keenly interested to see what happens. Malcolm the Destroyer was scourge and sword against the Saxons and the Northmen for decades. At times his fierceness alone was enough to keep either sort from coming into Scotland."

"And now?" I glanced up at him.

"Now the ravens gather to watch Duncan, and see what sort of mettle makes him."

"THE OLD warhorse battled his way out of life, ambushed near one of his own royal holdings," Constantine told us. We walked from the docking at Scone up the hill to the church, where we would be welcomed by the archbishop. "Surprised and swiftly killed—November's early darkness encourages raids for killing and thieving. His assailants are still unknown."

"May never be known," Macbeth said. "His kinsmen and his enemies are legion."

Constantine shrugged. "I have heard some names mentioned, and I will warn you that some say you had a hand in this. The rumor is that your lady urged you to avenge the deaths of the men of Fife, and that you complied."

I began to speak, but Macbeth sent me a frown. "Those who know us will know the truth. The opinion of the rest does not matter."

Constantine nodded. "In the same breath, those who mention Lady Gruadh then discount the deed as unthinkable for a woman, especially for one as young and finely bred as Bodhe's daughter."

"Vengeance did appeal to me," I admitted. "And Malcolm's death is so similar to Bodhe's, some will say we arranged it. But we never did. Besides, Macbeth has been recovering from an injury for the last few weeks."

"We make no excuses," my husband replied. "Let them say what they will."

"The attack near Glamis was much like any raid," Constantine said. "But the men who killed the old king were not thieves in the night.

They made a harsh decision and pursued it. Soon or later, it was destined to happen," he added low.

"A man who lives by his sword invites a blade-death," Macbeth said.

I shuddered. The guilt of wishing the old man dead grew strong in me, suddenly. "Now I am thankful for your injury," I told my husband. "None can say you had direct involvement. Whether you gave some word otherwise . . ." I let that hang in the air, for even I wondered. He always had secrets.

"If honor held me back for over a year," he growled, "why would I act now, in such a way?"

"Duncan and Crinan had good reason to hasten the old king's death, and less principle, I am thinking," Constantine said.

"It is done, and what matter who," Macbeth said. "Malcolm was surrounded by enemies and schemers. We were among them."

"There are other matters to think on now," Constantine said. "Many expect Duncan to be a poor king, and wonder how long he can last. The damage the new king could wreak may be more than any of us can imagine."

"Why so?" I asked.

"He bears the ambitions of three—himself, his father, and his grandfather," Macbeth answered. "But he lacks the wit or judgment of the others."

"I heard it from Duncan's own lips that he will ask you, Macbeth, to act as his general," Constantine said then, "as you served for your grandfather. He wants to offer a branch of peace between you. As king, he greatly needs the strength of Moray."

"Very well," Macbeth murmured, "and Moray needs the crown."

Though we Celts are fond of puns, none of us smiled at this one.

Chapter Twenty-Two

C andlelight vigils were held for old Malcolm in the nave of the church at Scone, where the body rested on a draped bier. Macbeth and I made our respects and prayers with the rest, and if anyone thought me a murderess or instigator, none dared say so in our hearing. I mustered dignity, dredged up grace, and said nothing outside of polite. And as I gazed down on that old face with its hard sculpted planes, I silently asked Malcolm for forgiveness, though offered none of my own.

Burial would take place on Iona the next week, and Macbeth and others would accompany the body. Three days after the murder, we had joined an assembly at Scone to see Duncan crowned *Ard Rí Alban*, High King of Scots, as is properly termed, for the Scottish kings are revered as rulers of people, not land. The inaugural ritual was age-old, and while earlier generations had seen a new warrior-king crowned every few years, Malcolm had held the throne for over thirty years.

Macbeth stood with Duncan on the flat-topped earth mound at Scone that day, though other mormaers had not appeared. No matter my husband's personal views, his plans were better served through this show of loyalty. I stood on the mound, too, as companion to Lady Sybilla. We were the only women amid the warlords, housecarls, kinsmen, priests, and bards.

Encircling the hill was a great crowd of witnesses and warriors. Years before, I had stood in such a crowd to watch a golden-haired boy with grief like a rock in his heart. Now the tallest man on that hill, he looked far more a king than plain, stocky Duncan.

When the red robe of kingship was set upon Duncan's shoulders, he smiled; and when blessings were said over him and a bard recited the long list of kings upon kings, he smiled again. The December day was chill and windy, and I lifted my cloak hood over my veil and did not smile at all.

The stone kept at Scone is a revered object, the basis of Scotland's ancient right of kingship. The *Lia-Fàil,* or Stone of Destiny, is a roundish chunk of pale stone said to have been the pillow of the biblical Jacob, somehow come to Ireland first. Anciently, old King Kenneth mac Alpin took the stone from Pictish Dunadd to his new capital of Sgian, or Scone, and all rightful kings of Scots must be crowned on it. Marked with Pictish symbols, it rests atop a rectangular block of sandstone that raises the seat high enough for a man to sit. Carvings mark the larger stone, too, which is fitted with iron rings for carrying. The Stone of Destiny contains the power of kingship in Scotland, and so the monks of Scone must swear a vow that if the stone is ever in danger, they will hide the smaller one and relinquish the larger, uglier stone instead.

Ours is not a coronation, or an anointing with oils and prayers with a crown bestowed by holy right of a priest's hands; ours is a crowning, where a warrior is declared leader through ancient, mystical rite by a crowner representing the Scots. The presence of the Church and the blessings of the faith are welcome, but the stone itself is the king-maker.

It was Crinan, abbot of Dunkeld, who set the red mantle on his son's shoulders, and the rod and crystal in his grip; and Crinan who set the crown on Duncan's head: a circlet of beaten gold with a twist of golden leaves, very old. The choice of crowner smacked of conspiracy to some.

All that day, through the crowning and the feast that followed, with its music and poems of praise honoring that new and satisfied king, I had a dark feeling within, like the coming of a storm.

· · ·

THE OLD king was taken to Iona for burial, the caravan heading northward over land and by boat along the chain of lochs and rivers that cut
through Scotland's heart toward Argyll and the coast. With Macbeth
gone for weeks as part of that escort, I remained at Dunsinnan.

I witnessed Lady Sybilla made king's consort and effectively queen,
with Crinan resting a small crown upon her blond hair in brief ceremony. Being Saxon, she could not be a full queen by Celtic tradition.
Now we would refer to her as the Lady, for our queen is also Lady of
Scotland.

Wondering if I might have that title one day, I knew it was a sin to
covet, a sin to scheme. I set the thoughts aside and smiled, for I liked
Lady Sybilla. She was heavy with her third child, and being early with
child myself, and both of us with little sons in breeches, we found much
to talk about despite our husbands' differences.

We marked her day with another feast at Dunsinnan. King Duncan
was near raucous in his jovial mood, which, considering that his murdered grandfather's body was on its way to Iona, seemed wrong to
many. Too much joyfulness, the Celts say, often precedes a person's
own death.

The next morning, as I was preparing to depart Dunsinnan, Lady
Sybilla summoned me to her bedchamber. I presented her with a gift of
peace and friendship, a piece of floral embroidery that had taken me
months to finish, which could be sewn round the hem of a robe or
gown. In return, she gave me a ring from her own finger, a pretty twist
of silver set with a river pearl. We embraced, and I saw a sheen of tears
in her hazel eyes. Being far gone with child, she was a victim of senti-
ment; I had been wild-swung by moods myself before Lulach's birth.

"Lady Rue," she said, "promise me that if I do not survive this
delivery, you will watch over my children."

I blinked, stunned. "Lady, you have borne two healthy sons already. And your children have a good father with a legion of kin and
friends. They would not want them to foster in remote Moray." I could
not add that my own husband planned to contest her husband's throne.

She shook her head. "Not fostering. If anything befalls me, or Duncan, the beast of war will rise up in Scotland. Some may wish to harm my children. I can trust you to protect them."

The dear lady did not know the whole of what she asked. Kissing her cheek, I nodded in silence.

A s we traveled home, heading northward again by longboat to Moray's fastnesses, Macbeth told me of the serenity of the Isle of Iona, where an ancient graveyard beside a stone church holds the Scottish kings. Their marker stones lie in neat rows beneath the vast blue sky, with the sea winds blowing soft over them. His eyes shone when he spoke of that holy isle, and I knew he hoped to rest there himself one day, as a rightful king.

I said little, striving to keep my thoughts on life, not death.

At Elgin, reports continued of Viking ships seen in greater numbers off Moray's shores, a concern to all. Macbeth rode out on patrol, often gone for days, and I wondered if he arranged a meeting with Thorfin, who likely had ordered those ships. But my husband did not mention his Orkney cousin, and if he met with him, or with Catriona when he rode in that direction, I did not want to know.

After the new year came a message that Sybilla, Lady of Scotland, had been delivered of a small but thriving daughter, and all was well. I breathed in relief on behalf of my friend. Bethoc made up a lavender balm for the mother and a bathing potion for the child, and I sent them by messenger with a length of soft woolen plaid.

I felt well and hopeful, and just into Lent, my tiny hatchling slipped out of me on a slide of blood. Maeve called it a son, and my women got me to bed. This time I cried into my pillows in muffled agony and kept to my bed, while Bethoc treated me with hot infusions and cool poultices, and some of that same calming lavender. The fragrance came to mean sadness to me, and despair.

A few days after, I looked up to see my husband leaning in the doorway, his hair mussed, cloak wet with rain, his cheeks sanded with a week's beard growth. Dark circles showed under his eyes. He seemed hesitant to step inside, as if he did not know what to do. I did not know either. "Are you well?" he asked, somber.

I nodded in silence, ashamed to have kept such ill care of the little souls we invited between us.

"Then that is what matters," he said.

WEEKS LATER, Finn and Ruari rode out at the front of a host of men to head west, though no one told me why. That very day, my husband left, too, taking Giric and a smaller contingent to ride southward, leaving Mungo in charge at Elgin.

"Judgment courts," Macbeth had explained curtly, "and other business."

"What business? Are we to go on progress soon?" I asked.

"Perhaps later this year," he answered vaguely.

This was in April, around the blooming time of the bog violet. Bethoc had plucked a basketful to be made into the love potions much in demand among local women, but of no use to me. I waited, idle and out of sorts, frustration gathering in me. Something was afoot, and my husband had not conferred with me.

Although I had a place on his war council, lately he had not included me, claiming I needed rest. I did not. I needed something more to do, for my household was smoothly run, and my son was finding his way in his world more and more without his mother. With no other little ones to fill my arms, as I should have had by then, I lacked enough to do. One day I set down my needlework and looked at my women.

"I want to do more charitable work. It is spring, and time to be visiting about. We always send baskets of food and supplies to the tenants in the winter months," I said, "and Bethoc often tends to the sick or wounded, and if someone is ill or dying . . . but I should know our tenants better than I do."

"You have been well occupied with other matters, and your husband is adamant that you stay safe and keep guarded," Aella pointed out.

"It is important for me to be useful in Moray, now more than ever." My arms were so empty. Besides, my husband needed all the loyalty of his people, and I could take a hand in that.

Summoning my guard, Angus and Conn and several more, I went out often with Bethoc or Aella, or both. We visited one home after another with baskets and staples, asking after the well-being of the household. If food or medicines were needed, or a carpenter, blacksmith, or weaver wanted, we would send word; if someone lay ill or dying, and a priest came there, I quietly paid a donation to the parish. Our Moray folk were not helpless by any means. Highland sorts are tough and resourceful, and they have great pride, but our visits and gifts were welcome. Hospitality, even in the meanest Highland hut, was freely offered us.

And I set to learning more closely their names and stories: Tomás the shepherd, his wife Esa, their five little ones and four hounds, all a big, noisy family; Hector, who had cut peat for fifty years, whose shoulders were bowed with age and work, whose wife had recently died; the widow Mairead, who spun flax and wove it into good linen, and her three young daughters, one blind, each pretty as an apple; Ewan the weaver and his wife Annot, with their fine house, had two sons in Macbeth's service, and another had died with my first husband. We visited, as well, Una the charcoal burner's wife and her husband, old Colum, who squinted and coughed constantly from years of smoke; we increased Elgin's order for charcoal, always needed. Yet I said nothing to Una of dreams or the future, or that I had impulsively buried her gift of a stone.

Feeling a better satisfaction in my days, I watched carefully as I could over Macbeth's Moray in his absence, and the responsibility was no chore. Later I realized that in small and large ways, I had begun to prepare myself for what might come. Queenship in its many aspects was not a teachable thing, yet instinctively I tutored myself with charitable works and sword training. Inch by ell, I became the small queen of Moray in more than name alone.

The goodwill came back, for people brought gifts to Elgin: lambs in lambing season, baskets of new wool, lengths of plaid and linen; barrels of nut oils pressed over the winter, and ale made fresh; and more loyalty than could be measured in all the bowl of the sea.

Spring turned to summer, and I worried more about Macbeth and our men, for they were still away, and little word had come. Finally a terse message was brought by a boy. Both parties of men would return by midsummer.

Finn and Ruari arrived first, and brought with them two thousand men.

"MACBETH WANTS new swords and daggers, helmets and armor made," Finn said, as they sat with me later, drinking a welcome ale in the great hall. "By the time he arrives, I will be well started on it. I am fostering four strong youths to work in the smithy, and we will build more forges. The undertaking is large and will take months, but we will produce much of what is needed ourselves from Moray ore, which will be carted here soon."

"You are preparing for war," I said, frowning. "The men you brought, now camping in the fields beyond Elgin—that is an army, not an expanded retinue for the mormaer of Moray! How shall we feed them all? And how many will Macbeth bring with him when he returns?"

"Perhaps more than we found," Ruari said, leaning back in his chair. He looked tired, yet there was a taut excitement about him as well. "We have promises from other thanes—we could gather thousands more, six or seven perhaps, if we need them."

"Why all this now?" I asked. "My husband expected trouble once Duncan was installed as king, particularly from the Vikings, since we have seen the longships for months. But nothing has occurred, so far as I know."

Finn and Ruari exchanged glances. Seeing this, I leaned forward. "Tell me true. You both rode west, and Macbeth south. You found smiths, bought ore for weaponry, and gathered troops. Is the effort to support King Duncan—or is it for Macbeth?"

"Macbeth is Duncan's *dux bellorum,*" Ruari said evasively. "The king asked for troops from the reaches of Moray, which we have done."

"Does Macbeth intend to go against the king?" I asked bluntly.

"He means to hold, and wait," Ruari replied. "Then he will spring fast."

"He is doing what the king asked, and strengthening his own forces at the same time," Finn said. "That is all. The new king is unpredictable."

"Neither is Macbeth predictable," I answered. "He has a larger plan in mind."

Sixteen hundred men followed Macbeth when he arrived. Immediately, he and his retainers set about making arrangements to provide for them—new garrison buildings to be constructed, lists made of names and homesteads, weapons and armor owned, months or years of service pledged. He gave the newcomers the choice to stay in Elgin's garrison or to return to their homes on condition of answering his call quickly, and over half the men chose to stay, thinking they might be needed sooner.

"An army to hand is well and good," I said, "but they must be fed and sheltered."

"The patrols and hunting parties will be larger and more frequent, and I will send contingents of men out to collect supplies, grain and cattle, timber and stone, ore and cloth. And priests," Macbeth replied. "We must have more priests. I will send word out to the bishop of Saint Andrews that we will need religious sustenance for the king's men."

"The king's men," I said, skeptical. He inclined his head and strode away.

He was so occupied then that some days we scarcely spoke. One day he stood with me in the yard as we looked at the spread of tents in the glen. "Duncan may call for men soon. Word is that he disputes a border with the Saxons."

"But Malcolm and Cnut agreed on the border, and made some peace."

"Duncan has his own plans for Scotland's expansion." He looked up at the afternoon sun. "And I have mine."

"I know. When will you bring me back into your council?"

"Be patient." Someone called out to him, and he began to move away.

"I want to do more," I said, quick and fervent. "Once I made a sword vow to protect my son and my lineage. I want to help if you are readying for what may come."

"For what *will* come," he corrected. "Wait and see."

"How can I claim the right of my own ancestry if my husband does for us all? This is my obligation as well as yours. I cannot just wait and see."

He narrowed his eyes in thought. "The time will come for you."

Summer's heat and inclement fall, then into winter's freeze and out again, and all the while Macbeth traveled about so much that we hardly saw him—he rode patrol and sat court at distant thanages, and twice went down to Scone and Dunsinnan to attend the king's council. I watched my son grow toward a rowdy little boy, and my women and I visited tenants often—and did so much stitchery, with such efficiency between us, that each person in Dun Elgin, I believe, had a neat new garment by Christmastime. I even took to kitchen and herb gardening, a pastime that did not come naturally to me.

My heart still ached for a child. I wanted to grow something, make something. I spoke to Father Osgar of my despair. "My husband wants a son," I said, "yet I am reluctant to risk another loss. Nor can I give up either." Uncertainty was not like me, but in the matter of babes lost and my failures there, my heart sparred with itself.

"What heaven wills, that is our lot, and what clay is given us, we shape as we can," he answered. "Go to your husband, and trust in God to decide what is best. Ask your women to help you using the wisdom of healing herbs."

Osgar had respect for such things. Bethoc had done her best, and there remained Catriona, but for my pride. I shook my head, took my penances, and knelt often to pray.

I brought my dilemma to Macbeth, too. "What if God is punishing me for grievances and ambitions, for sometimes wanting you to be king, no matter the cost?"

"Be patient," he said, as he often did. "What will we give our children without the kingdom that is our lineage, and theirs? All will come to us in time, including sons."

Maeve, who wanted me to produce another babe so that she could knee-nurse again before she was too old, said she knew what was wrong. "It is willfulness and old grief, poisoning your womb. You want to be a warrior, and you want to be a mother. A woman keeps to home and family, and tends to matters inside the home. A man keeps to war games and tends to matters outside."

A queen tends to both, I wanted to say, but did not. She would not understand.

"THAT IS a servant's task," Macbeth said as he entered the great hall, where I was pouring new ale from a jug into several bladder flasks. He waved a parchment, its red waxen seal broken. "A messenger came from the king. We have a matter to discuss, you and I."

I set the jug away. "I hope that is not a summons to war."

He unfolded the leaf and read it quickly. "Duncan is offering compensation for the deaths of your kinsmen."

"What, a herd of cows?" I asked in disdain.

"Listen. He agrees that Bodhe's kin deserve some justice." He handed the page to me. "I give the man credit. I did not think him half so clever."

I scanned the tight black handscript. "Crowning rights! What is this?"

"Duncan grants you, and all descendants through Duff of Fife through Bodhe's line, the right to crown the kings of Scots in future. This recognizes your bloodline as second in rank to the current king and his line of descent. He expects you to sign it. The messenger is waiting."

I frowned. "Is this a compliment, or an insult? My acceptance would acknowledge a secondary position when we deserve a higher rank. A monarch's rank." Pausing, I studied the script again. "If I sign, what good comes of it for us?"

"You or your children could crown kings for generations. But by signing, you would dilute your claim to the throne. And refusal would be rebellious." He took the page again to read aloud. " 'The crowner shall retain right and privilege to set the crown itself upon the head of any rightful king of Scots at his inauguration on the hill at Scone.' It goes on to declare the descendants of the line of Duff as king-makers. It is a great honor."

"And it is a sly move for Duncan. Crinan is behind this, too."

"No doubt. They must appease the claim of Fife to protect Duncan's throne. By doing this, they have to admit the strength of your royal blood. And you or Lulach could crown the next king after Duncan."

"If I live so long. Your grandfather nearly outlasted Job. Duncan could, too."

"Will you accept?" he asked softly. "You must send a reply soon."

I folded my arms, thinking, aware of the veiled insult in the document. "Very well. I will sign." I snatched the page. "But my name is written here as *Gruoch,* some cleric's guess in Latin. I will write my name in the Gaelic—*Gruadh inghean Bodhe mac Cineadh mhic Dubh*—so that Duncan will know to whose hands he entrusts the crown."

Macbeth poured ale, handing a cup to me. "*Sláinte,*" he said, "to health and salvation."

Chapter Twenty-Three

"Saints in heaven," I breathed, seeing the men led by Constantine mac Artair gathered in the bailey. They had arrived just as the household was kneeling to morning prayers. Banchorrie's expression was grim, and he and his men were dressed in war gear, with shields strapped to saddles and upright spears thrust into saddle loops. "What is this?"

"Warships," Constantine told us. "Eleven of them were seen far off the Moray coast, sailing out into open water, northeast and away from Scotland."

I drew my plaid shawl tight around my shoulders and glanced at Macbeth. "Whose ships?" he demanded.

"Scottish," Constantine said. "Flying the lion banner."

"*Jesu,*" Macbeth said. "So Duncan is with them. Did you see this yourself?"

"I had the message from the thane of Banff," he replied. I knew Banff was a seaport along Moray's southeast coast. "He sent word to me of the longships, knowing I could reach you quickest. Months ago, Duncan spoke of having merchant vessels built in Berwick. Clearly he ordered warships instead."

Macbeth sighed. "So Duncan means to attack Orkney."

I put a hand to my throat. "Why would he challenge Thorfin?"

Macbeth shook his head. "He sent word to Thorfin to demand tribute and homage for the province of Caithness, which Thorfin holds by grant of the old king. Thorfin refused. He owes no tribute—old Malcolm granted those lands to him outright when he was a boy, after the death of his father. A land bribe, of sorts, to content the Vikings and buy some peace between the Norsemen and Scotland."

We all turned to head for the keep. "Duncan wants revenues from all mainland provinces now that he is king," Constantine said. "He declared that old agreement invalid. Either Thorfin pays, or there is war."

Inside the hall, a servant stoked the banked fire, and turned to light the candles in iron stands on the long table. Finella, a serving girl and kinswoman of Moray, brought ale and cups, and I poured out the welcome measure in silence. Then I sent her running to tell Cook to set the soup kettles to bubbling, though it was early, and see that Constantine's men were fed.

"Duncan does not have the right to declare himself king over all the mainland, if parts are not deeded to the crown," Macbeth was saying.

"I suspect Duncan has planned all along to attack Orkney, and set the tribute demand very high to have the excuse." Constantine accepted more ale.

"He wants more land for Scotland—Caithness in particular," Macbeth said, "and he wants to expand exports. Provoking our old Viking enemies could invite more trouble than Duncan can imagine. For years, Thorfin has restrained his hand, when he could have attacked Scotland to claim more territory."

"The northern regions are too remote for a king of Scots to oversee effectively," Constantine answered. "Let the Norse have those fastnesses if they want, I say."

"If Duncan cannot effectively rule up there," I said, "what does he want?"

"To show his might," Macbeth explained. "Every king, when he takes the crown, wants to prove himself. Old Malcolm marched on Carham as soon as he could muster the men for it."

"That campaign made more sense than this," Constantine said. "This move of Duncan's will accomplish nothing but disaster."

"The dragon of the north should not be awakened from slumbering." Macbeth looked grim and troubled.

I leaned forward. "Can Duncan be stopped?"

"Eleven ships, already sailed?" Macbeth shook his head. "Duncan has invited the devil to play. If he brings eleven ships, Thorfin will respond with twenty-two or more. Only a madman would think he could best the Vikings on the sea."

"Duncan will find out for himself." Constantine glanced at Macbeth. "If he loses his supporters in Scotland, or loses his life, it will only aid the cause we favor most."

"So be it," Macbeth said, leaning back in his chair. "For now, we wait."

D AYS LATER, dressed for riding out, I opened my brass jewel box to find a cloak pin. There my fingertips touched the jet-and-bronze penannular brooch that, years ago, I had torn from the cloak of a man who had tried to abduct me as a child. Setting the brooch back, I chose a plain silver piece. No matter what might come, if war indeed came to our shores and gates over Duncan's actions, I would stand strong beside my own and do whatever I must to protect what I held most dear.

Reports soon trickled in from men nearer the coast of a battle fought in the North Sea off Orkney. Five of Duncan's ships had sunk and the rest retreated, said the messenger. King Duncan had leaped from his burning ship into the sea, swimming to one of his escaping ships while Viking curses rang over the water.

Armed and fierce, Macbeth and Constantine gathered troops and rode for the coast. Before he departed, my husband told me to have the servants pack necessary items to be ready for a quick move to another location. "I intend to keep you all safe," he said.

I could not easily stand by to wait. With an intention of my own, I set about to see it done.

. . .

THE WALK from Elgin to Pitgaveny, where Finn's smithy was located, was a distance of two leagues or so. Aella came with me, and several guards, my usual contingent now. We took a basket of cheese and sweetmeats, letting a guard carry the thing. As we walked, Aella confided in me that Giric had asked her to marry him. Delighted, I was not surprised, for I knew they had been stealing away for walks and more. She blushed now to tell me of their plans.

"Macbeth promised Giric a parcel of land in Moray close to Elgin on the day we have our first child." She beamed, my frail and pretty friend. "And a fine wedding. For now, we will stay at Dun Elgin, or wherever you and the mormaer stay."

"I am so glad for you," I said, putting an arm around her for a moment. Ahead, the smithy forge glowed through the open door, and smoke curled from the roof. The house beyond was cozy, with pale smoke wafting above the thatch and two goats and a few sheep nuzzling in the kailyard outside the door.

"Perhaps Finn's wife would be the harper for our wedding," Aella said.

"Go ask her. I will be along—I wish to speak with Finn."

Aella hurried toward the house with the guard toting the basket. Lilias, Finn's wife, came to the door to greet them, waving toward me, too. Her belly was rounding with a child, and I felt a heart tug as I waved back. While the rest of the guards waited in the kailyard, I went toward the main forge. The clang of a hammer ceased, and Finn came outside, wiping a hand on his leather apron.

"We have worked hard to enlarge the smithy to complete all the work your husband has given us," Finn told me as I entered the dim, hot smithy. Three apprentices were busy near the forge, and the heat of the central fire was intense, despite a breeze from the open door and windows. The smell of charcoal and metal was strong, and the rhythmic shush of the bellows, worked by one tall lad, was steady.

Finn showed me some of the blades that he and his apprentices were working on. "I have adopted some Viking methods of sword making," he explained. "Viking steel is the finest I have ever seen, poured together with molten iron to form designs in the blade that vary with the pouring and twisting of the metal." Swirls like oil on water patterned the steel blade as he turned it for me.

"Beautiful," I murmured. "I came here on an errand. I want you to make a helmet and shape a hauberk to fit me."

He looked surprised. "Bodhe gave you a helmet and leather hauberk years ago."

"Ceremonial. I need gear that will hold for fighting. Battle gear." He frowned and began to protest, and I drew him aside so that his helpers could not hear. "If Duncan and Thorfin continue their war, the land of Moray may ring with steel and run with blood. Macbeth is mustering troops, commissioning weapons, preparing. I must be ready, too. I cannot sit by," I said fervently. "All is at risk if the fighting comes to Moray soil."

"And you think to fight? You have some skill, but your husband would never allow it."

"I will make him understand. I cannot fill a fighting man's spot, but we have a tradition of women warriors in our history, and that is my purpose. Now I am the small queen of Moray, and someday may be more than that. It is essential that I am seen as supportive of all Macbeth does, but strong in my own right, too. For him, for Moray, for Lulach. And Scotland."

Finn rubbed his fingers over his jaw. "It is not safe for a woman, regardless of her sword training, to enter battle. You have other concerns—family, children, home, and husband."

"Am I not doing this for Bodhe and his grandfathers, for my son and husband, for our home? Please, I ask your help in this."

He turned toward a small table and played with the items there, a few twists of iron, scissors, other things. Nodding to himself, he took up a piece of twine and a bit of charcoal. "Macbeth will have my head for this."

"It is my doing. As for the expense, I have revenue from my Fife lands—"

He held up a hand. "It is my gift, unless I can persuade you to change your mind."

I shook my head. "No one can."

"Well then. Stand tall, lift your chin—there." He wrapped the twine about my brow, then measured nape to nose, and made charcoal marks upon the string. As he worked, he suggested features for the helmet. "You will need a nasal plate. Eye pieces add even more protection."

"Danish style? Not that."

"It will be iron and heavy, but I will add extra padding. Perhaps the weight of the thing will convince you not to wear it." He touched my shoulders. "Stand still and lift your arms."

Around the chest and down, around the hips, the twine stretched; nape to spine's base, length of arm. His hands were gentle but without allure, the capable hands of a friend. What fire had once existed between us had long ago transmuted into steady friendship. Then he stepped back. "I have a sheet of steel mesh that is more lightweight than most. I will remake it for you. When the gear is done, I will send a message."

Thanking him, I left the smithy and went in search of Aella and Lilias.

THE THREAT of war remained just that, and long weeks passed while Macbeth and the others were gone, with days of rain and drizzling, until the ground grew boggy and all inside the keep seemed damp. I ordered the servants to mix bog myrtle in the rushes and the bedding and pillows to lessen the mildew. And I told myself that poor weather, not danger, kept Macbeth away.

Finn brought the armor at a time when others were so busy at Elgin that no one knew as I tried it on. The hauberk was a good fit, flexible and secure; the helmet handsome and not overly heavy. I thanked him for his work and his secrecy.

"It is my hope you will never wear it," he said, sounding almost sad.

Spring peaked, a damp season with much work to be done in household, garden, fields. Time passed quickly for some, but crept for me. I wanted desperately to hear word from Macbeth. We had reports from various thanes and men who returned, but all they said was what we knew—battles at sea and risk of same on land, and neither Duncan nor Thorfin willing to compromise. During those months, Lulach was a blessed distraction, finding daily mischief as he ran about, wearing out his young nurse and his elderly one, too. Complaining of her joints in the dampness, Maeve gave her chasing duties over to the younger women. My little son played at swords and staves too often for my comfort, so keen on growing into a warrior that he spoke of nothing else. But who was I, really, to discourage a warrior's son?

Finally a messenger came at dawn to the gates, a tall and robust man in full armor, with a blond beard and the trousers and gear of a Viking. He came alone, without weapons, and was wounded—a bandaged arm and stitches to his cheek. At our gate, he asked for peace and a word with the lady. Hurrying when Angus told me, I greeted the man inside the gates.

When he removed his helmet, I started in surprise. "Ketill Brusisson!" Years had passed, but I would always feel a bond of trust there. "Welcome! Is there news?"

"Lady Gruadh, greetings," Ketill said in his good Gaelic. "I am glad to see you well and thriving." He looked past me to where Lulach sat in Aella's arms. "And your small son, too. I cannot stay. I bear a message for you." He refused refreshment, but I sent a groom running to fetch fresh ale for him nonetheless.

"State your news," I said, as my men gathered in a protective circle around us.

"Mac bethad mac Finlach of Moray," Ketill said, "rode south in the time of Lent to urge the King of Scots to consider peace or truce with the Jarl of Orkney. The three—Moray, Orkney, and Scotland— met together on a Moray beach, with troops at a distance, to negotiate. The son of Finlach argued for the setting aside of weapons and the docking of warships, before all blades were bloodied and all boats sunk to the depths. King Duncan refused, and Jarl Thorfin will never surrender. He returned to Orkney to gather his forces. Now comes word that the king rides south and calls for more ships to be constructed."

"Where is my husband now?" I asked, heart beating fast.

"Gone with the king to Dunsinnan, we heard."

"Then who sent this word for me?"

"Thorfin Sigurdsson of Orkney, lady." He met my gaze evenly.

I gasped. "Give him my thanks, and tell him that I wish for peace between Moray and Orkney, no matter what else prevails." That much I could offer in return for this.

Ketill swallowed the ale thirstily under the wary gazes of my men. Then he nodded farewell and walked away through the gates. In the distance we saw a line of warriors waiting for him, but they only turned and left together. When Angus took some men to ride out there, they returned, saying the Vikings had vanished.

"How did they get so far inland, all the way to Elgin?" I asked.

"Cleverness," Angus said. "Do not trust your old friend Ketill so well. It is death to underestimate their sort."

MACBETH STOOD in the yard in the red light of sunset with his guards dismounting around him, home at last, a sudden return without warning. As I hastened toward him, he turned. "Gather your household, lady," he said. "You cannot remain at Elgin."

"Gone for weeks with little word, and now you want to dismantle my home before you so much as greet me properly?" I smiled, striving not to show my concern.

"Greetings, then. I am grateful you are well." He leaned down to kiss my cheek, his jaw beard-bristled. "What news here?"

"All are well, though hungry for word of peace and resolution. We had a visitor with an interesting message." I told him how Thorfin sent Ketill to me.

He exhaled slowly. "Then you know of the attacks in Orkney waters, and my attempt to arrange a truce." He had removed his helmet, and his eyes were darkly shadowed. "Duncan mustered more ships to go after Orkney again. Thorfin threatens to march on Duncan's lands, entering Scotland, and he has asked for my support."

"Support for Vikings to ruin Scotland? Does he want prayers, or warriors?"

"Both. He believes we should join forces and work together to destroy Duncan. That would win Thorfin's cause, and aid my own cause."

"You confided your ambitions to *Thorfin,* of all men, our enemy?"

"He is not my enemy so much as others. And long ago, he surmised my thoughts on the matter of the crown. In fact, he has offered to be at my back if I need help."

"The Vikings think to benefit with Thorfin's cousin as king of Scots!"

"For now, our concern is not that, but Orkney's quarrel with Duncan. We do not know which gateway Thorfin might use into Scotland, but we can be certain he will try. He could land on Moray shores, or sail to Fife to march direct on Duncan's lands. Or he could enter through his own property of Caithness—the longest route and least likely."

"What will you do?"

"If Thorfin sets foot in Moray, I will meet him with troops to push him back. Let him go after Duncan if he will, but he will not raze a path through my lands." He looked gaunt, determined. "It is best that you leave Elgin with most of the household."

"I want to stay wherever you are, and fight alongside you."

"Rue." He sighed. "You have a child. Think of him."

"I do. My son needs a home, a lineage. A stepfather."

"Go," he said wearily. "I want you to go."

Ordering me was like a spark for fire. I began to argue, but men shouted at the gate and the thudding of hoofbeats sounded beyond the palisade.

"Rue, give me a measure of peace over this. I want to know that you are safe."

I sighed and turned to hurry the servants into packing, while servants lit tall torches against the purple darkness.

THE DAY of Avoiding, marking when certain angels fell to earth, is a time when we must avoid bad deeds and risks, or plummet as well. On that May afternoon, my household and I arrived at the fortress of Crom

Allt, a very old place with a stone foundation and a small fort with wooden walls that reeked of mildew, kept by a few lazy servants who had let the place fall into neglect. Dolina would have approved of the way I set the household on its ear. Maeve and I were demanding and unflinching house generals, and within a week the place was much improved.

The fortress overlooked a river, where I took Lulach, in the company of Angus and some guards, to go fishing along the banks. The river was fast and deep in some places and spilled over rocks in others, and a boatman took us out in a curragh, the wind blowing deliciously in our faces. We caught plenty of fish between us, and Angus taught Lulach how to wade knee-deep into the water to catch small fish in the Highland manner with bare hands. My son was never so happy as on the day he snatched his first trout.

We stayed peacefully at Crom Allt, while Macbeth kept Elgin, sending word that he would ride south to meet with Duncan again. Weeks later, he visited us for a few days, warming our bed in a way I had dearly missed, and again I dared hope I might catch, even in such circumstances.

Constantine came from Banchorrie to meet with him. "Once again Thorfin refuses to pay so much as a groat of revenue to Duncan, nor will he give up his north mainland holdings," Constantine told us. "He will destroy Caithness before he would hand it back. If he does, it would not surprise me if he marched straight through Moray next."

"Are we not safe in Crom Allt?" I asked Macbeth. "Must we move again?"

"Safe here as anywhere," he replied, concern like a shadow on his face.

In August's steam, King Duncan sent another sea envoy to warn Thorfin. Those boats, too, were sunk by the Orkneyings. Then Thorfin gathered troops and longships, and sailed across the gray swath of ocean to step onto Caithness soil. They swept a burning path southward, wrecking and killing as they came.

And so began years of war.

III.

... the golden round, which fate and metaphysical aid
doth seem to have thee crown'd withal.

—*Macbeth,* act 2, scene 5

Chapter Twenty-Four

I had need of magic.

This I decided as I listened to the bard Dermot mac Conall reciting a praise poem for Macbeth. Dermot spoke of battles fought and
won over the last year, hinting that magic had aided our enemies. *Why
not us as well?* I thought. *We, too, have need of charms and blessings for victory
and protection.*

"Thorfin the Raven-Feeder," Dermot said, rippling a low chord on
his harp to signify the man, "used his wily wizard magic on Scottish
soil, and burned a scythe's path down the length of Caithness into
Ross. The Vikings survived only by the spell-cast luck of the raven
banner. When Thorfin met Macbeth and three thousand men at the
Moray border, he walked away with his life, for raven's luck, and by
mercy of his cousin."

"Walked!" Our dinner guest, the fugitive Eric of Ross, hooted. "I
heard he ran like an old woman."

"So the Scots report," Macbeth answered in a wry tone.

I glanced at Macbeth beside me. It was a rare evening that he was
with us at Crom Allt. He was often gone for weeks and months at a
time, resisting Thorfin or restraining Duncan. I saw him so infrequently now that I noticed changes more keenly—he was leaner,
harder, darker in beard and glower, with a deep and serious air. His

hair, too long and unkempt, was bleached to straw, and deep lines etched the skin around his eyes. He had a reddish tone from the beating sun and wind, and he bore a few new scars, a jagged line on his forearm, and a healing crease in his chin to match the jaw nick that Gilcomgan had once given him in my father's hall.

The months spent protecting his borders from his Orkney cousin, once trusted, had taken their price of him. The need to wrest Scotland from Duncan's increasingly foul grip had become obvious to all. Other mormaers sent offers of assistance against Thorfin's troops, and covertly against Duncan's forces as well, when the time came.

More and more, it was whispered that Scotland's truest and best king resided uncrowned in Moray. All saw, as the months wore into years, how Macbeth strived to keep Thorfin the Raven-Feeder and his Vikings from the gates of Moray and Scotland, and how he worked to convince the king to cease sending more troops and manned ships after the Orkneyings. But Duncan remained determined to overtake and control Caithness.

"Incensed by the demands of the King of Scots," Dermot said, "and angered by the loss of his kinsmen on his ships, twice facing Duncan's fleet, Thorfin swore high vengeance. He set foot with his Vikings on Caithness soil and marched southward, burning and ruining as they went. Nothing would be left for Duncan to claim, so the Raven-Feeder swore."

As I listened, I made up my mind. Once we moved north again, I would seek out Thorfin's grandmother, the witch. Thorfin had learned magic at his Irish grandmother's knee. She, too, lived in Moray now— she, too, must want this madness to end, as I surely did. And I had other, private and desperate, reasons to seek her out.

"At the border of Ross, Macbeth and his men saw black smoke," Dermot said then. "'Dare to come over into Moray,' he shouted to the Viking horde, 'and I will see you dead, each of you!'"

After a ripple of applause, the bard continued. "'A Moreb!' Macbeth cried, and with three thousand men at his back, he clashed hard with Thorfin and the Vikings in battle. The Orkneyings insulted our mormaer by calling him Karl Hundisson—'peasant son of a dog.' But the wild Moray men drove the Vikings back to the sea, and the Norsemen sailed home to nurse their wounds over the long winter nights."

Eric of Ross thumped the table loudly, hooting his heartfelt approval of the defeat at Tarbet Ness. Others did the same, so that feet stamped and cups banged on the table, and ale sprayed from drinking horns hoisted upward. Lulach, seated across the table from me, hooted and banged his wooden cup until Aella put a stern hand on his shoulder.

He had begged the treat of staying late to hear Dermot's praise poem, and I had relented—anything for my dearling son. Macbeth said I would spoil the child to uselessness if I indulged his whims and wishes. But he was my treasure, and generous affection could not ruin him—he was a cheerful soul by nature. Macbeth, for all his talk to me, already had leather armor and wooden weaponry fashioned for the child, with a helmet of leather decked with a hawk's plume. So when the boy whacked his cup, spilling well-diluted ale, and shouted with the rest of the warrior company, his stepfather smiled. He wanted a rambunctious warrior for a stepson.

Dermot struck loud chords on his harp to call for quiet. "Macbeth the Mighty," he said, "acted fairly as King Duncan's *dux,* for the king lacked war skills, men, and support to come so far north." Low hisses and laughter sounded at the king's name.

"And lacked wit enough for the task, too!" Eric shouted. His wife shushed him.

"Macbeth *Fiadhaich,*" Dermot said, "Macbeth the Fierce, heard the cheers of the people of Moray, having saved their land from the invaders. After slaughter of Gaels, after slaughter of Vikings, the generous king of Moray will take sovereignty," he continued. We all cheered at that.

Dermot stood and inclined his head. "For now, that concludes my praise poem, which will be complete only when Macbeth achieves his destiny. Greatness is in his stars. We have only to wait, now, to see it unfold."

For a moment, silence—then loud applause from the friends and housecarls gathered there. We were among friends, in a circle of trust. Macbeth shook his head, held up a hand, for he had a strong measure of humility. But we knew the truth, all of us.

"Good Dermot, thank you," I said, speaking for all. "Let us hear a song now, to soothe us at this late hour." The bard picked up his harp and began one of the melodies of sleeping, to ease the company toward the resting hours.

Magic, I thought, was definitely needed, to ensure the very destiny that the bard had mentioned.

Spring was thin and cool when we traveled back to Elgin. I expected a few undisturbed months at home, for my Argyll kinsmen had sent word that Thorfin had gone to the Western Isles and would remain there for a length of time.

"He is embroiled in a dispute over some lands in Orkney that he had promised to his nephew, in return for help in fighting Duncan," Macbeth said. "But his nephew betrayed him, burning a house that Thorfin slept in, so that the jarl had to flee in the night with his wife in his arms, and his daughter, Ingebjorg, carried by another. So Thorfin, in a fury, had his nephew killed."

I gasped. "Nephew? Not Ketill!"

"Another, called Ragnvald," Macbeth said. "Half brother to your Ketill."

"You cannot trust Thorfin. Murdering a nephew takes a black heart."

"My father was murdered by his nephews," Macbeth reminded me. "Old Malcolm likely ordered the death of his cousins, Bodhe and the others. And I brought on the death of Gilcomgan, my own close cousin. When kin slaughters kin, it cannot always be judged poorly. It may look like the devil's work, but sometimes it is necessary."

"I know. It is the way of things," I replied softly, as Bodhe so often said. Macbeth reached for my hand, squeezed my fingers, let go.

. . .

Duncan's consort, the Lady Sybilla, died birthing a weakling son who did not survive her. When Constantine brought the news, I shed tears over this, deep sobs one rainy afternoon, grieving for my friend and her little son, and anew for my own little lost ones. And I remembered my promise to Sybilla to watch over her children, two boys and a small girl. I had never told Macbeth of that, and now wondered how I could ever fulfill it.

Grief cracked Duncan further, and he took to snarling at the Saxons. He gathered troops to dispute a border that old Malcolm had settled years before, and several mormaers sent word to Macbeth, urging him to help quell Duncan's erratic actions.

"My cousin the king arrogantly believes that his heavy-handedness makes him as good a warrior-king as his grandfather," Macbeth told me. "Duncan goes too far—negotiations and compromise will expand Scotland, too, and peacefully. He refuses to consider it. Short of outright war between the mormaers and our king, and outside of simply taking him down in ambush, it may be impossible to stop him."

"Has it come to that?" I asked. "Killing a king? Surely not your hand."

"There are other hands eager to do the job," he said curtly.

Soon after, he rode out with a war band to head south for Dunsinnan. Before he left, Macbeth sent men out to summon four thousand warriors to Elgin from the reaches of Moray, and told them to set by.

Praying, worrying, I did not sleep well for days. When I dozed, my dreams were filled with men fighting in bloody disarray on sunlit fields, while I searched for Macbeth, and Lulach, too. Not finding them, I woke in a panic. *Be strong for what will come,* my mother had told me. I felt whatever it was approaching like a dark whirlwind.

"It is dangerous and foolish to go there," Angus grumbled as we set out to find Thorfin's grandmother. "With Vikings all about and who knows where, we will be sent to the trolls if we are caught." He drew a finger across his throat.

"She lives in Moray under the protection of my husband. The Vikings will not harm us if we go to visit—"

"The witch of Colbin," he muttered. "No one dares say her true name!"

"Enya, widow of the first Fat Sigurd?" I smiled when Angus shushed me.

I rode Solus, my white mare, accompanied by Aella—happy in her marriage to Giric several months earlier—and Angus, as well as several other guards. We took secret routes through forestland, riding for much of the morning toward the sea. The air was fresh, the ride peaceful. Finally we reached the little house, having asked along the way where the witch of Colbin lived. Her parcel of land lay near a small northeastern cove, where the sound of the ocean was constant, the wind salt and damp. The sturdy little stone house, topped with thatch, sat in the lee of a hill, overlooking a crescent beach and the gray-green sweep of the bay.

Dismounting, I asked the others to wait and went to the door to knock. Moments passed, and then a voice called from within. I creaked open the door.

She sat in shadow, the firelight playing over her, a tall woman, long and thin, with a dark veil that only partly covered her gray hair. A thick silvery braid cascaded over one shoulder, so long it spiraled on the floor. "I know you," she said. "Queen Gruadh."

"Lady Gruadh," I told her, giving her a willow basket of cheese and spices, and beeswax candles, which she set aside. "And you are Lady Enya."

"Only Mother Enya now," she said in a raspy voice, and by her Gaelic I knew her to be full Irish. She gestured for me to sit beside her on a three-legged stool, which placed me below her eye level. I felt like a pupil looking at a mentor.

"I know what you want." She leaned down. "You want an end to sorrow."

"I do," I answered, stunned. She took my hand, turned it, then took my chin in her hand. The light of the peat fire was low, its smoke fragrant as she studied me.

"Why come to me?" she asked. "You can already see what you would know. And you bear a sign that gives you strength and vision." She tapped my left shoulder.

Startled, I set my hand where the sign of Brigid still marked my skin. "Things come to me in dreams, mostly. I have tried to look in water for signs, but I am not good at it."

"Look for answers in flames, too, for fire suits your nature. There are omens all around us, and you have the wit and the Sight"—*Da Shealladh,* she said—"to see their meaning in fire, water, anywhere. You do not need *me* to tell your future, girl."

"I came here to ask you for good omens and powerful charms." I drew a breath. "Perhaps some true magic to bring good fortune to . . . me and my own."

"I know your husband. He is an ambitious one, a strong one. But he did not send you here, did he?" She paused, holding both my hands. "Watch for omens yourself. Cast now and then for the future, but do not look too far, or try to guess. By nature, you are one to rush on and think after." She leaned toward me, let go my hands. "A queen of Scots must think first."

"I am Lady of Moray. Not queen."

"Not yet." Her eyes, brown and clouded, narrowed. Her smile lacked humor.

"Tell me what you know," I said.

"We will look into the water together. Over there, in that pitcher. Fetch it here. Get a bowl from that shelf."

Walking through the dim room, I found the table with the pitcher, then a wall shelf with a few stacked wooden bowls. I filled a bowl and set it on the hearthstones before the peat fire. Next she sent me to a dark corner to fetch branches of hazelwood and juniper from a basket. She tossed the kindling onto the peat bricks: smoke, mingled fragrances, and then a leap of golden light, reflected in the surface of the water. Enya scooped up some herbs from a little dish and sprinkled them into the flames. I caught the scent of precious cinnamon, followed by the sharper smell of thyme.

She murmured a chant in Gaelic, and I heard a few words: *protection . . . Brigid . . . gift . . . blessing.* She waved gnarled fingers over the water. "You will have . . . sons."

I sat forward. "I have one now. There will be more? How many?"

"Perhaps two." She sat back and frowned at me, her eyes dark and deep, so piercing that I leaned back a little. "No daughters. Your sons remain in God's hands, and it is for Him to decide, not you, or any seer, what becomes of them."

"Ah," I said softly. No promises, then. "I did hope for better news."

"There are always bitter berries among the sweet. You have a healthy son who will be a strong warrior. For the rest . . . wait—and pray—and accept what you must."

A dark feeling turned in my belly. "Can you . . . help me to conceive, and keep the babe through to its birthing?"

"Your husband will help you to conceive, not I," she said bluntly. "As for the rest, you must seek out a healer and womb wife you can trust. Put it in your prayers, as I am sure you do, and ask the holy Brigid for help. If she has not aided you yet, she has her reasons." She took my shoulder to turn me, so that I could look into the bowl. "Tell me what you see."

Fire danced on the skin of the water. My face, hers. Flames. "Nothing much. I cannot do this, what you do. I have tried, and it does not come to me."

"*Tcha!* Look deeper, past the water, past the bowl, beyond this place where we sit." Quietly, she repeated the words. I breathed, closed my eyes.

When next I opened them, the water seemed to glow, and I found I could see beneath the surface, and beyond the very bowl, somehow, to a glimmering of golden fog. "A longship," I said, for it appeared suddenly. "I see a boat, and people on it . . . the sails are black and purple. A warrior has died." Breathing deeply, I felt awed and excited. "I sail there, with several warriors. But I do not know who—" *A king.* It came to me like a voice. "A king is dying."

She was silent. Now the bowl showed only flames and my own face.

I sat back. "A king in a boat . . . perhaps a funeral, but whose?"

"Knowing too much of what will come is not good for our souls, or our sleep." Enya removed the bowl. "You have a seer's gift. As I did, many years ago." She smiled, then, and instead of the crone, for a moment I saw the beauty she had been, the ghost of her young face framed in long dark hair, a slim and proud woman.

"Where did you learn magic?" I asked.

"From my mother, and my grandmother. I had years of learning with them. My father, a small king in Ireland, married me off to a Norwegian prince. I was a peace weaver between our land and theirs. For many years I lived in Norway, and Orkney, and learned much of spellcraft there from an old woman. Viking magic is very potent."

"Orkney," I said. "You made the raven banner. Many know of its power."

"I made it using certain spells and charms, to give it power to protect men."

"Mother Enya, I did not come here to ask for foretelling, but to ask about magic."

"*Tcha,* that. We only ever need a little of that, when we need it at all. Though queens have use of it, I admit." Quick and keen, she glanced at me. "Did you come here to ask for a spell to be put upon your husband's banner? Think you I would strengthen Macbeth against my grandson? You may leave, if that is your intent here."

"I want to help my husband," I said, "not destroy Thorfin."

"Well then. That we may do." She watched me. "Know this. I never made leaders, nor ruined them. That they did themselves, my husband, son, and grandson among them."

"What of Jarl Thorfin? It is said that he knows magic."

"I taught him some skills and charms, but if he uses them or not, I cannot say. Beware Thorfin," she added low. "He has a raven's soul, that one. Whoever crosses him regrets it. But if you have his loyalty, there is none stronger at your back."

"My husband believes so, but Thorfin and I have had our differences."

"He has done some stupid things, though a clever man. Power is a craving, like strong wine, and he has a weakness for both. There are ways to make peace with him."

I did not want to do that. "Unlike Macbeth, I have never trusted Thorfin."

She nodded as if she understood. "If you wish, I will teach you to use your Sight, and to weave spells when you need them."

"Better to let others do that than delve myself and be called a witch for it."

"So the small queen who would be a greater queen is cautious." Her eyes gleamed. "You have the gift. Use it or not, but it will not go away. Your dreams will continue, if you do not choose to look into the Otherworld some other way."

"I only came here to ask for your help, for myself, and for our cause—"

"Fah, not for you or Macbeth would I do what I did before! But you can, if you wish." She tapped my shoulder. "A little magic is not so hard a task, for it is all around us. We see it and honor it, or we are blind to it and fear it. Smoke and herbs, elements and chants, a wish for what you will . . . I can teach you this and more. But you would have to choose between the study of it and the queenship."

"It is certain, the queenship?" I asked. Enya nodded, shrugged. "If so, then I must help my husband however I can."

"Best you can do is to be the strong queen he will need," she said.

"Strong. I know. Please, Mother Enya, teach me a powerful charm or—"

Impatiently she waved her hand. "Very well. But I do no ill deeds. Remember it."

"I would not ask that of you."

She stood and went to a table in the corner, opening a wooden box with brass latches and a small key. I saw the gleam of silver and gold as her fingers sifted through brooches and bracelets, rings, coins—the treasure of a princess who had once been lady to a Norwegian jarl.

I stood when she beckoned, and she pressed a large brooch against my palm. "This guards its wearer. Each day say this spell of protection over it, for nine days." She spoke a breathy swirl of rhyming Gaelic. "Set it in sunlight, in moonlight, and in mist, and each time say the chant over it to ask for help from the elements."

I repeated the verses to commit them to memory, and opened my fingers to study the silver cloak pin: it was round and open, with the triple spiral design of Brigid swirling at its center. A single ruby was set in the middle, red as blood.

She closed my fingers over it. "This is Irish make. My father wore it, long ago. Take it, work the magic, then give it to your husband when he rides to war."

When I thanked her, she nodded and guided me to the door. "Your friends are waiting. Come back another day. I am a lonely old woman."

I joined the others, who had found an otter to watch in a sea pool, and I glanced back at Mother Enya. She stood in the doorway, long braid trailing on the step, looking a bit of a madwoman, which was often, and unfairly, said of her.

KING DUNCAN went after Thorfin again by sea, losing more Scottish ships, yet somehow he escaped his own drowning. "The very sea monsters will not have him," Constantine said when he brought the news of Duncan's latest defeat by the Orkneyings.

"He should know by now that Vikings own the sea and cannot be defeated there," Macbeth said. This time he had not summoned men to arms, though the king sent word. "Let Duncan weave the rest of his fate, for he seems determined," he said.

Sometimes that summer, looking north, we would see the wild jeweled colors of the northern lights. Their beauty was fervent, especially so around the time of our summer birth anniversaries—Macbeth marking thirty-three; myself, twenty-three. Watching the lights, he took my hand. "I wonder what magic makes them, and what omen they might be when we see them," I whispered.

"Celebration for a king and queen," he said. "The time is approaching. Rue," he went on, "if we never make a son between us, I will name Lulach my heir. He is the son of my cousin, and by the Celtic laws of succession, it would be his turn, after mine, to lead Moray. And he is my son in all ways but one."

My throat tightened so that I could not speak. I only nodded. He put an arm around me—which, for him, was a good deal said.

Chapter Twenty-Five

Season to season and round a full year, and King Duncan sent more boats and men after Thorfin, demanding Sutherland as well as Caithness. No peace could exist between those two. Twice more they met at sea, and each time Scottish boats sank, Scotsmen drowned, Duncan swam, and the Raven-Feeder retained disputed territory.

We moved between Elgin and Crom Allt over the year, and I rarely saw my husband, my bed cold at night, my days long but for the joys of my son and my friends. I sewed more stitches into more ells of linen than I cared to count, my thimbles dented where I pushed the needle in and out, in and out, the rhythm quelling fretfulness. New wool came to us from our tenants, and Bethoc and Aella dyed it in great tubs of boiling water with colors from herbs and plants, mixed with salt or apple vinegar.

When the yarns were dried and spun fine, I chose colors to suit my mood and thoughts: the blood reds of sorrel and the blacks and browns of walnut and alder. Embroidered onto pale or dun-colored linen, the contrasts were striking. I covered curtain panels and seat covers with images of armored men, horses, ships on the sea. Lulach was fascinated with yarn or wooden warriors, and I wished he was not. Books and monkishness might save his life in future, I reasoned, so I pushed him to his lessons. And then Father Osgar learned him about Hadrian, Alexander, the Saints Michael, George, and Mercurius—warriors all.

Bitter winter came, and Macbeth returned home. The steel-games stopped for a bit, and behind my embroidered panels we resumed bed games that pleased us both, tenderness and ease, comfort beyond words. Still I did not catch, though Macbeth never asked, and I ceased to weep when I came into my flowers.

A wife who gave her husband no children, perhaps a queen who never produced a prince—I began to wonder if, and when, Macbeth might set me aside for a woman with a more fertile womb to bear his babes.

So we went on. In the cold months armies cannot move about easily, nor find food for men and horses. And Vikings disdain to sail cold waters with ice in their beards and snow on their cloaks, choosing instead to sit by warm hearths and listen to their *skälda* poets, as we listened to our *seanchaidhean*. War disputes go dormant over winter, like many things that grow for good or ill, and in spring and summer heat up again.

TRUSTED BY both Duncan and Macbeth, Constantine brought news back and forth, and this time arrived with the news that a large party of Northumbrians had raided the Britons of Strathclyde, who were under the protection of the King of Scots.

"Duncan thrashed about in a temper, threatening retaliation," he told Macbeth, while I stood listening. "He wants you to muster thousands of men from Moray."

"To attack the Saxons? I will not," my husband answered.

"Without Moray men, Duncan lacks enough Lothian and Lowland warriors for an army. He depleted his forces and ruined the goodwill of the rest after his Caithness campaigns."

"Tell him to wait," Macbeth said, "and to cool his head."

With a dubious roll of his eyes, Constantine departed for the south.

A fortnight later, another messenger arrived. King Duncan sent gifts as plea and placation to Macbeth, his *dux* and chief mormaer. The few guards arrived with a packhorse and a monk from Saint Serf's at Loch Leven: Drostan.

My good friend had never traveled so far north, and we gladly welcomed him. His monastery hoped for reports for the annals, and we all enjoyed a reunion of sorts. The sons of Fergus—Ruari, Angus, and Conn—were also at Dun Elgin, and Finn came from Pitgaveny to see his foster brother, bringing his wife and small son. Everyone gathered at supper, where I ordered a fine table laid with the best we had. Dermot played soft tunes on the harp while we talked and laughed, and sat late into the evening.

After the guests had eaten, Macbeth asked to see Duncan's gifts. The big willow baskets held two handsome drinking horns banded in bronze, with neat bronze stands for setting them down; one cask of mead from Fife, and a keg of red wine from Rome itself; a small brass box filled with sweetmeats, honeyed nuts rolled in spices, and another box of pepper. While the others were delighted, I felt sour. Macbeth seemed so as well.

"The king must be desperate for Moray's assistance and favor, to send so many excellent gifts," I said.

"He knows I condemned his attacks on the Orkneyings, and will not condone his attacks on the Saxons," Macbeth said. "Neither will most mormaers, but for Crinan of Atholl, his father."

"And Duncan would never send gifts without wanting something more," Ruari said, and I saw that he, too, wondered what the king wanted of Moray now.

When the waxen seal on the mead keg was peeled away, a servant transferred the mead to a large leather flask, and I poured the amber liquid into cups. I saved the last for the two new drinking horns, handing the larger to Macbeth, and the other to Drostan as our guest that evening. Having no taste for mead himself, he shared its contents with Maeve beside him, who had been admiring the new horn. I sipped some from my own ordinary cup, and the mead was excellent stuff, strong, sweet, and potent. When Angus sat down quick, we all made a jest of it.

Macbeth quaffed his fast, talking with Ruari and Finn, while Dermot played a lively tune on the harp. I walked over to hand the bard some of the mead in a wooden cup. Hearing a cry, I turned to see Drostan bent over Maeve, who clutched at her chest.

As Bethoc and Drostan helped Maeve away from the table's bench to one of the cushioned seats by the fire, I sank to my knees beside her. Taking her hand, I saw her gasp for breath and pound a weak fist upon her own chest. "O *Dhia, Dhia,*" she whispered frantically, clutching at my arm. "I am dead."

"Her heart," Bethoc murmured, and slipped her hand alongside Maeve's neck to count the beats. "Very fast, and not in a rhythm." She tapped the old woman's cheeks gently, calling her name. My old nurse sank against me, and I put my arms around her, my own heart thumping fiercely.

"I have some remedies that may help." Rising, Bethoc ran from the room, leaving Maeve slumped in my arms. I glanced frantically toward Drostan, then my husband.

Macbeth sat at the table, pale as linen, and I saw him tilt forward. Ruari reached out to grab him just as my husband began to retch out the mead. In my arms, Maeve sank heavily, and Drostan helped me set her on the floor. Her hands were damp, her lips bloodless. "Fetch her some strong wine from our own stores," I called to Aella. "Hurry!" I could think of nothing else to do, hoping that might revive her until Bethoc returned.

Maeve's breathing was too shallow, too fast, even I knew it. Drostan placed his hand on her brow, praying, and I realized he was murmuring the last rites.

"I am here," I told her, and my nurse's fingers clutched, moved in mine. Glancing toward Macbeth, I could not see him for his men around him. Then a raspiness sounded in Maeve's chest, awful to hear, and just as suddenly, went silent.

So fast, and she was gone. Holding her, I rocked gently and sang a chant, as she had done as knee-nurse to me and other babes—but my verse was to ease a departing soul.

Together Drostan and I covered her with someone's cloak. Rising to my feet, I had no tears, just a dark depth within.

Turning, I saw Ruari and another man assist my husband from the room. I hastened to follow, bumping into Bethoc as she returned, vials grasped in her hands.

"Maeve is dead," I told her. "Fetch whatever you have to counter poison."

COOL CLOTHS against Macbeth's head while he vomited, and my hand in his as he subsided back against the pillows, only to retch again—this seemed all I could do. The moon sailed and darkness edged toward dawn, and my husband grew weaker, sweating cold, trembling, his heartbeat thundering under my fingers, his mouth and lips dry. Bethoc brought whatever remedies she had, and between us, with Drostan's help, we dosed Macbeth. Sips of this, a poultice of that, a spooned infusion. Father Osgar came to kneel in prayer, then stood to lend a practical hand for messy work, good fellow that he was.

And I, realizing nothing we had tried was strong enough to turn the tide of this, knew what must be done. Hastening to find Angus and Ruari, I pulled them aside.

"Ride north," I said, "and fetch Catriona."

Drawn and grim, they left.

"I know you have given him every antidote you have, but what poison is it?" I whispered to Bethoc in the corridor outside the bedchamber. Aella—having tended to Maeve's body, and a harder task I think that girl never had—now watched over my husband with Father Osgar.

"I think it was what is called purple fairy flower," Bethoc said. "A good plant in small drops for those with weak hearts, but a terrible poison. And something more with it, but I do not know what that might be." I knew she wondered if he would live.

"How did he and Maeve take ill, when we did not? And who would—"

"Duncan," Drostan said, for he came round the corner just then. "The king must have had a deliberate hand in this. He sent me to bear a killing poison to your husband—and to you. For that, I cannot forgive Duncan, or myself."

"You had no hand in this," Bethoc said.

He shook his head. "The mead came from Saint Serf's. I brought it to the king myself, when he summoned me to act as his messenger. I know the two monks who make our mead, who sealed the cask. No one there would have tainted that wine."

"It is Fife wine, and Duncan would see irony in that," I said. "He must have meant it for both Macbeth and me, but we all drank of it."

"The poison was not in the honey wine," Drostan said. "It was in the horns." He leaned a shoulder to the wall. "Only two took ill. Macbeth drank his portion from the larger horn, and the smaller horn was meant for you. I held that one, but I am forsworn against strong drink. Maeve had a good bit of it. I tasted only a sip."

I gasped. "The horns—of course."

"Yet you have no signs of illness," Bethoc said.

"I have," he answered. "My heart has been pounding oddly and my stomach feels ill—sometimes there is a strange yellowish hue around things. But I have endured."

"The drinking horns were dry and new until I poured into them," I said.

"Poison could have been rubbed inside the horns, or a residue left in the bottom tip to mix with the liquid when filled," Bethoc replied. "The sweetness of the mead would have masked the taste."

"Someone ordered this done, or did it by his own hand," Drostan said. "And Duncan could have deposited the poison himself, or paid someone to do it. Surely it was meant to kill Macbeth and Rue both."

Fury mounted in me, overtaking grief. "Then Maeve has died in my place, and we do not know if Macbeth will survive."

"He will," a voice said from behind us. I turned to see Catriona, her cloak rain-damp, with Angus and Ruari just behind her. "I will make sure of it."

Within minutes, she had us running to her will—Bethoc to fetch oils to mix with the fresh and dried herbs Catriona brought, Ruari and Angus to lift Macbeth, a bigger man than either of them, to sit so that he could better breathe, Osgar and Drostan to praying, Aella to fetch more water and clean linens. I was not ordered, though I would have been willing and obedient. Instead, I stood by and watched her, how she bent over him, touched her cool fingers to his brow, how she spoke so gently.

And I saw him gaze at her in his weakness, as if he could cling to life along the line of that glance. That I felt like a blow, but said nothing, nor would I allow old feelings to take me down. Whatever gave him the strength to climb from the abyss, that I would love too, as best I could.

Catriona bent forward to listen a long while to his heart, her ear against his bare chest, so scarred and powerful, and she had Angus and Drostan lean him forward so that she could listen at his back. Her hands splayed gently there, terrain familiar to her fingers—that I could tell. Then she sniffed at his skin and lifted his arms to smell the inner side of his elbow.

"Macbeth has taken the poison of the *lus-nam-ban-sìth*," Catriona said, glancing at me. "The plant of the fairy woman, or purple fairy flower, we call it. Others call it folk's-glove or foxglove for the shape of the flowers. Your Bethoc was right."

"Bethoc thinks there was more to the poison than the fairy flower alone."

Catriona nodded. "By the signs and the quickness of it, I believe there is also *lus-na-h-oidhche*. The plant of the night. A sleeping draft in small doses. But it is said to be used by witches, and it is an evil poison in larger amounts. With that tainting his blood, he could die seeing demons."

I cupped a hand over my mouth, listening. This was no death for such a man.

"If we can counter both poisons and dilute their power, he will have time and strength to defeat it, and recover, by grace of God. Sit with him," Catriona told me. "He will know you are there." She left the room.

I sat on the edge of the bed, the down mattresses sinking beneath me. When I took his hand, it was cool, limp. With my fingers on his wrist, I could feel the wrong rhythms of his heart. He moaned, writhed, whispered frantically. I closed my eyes and murmured a prayer, and an appeal. *"Mhiceil nam buadh. . . ."*—Michael the victorious—"be shielding him, this day and night."

Bethoc and Catriona returned with an infusion of herbs and oil, which we spooned into his mouth. Macbeth stirred, mumbling in half sleep, and called out a name. Two. *Malcolm,* he said. *Finlach.* He shrieked, struggled. We pressed him down, we three.

"He wanders on the back of the night-mare," Catriona said. "Bethoc, go out and find men to help hold him down. Send Aella to the kitchens to tell Cook to make a soup of lentils, kale, beans, carrots. A mild salty broth with those certain vegetables. They have a restorative power to counter part of the poison when he wakes."

Should he wake, I could not help thinking. Dragging a stool toward the bed, Catriona sat on the side opposite me, with my husband between us. I picked up the bowl Bethoc had brought, and at Catriona's nod, spooned some of the herbal stuff between his lips. He took it, eyes closed.

"This is a strong mixture, and not to be used often, or too much," Catriona said. "It is very powerful against certain poisons, but potent enough to harm him too, so we will dose carefully. If any potion will bring him around, this would be the one." She sent me an odd look, something poignant, something pleading, then she glanced quick away.

"What herbs are in it?" I asked. "Will it truly save him?"

"The main herb is *ruigh*," she murmured, and lifted her hand to gently sift the damp, tousled hair away from his brow. "It is not grown near here, but I keep a little store of it set by. Herb of grace, they call it in the south, and use it as a brush to waft holy incense in churches. Its other name is rue." She smiled, wistful and quick. "As it happens, it is the remedy for this poison."

Rue. The name had followed me with its sadness, but now it showed a better power to save. I took his hand, and we two sat with him in silence. She bathed his brow with a cloth, and I stroked his fingers in mine. He did not stir, but seemed to settle for the first time in all those hours, as the strength of the herbs, and more, took hold.

· · ·

Maeve's funeral was small and somber, and I missed her deeply in the smallest of things—who to admonish me when I was impulsive, who to make me laugh at my own pridefulness? Losing her made me miss my own mother again, sharply, though so many years had passed. Who to be the knee-nurse for my next little one, if, when?

Once Macbeth was well enough for us to share a bed again, I slept more soundly, though I dreamed now and then of battlefields. I saw Macbeth face a giant in combat, a stranger whose great, hairy head was encircled by a crown; with limbs like hewn oak, he tossed Macbeth upward and outward to spin against a pearl gray sky over the mountains. Such dreams, Mother Enya told me—for I saw her when time allowed—might always haunt me. Some nights, I dreaded sleep.

"No doubt Duncan expected word of your death, and Lady Rue's as well," Ruari said. He had returned after escorting Drostan south during the weeks of Macbeth's recovery, and we sat very late by the fireside to hear his report. "We made sure Duncan heard that Macbeth and his lady are hale and well at Elgin. Soon after, he went into Northumbria with an army."

Macbeth sat forward, sharply interested. "What news of that?"

Ruari hesitated, a quick crease between his brows. "Duncan and his men pushed deep into Northumbria and down to Durham, where the relics of the holy Saint Cuthbert are kept."

"Ah. If the king can capture Durham's treasure, he proves his might to the Saxons," Macbeth replied. "Go on. And the Scots? How did we fare?"

"Horsed and on foot," Ruari said, "slaughtered nearly to a man."

My husband sucked in a breath. "Tell the rest of it."

"Duncan fled with a few men, and they made their way north. In Durham, Scottish heads were taken and piked in the marketplace, hundreds to form a palisade. They said it was in answer to old Malcolm, who made a gruesome display of Saxon heads years ago."

I listened, silent and horrified. I had seen the like myself, once.

"And now?" Macbeth asked in a rough voice. "What for Duncan?"

"He is back in Dunsinnan, calling the Saxons barbarians, and blaming you for his failures, since he asked for Moray troops and you refused. A few mormaers have already met in secret, under the protection of Neill of Angus and the mormaer of the Mearns. They know the truth—that you were ill, most likely poisoned by Duncan's order. The word has gone round, and many are incensed over it. Another black deed to add to his roster, they say. They meet to decide further what should be done."

Macbeth nodded, thoughtful. "We should all fear for Scotland now. Thanks to Duncan's actions, both the Saxons and the Vikings may retaliate."

"Some feel," Ruari said, "that you are the only mormaer in Scotland who can repair the damage Duncan has wrought."

"He is," I said quietly.

Loops and currents in the wind had our hawks eager to fly one golden morning in early August, or *Iuchar,* the hot month. I went with the men as they hunted, walking over miles of hills through thickening heather, with hawks and bows and arrows. The view was wide and generous over the glen to the mountains, and as we headed back to Dun Elgin, we saw thunderstorms approaching—and riders coming fast from the mountain passes to the south. They rode with purpose, the banners among them an astonishing array that identified the leaders. We hastened to Elgin's gates, where Macbeth took my arm.

"Order your servants to leaping and doing. We will have guests for supper. This has the look of a war council," he added.

I stood with him while our hunting party hurried through the gates. The wind increased, and where the men rode through the glen with bright banners flying, I saw gray veils of rain slanting down from the ominous sky. "There are the colors of Angus and Buchan. And priests ride with them as well—a bishop, too, by the robes," I said.

"The other standards look like Mar and the Mearns, Argyll—and by the saints, Imergi of the Isles as well. The bishop of Saint Andrews, too," Macbeth added.

Men of high importance on a sober matter. Although we had expected this someday, my heart fluttered hard. The escort was not a war band, though armor and weaponry flashed in the light. These were allies, and there was secrecy and urgency in their mission. I felt it keen as the storm clouds that hurtled toward us.

Just as the men entered the bailey, the storm struck with dousing fury. I stood at a window inside and watched as Macbeth ushered our guests toward the keep, out of the wind and the lashing rain. Then I turned away to hasten the servants to their tasks.

"He must be stopped," Constantine said low and clear. "Either we make an end to it, or Duncan will lead Scotland into ruin!"

"If he is left to do as he pleases, we will be called either Saxon or Norse by the time we all die on battlefields. We will have no peaceful aging in our homes," remarked Nechtan, a cousin to me from Argyll. "Scots will be no longer Celtic, but a defeated lot, constantly at war. This cannot be allowed to happen."

The servants had been excused, doors and windows shut and bolted. As the fire crackled and shadows grew deep around us, the men spoke in turn, some quiet and others insistent. I sat with them, committing all to memory. Wine met water in my cup, and so my mind was sharp, my tongue discreet.

"We need an elected king," said Neill of Angus. "One who rules by Celtic right. We are agreed on it." He looked square at Macbeth. My husband listened, silent, somber.

"Even more than blood right, we agree that Scotland needs a king with not only warrior skill, but the wit and calm to rule fairly." This from the mormaer of the Mearns, a large, gruff, elderly man with copper-and-silver hair, who reminded me much of old Malcolm. They had been first cousins, I knew.

"So we come to you," Constantine told Macbeth. "Duncan must be defeated."

"Taken down, one way or another," added Neill of Angus.

"How?" I asked quietly. No one looked at me, but they heard.

"Ambush or war," the mormaer of the Mearns answered. "Or poison."

Macbeth tapped his fingers slowly on the table, and looked from one man to the next. "Very well. Moray," he said, "will rise in rebellion."

H E C A M E late to our chamber, having lingered nearly to dawn with the others in the great hall. I felt the bed shift as he sat on the edge to remove his boots and tunic. In the hall below, the wooden floors creaked as men settled down to rest on pallets near the fire basket. Macbeth glanced over his shoulder in the darkness.

"You know what they want of me," he murmured.

"They believe you would be a far better king than Duncan, and they are right."

He laughed, bitter and quick. "Anyone would be better. But there is more to their request." He rubbed a hand over his face, sighed out. "They want me to kill Duncan myself, and win the crown through victory, by old Celtic tradition."

I sat up. "With or without you, there is conspiracy. Duncan will not live long."

In the dim moonlight through the unshuttered window, I saw the sorry shake of his head. "I have killed many men," he said. "And one first cousin. It haunts me still, that. Shall I slay another of my own close kin to gain what I want?"

The light played over muscle, sheened skin, old scars. I rested my hand on his shoulder. "Many are with you in this. I am with you."

"There is much sin in forcing fate." He leaned forward, arms resting on knees.

"Sin is a choice," I said, "and so is this path."

"My ambition was always for Scotland as much as myself. We must be careful to preserve the heart of what is called Gaelic, the honor, the power in it, when the outer world—the Church, our enemies, the trade, all the rest—stands to change us. Duncan is hastening the end of the Gaels, if he even knows it."

"You can honor that heritage and vindicate your kin, and mine," I reminded him. I thought of Bodhe and old Malcolm, and the turmoil we had suffered for the sake of revenge. "Duncan cannot be permitted to remain king longer. Mac bethad," I said then, "the others are right. There is no choice but to see him gone, and another in his place."

"If this must be done," he said, "best it be done quick. We ride out soon." He glanced at me over his shoulder. "Tonight we dispatched men south to Lothian with the word that Moray gathers forces to challenge the king."

"So Duncan will come north. Will you meet him in ambush?"

"Not a trap," he said, "but a lure."

Chapter Twenty-Six

A fortnight gone to planning and visitors, and swift horses carrying men and messages, and one day I woke to the sound of impatient hoof stomps, of men murmuring, of the cold chink of mail. I rushed to the bailey, throwing a cloak hastily over my gown.

Macbeth stood on the wall walk behind the palisade, looking out at the vast body of the army that he had ordered to gather beyond our gates. Climbing the steps, I hurried toward him. Over the hills, a pink glow rimmed the mountains.

"Almost light," he said. "Word came that Duncan has sailed up from Berwick with more ships. He has landed on Moray shores with an army, and they are marching this way. There is no time to move the household," he added. "You will be safe at Elgin for now. Buchan, Mar, Angus, and the Mearns have sent messages. They bring men, but may not be here in time."

"Will you ride to battle, or to make a truce?"

"We ride," he said, "to make an end of this." He cupped my face in his palm then, so rare a gesture for him, and I leaned my cheek into that cradle for an instant.

"I will go with you," I said.

He shook his head. "Stay here, and look to your son. This day will be over soon enough. You need wait but a little while."

"Take this." I had brought the silver brooch that Enya had given me. With shaking fingers, I slipped the pin into the weave of his red cloak and hooked the catch. "This has protective power. And let me put a battle charm around you. Please." He nodded and stood while I walked round him *deiseil,* sunwise, murmuring the words Enya had taught me:

A shield of mist I put on you
To guard against arrow, against blade, against faery
To guard you front to back, crown to sole, until you return to me.

Then I touched my fingers to the silver circlet. "Power of wolf, power of raven, power of air, power of earth, power of stone be yours."

"So be it." My husband kissed my brow, my lips. Then he strode away and down to the bailey, calling for his horse. An unworried farewell, when I felt such dread.

Slowly I walked through the bailey as the men organized their force. Macbeth called orders for a large number of men to stay and guard Elgin, while he and the others, so very many of them—thousands—would ride out in a body.

"Duncan will bring his troops along the coast," he said. "We will meet them on the moorland a few miles beyond Pitgaveny."

So close. Hearing that, knowing what I must do, I hurried toward the keep. If Macbeth would face death that day for the sake of my kin group, I had to be there too. First, though, I ran to find my son. Kneeling, I put my arms around Lulach and held him, though he was stiff, a little embarrassed. I kissed that sunlit hair, smelled the little-boy scent—warm and sweaty, earthy yet innocent, like a new spring bud with the soil still upon it—and then I rubbed his cheek and tugged his ear, and told him that I loved him.

By the time Macbeth called for his horse to mount and ride out, I sat a horse of my own—not Solus, but a large dappled stallion—and I wore the chain mail hauberk and iron helmet that Finn had made for me. Macbeth walked past me, then stopped and turned on his heel.

The helmet had a brass nasal plate that divided my sight, though I had a fair view ahead, and I lifted my chin and waited. The chain mesh hauberk covered me neck to knee, with a quilted tunic beneath to make the weight more tolerable, and I wore leather brogans on my feet and thick cloths wrapped foot to knee. I had the sheathed sword Bodhe had given me, along with Macbeth's dagger; a bow, quiver, and arrows were strapped to my saddle. I had bullied Aella, fretful soul, into helping me dress. She had already helped her husband, Giric, and was in no mood to turn me into a warrior, too.

"What in the name of all that is holy," Macbeth said, low and terrible, "is this?"

Behind him, Ruari walked Macbeth's horse toward us and stood by, as did the others who gathered around. My own horse sidestepped a little, but I held the reins steady. "I mean to come with you," I said. "I will not wait in the hall with my needlework to hear word of your fate. Or any of yours," I added more loudly for the rest.

"A little stitchery, and more patience, would suit you," Macbeth said.

"You are Moray, and I am the lady here. Our region, and your very life, are threatened this day. If the people see both of us riding at the head of our army, I believe they will rally behind Macbeth with greater loyalty than ever before." I made my voice loud enough for his housecarls to hear. "All of us together will protect our homes and our Celtic way of life, because that is what we fight for against Duncan the king. We will rout the invaders like a flock of birds fleeing from a great storm."

I saw a spark of true thunder in his gaze. "Some would call you foolish," he said, "or a disobedient and defiant wife."

"Better defiance this way than some other way," I answered. "I made a sword vow years ago to protect my own, and I will keep it. I have a home and a son to protect, and I have a husband to support as best I can. All my life I have lived a female among Celtic warriors. My sword arm is trained, my bow and arrow are swift, and I have already bloodied the blade. Know this—my determination is in place. I will go with you."

Macbeth took my horse's bridle. "Each one who rides with me contributes to the whole. Your skill I will not argue, but your fortitude is little tested. You would require guards to protect you, and that detracts from the whole."

"Have you not made it your purpose to uphold the old ways, the ancient ways, of the Gaels and the Celts?" The horse shifted under me, and I pulled the reins. Macbeth still held the bridle. "Celtic women have always fought beside their men."

"You do not need to revive the old tradition."

"I do," I said fiercely. "Today, for this, I do. Duncan sent poison to you, and to me. He nearly killed you in a coward's fashion, and he took Maeve from us, and my kinsmen before," I said. "I have full reason of my own to ride out this day."

His gaze was intent, but my point was made. He let go of the bridle and stepped back, silent, glowering, accepting.

We rumbled through the gates and down the slope to the glen floor, a dark stream of warriors like the whip of a giant horse's tail. Macbeth kept me just behind him, and assigned Giric, Conn, and two others to ride close by me as a phalanx. Riding with us at the head of the army were Dermot mac Conall—a warlord's bard was essential for the ritual of battle—and the groom who carried the banner of Moray tied to a spear. Father Osgar was there, too, along with two other priests robed in white, members of the Culdees. They carried a brass reliquary with the finger bone of our local saint, and they brought a large cross as well.

Macbeth sent lads ahead on foot, two who were swift footed as deer, to climb the hills and spy out what they could. We rode on, and the lads returned to say that Duncan's army was very large, coming over land as well as sea, and moving from the opposite direction. We would meet within miles.

After a while, Macbeth looked over his shoulder. We all turned, and I could see, then, a great mass of people gathering to follow behind us. As we neared Pitgaveny, where Finn had his smithy and home, I saw our blacksmith friend riding toward us, horsed and armed. He joined our group, too, falling into the stream of us without a word.

"Some of my retainers have gone around, farm to farm," Macbeth told me then, "to order able-bodied tenants to bring what weapons they have. My housecarls are letting them know that the mormaer's lady rides with him where he goes. Your presence is attracting more to our army, just as you thought."

I smiled, holding my head high, though truly I felt frightened.

Within the next two leagues, we gained farmers, sons, old men, youths, all with weapons, a bristling sea of spears and swords, rakes and scythes. Our ranks grew, much as a river widens as it nears the sea. We rode on, daylight brightening over us.

Seeing me with Macbeth, some women came, too, fitting themselves with helms, swords, spears, or rakes—whatever came to hand. Those who were able to leave their homes, who had no children, women who had husbands, lovers, brothers, and fathers to follow— they came. They, too, knew of the old ways, the rightfulness of men and women fighting side by side to defend their own.

In that moment, perhaps for the first time in my life, I felt like a monarch; we had powerful loyalty among us, and that unity gave me the heart of a leader. Macbeth and I formed the head, the crown, and the people of Moray the body, and we moved as one in a tide toward the sea. The entity of Moray would not tolerate the invasion or destruction of our land.

At the top of a ridge, we saw the dark mass of Duncan's army spilling into the glen beyond Pitgaveny. I saw Duncan was there, too, for his standard, the red and yellow with lion roaring, flapped in the wind.

"So you have come over into Moray with arms," Macbeth growled, as we sat and looked down on that scene, "and king or none, you will pay for the trespass."

He gathered his retainers to confer, then he gestured, and in a great body, we all moved along the bare crest of the hill to stand in a long line, thick as trees, where we could be seen. Warriors, tenants, old men, youths, women—all stood or sat horses on that long ridge, the whole of the Moravian throng, to give the appearance of a daunting force many thousands strong. Bristling and severe, we formed the spiny-backed war monster.

Macbeth and his close guard rode back and forth, explaining, calling out, marshaling force and spirit among us all. The women and the old ones were thanked and told to return to their homes, though many did not. The rest, other than armed warriors, were asked to keep far back from any fighting, and to stay at the top of the hill to show our Moray strength. I stayed with Macbeth's men, and my own.

A king's man rode toward us waving a white banner, and was permitted to approach Macbeth. They spoke, and the messenger rode away. Without explanation, Macbeth led us to a long slope, and we began to move down toward the moor.

"What is happening?" I asked Giric, for the movement of the warriors and the quick decisions made around me were confusing.

"Duncan wants to meet with Macbeth. We are going to the moor to wait," Giric said. "Only a few will meet at first," he said, gesturing toward the king's army. "Soon, though, red blades will feed Duncan's men to the wolves and ravens for supper."

I shuddered. The world I had thrust myself into that day, spurred by my own will and a noble intent, was foreign to me, not a whit like the practice yard, or even a skirmish. This place was brutal and cruel. Yet I had promised to be equal to the task. I was glad to have trust in Giric and the others beside me.

Looking past the moorland, over vast miles to the coast, I could see ships. "Warboats," I said, and Giric raised a hand to his brow.

"Not Duncan's, which have a Saxon shape," he said. "Those are Viking ships. No doubt Thorfin and others wait to see who will win Moray, and Scotland, this day."

Suddenly, two of Macbeth's retainers began to ride around the perimeter, shouting for all to take up sticks and mark them. Wooden sticks were produced from belts and pouches, and those who did not have them dismounted to crack thin branches from trees, or pluck fallen ones from the ground. My husband joined us and reined his horse near me. He thrust a fat stick into my gloved hand.

"What am I to do with this?" I asked.

"Mark it," he said. "Carve something into it—anything to identify you. Break it in half, and mark the other with the same symbol. Tuck one into your belt, your boot, anything. Leave the other half here—end first into the ground, back there with the rest."

Behind us, I saw a growing forest of sticks thrust into the ground. Somehow this panicked me. "Why?"

"Warriors who go into battle," he said, "must leave their marker behind. If they live, they fetch it again. If they die . . . we will know who is missing."

A Dhia. I took out my dagger and hastily marked the stick, my fingers shaking. I cut a G for Gruadh in both ends, scratched the triple spiral of Brigid, snapped the stick in two. Macbeth took one from me. "I will put this in the ground beside mine. We will fetch them again. I swear it, Rue." He looked hard at me then.

"Mac bethad—" I reached out.

He pressed my fingers in his, through our thick leather gauntlets. I wondered if I might ever touch him, skin to skin, again. Then he guided his horse's head around and rode off, cutting through the throng toward the growing field of sticks, where men planted their signs.

I knew then that this was real, horribly so. We might not come back—we might suffer terribly. And whatever happened, I would be changed utterly that day. For all my fine talk and boastfulness, I was not prepared to be lost in the whirlwind about to be unleashed. *Cuidich mi a Bhride.* I began a protective chant as a great trembling filled my body. *Mhiceil nam buadh, bi fein mi ro chul.*

In the tradition of the Gaels, those who enter battle go with blessings and chants. Now I heard, all around me like the rush of the sea, chants and prayers among the men.

> *No fire shall burn me*
> *Nor wind cool me*
> *Nor water drown me*
> *Nor stone fell me*

I looked for my husband and saw that he was riding out to meet Duncan. In the glen, Macbeth's army was far larger than Duncan's force; much of Duncan's Scottish army had been decimated by the Saxons months before.

"We outnumber them," Giric said beside me. "Duncan may turn tail and run."

"In six years of warring," said Angus, who had joined us, "he has not won a single encounter. By the lay of this battle, he cannot win against Moray either."

Silent, I watched my husband as he and a few retainers—Ruari, Finn, Mungo, and others—rode toward the center under the silver-and-blue banner, along with the priests and the bard. From the other side, the king led his own party. Then Macbeth dispatched a messenger to ride to Duncan, along with Father Osgar.

From my vantage point, I could see that the messenger delivered Macbeth's words, whatever they were. Duncan conferred with his men and gave an answer, and the messenger and Osgar returned for more conference on Macbeth's side. I shifted, and my horse moved under me, impatient too. A kingship would be decided here; we all felt the certainty of it.

Finally Macbeth rode forward into the middle area. With him was Ruari, whom I recognized by his huge black horse and blue hauberk over chain mail. Six other housecarls rode with them. Macbeth dismounted then, removing weaponry from the saddle loops. He strode forward. On the other side, fifty or so feet away, Duncan did the same. They met, and around them, their several housecarls formed a wide circle.

"What are they doing?" I asked Giric. "Will they fight, just the two?"

"It looks so," he answered. "There is an ancient tradition among Gaels and Picts that a difference, even between armies, may be settled between the two leaders, or their appointed fighters. Hand to hand. Whoever survives here," he went on, "will rule Scotland. Macbeth should beware. For all Duncan's blunders in war and leading armies, the king is a powerful fighter all on his own, I hear," Giric muttered. "Strong and sly."

"Duncan is a strong fighter," Angus agreed, "but Macbeth has the true skill and instinct of a natural warrior. Besides, Moray's cause is the better."

"Clever of Moray to suggest the old Celtic tradition of a fight be-tween kings," Giric said. "He knows who can best win this."

A housecarl rode toward us. "Giric, Macbeth wants you to lead three hundred men forward to the field. The rest stay back. The king has five hundred on this field, and Macbeth wants him to see a lesser force."

"Why?" I asked. "Why not more?"

"He wants Duncan to feel overconfident," Angus replied. "I sus-pect we will not fight today. Macbeth and the king will settle this on foot, with two blades, and quick."

I pretended courage, but felt a flash of relief, knowing we might not face physical danger that day. Yet my husband was at imminent risk, and that terrified me. "Quick for you to watch, perhaps," I told Angus. "Endless for me."

He grunted agreement. With the others, I urged my horse forward with the three hundred, for I would help form a part of the great shield at Macbeth's back. Slowly, we went closer until Giric raised a hand to halt us. Peering past him, I removed my helmet to view the field more fully.

The combat of the two was already under way.

It was brutal and fast. Duncan was powerful, bullish, and persis-tent. But Macbeth had the greater skill, and his sword was swift and sure; a taller man, he had the longer reach. They each gripped a simple broadsword in the right hand, and braced a round shield on the left arm, and each man clenched a dagger in the left hand like a wicked spike beside the shield. One sword strike after another rang out as the blades met high, met low, scraped against one another, withdrew, clashed again.

I pressed a fist to my mouth as I watched. Macbeth sidestepped a downward swipe that could have taken his hand, all of it, had he not been quick. Macbeth then smacked his hilt upward against Duncan's dagger hand. The king lost his grip on the smaller blade; it tumbled away. Macbeth struck again, Duncan blocked, skittered sideways, lunged. They moved so fast that I could scarcely follow each move.

The king struck again, and Macbeth deflected, using his shield arm to slam his targe against Duncan's head. Circling away, Duncan shuffled as if dazed, and Macbeth caught him hard with the hilt of the sword, knocking him in the jawbone, so that Duncan's head jerked backward. The king stumbled, then arced his blade just as Macbeth turned, catching Macbeth at the back of the leg. I saw my husband bend one knee deep, and struggle to rise again.

All in an instant, longer to say than see.

The blades met again, the men pressing forward in hard resistance. Then Macbeth slid his blade fast along the edge of Duncan's—we heard the screech of it—and the steel bit deep into Duncan's shoulder. The king, already weakened, fell to his knees on the turf, sought to rise, then fell. Yet he moved, though Macbeth stood over him, sword hilt in hand. Every man there, I think, held his breath, knowing Macbeth had the right to make the killing blow. Duncan lay on his back, and Macbeth still held his sword.

A moment later, he thrust it hard into the ground and walked away.

Men were already dashing across the field toward them from opposite sides. Now some of them dropped to their knees beside Duncan. The king seemed unable to stand up. His retainers bent over him; one called for a litter. Now we were moving closer, but not for battle. Ahead, Macbeth spoke with Ruari, Finn, Mungo, others, and I dismounted from my horse and began to run, Giric and Angus following.

Mungo met us. "The king has taken a deep wound to the shoulder and his jaw seems broken. They will move him to the smithy, where Finn can cauterize the wound."

On the field, the king's housecarls were lifting Duncan onto a litter made hastily from a cloak and spears. It was the dark red cloak Macbeth had worn.

Men were moving, dashing about, shouting everywhere. I looked about for my husband and saw him at last.

He stood apart on that field, alone in the midst of many. I saw him bend a knee to the ground and dip his head in prayer, hands crossed on the hilt of his upright sword. Then he stood, pulled the blade free, wiped the bloody steel on the grass. He balanced the long blade on his shoulder to carry the sword. No celebration, no victory mantled him. He moved slowly, he limped, his head was bowed low.

THE TIME-between-times, say the Celts, has the power of magic. Such moments of transition—dawn and sunset, mist and snow, birth and death, breathing in and breathing out—suspend us between one realm and the next, and mystical doors fly open. Through that night, Duncan lingered in such a place: king but no king, alive yet not.

The worst of his wounds was the deep sword cut that had bitten along the neck of the chain mail and down into the shoulder, breaking bone and severing muscle. With a wadded cloth, I pressed upon the bloody wound while Finn looked at the rest. Duncan's jawbone was broken from the strike of the hilt against his face, and he could not properly talk, could scarcely breathe or swallow.

While Father Osgar led prayers over the king, Finn worked quickly, cutting away the chain mail. He gave the king a strong dose of Danish aqua vitae, and then seared the deep gash with the glowing tip of a hot iron, while Macbeth and another man held the king steady, for Duncan arched, shrieked. Then Finn stitched the wound with silk thread and a steel needle brought by his wife, and poured wine into the wound. Watching, I flinched, felt ill, but would not turn away.

I rinsed my hands clean of Duncan's blood, and stayed close by him. Macbeth did the same, and we stood with the king's closest retainers. Those men were nameless to me, but they were quiet and concerned, and seemed accepting of Duncan's defeat.

"He will not die alone," Macbeth said. "And if he recovers, so be it."

Finn had already sent for the healing woman from the nearest clachan, and we waited. Osgar and another priest, one of Duncan's entourage, knelt to give the king the last rites in case he should not live. When the herb woman arrived, we stood back to let her work. She applied ointments and a poultice that was pungent with onion to the flesh wound, and said she could do little for the broken jaw. The old woman walked around him in a circle, murmuring charms and prayers. Then she knelt beside Duncan, and when she rose, she came toward us. I remember the cloying heat of the smithy on that August evening. I remember that she was very old, and I did not know her name.

"He is not dead, but dead," she told us. "He is a broken man. His spirit will soon find its way out of this life."

Finn's wife, Lilias, went to the house for her harp, and she sat with it in her lap to play for the dying king while the light faded to purple but did not vanish, for a Highland summer carries a perpetual light of its own.

Three kinds of harping exist, they say: music for laughing, for crying, and for sleeping. Lilias played the crying sort: soft melodies so exquisite that my heart turned within me. While we were sitting quiet in the dark hour before dawn, Duncan died.

In silence, Macbeth walked through the doorway and took up the reins of his horse, waiting just outside. He rode away alone.

Chapter Twenty-Seven

Thorfin's ships were visible at dawn, floating off the coast. Someone left the smithy at first light and saw them there, running back to report that, and to say that some of Macbeth's men were heading up the hill toward us.

Macbeth, who had come back from his solitary ride, was with us when Duncan's body was shrouded in clean linen, brought by Lilias; every woman keeps a winding cloth tucked away, for sooner or later it is always needed. My husband and I knelt with the corpse, and Osgar was praying, when Ruari found us.

"The Vikings sent a boat to shore to ask about the outcome of the battle, and were told the news," he said. "Now Thorfin sends back word that he will offer his boats if we wish to sail Duncan's body down the firth and river to Scone."

"Send word of thanks," Macbeth murmured. "But to have such an escort would lead some to believe that Moray is allied too close with the Orkneyings. We will take Duncan back on one of his own ships, for that is the way he came here. We will leave shortly. Arrange it." Ruari nodded and left.

Not only must Duncan be buried, I knew, but a new king must be elected and crowned at Scone. I looked at my husband, saw the deep fatigue creasing his face, and said nothing of my thoughts.

We shared a somber, simple meal of oatcakes and a thick soup that Lilias prepared, and then we readied to depart for Scone. Earlier I had asked Giric to return to Dun Elgin to fetch Aella for my handmaid, and she brought me two good gowns, green and blue, a veil and cloak, and other things I required. Though I wanted Lulach with us, Macbeth would not have it. He feared repercussions after Duncan's death, and reminded me that we could not allow the child to be exposed to harm.

By midday we sailed amid an escort of Duncan's ships, swift and long, with a wind that carried us quickly southward around the curving eastern coast and deep into the firth of the River Tay. The king's shrouded body, covered in a cloak, lay on a bier in the boat. We followed the shining course of the river down to Scone, and the people gathered along the banks.

I remembered the vision I had seen in the bowl of water by Enya's fire: a longboat carrying a dead king, and I was there with warriors. So my vision had portended Duncan's death, and had showed our silent journey to become king and queen.

My husband said little as we sailed. Pensive, he was, and I sensed within him both sadness and long-held anticipation. I shared those feelings myself—sharp regret over a painful death and a life gone, and excitement building for what would follow.

Along the banks by the docking ship at Scone, hundreds of warriors appeared, but again none challenged the victor, the king-slayer. They came to accept the body of the deceased king, and scarce spoke otherwise. A strange tension quivered in the air. We walked up the hill to the church at Scone behind the litter held by several of Duncan's men.

We saw no funeral beyond the Mass and Office of the Dead performed at Scone. Crinan had demanded only that his son be brought to him at Dunkeld, which was quickly done. Relief swept all of us, I think, that Crinan stayed apart.

"Atholl will take his son's body to Iona immediately for burial with the other Scottish kings," Macbeth told us, after speaking with one of Duncan's housecarls. We walked alone in the bottom of the garden at Scone's monastery.

"Crinan will come after you seeking revenge when he returns from Iona," I said.

"He has made no threat so far, even in the heat of his grief. His son was slain in a fair contest, before thousands of witnesses who can attest that Duncan agreed beforehand, as I did, that our combat would decide the dispute for Moray."

"And kingship?" I had found no moment yet to ask this.

"I told Duncan, when we faced each other on that field," he said, "that his crown would be mine if I took the fight. He laughed and was sure he would win. I could just as easily have lost that contest. Duncan was a powerful fighter."

"He thought he would win every battle he entered, yet never did. Crinan will dispute his death." I dreaded more war.

"He may, but he would find little support. Duncan's battles over the past several years so decimated his armies that Crinan would have to wait for boys to grow into warriors. Most men, here and now, are glad for an end to Duncan's recklessness." He touched my shoulder. "No one will argue this—at least not yet."

"Not yet?" I asked. He shook his head without answer.

W ITHIN A day of our arrival at Scone, mormaers, thanes, priests, and warriors came from all corners. By the second evening, they gathered in the great hall at the palace of Scone—we stayed ourselves in the monastery, not willing to claim residence in Duncan's royal palace— and met to elect a new king.

That night I paced my modest bedchamber, which I shared with Aella rather than my husband, for the usual separation rules at the monastery were observed even for guests. Finally I could bear the waiting no more. Aella and I left, found our guards, Angus and Lachlann, and went to the church of Scone for prayers. There, in the quiet, deserted nave, Aella and I went on our knees on hard slate and bowed our heads.

Dull darkness fell, and finally Macbeth appeared. Aella was already on her feet, hurrying toward the door to leave us alone. He sighed, looking up at the planked ceiling over our heads, rooftrees topped by timber. A candle burned on an altar, all the light we had. I burned to ask, yet kept silent.

"It is done," he murmured. "I am to be crowned High King of Scots."

My heart pounded hard. "They agreed, all of them?"

"To a man, but for the one mormaer absent—Crinan of Atholl." He put an arm around my shoulders. "They want it done quickly, before Crinan returns from the burial at Iona. The crowning is tomorrow."

I leaned against him, silent for a moment, sending up a prayer of relief and gratitude. When a long-held desire, into which many fears and dreams have been poured, springs to life at last—it is joyful, humbling, and terrifying. Taking his hand, I cradled it in both of mine.

"They elected me by old process—as a candidate by right of blood and claim, by consensus of the mormaers. And there was more that convinced them," he said then. "With you as my wife, our combined claim could not be denied. Your ancient bloodline holds the key in this. They saw that we bring the two branches of the oldest ruling tree in all Scotland's history to the throne. Because of your blood, you will not be called consort, but full queen, and crowned as such." He looked down at me. "Bodhe's line comes to the throne at last."

The waiting, the strife, the losses of those I loved: all of it struck me like a blow. Tears stung my eyes, and I bowed my head and wept for all the kin and ancestors whose blood had made mine that pure, to lead to this. And I cried for their vindication, for they had regained the throne after generations of being held back from it, gained it through me, and Macbeth.

H E HAD brought the soil of Moray to the great moot hill at Scone, carried in his boot, in keeping with an old tradition. In the dark hour before dawn, Macbeth went to the mound, pulled off his boot, and tipped it. Reverently, he let Moray's earth sift down to add to the hill. I watched from a distance, having gone with him in that early misted hour, the day of his crowning. He climbed the hill alone to honor custom, and kingship.

Legend says the hill at Scone was formed gradually over generations, handful by handful, as men carried soil, turf, and stone from their homes in all the regions and reaches of Scotland, and left it there at that central place. So the deepest part of the mound, they say, was created by Picts, while the most recent layer was left by those who still breathe Scotland's pristine air.

In a few hours, a huge throng would gather here. Already they were crossing hills and moorlands, rowing along rivers, coming by foot, horse, and boat to witness the making of a new king, a warlord who would defend them and uphold the Celtic customs. Later he would accept a handful of soil each from his mormaers in homage when he was made king. Now, in this hour, he was but a man. He knelt in the grass and the mist wrapped around him, and he prayed.

I whispered prayers myself, and a chant, and I walked three times round, left to right, before we left the mound that morning. I felt the old spirits watching.

IN SOLEMN procession we climbed the hill under the late summer sun, myself and Macbeth, with the several warlords of Scotland, a host of retainers, the priests, and the bard. The mound was surrounded by a depth of a thousand and more witnesses, and the shields and spears many of them held formed a palisade of strength around the hill.

The Stone of Destiny, the *Lia-Fàil,* was already in place, stacked upon its larger companion stone and draped with a woolen fabric woven in the crisscrossed pattern favored by the Scots—this one included the colors green for growth, blue for sea and sky, red for blood, purple for our heathered hills. The priests carried a cross the long length of the hilltop, chanting a kyrie in glorious harmonies to invoke heavenly protection and blessing.

Macbeth stood in bare feet, dressed humbly in an unbleached woolen tunic, his hair thick gold, his beard clean shaven. He circled the stone three times, while Dermot, our *seanchaidh,* murmured a blessing of a Celtic nature. Then Macbeth sat upon the stone. Arranged behind him were the mormaers of all the ancient provinces and regions of Scotland, with the exception of Atholl. With them were their elite guards, the tall, strong, most trusted of warriors.

A bishop brought hurriedly from Saint Andrews came forward to lead prayers, and then spoke the vows, in Gaelic and Latin, that Macbeth repeated. The abbot of Scone placed upon Macbeth's shoulders a red mantle of rich woolen weave, lined with fur and edged with eagle and raven feathers, a magnificent thing, said to be very ancient and kept in the church at Scone with other precious royal items held through generations.

Then he placed a scepter in Macbeth's hand, a shining rod of Scottish gold and silver, crowned with a crystal from Moray's own ancient mountains. Dermot mac Conall began to recite an invocation of power, its verses written ages past by Amergin, the first poet of Ireland, where Scotland began. *I am a wave of the sea, I am a hawk on a cliff.* When the mantling of the king was done, with the rod and crystal in his hand, the priest and bard stepped back.

I walked forward, heart pounding, followed by a boy from the monastery, who carried a square of red silk, and on it a golden circlet, the crown of our kings. As the designated crowner of the kings of Scotland, the right Duncan himself had given me, it was mine to place the crown on my husband's head. Standing behind Macbeth, I lifted the circlet in my hands, fingers trembling, raising it up for all to see. The precious sunlit metal glinted. Then I set the golden round gently upon his head.

Cheers rose up from the crowd now, and hands, feet, shields, and spears beat a powerful rhythm. The joyous, wild thump-thump drumming echoed and swelled, and went through me to blood and bone and spirit.

Macbeth stood, mantled and rightfully crowned King of Scots. He lifted his arms high, the golden circlet shining on his head, and for an instant he looked more sun god than man. He laughed—he so rarely did, the sound joyous to hear—and he took my hand and brought me around, three times circling the stone. I sat upon the *Lia-Fàil*.

A chunk of plain sandstone, yet I felt a power rise up through me like a swelling of spirit within, and I breathed deep with that. Dermot the bard said the old words of power over me, too, and I echoed: *I am a wind, I am a wave, I am a hawk. . . .*

The abbot sent the boy forward again, this time with a smaller circle of gold on the cloth. I dropped back my veil to expose my hair, shining like bronze in two long braids. Moments later, Macbeth set the circlet on my head.

Queen. By right of the blood that flows in me, by the right of Bodhe and all before him, I was Queen of Scots. Bowing my head, I thought of my kin and especially my parents, while the cheering sounded and grew all around the hill. Bodhe. Ailsa. I swallowed tears. Macbeth brought me to my feet, and we stood together, turning, surrounded by the great heartbeat of that crowd. Dermot stepped forward again for the last part of the ritual, the full recitation of the long list of the kings.

"Mac bethad mac Finlach," he finished, "*Ard Rí Alban.*"

STANDING ON the shore of Loch Leven, I waited for the ferryman to come over from the island. When he glided the barge smoothly to the little stone beach, he stepped out and bowed. Though I was queen, I was not accustomed to such. Nodding, I smiled. My escort, Angus and the dozen retainers who followed me everywhere now, stepped forward with me, and Angus made a show of bowing and asking if I was ready to board. I knew that politeness would wear off him quick enough, like a shine on silver.

Two of the housecarls made a chair of their arms and carried me to the barge, another surprise. I would not have hesitated to lift my skirt hems to wade into the water, but I was glad, for I wore two silken tunics and a woolen cloak with fine embroidery, gifts from mormaers' wives. The housecarls set me down gently on the barge.

We were all a little awkward in those early days, finding our ways and our roles.

And that morning, I had assigned myself a task. I visited my property near Loch Leven, and saw my stepmother Dolina, inviting her to join us in our household if she wished. She was content in her little house for the time being, and declined, disliking the sort of travel a king's household would take on, though I told her she could stay permanently in any of the several residences we now would own, both in Moray and around the kingdom. In truth, I wanted her help, and she finally promised to consider it. Before I left, she pressed upon me a pretty embroidered veil that she had made for me as a gift. I promised to see her soon, then left for the shore of the loch, intending another errand before day's end.

The barge nosed onto the shore of the island, and the abbot of Saint Servanus came down from the monastery to meet me himself. The isle is a gentle hillock rising up from the water, and buildings clustered at its center contain an air of serenity.

"Queen Gruadh, welcome." The abbot greeted me, and we began to walk. "We are doubly honored. Not only are you queen, but also the gracious lady who owns the land around our loch. I only received your message last evening—let me show you around our enclave."

Within moments, we reached the gates and were met by several monks, one of whom offered me a welcoming cup of the mead they produced from their beehives. The abbot took me on a tour of the grounds, past the dormitories, the gardens, and into the chapel. We all knelt in prayer there, my guards and I, for a few moments of peace. Once outside, I asked to see Brother Drostan.

"He is generally in the scriptorium," the abbot said, and sent a young boy to find him. Within minutes, Drostan met us, his cordial but stilted congratulations making me smile. Neither of us knew quite how to behave as yet.

"Come, let me show you where I work," he said, sounding more like my friend then. He and I walked ahead, with Angus and my guards following.

The library and scriptorium, where the books were kept and copied, were contained in a stone building, whitewashed inside, to protect the treasures within from dampness. The walls were fitted with thick shelves, and the books were stacked flat, many on long chains that attached to the shelves. A few tables and stiff little stools were arranged in rows. Drostan proudly showed me a few of the books, removing them from the shelves so that I could see their intricate covers, some of metal inlaid and enameled, some of leather. The most prized of the books at Saint Serf's included a very old copy of Adomnan's Irish laws, and another of his life of Saint Columba. The gilt covers were studded with crystals, and the pages were illustrated with elaborate ink drawings, delicately colored.

"Macbeth will be interested to know that the books of laws are kept here," I said. "I am sure he will want to visit and spend time reading them."

"The abbot would be very pleased." Drostan showed me his own copying desk, a tall narrow table with slanted top. He had been copying a manuscript just that day, and a loose page filled with his work was half-finished, the lettering not yet complete.

"Only so many pieces are ruled and ready—preparing them takes time," he said, and then told me how he would take a leaf of vellum or sheepskin parchment, carefully scraped—the work of other monks—and rule it in pale red-brown ink, top to bottom, before precisely copying or writing the letters and words. A little space was left in the margins for decorations and notes, before the final decorating. Each page would then be decorated with rubrics, large single letters in red ink inserted as headings, often intricate, curling flourishes embellished with plants or creatures.

"I have scant talent for that, so the pages are given to a more artistic soul for the decorating," he said. "Good scraped vellum pages come dear and should be used wisely, though oak-gall ink is plentiful enough if one knows how to extract and boil it. I prefer the brownish sort, mixed with iron scrapings to turn its color just so. I find ink made from iron salts less good, though I have a store of that set away too—" He stopped then, laughed. "I love my work."

"You do," I said, smiling.

Later I took my leave of the abbot, and Drostan walked with me, and my constant escort, Angus and the others, down to the barge. I turned. "Drostan, we want you to join the royal household," I said.

"We have need of a good cleric to write out our documents and corre-
spondence."

"I am honored," he said, sounding cautious. Years of prayerful
meditation had enhanced the solitary part of him. "But many could do
that for you better than I."

"None of them are trusted friends," I said quietly.

"You have more friends than you can count now that you are
Queen Rue."

"And how am I to sort the enemies from the allies without your
help?"

He smiled. "Very well. I will ask the abbot if he will allow me to
leave here. There are two books I have been copying, and I have not yet
finished my studies, but perhaps he will consider it."

"Excellent. I will make a formal request."

"Make a gentle suggestion," he said, "and he will consider it
kindly."

"I knew I would need your advice."

"Go on, now," he said, "your barge awaits."

My guards formed a chair with their arms, and this time I sat as if
I expected it.

Chapter Twenty-Eight

We left Scone behind for an old fortress on a rolling hill at Kincardine O'Neil—*Ceann-na-Cearn,* headland of the hill—in the region of an old thanage. This place reminded me of Crom Allt, for it was very near the River Dee, swift and deep, and near the mountain pass into Moray. I loved its tranquility of golden moor and river, but it was very near the ancient ring of stones at Lanfinnan, where three ravens had once watched us ride beneath them. That poor omen still haunted me.

Nonetheless, it was a good house for a king, and we stayed there, except for a brief return to Elgin to fetch Lulach, who was delighted with his status as royal and only prince of Scotland. While we were at Elgin, I set myself another task, a secret one. For too long I had not had so much as a conception to give me hope. As queen, part of my obligation remained unfulfilled: to give the king an heir of his own blood.

Bethoc and I went into Elgin's orchard, with the apples of September heavy in the trees and blackberries still on the bushes. We brought Lulach and Finn's oldest son, whom Macbeth had agreed to foster when he was older. In that privacy, I spoke to Bethoc while we plucked berries with the children's help, filling buckets from the wild array there.

"Raspberry leaf is a good remedy for many female matters," Bethoc said.

"I have been drinking raspberry infusions since Lulach's birth, with other herbs," I said. "Surely there must be something more. Shall we send word to your mother?"

"We could, but she remains so busy with the people who come to her, she will not be free to come north. And you are not so free to travel about." Bethoc dipped a loaded bough downward so that Lulach, intent on filling his bucket, could reach more fruit. "You could go to Catriona of Kinlossie," she said. "I will admit she knows as much as my mother. And Macbeth is alive now, I think, because of her skill."

"I could go to her," I said carefully, "if you would not take offense."

"I told you to do it, did I not?" She smiled a little. "If I had her knowledge and experience, you might well have another child by now. Despite what happened between you two, and my own resentment of her, to which I own—I believe she can help you."

We picked the next berry bush clean before we spoke again, the decision made.

STIFLING MY pride, I searched out Catriona when Macbeth left on a short progress through his Moray properties. He had appointed Mungo and Constantine to help him there, giving them large thanages so that they would have authority to oversee parts of Moray in his absences. Meanwhile, I went to Cawdor with a guard to visit the thane's wife there for a few days. Flattered by a visit from the queen, she asked no questions when I rode out with two guards and Bethoc, and went to Kinlossie.

Catriona's house was as I remembered, peacefully nestled at the foot of a hill. The chip in the door where my arrow had embedded, years before, had been painted over. I felt in some ways like a different woman than the jealous, impulsive young wife who had loosed that arrow. I knocked, for smoke curled from the roof opening, and I chanced that she was inside. The door opened to her surprised, lovely face. Looking alarmed, she glanced past me. "Queen Gruadh," she said hastily. Awkwardly. "Is something wrong? Your husband is not here."

"I know," I replied. "May I come in?"

She stepped back. Her son, Anselan, sat by the central fire playing tug-the-rope with a small terrier. He had grown into a beautiful sturdy boy, his hair darkening now like his mother's. I smiled and greeted him. Catriona poured drinks and sent a jug and cups outside to my guards and handmaid. She gave a cup to me. It was delicious, berries and spices. I thanked her.

"Your son is handsome. And must be old enough for fostering now," I said.

"He is. Your husband has offered to take him," she said. "But I have not accepted as yet, though Anselan would—please sit, Lady," she then said, and I took a bench at the table opposite her. "Can I be of some assistance?" she asked.

I sighed. "Since Lulach, I have lost every babe I have conceived, very early. And I have not caught since."

She nodded as if she knew, and asked me a few questions so personal that I hesitated, but the frankness in my nature won out; after all, she had pulled a babe out of me with her own hands, and though I was loathe to admit it, she knew my husband's body as well as I did. Suddenly, I felt at better ease with that. In the past, I had been harsh, jealous of what had been between them before I became part of the knotwork. I had been envious, territorial as a she-wolf, but Catriona had saved Macbeth's life as well as my own and Lulach's, and I wanted to trust her again.

"I will prepare something for you," Catriona said, and she rummaged through some small clay vials and little cloth sacks on cluttered shelves over a corner table. Herbs hung from the rafters there, and tools were neatly laid out—pestle and mortar, small knife, glass container of oils, small clay jars with waxen plugs. Choosing several herbs, she sprinkled dried leaves and stems, flower petals, and tiny dried berries into a little water set to boil.

"Raspberry leaves and dried berries," she said. "You also need chamomile, feverfew, and others." When the brew was to her liking, she set it aside to cool, then took up another vial and handed it to me. "This infusion is already prepared. It is *copan an druichd,* or what is sometimes called lady's mantle, blended with other flowers good for women's matters. Mix it with water from a healing well and drink it for three weeks, after your next cycle comes and goes. Use them in baths as well."

"I will," I said, taking the vials.

"And lie with your husband as often as . . . you both like. The tonics should help your womb to conceive." She turned away. "If you need more, send word to me."

I watched her pour out the fresh infusion into little clay jars and cap them with wax. "I am grateful," I said then. "Catriona, I have never forgotten what I owe you. We are all in your debt. And I have been . . . unfair to you." The words stuck in my throat a little, but I forced them out.

Folding her hands like a natural queen, she sighed. "We have each wronged the other."

I could not offer lifelong friendship, but I felt a truce forming. "Bethoc is outside," I said. "She is impressed by your skills and knowledge." I told her of the medicines Bethoc had made for me.

"Good," she said. "I have been thinking of sharing my work with an apprentice, but no local girl has the talent for it. I wonder if Bethoc—" She stopped.

"Speak to her about it." As we went to the door, I turned to say farewell.

"Lady," she said, using the formal title, "the thane of Kinlossie, my late husband's cousin, has asked me to marry him more than once. I have decided to accept."

"I wish you well of it. I truly do."

"Will we have peace?" she asked suddenly, near a whisper. Her eyes were large, gray, and beautiful, and seemed vulnerable just then.

"Amends," I said. "And I think your son would do well as Macbeth's fosterling. I will tell him that you accept, if you like."

"Thank you." She came outside with me to speak to Bethoc. "Send word to me when you are caught with child, and I will give you something for the keeping of it, until you come to the birthing. And I will come to you for that, if you like."

"Let us hope there will be one for you to assist." I smiled, my throat tight as I turned away. If Macbeth had loved her, or did still, I could understand it, though it hurt deep to contemplate. Always would.

I DRANK the herbs, steeped in the baths, and tumbled with my husband as often as he wanted when he was there at Elgin or Kincardine. Courage became a kind of fire within me: I desperately wanted to bear a child for him, for our lineage. This time, I felt more assured that I would catch one safely, and nest it surely, until the birth time came.

By Christmas, when we were hanging juniper boughs and burning sweet branches, and singing the blessings of that time of year, I knew I had caught firm and caught well. I was careful, took no chances. Even Macbeth remarked upon my new devotion to quiet activities, to the diligent reading of my little gospel book, embroidery with my women, and hours spent with Drostan learning the laws of Scotland. I did not tell him, for a while, why I sat by. My women soon knew. I sent word to Catriona, who sent back by messenger—bless Bethoc for her discretion and knowledge—packets of herbs and blessing charms made of straw and red thread, another of rowan branches, and some beneficial chants to be said. I dared not speak of what we did, lest the sorrow that knows my name find me again.

And one day I felt a stir within me, light as the slip of a fish, the flutter of a wing.

HEARING A loud argument in Kincardine's hall, I left my place with Aella and Bethoc, where we sat in my bedchamber with our stitchery. Belowstairs, Macbeth was meeting with a few mormaers and thanes who had arrived earlier, sharing supper with us. Feeling tired due to my increase, I had gone to my chamber early. Now, as shouts reverberated, I hurried to the hall.

The retainer at the door was a new housecarl who hesitated to admit me. When I gave him a cool glance that asked how dare he stop the queen—a skill I was honing—he relented. The shouting ceased when I entered, as if cut off with a knife.

"Queen Gruadh." Macbeth stood. His manner was stiff and formal; either he did not want me there, or some of his guests did not. The familiar ones greeted me, and others glowered. Ruari drew up a chair, and I sat between him and Macbeth.

"We do not need the young queen on this council," the mormaer of Mar growled. I scarcely knew him, a large and gaunt man whose face looked as if a grimace had been carved there.

"The queen has a place on this council," Macbeth said. He sat back in his chair, fingers casually together, a thoughtful pose that guarded his thoughts.

Ruari leaned toward me. "We have heard that Crinan of Atholl has sent Duncan's children out of Scotland, the younger boy to the Norse-held Isles, and the oldest, Malcolm, with his sister south to the protection of their uncle, the earl of Northumbria."

"They never should have left Scotland," Mar said then.

"Their kin took care of them, as seems fitting," I said.

"Duncan's pups should have been killed," he said bluntly.

A few agreed in a rumble of voices. Some were silent. Immediately I thought of my promise to Lady Sybilla, the late mother of that brood. "You cannot mean that."

"The line of old Malcolm must be eliminated, just as he tried to end Bodhe's line. You, of all, should understand that." Mar stared at me.

"But they are gone from Scotland," I said. "Crinan took his grandchildren away from Scone when he moved Duncan's body to Iona. We will not see them again."

"Until they are grown," one of the thanes said. "So long as they live, they are a threat to King Macbeth and the throne of Scotland."

My husband simmered quiet as a banked fire, thoughtful, listening. "Go on."

"I am their kin," the mormaer of the Mearns said, "and even I say they are a threat and must be dealt with, especially now that they are in the keeping of their Saxon kin."

"Malcolm and his brother will grow into warriors and return," Neill pointed out.

"Or they will stay in exile," Finn said. "Macbeth has banished them all."

"They are children," I said then. "What do they know of war?"

"Their kinsmen know and will train them up!" The old man of the Mearns, as some called him, pounded a fist on the table. A dog, hidden under our feet, got up and left the room. "Duncan's whelps will grow. They will be strong men with strong allies—their grandfather is Atholl, their uncle is Northumbria, their father is a murdered king!" He slammed his fist again. "They will never be allowed to forget that."

"They pose a danger," Neill agreed. "Even the girl—someday she will marry a warrior who will join that cause."

The mormaer of the Mearns leaned forward. "I knew Malcolm the Destroyer," he said. "I fought beside him, was with him when he razed Carham and set heads on pikes. They do not forget, nor do we. Duncan's pups will become a danger and should not be allowed to grow into warriors. Old Malcolm would have seen to it, if such whelps had threatened his future."

"I am not the Destroyer," Macbeth answered.

"You are his ilk," old Mearns said. "You hold his throne now. He would not have drummed this round his war council, but would have simply seen to it. Were they my own pups, I would pluck them up and drown them."

I smothered a gasp. "The oldest is but ten years old!"

Most of the men ignored me, talking over one another, though my husband glanced at me. I had heard enough. Standing, I left the room in seething silence. Likely they breathed in relief, but I was not done.

Marching to my chambers, I opened the door where Lulach lay sleeping, and gazed down at him, swept a hand over his brow to wake him gently. Then I beckoned to his young nurse. "Bring him," I said, and we did.

Within moments, I ushered my son into the hall, his cheeks flushed with sleep, a hand rubbing his eyes. Guiding him forward, I rested a hand on his head.

"Lulach is eight years old," I said. "Duncan's Malcolm is not much older. Is this child a threat to Scotland?" I met the gazes of the men who had the courage to meet mine. "Many of you are fathers, and you follow the teachings of the Church. And as warriors, you must protect your lands. Now you must weave all that together in this decision, so that the sum is not only powerful, but merciful and rightful."

Some watched Lulach, some looked away or down. I kissed my son's head and sent him back to his waiting nurse. On the way, of his own impulse, Lulach went to Macbeth and set a hand on his shoulder in tender good night, son to a father.

"Go on, now," Macbeth murmured.

I waited until the door closed. "If you kill Duncan's heirs," I said, "you slay children, not enemies of the crown. They are precious to come by, each one." Here I set a hand to the rounding of my own belly.

"We do not know what sort of men Duncan's boys will become," Neill said quietly. "They could be warriors with the armies of the Saxons or the Norse, or both, behind them. They could destroy Scotland, and Macbeth."

"They might be monks, holy men, or warriors seeking peace, not destruction," I replied. "It is a risk. Yet some of you would prefer to have the sin of infanticide on your souls forever."

"The deaths of Duncan's children would create martyrs," Ruari pointed out. "King Macbeth would be vilified as a tyrant, and the people might turn their backs on him then. No matter who turned the blade, the blame would go to Macbeth."

"Such killings would blacken our reign, not relieve it," I said.

Beside me, Macbeth was silent but taut, allowing us to speak our minds. The certainty of my rightful argument filled me. Beyond my promise to Sybilla, saving any child greatly concerned me, given my tender state.

The men grew silent, each one considering home, or hell, or revenge. I waited.

Then Macbeth leaned forward, placed his fist on the table, opened it. "We will leave Duncan's offspring be. For now, they are protected by their kinsmen. When the two boys are grown warriors, I will deal with them then, if it comes to that. But they are banished and forbidden to set foot in this land for all their lives."

Old Mearns cleared his throat. "It is a mistake to let Malcolm mac Duncan, the elder, reach his age of majority, let alone become a warrior."

"We do not kill children in Scotland," I responded.

"You, Lady," Mearns rumbled, "have sealed your husband's fate."

LATER, I lay tossing in my bed, where Macbeth had not yet come for sleep. I remembered, suddenly, the prophetic riddle the old charcoal burner's wife had once uttered.

Beware the son of the warrior whose spilled blood will make Macbeth a king.

Had she meant young Malcolm—whose father's spilled blood had made Macbeth king? I had kept my solemn promise to Lady Sybilla, doing what I could to protect her children. And I had dismissed Una as a madwoman, diminishing her prophecy as spite and foolishness.

You have sealed your husband's fate. Mearns's voice echoed. I could not rest, wondering if I should have kept silent when the men proposed slaying children who might become a future danger. Had they been right, and I wrong? Was the taking of so sweet and simple a life—a soul swiftly sent to heaven, and rewards there—scant price to pay to protect a kingdom?

If the whelps proved wolves one day, then I would know the depth of my error.

IV.

After slaughter of Gaels, after slaughter of Vikings,

the generous king . . . will take sovereignty. . . .

Scotland will be brimful, west and east. . . .

—Eleventh-century *Prophecy of Berchán,* on the reign of Macbeth
(translated from Old Irish by Benjamin Hudson)

Chapter Twenty-Nine

ANNO DOMINI 1050

Gulls called and swooped overhead as we rode toward the seacoast, my guards and I. The horses' footfalls thudded where the ground grew damp, and the breezes blew light and salty. In the distance, the sea shushed in thin, foaming waves. I pulled up on the reins of my dark mare—Solus had retired to a quieter life, and this was a spirited young mare of glossy brown brought from Fife to Moray. Slowing, I waited for the others, for I had pulled ahead as we headed for the hidden bay where Mother Enya lived.

Only six of them followed me about that day, for Scotland had been a peaceful place for several years. We had few enemies now—some among the Saxons, to be sure, but none in Moray, its mountains safe as a citadel about us. My husband had crafted that peace with a steady head for reasoning, a just heart, and a strong hand on the sword.

Angus, his beard grizzled and reddish and his cheeks fuller these days from the good meals fed him by his wife, a daughter of Eric of Ross, now approached me. Behind him rode Bethoc's brother Lachlann, Conn mac Fergus, and Catriona's son Anselan, who had fostered with Macbeth and had entered his service.

I had dispensed, sometimes, with bringing a lady about with me. Bethoc remained part of my daily household, unmarried and busy with her herbs and healing; and Aella had long made her home with her husband Giric, now a local thane as well as Macbeth's retainer. She brought their two daughters to visit whenever I was in the north, and for those days she would once again be my handmaiden. Daily, though, I still missed her gentle presence.

I looked at Angus. "I will leave my horse with you here, and go on alone."

"We will accompany you," he said. "On foot, with weapons. Lachlann, keep the horses." He helped me dismount, and we began to walk over sand and grasses.

"I hardly need an armed guard to visit Mother Enya," I protested.

Angus looked toward the sea, his iron-studded leather hauberk creaking as he lifted an arm to shadow his eyes. "We saw ships off the coast. Viking make, close enough to sail and beach if they want. We stay with you."

"Thorfin is Enya's grandson, and visits her now and then. But he is traveling in Rome, I hear." I shrugged. "Besides, Macbeth has a good truce with the Norsemen. Scotland has seen no Viking threat since the year my husband took the throne."

"He and Thorfin have made some peace," Angus agreed, "because Macbeth asks no revenues of Caithness and Sutherland, nor homage of Thorfin. They let each other be, neither friends nor enemies."

"The true threat comes from the south, not the sea," I pointed out. Six years earlier, Macbeth had met Crinan of Atholl in hard battle lasting two full days, until Duncan's fierce, angry father, grandfather to Duncan's three, had been killed. So ended Atholl's threat, bolstering unity among Scotland's mormaers. Just two years after, Earl Siward of Northumbria, uncle to Sybilla's well-defended brood, marched a troop of thousands over the border to meet Macbeth in devastating battle. More of our Scottish warriors had been lost, grieving my husband deeply, and Macbeth took such a wound to the leg that he now limped in cold weather. The Scots had earned victory that day.

"Four years have passed since Siward's Northumbrian troops showed their backs to the Scots," I said. "He came north that year because Malcolm mac Duncan had reached his majority. Macbeth defeated Siward then. Still, I know we should be wary. I know it well."

Angus grunted. "Malcolm mac Duncan has a supporter in King Edward, that would-be confessor—a man who limits himself to sour wine and dry bread, and bears bitterness like a banner, calling it saintliness." He spat on the ground. "A boy fostered in that court and raised up to be a warrior will nurse hatred for the man who defeated his father. Though Malcolm's own life was spared by Macbeth's generosity," he added, with a glance for me, "now he is older. With Edward's troops and ships at his call, we will stay on guard, always."

"Malcolm will learn that he cannot breach Scotland, and should stay south and well away, where my husband banished him."

"Banishments exist on parchment, and borders are just turf, water, or rock. When we see longships on the water, we are alert, and that is the way of it. So Mother Enya must entertain several guests this day."

"She will not let you in. She never does."

"Standing about suits us," he replied. With Conn and Anselan, we walked over the boggy expanse of turf leading to the little cove where the witch of Colbin lived. "When King Macbeth returns from Rome, we cannot tell him that we let his queen go about alone. He should be back soon enough from seeing the holy father in Rome, I think," Angus added.

"Within a fortnight, if the messages we had from the merchant ships coming in to Banff were correct. They said he made his way to a port in the Low Countries and expected to sail back to Scotland from there." I slowed to admire the boundless gray sea and sky above it, where high clouds rode the swift breezes of late summer. I set a hand to my brow, where my veil blew back, and watched.

I saw the longships then—three, four, far out. A beautiful, lethal sight.

But Thorfin, and Macbeth, were away. A few months earlier, Macbeth had sailed from Scotland to go on pilgrimage, something no Scottish king had ever done before him. He was still gone, having traveled at the invitation of the newly elected Pope Leo IX.

The reasons for Macbeth's journey were multiple—personal and kingly. Leo, a Frankish pope, was keen to host a meeting of kings and key leaders, and he invited Macbeth and others, including Thorfin of

Orkney, to Rome. This pope, we heard, dreamed of unity among leaders in the West—though privately some said he wanted coin and support for his own ends, for he plotted to dismiss the powerful Eastern Church, centered at Constantinople, from Rome's protective mantle.

"Little of that is Scotland's concern just now," Macbeth had said, after reading the parchment delivered by foreign messengers come a long way to reach Britain, Scotland, and the Viking countries. "But I will go, for my own reasons more than the pope's."

He had departed Scotland's shore in April, a king and his entourage in a wide merchant ship of a hundred oars, carrying fifty armed and armored housecarls and a dozen Culdees—Drostan went too, as did Father Osgar and other priests from the monasteries at Scone, Deer, Saint Andrews, and Loch Leven, which was a favorite holy center for Scotland's king and queen. With a guard of several ships, they would travel south over the water past Britain and deep into foreign rivers that would conduct their party closer to Rome.

Though on holy pilgrimage, he brought with him the garments of a pilgrim for days when he reached holy sites: a simple woven tunic and cloak, with the seashell badge, a walking staff, and plain shoes. When he left, he carried with him a small sack with the earth of Scotland tied snug and kept in his belt pouch. That way he would not leave Scotland entirely.

He left the rest of Scotland in my hands as sole regent. Mine it was to see to the welfare of the people and the land, and I had done so for months, with the help of a few trusted mormaers and thanes. Within a peaceful land, the challenges were those of benefit and trade, and small disputes. I even sat moot courts in Lothian and Moray, though I disliked passing judgment, but matters had to be decided. In one place, a thane had pledged his daughter to marry two men, and both now pressed for her hand. I let her decide. She took the quiet one, and I fined her father a dozen cows to be given to the loud one.

Be strong, my mother had once told me, and I relied on that advice.

I had Lulach's help as well, in Macbeth's absence. My son had grown tall and handsome in his eighteenth year, proud to be among the king's elite guards—his stepfather required that Lulach learn all the roles a warrior and warlord might play—and he showed the promise of a prince in his responsibilities of late. I was pleased with my treasure, my only child.

Another son had been born at Elgin near our year's anniversary as monarchs, after hours of steady pain yet an easy birth, with Bethoc my calm and competent womb-woman. She had learned much under Catriona's mentoring. The boy had his father's blue eyes and black hair like Bodhe, and was called Farquhar for my brother; Ferchar in the Gaelic, "very dear one." In his second year, he was quick lost to a winter's chill and fever. He lies in a hillside near Kincardine and Lanfinnan.

Heaven, and Catriona's herbs and efforts, blessed us with another son after that: Cormac, delicate as a fairy child. He suffered from the moment of his hard birth to his quiet death six months later, and I suffered every moment with him. That grief made ruts in my heart ever after. He is with his brother inside that green hill, and whenever I pass that place on our way on royal progress, I pray they are not cold there, or lonely, but play like the fairy ilk in the hill, or with angels. Innocent babes go fast to heaven, and do not linger in purgatory until Judgment Day with we sinful ones.

No doubt history will say the *mulier bona Macbeth,* the good wife of Macbeth, was barren. Some will wonder that a powerful Celtic king did not set his unsatisfactory wife aside, as custom goes, to find another mate to continue his line. But they will reason that Macbeth needed the bloodline of his *mulier bona* to secure his claim to the throne. In part, that was true; but we suited, we two, and knew it well.

Before Macbeth left for Rome, we dedicated a parcel of my Fife land with grazing rights to the monastery of Saint Serf's at Loch Leven, in exchange for prayers said in perpetuity for the souls of our children. Then he left for Rome, intending the larger world to see that the King of Scots was powerful, godly, and generous: let our enemies take note. For himself, he sought private penance and absolution from the Holy Father.

Since the deaths of his small sons, Macbeth took increasing solace in his faith and in extended prayer. He spent more hours with Father

Osgar, now his private priest, and spent hours conferring with the bishops he had the right to appoint in Scotland. Tortured within by his blackest sins—the murders of his first cousins, Gilcomgan and Duncan, who had left small fatherless children—Macbeth feared that he had invited the sorrow of having no surviving child of his own.

"Much of the fault is mine," I told him once. "You married rue, after all."

"Sorrow and life go hand in hand," Macbeth reminded me.

INSIDE ENYA's house, I settled beside her at the fire, the sweet, musky peat smoke wafting up to the roof draft, with the door gapped open for air. Enya had sent her servant, a simple woman called Muirne, efficient and nonquestioning, outside to tend to the kitchen garden. I had brought my friend a length of good woven wool, which she spread over her lap.

"I have too many of these blankets, but I will take another, for I am sometimes cold in my elder days. But where are my gifts from Rome?" This she often asked, a teasing of sorts. "I want southern gold, and holy water blessed by this Leo of Rome. I am less of a pagan in my elder years," she added, "just to be safe."

"I expect Macbeth home by next month, Mother Enya. And when Thorfin returns, he, too, will have remembered you."

"He is back," she said. "And brought me only green glass cups and some wine."

Mother Enya and I had forged a friendship in those years, and I visited her as often as I could for companionship and lessons. Orkney's support of his cousin of Moray and Scotland fostered a peaceful relationship with the Norwegian and Danish Vikings as well. Enya enjoyed fine treatment from Moray and Orkney, for not only was she elderly and knowledgeable of mysteries, she linked cultures and generations. Yet she refused Macbeth's offer of a fine house in Moray, with stone walls and a garden, and servants to do for her. She wanted her own little house, one servant to help her in her elder years, and a cow, for hers had died.

"King Macbeth will be home sooner than you know," Enya said then. "I saw it myself last night. Go get water and a bowl. Hurry, girl!" Eyes twinkling, she gestured.

I did, and she tossed kindling onto the hearth, and we waited. Brightness leaped, and the smooth water gleamed. I closed my eyes, breathed. Enya droned a chant, tossed fragrant herbs on the fire; lavender, though it made me sad, also brought clarity.

"There, I see him," she whispered.

Looking, I saw water, flames. "I do not see anything today."

"Fah, your head is elsewhere, since he made you both queen and king in his stead these months. Let that go, and remember what I have told you."

By looking in water or flames, or even just closing her eyes, Mother Enya could see what was happening at the same moment in another place. This, along with other secrets, she had taught me. I knew how to use breath, quiet, and desire to open that mystical window. "Know this," she would say, finger jabbing the air. "Magic, mundane matters, dark mayhem—they are all the same, beneath it all. The difference is what we think, whether we fear or welcome these elements. If we are caught fast in the threads of the world's fabric, like a spider on a web, we will see the web itself, and not the magic that made it. But when we draw back, ah, the whole of it is there," she often said. "Look past the surface of the water, the yellow of the flame, and you will see the magic itself."

Now I nodded. "What do you see, Mother Enya?"

She leaned forward. "Ships sailing. A man upon the deck, looking homeward. He is nearer than you think. A day, a little more. He will be here." She paused. "Other ships, too, come over the water."

"There were Viking ships out past the bay when we came here."

"Thorfin." She did not sound surprised. "But this is Macbeth I see. Your husband stands beside the mast, watching for the shores of home."

My heart turned a little to hear it, for I had missed him deeply, especially in the solitary nights. His long journey had such natural risks that I would remain concerned until I saw him solid before me. "What else can you tell me?"

"I see the cliffs and sands of Britain. He comes north even now."

"I expect he will go to the firth near Dun Edin." Recently Macbeth had rebuilt the old fortress on its immense rock overlooking a firth where trade ships came and went.

"A king might go there," Enya said dismissively. "The man sails for home."

"What of the Viking ships I saw today? Thorfin and Macbeth have a truce."

"They do." She frowned. "I think several warboats will come over the water to Moray. And you, Queen Rue, must act. I sent for you today to tell you so. It is up to you if your king sets foot on Scottish soil again."

A chill came over me. "Mother Enya—"

"Out, now." She stood to usher me through the door. "Hurry, girl!"

With mounting dread, I urged my men to leave the cove quickly. As we rode along the beach, two men came toward us over the sand— Vikings, by the look of them, their trews and tunics distinctive, as were their helms and armor. Clearly they had come from the direction of the cove, for their footsteps on sand led back to a ten-oared birlinn, where other men waited. They, too, were armed.

Immediately, my guards circled their horses around me, hands clapped over sword hilts. We had an archer with us, too, ready to snatch bow and arrow if needed. I reined in and watched the men walking toward us.

"The Raven-Feeder," Angus said warily.

I backed my horse a few steps, not eager to see Thorfin Sigurdsson. I had never forgotten my first encounter with him, and still bore the indelible blot of a child's grudge and fear.

"You two take the queen away," Angus ordered his brother and Anselan in a low tone. "Northmen on foot are no challenge for us," he told the others confidently. Conn turned the head of my horse, but as we passed a dune, I looked over my shoulder. What I saw made me pull up on the reins.

"Hold," I said, and against their will, the men paused. We watched as Angus and the other guards rode along the sand toward the two men, intending to stop them from coming near Scotland's queen. Still Thorfin came boldly on, and suddenly—whether they spoke, or some subtle threat was made—swords were drawn. With my two guards thudding after me, I turned my horse to ride back to try to stop the bloodshed, for mine was the authority over guards and usurpers.

Flashing swords, hurtling horsemen, and then suddenly, abruptly, Thorfin raised his arm, palm flattened outward, his black cloak billowing, and my men drew up. Stopped, all of them, as if commanded. Thorfin's gesture and manner intimidated—yet it was more than that, more subtle. His gaze alone seemed sharp enough to bore straight through us.

I stopped, too, and stared, my heart pounding. I had never seen anything quite like this. Had he summoned fireballs, I could not have been more startled. We all obeyed. Even the horses stilled, snorted.

Often it was said that Thorfin Raven-Feeder had a touch of wizardry to him, but I had never seen proof. His grandmother admitted to me that she had taught him some magic, and I saw true power in the simple gesture he made. Suddenly I was sure that the Raven-Feeder had used more than Viking sea power to sink ten or more of King Duncan's ships.

My guards gathered their wits and raised swords again. In answer, the tall Viking behind Thorfin showed part of his sword blade in its sheath.

"Hold!" I called loudly, and rode forward. "Jarl Thorfin."

"Queen Gruadh," he replied smoothly. "You and I must talk. Get down."

Ignoring his order, I glanced past him, recognizing his comrade as Ketill Brusisson, who gave me a somber nod. "We will talk here, before my guards," I said.

Thorfin grabbed the bridle of my horse and led me away, though my men drew blades and came after us. Once again Thorfin raised his hand in that stern warning gesture, and this time I gestured too, so that my guards subsided, glowering. Ketill stood with them; Angus, at least, knew he could be trusted.

Thorfin walked the horse with me astride farther down the beach, where the water lapped at the horse's hooves, and the rushing waves would muffle conversation. "Are you frightened, Lady?" he asked, pausing to look up, his hand still on the bridle.

I felt angry, though it was not the sparking fury of my youth, but rather the steady heat of a woman slow to forgive. "I am no longer a child, nor small queen of Moray, to be frightened by you," I said. "I am rightful Queen of Scots, and you are standing on my shore. It is you who should be wary."

"Queen, and regent in your husband's absence." He had a smugness about him with a cruel edge to it, and I could not easily decipher him.

"What do you want here? Do you think to take Scotland before Macbeth returns? Is that why you have longships in the bay, to bring your war bands onshore?"

"You are wrong," he replied. We spoke Gaelic, for I had no Norse. "I returned a few weeks ago from Rome, where I saw your husband. I have a message for you."

I wanted to know more. "What message?"

"He fares well and will return within days. He impressed Rome and the foreign leaders as a good and generous monarch. When he entered the city, he scattered Scottish silver and gold like stars. A magnanimous gesture that will be recorded as such, and he knew it when he did so. Today I seek you out on my own account," Thorfin continued, fingers tight on my horse's fitting strap, "to suggest our alliance, you and me."

I laughed outright. "Allies, us? Not since the day you ordered me stolen from my home. Not since the day my father risked his life and others died to take me back again."

"Years ago," he said impatiently. "We will make a truce now."

"Or you will attack? Your ship carries a dragon's head today. War, it says to me." I leaned slightly back, as if to avoid whatever spell he might cast—I knew Enya's ways, had some of them myself now, though I felt my own modest skills no match for his. With one hand, I touched my shoulder where my faded blue spiral sat, and in my mind, asked for protection in his sinister presence. *Cuidich mi a Bhride, help me O Brigid.*

"War?" He gave a scoffing laugh. "I do not want Scotland for my own. Listen well. Saxon ships are approaching. We counted three. They are not merchants."

"We had no word of that." I wondered if the Raven set some trap for us. Gripping the reins, I looked out toward the water.

"Word came to me. My longboats patrol the North Sea routes to protect our interests." He gestured toward the water. "Nothing escapes our watch on the sea."

I watched the ocean, seeing only the graceful curves of the Orkney ships, far out. "Why would Malcolm mac Duncan sail this far north?"

"King Macbeth is not in Scotland," Thorfin said. "The son of Duncan knows this. If Malcolm should sink the king's ship out in the firth, in full sight of his people, and then invade Scotland, he could take the kingship." He looked at me intently. "Only a queen and her untested son hold Scotland now, so what is to stop him?"

I heard a sneer in his voice, but realized it was not for me, and I knew he told the truth. "Then Ceann Mór must be stopped." Big Head, I said, using the name Malcolm had acquired from the Scots. I pulled to turn my horse's direction, but Thorfin kept hold of the rein. "Let go."

"Malcolm Canmore has gained in strength and cunning," he said, "and now has the favor of the English king, who has an army to lend for conquering Scotland. This warrior is not to be dismissed—he has been raised by Scotland's enemies with the ambition to take Scotland's throne as his right."

That was my doing. Malcolm lived now because of me. "I can summon Macbeth's army quickly by sending runners out. But Malcolm comes by sea, as does Macbeth. Our warships are kept at Banff—too far, now, for this."

"So long as Malcolm is on the sea, he is in the realm of Vikings," Thorfin said.

"You would offer Viking help?"

"I do not wish to see young Malcolm as king in Scotland, any more than I did his father. But the son is not the fool the father was. Remember that." He released the bridle and stepped back.

"What of Macbeth, and his ship?" I gathered my reins.

"The Vikings will keep the sea. The Scots keep Scotland. Go," he said brusquely, then turned. Beckoning to Ketill, the two of them returned to the waiting boat.

My guards and I rode hard for Elgin.

Two banners fluttered and snapped in the dawn winds: Moray's blue silk sewn with silver stars, and the red lion on yellow of the monarchs of Scotland, were tied to spears hoisted high above my head, where I sat my horse. I had twelve hundred warriors behind me, two hundred horse and a thousand foot, with dozens of equestrian warriors arranged to either side, there at the head of that force. We gathered on the high cliff tops of Moray near Burghead, where my first husband had been burned in a tower eighteen years earlier.

His son sat beside me now. Lulach was tall and fair, with the height and clean-sculpted features of my kin, along with his true father's fair coloring and genial nature in good company. My amiable boy had grown into a fierce, lean warrior, well-trained by his stepfather and as yet untested. The last troubled me that day. But a prince could not sit back in the ranks by his mother's whim.

Others with me included the men of Fife who had supported me for years, especially so in my months as regent—Ruari, Angus, Conn, and Brendan, the sons of Fergus; Finn, and Lachlann. Leading our Moray men were Lulach and Anselan. Not with us were Giric, Mungo, and Drostan, who had gone with Macbeth's large entourage to Rome. If we faced battle on these shores—as I prayed would not happen—the lot of us were strong together.

The winds whipped cool as we waited on the headland, and the dawn sky was colored as delicate as the inner curve of a seashell. As the sun climbed, seagulls skimmed and soared over the water; I saw a cormorant or two far out, and in the distance, dolphins in the firth, and a few seals near the rocks. Boats, too: the distinct shapes of the Orkney vessels could be seen, moving to and fro across the firth.

Though it was chill so near the ocean, I was warm enough in my heavy gear, including a padded tunic over my gown, under the mail armor Finn had once shaped for me, and the helmet, which I now slid on. From the high headland, the wide view swept ocean and sky, as well as the glens and hills of various regions. They say that from the Burghead promontory looking toward land, one can see seven regions from Orkney to Moray, all in a glance. That morning, it was misted beauty in all directions.

Gray clouds scudded overhead as we waited, shifting in our saddles. I dismounted to walk about and speak to some of the men. Repeatedly I asked Ruari mac Fergus if any messengers had returned of the several gone out along the coast to seek news. I paced, growing anxious.

Rain pattered the earth now, tapped on armor, pocked the surface of the sea. I went to the cliffside to stand there in the whipping winds. The drear weather and endless waiting made me feel humbled, and it keenly reminded me that a power larger than any of us always prevailed. No one could presume the day's outcome. I could only pray, and recite blessing chants to myself to wish safety for all.

Eventually more ships moved into sight, and I raised a hand to my brow. Several longships arrowed from the North Sea and outer firth toward our shore. Thorfin's Viking ships were painted red and black, bearing the dragon head prows that signaled menace. Graceful and awful birds on the water, they were, oars up and square sails, yellow and black stripes, filling. Along the side of each vessel, round shields were strung like the bright beads of a necklace.

The longship in the lead carried Thorfin's raven banner. Six were huge boats with more than a hundred men each on their decks, and the rest were smaller, the total count of men formidable. To any who met them out on that water, their warlike purpose would be clear. This time, they sailed on Scotland's behalf.

Ruari and Finn joined me near the cliff edge. "Saxon ships are coming along the coast of Scotland," Finn said. "Word is spreading fast. I sent men south, as you asked, to carry messages to the mormaers of Buchan, Mar, the Mearns, and so on. They will have seen the Saxon ships by now too. We have local boats in the water, running close to the coast." He pointed, and I looked down toward the base of the cliffs to see agile birlinns but ten or twelve oars each.

"What other news?" I asked.

"See for yourself," Finn answered. "There." Out on the water, the Orkney ships were deep in the firth now, and coming swiftly toward the rocky cliffsides. Much of Burghead's shoreline consisted of white sand, though there were high cliffs like the one where we stood. "Thorfin will hide his fleet in the inlets and coves tucked along the shoreline. He is positioning now. Look." He pointed.

Within range of the beach, some of the Viking ships slipped into the great drape of rocky curtain that made up the cliffsides. When they lowered their bright striped sails, they all but vanished.

I peered outward again. "Far out, there is a ship alone, not a Viking boat but a trade vessel. There are smaller ships alongside it. Macbeth," I said suddenly.

Ruari nodded. "Likely so, but too far out to tell for certain. A wide-bellied knorr like that one, a merchant ship sailing this far north, past the Banff port and into the Moray firth—that boat will carry Macbeth. The Vikings, and Malcolm Canmore, will see it too."

My heart pounded, dread and excitement. "Thorfin could still trick us."

"We take the chance," Ruari answered simply.

Out on the ocean, where the waves lapped, roughened by the passing storms, we watched as the knorr vessel and its attendant boats entered the firth, miles yet from our coast. Then, from the south and behind the merchant vessel, I could see other ships, sleek and dark shapes through the blur of rain.

"Saxons," Finn said. "Their longboats have plainer curves, plain sails, without the artistry of the Viking boats. Saxons for sure. Those would be commanded by young Malcolm." He glanced at us.

Suddenly the scope of it came together for me—Malcolm's scheme, Macbeth's chances. "Canmore and his fleet must have waited for Macbeth's ship, and now pursue him into the firth to trap him there. But none of them know that the Orkney Vikings wait in the coves and inlets."

We could lose all we had, all we loved, heritage and pride and our very selves. I felt danger keen as a blade then. Turning, I began to run, my cloak snapping in the wind. Ruari and Finn went with me down the slope of the headland toward the scores of men waiting, ready, on the meadow beyond the dunes.

"To the beach," I shouted. "We must be seen in force! Malcolm mac Duncan must know that no matter what happens on the sea today, he will not set foot on this land!"

Somehow I found the courage to call out, to order them, to be a warrior queen for them. Duncan's pup could not be permitted to come ashore—even if he succeeded out on the ocean. Rank upon rank, we collected, and moved past the dunes toward the white sand that edged the firth. I would not think beyond that, would not dwell on the risks.

Soon I sat my horse beside Lulach, all of us gathered in a mass that stretched along the beach, representing the might of Moray and Scotland. From the water we would be seen as rows and rows of ready warriors. Once, years ago, we had gathered on a field to show our strength when King Duncan came to quell Macbeth. Now I headed a similar display for his son's benefit.

If Lulach was nervous or fearful, he did not show it, but sat his horse stiffly, set his jaw, and steeled his eye, waiting motionless with the rest of us. My heart swelled with pride to see him like that, the first true budding of the king he could one day become. Then I turned my attention back to the sea.

The longships and other boats were easily visible from where we sat on the beach. Macbeth's wide knorr sailed deeper into the firth, with Malcolm's seven ships in pursuit. I saw what appeared to be sheets of rain, then realized it was a hail of arrows arcing from one of Malcolm's ships toward the merchant vessel. Another cluster launched and fell, and we watched, made helpless by distance, but for our display of power, a dare to Malcolm, a boon for Macbeth.

Just as Malcolm's ships chased the knorr and its sister ships, and seemed about to overtake the large one from three sides, the Viking longboats left their inlets and niches among the cliff rocks. They glided out to intersect the path of the Saxon ships.

Angus hooted. "I can almost hear Malcolm cursing," he said. "He did not expect swift dragon boats to be waiting for him. He only thought to ambush Macbeth's vessel!"

"Thorfin sank his father's ships," Ruari said, beside me. "Malcolm will do well to remember that."

"He is clever enough to know risk from danger," I replied.

"And sensible, too," Lulach said. "The Saxon ships are already turning around."

Out on the bay, the rain of arrows had stopped, and the Saxon ships curved a path through the water as they began to turn. Several of Thorfin's ships moved after the Saxon boats, chasing them out toward the North Sea. One by one, Malcolm's ships disappeared around the headland.

"Turned tail," Angus said with satisfaction. "Thorfin will chase them all the way back to England, and will patrol in their outer waters—as we will—to make certain they do not slip out to head northward again. He is no fool, is Thorfin Raven-Feeder."

"Nor is Malcolm mac Duncan. He will return," Lulach said, and glanced at me. "Next time he will come by land, now that he knows we have solid friends in the Orkneyings. And he will wait, knowing that King Macbeth will be on alert for him. But sooner or later, Malcolm will find a way to breach Scotland's borders. He will not give up, if it takes his lifetime."

My son had a king's cleverness, even so young. He knew, as did we all, that the wolf at our gates was determined to find its way inside. I nodded, silent, aware that I had brought on this threat—I more than anyone.

Now one boat sailed for the shore, with Orkney ships running alongside and behind. From my saddle perch on that strip of sand, I could see the men on the deck of the knorr. One of them, taller than the rest, golden-haired, lifted a hand in salute as they came closer. The wind was up, the rain soft, and strong waves carried them toward the shore.

I stepped the horse forward until the water foamed and swirled around its hooves. Then I removed my helmet, hair blowing free, a beacon to be seen. And I waited.

Chapter Thirty

ANNO DOMINI 1058

DUN ELGIN

Last night I dreamed of a stone citadel, a magnificent fortress on a green hill beneath a summer sky. Inside were marble halls and bright glass windows like sliced jewels. Yet the place seemed no marvel to me, but home and haven, and familiar. As I opened a polished door to the expansive great hall, a man I love dearly sat in a fine chair, warming his feet beside the hearth. He stood, drew forth another chair for me. A smile, a sparkle of blue eyes, and he reached out his hand in welcome, a longed-for reunion. Through an open window, I noticed black smoke and flames in the glen, where a wooden fortress was burning to its foundation. Suddenly I was there, not in the hall, and I ran frightened through darkness and smoke. I heard screams, and the sound of steel clashing—

I wake on a startle, a gasp, alone in my bed.

Fear, presage, yearning—my dreams still bring such to me, at times so vivid that I am grateful to wake. Sometimes I resist sleep in case of those dreams.

Rising, I go shivering to the small privy connected to my bedchamber, and return to break the skim of ice on the water in my washing bowl. Then I contemplate red or blue: my sorrel red gown is warm and lined with otter fur, but I have worn it often of late. Blue it will be, then, a dark woad color, worn over a tight-sleeved undergown pale as cream. I tug the undersleeves down to show their embroidery and slide on my rings: the little silver with a pearl that a tragic queen once gave to me, a gold twist set with a garnet, another of silver and crystal. They glint on my fingers.

Comfort exists in the smallness of routine, especially when unwanted thoughts loom. These several days, as I have contemplated my story, I am reluctant to reveal all of the events. Certain memories cut deep, and others are too private.

Finella arrives, surly and sloe-eyed, to braid my hair, which has a bronze burnish as yet, and no silver strands. A pity to cover its gleam with a veil, but a widow and a former queen cannot go about like a virgin girl with a bare head but for a ribbon fillet. The silk is creamy and soft as Finella drapes it just so, wrapped about the head, under the chin, draped over the shoulders. A polished steel mirror shows how the color flatters my complexion.

I pause—my skin is smooth yet, cheekbones high, jaw still firm, with just a hint of fine lines beside the lips, where sorrows have taken their toll, and at the eyes, where joys are counted. My eyes remind me of my father's, pale blue with hints of silver.

In the brisk early chill, I wait as Finella drapes an indoor cloak over my shoulders, a soft weaving of plaid in cream, brown, purple. I attach the pin myself, the circular triple spiral that Macbeth often wore, blessed by a princess and a witch. When my handmaid opens the door, I glide through, hems whispering over the floor.

In the great hall—not the grand chamber of my dream, but whitewashed wooden walls hung with embroidered panels—a young man I have never seen sits at the table with Drostan. Both rise, the boy spilling porridge from his bowl. His spoon clatters away, and he picks it up.

"Another messenger has arrived from Malcolm mac Duncan, king in the south," Drostan says. The boy greets me, and I nod for him to sit and eat. He crams himself with coddled eggs, dried beef, a buttery porridge. Two tall hounds lope over to the table to greet me. Faithful Diarmid, who belonged to my husband, quietly nudges his woolly head under my hand, while the other, a year-old pup named Flann, leggy and gray and always curious, laps up spilled food.

"What does Malcolm send this time?" I ask. "More silk? Sweetmeats?"

"Lady Gruadh," the boy says, "the king sent me with a gift of figs for you."

"I am amazed they survived your hearty appetite," I say.

"And a written message," Drostan adds. He hands me the parchment, still sealed by a glob of bloodred wax.

The message is in black ink, the script in Latin. " 'Malcolm mac Duncan, rex Scotorum, sends felicitations to Lady Gruadh of Elgin,' " I read. I hand it back to Drostan in disgust. *Rex Scotorum?* Self-declared king is all he is! And to him, I am merely Lady of Elgin? *Tcha!*"

Drostan draws me aside so that we may speak in private. "Malcolm informs you as a courtesy, since you hold lands in Fife, that he has just claimed Fife as his, now that your cousin MacDuff is dead. He is moving his garrison into Dun Abernethy."

"Damn both their souls, MacDuff and MacDuncan, for what they have wrought."

Drostan sighs. "Malcolm repeats his earlier messages to you that your son is no true king of Scotland, and that he will be forced to yield. He suggests again that you consent to marriage with him." The monk looks up from the page. "If you refuse again, he urges you to bid farewell to all you care about, and clear out to a convent."

"All the priories for women are south, in England, where I will not go. Besides, the snows prevent much travel now. And prevent Malcolm from coming here."

"Until the mountain passes are open," Drostan says.

I snatch back the letter, peruse it again, refold it, and touch its corner to the table: *tap, tap*. Thoughtful, I glance at Drostan. "No silk? Only figs?"

"Rue," Drostan says, "give me permission to send a note of this to Lulach."

"He is always on his guard," I say. "Macbeth's best are with him. And Lulach is coming to Elgin—we had word from him last week. He will be here as soon as weather permits, making his way back from Iona after—" Sighing, I fold my arms. "When Big Head hears what we have plotted, and what my son and Macbeth's men have done, he will not send silks or marriage proposals, but an army against me for treason."

"He may indeed," Drostan agrees. "At the very least, he will ruin Macbeth's name now through rumors, and permanently in the annals and chronicles. You know that."

"I do. And he knows that I can summon men myself and meet him in armor."

"No doubt he gambles you will not do that again," he replies.

The king's lanky messenger is still eating robustly. Lads that age are always hungry, and the sight tugs at my heart. I would have had two younger sons near his age now, but for fate. With my own hand, I pour him a cup of the heated, spiced ale that steams fragrant in a jug.

Dermot the bard enters the room, downs a cup of the same ale, and takes up his harp. A lovely sound fills the air. Droston leaves the room with the young messenger, who will return with no reply from Lady Gruadh, who stubbornly calls herself queen dowager.

Bethoc, who manages my household now, enters to scold Finella, for there was a spill of the dried herbs and petals used to freshen the linens. They depart the room to sweep it up and find the culprit. I am suspecting one of the cats.

I settle with a cup of warm ale, the dogs curl at my feet, and we listen to the bard's melody. The usurper's message has brought back pain and anger just months old. Music is no solace for that.

SEVEN SUMMERS passed from the day Malcolm Canmore's ships turned tail, to the night I saw him next. Only four years passed from that encounter until Macbeth saw him again. On that meeting all the rest turned, as if caught in a whirlpool.

I was helping to make and test new beer, batches of golden stuff, and laughing with Bethoc and Aella, who had come to Elgin to visit from her home in a thanage in Buchan, where she and Giric lived with their two daughters. I giggled like a girl with my dearest friends, not queen and ladies, but three friends reunited. Our attention was on whether the servants were slacking off, or had the same buzzing in their heads that we did; and whether we should break egg whites into bowls for the benefit of Aella's tall, dark-haired daughters, who at nine and seven years were already asking whom they might marry. We were laughing on the very day, far to the south, that Malcolm Canmore and his troops stepped over the border into Scotland.

That was in July of the year of our Lord 1054, on the Feast of the Seven Sleepers: a holy day of miracles, it is said, when seven ancient Christian martyrs were released from a tomb in which they slept, trapped for centuries yet still alive, as is told in the *Acta Sanctorum*. Now, in Scotland, the Feast of the Seven Sleepers is known as the day Birnam Wood came to Dunsinnan.

I heard of this battle from my husband himself, who survived, praise heaven. He brought the news north to Elgin—fled, some unfairly said. Malcolm had encamped his troops in Birnam Wood near Dunkeld, where a waterfall rushes into a stream. The forestland is so dense there that, between water and wood, the sounds of sly men cannot easily be heard.

And so Malcolm's men fooled Macbeth's guard by devious means when they approached Macbeth's own encampment between Dunkeld and Dunsinnan. In the darkness before dawn, the Saxons disguised themselves by draping branches and leaves to cover heads and shoulders as they hunched along like foxes and weasels to ambush the Scottish guard, bringing on a swift surprise attack.

Malcolm Canmore had attained the maturity of a tested warrior when he brought King Edward's army into Scotland that year. The only Scots who would support him with arms and loyalty were those who lived so close to the border that they were more Sassenach than Scottish. On a hillside in sweltering heat and unrelenting sunshine, the two armies met so ferociously that by day's end, many had cast off armor and garments to fight unencumbered and half-naked in the manner of the ancient Celts. Clusters of men fought on, exhausted, while the rest lay dead around them on that bloody hill.

The annals record that Malcolm mac Duncan routed Macbeth and sent him fleeing northward to the Moray mountains. Truth is, both leaders were sore wounded, and retreated with their ragged, devastated forces. With no victory for either side, Macbeth conceded to Malcolm mac Duncan the lands that had belonged to Duncan, old Malcolm, and Crinan of Atholl. By doing so, Macbeth wished to gain peace for Lowland Scotland, which had suffered greatly from Malcolm's persistence. Before wounds were healed, the half-Saxon, half-Scottish warrior was already gathering more men to replace the army he had lost.

Gaining his kinsmen's land and some leeway, Malcolm called himself King of Scots. But he could not force the steadfast priests, the keepers of the stone, the crown, and red mantle, to bend to his will. He was not crowned at Scone, though we heard he railed on about it.

Besides, by decree of his own father, I was the crowner.

And so Scotland was split like an apple.

Macbeth went north beyond Moray's mountain barrier and stayed there, wounded himself. He was twice Malcolm's age, yet he had held his own. But he took a severe blow to the cheekbone under the eye socket, splitting the lid and swelling the eye, and we feared he was half-blinded.

Catriona came to him at Elgin. The year of his crowning, she had married the thane of Kinlossie, and now they had a boisterous son, and a daughter, too, this last a simple child. Some called that gentle soul a changeling, but her mother loved her whether God or the fairies brought her. Catriona offered healing potions and gentle hands, and together she and Bethoc nursed Macbeth. Once the swelling reduced, he regained some skewed sight. The lid was scarred half-shut, and unpredictable shadows afflicted his vision. Yet as soon as he could, he returned to the practice yard to retrain his balance and learn to judge distance and depth in combat.

"Ironic," I told him and Lulach one afternoon, "that you took the same blow from Malcolm that you gave his father." I pressed one of Bethoc's cooling poultices to his eye.

"A back knock from the sword hilt? I put up my shield too late to stop it," he said.

"Not irony," Lulach said then. "That particular blow was meant as revenge. Mark it well." He seemed to understand young MacDuncan. They were of an age.

For three years we kept to Moray and the Highland provinces. Messages went back and forth swiftly, and mormaers were regular visitors wherever we were. Throughout Scotland, Macbeth was still regarded as true King of Scots, and young Malcolm the usurper. With that loyalty strong about us, we used others' eyes to watch Malcolm's every step, or nearly so.

The wolf was inside the gates now, drooling and seething as he watched the inner keep, where his chief prey stayed safe.

Chapter Thirty-One

Here is what the annals will say of Macbeth's kingship: very little. Seventeen years of plenty and peace for Scotland, give or take some strife. We suffered few battles and fewer enemies compared to other reigns. Scotland was brimful: fat cattle on the hillsides, fish in the streams, sheep thick with wool, the bellies of trading ships heavy with goods. Grain crops were golden and larders and byres filled; treasures accumulated, and all prospered, from shepherd to mormaer. Contentment is a thing not often recorded in the annals.

For much of Macbeth's reign, the strength of his reputation and presence and the loyal nature of his alliances protected Scotland as never before. We had respite from decades of wars and conflict. Given more time, he would have attained what he sought for Scotland: more fair-minded laws, and the blending of honored Celtic traditions with the ways of the Church and even the Saxons.

I protested this, arguing to protect the integrity of the old Celtic ways and not mingle them, such as choosing Gaelic over Latin in the documents Drostan wrote out for us so diligently, and maintaining the Sabbath on Saturdays, which the Celts honored and the Romans did not. As for Saxon primogeniture—that I could never accept. Lulach, as Macbeth's blood cousin and the last of Bodhe's line, had full right by old Celtic ways to claim Moray, and the crown of Scotland itself, one day.

"Scotland, its very soul, is threatened by the new manners and laws of the rest of the world," I said. "Do you want us to be Saxon, or Roman, with such ways? As a Celtic king, are you not obligated to fight and resist daily, in large and small ways, in order to preserve the Gaelic nature of your own heritage?"

"What I want," Macbeth told me fiercely, "is for Scotland to survive and prosper. To remain true to its Celtic nature always, but to keep pace with Britain and all the trading countries. Rue, if we insulate ourselves and remain Gaelic, as you prefer, if we do not allow outside influences—then Scotland and her great branches and roots will wither. We cannot desperately cling to our legacies, but must stay magnificent in those aspects."

I subsided, seeing the scope of his goal—not to succumb to other cultures, as I had once feared, but to absorb change heedfully, and grow in power and presence.

In Rome, Macbeth had appealed to Pope Leo for the rights of the Celtic church, which shepherded great flocks with its mix of spirituality and artistry. Gaining a deeper sense of his own faith, Macbeth gave land grants, founded some monasteries and small churches, and made more bishops. He wanted to establish additional chapels and priests in the vasty Highlands, an ambitious goal all on its own. He had met foreign leaders on his travels, and kept contact with some. When Norman knights were banished from England, Macbeth welcomed two, Hugo and Osbern, into his own elite house guard.

"We will do well to have some favor with the Normans, for they will take England one day, if King Edward the Monk does not watch his back," Macbeth told me the day I met these two men. Their lilting, soft-tumbled language, strangely shaped shields, stiff bearing, and precise manners made them an oddity among our rough-edged, brawny Celts. Soon enough, they became comrades with the rest, at first fighting to prove themselves, then teaching what they knew. And so, in that, we Scots expanded.

All this would have continued years into years, but for the banished son of a warrior-king. That young man made it his lifelong goal to take down Macbeth.

In the same year my husband was near blinded, we held a wedding in our household. Lulach, strong and handsome at twenty-one, suffered a fever of yearning for a girl he had met while traveling with his stepfather. Though Lulach was younger than most warriors when they marry, Macbeth knew the alliance was a good and significant one, and he arranged it.

Just after Martinmas, Lulach wed Thorfin's daughter, forging a powerful bond of kinship and loyalty between Moray and Orkney. Ingebjorg Thorfinsdotter shared a name and a sweet face with her mother, and the dark coloring and lean build of her father, in all, lovely. Quiet and given much to prayer, if she had not captivated Lulach when she was seventeen, she might have gone into the Church, for such was her devotion. We held the wedding at Inverness, inviting Orkney guests, and the feasting went on for near a week.

I pined a little, feeling the deep tug as my son moved on in life, his heart elsewhere—as it should be. Ingebjorg's gentle grace added into our household, where Lulach, as prince and retainer, lived as yet. Her dowry to Lulach included chests of Viking silver—coins, dishes, adornments—and Thorfin gave him a fine longship and a hundred cattle brought over on separate ships, lowing and complaining. Several Orkney housecarls joined Lulach's guard, headed by his friend Anselan, Catriona's eldest son, and though we did not enjoy their company at first, once more, we grew and absorbed.

In spring, Mother Enya died quietly while asleep. Thorfin sent word. I had seen her only weeks before, when she had looked into the water for me to speak of what might come. "You will be content one day," she said, and pushed the bowl away. "What more do you need to know but that? Heed your dreams," she added, "for they are your counselors."

Thorfin gave his Irish grandmother a Viking burial, sending her out at dusk in a graceful birlinn, torches blazing, into the little bay whose surf and beauty she had watched for years. When the boat drifted far out, Thorfin's guards sent fire arrows arching after it. She left a gap in my life, wider and deeper than I had thought possible after so many losses.

When I had time to myself, I went to her house, straightened its shelves and folded her things into a chest, then sat there in that peace. She had left her things to me—garments and blankets, herbs in packets and boxes, her box of jewels, the bowl where she poured the scrying water. I missed her deeply, like Ailsa, like Maeve and the others.

Within a year, Ingebjorg gave birth in a bedchamber at Elgin, clutching the linens and making no sound beyond a whimper. A lusty boy, my grandson Malsnechtan, entered our lives that autumn day. He was dark like his mother, and Thorfin and Bodhe, whose blood he combined. Macbeth fondly called him a troll. I loved him on sight, my heart turning full within me.

TREACHERY CAME at night.

We were spending August at Kincardine, our small fortress along the River Dee, not far from the ancient stones at Lanfinnan, where we had once seen three ravens perch. Fate sends signs and portents, then obscures their meaning enough to lure us forward.

They came late, while we slept on a stifling night. The first notice was the slam of arrows into thatch. Fire arrows, for I heard the shouts, and as I scrambled from bed, Macbeth grabbed his tunic and gear and urged me out the door. I grabbed a cloak to throw over my shift, and ran with him. We paused for a moment at a window. Fiery patches burned on the roofs of the outbuildings. Judging by the shouts and chaos in the yard, and by the smoke gathering in the room, the keep was on fire as well. I lingered long enough to see another volley of flaming arrows arching through the darkness, over the high wooden palisade, to embed—*thunk, thunk*—in roofs and walls.

The palisade, too, was on fire now. In that frightening brilliance, I saw Malcolm mac Duncan clear for a moment. He was a big man in his warrior prime at twenty-seven, with thick brown hair like a wild man, a towering height and build, and a scowl I cannot forget. The wolf was not only at our gate—he had near burned it down before we even left our beds.

Macbeth ran up the stairs to look for Lulach, Ingebjorg, and their babies, the boy and now an infant girl. Lulach was leading his family out, and I took my swaddled granddaughter so that Ingebjorg could carry her son. We met Bethoc by the great hall, and we all went out into the night, where smoke was billowing fast. Macbeth and my son ran into the main bailey yard, while Bethoc and I led Ingebjorg and the children toward the shadowed back of the bailey, which the fire had not touched. Leaving them secluded and safer there, I went in search of my husband.

Heat, firelight, smoke, and the burning smell assailed everywhere I turned. Men were shouting, some grabbing buckets of water, servants and housecarls alike. The few horses we kept there—most of the riding horses were kept in a tenanted field—and the other animals, some cows and goats, the chickens and the rest, were being herded and coaxed to the back palisade, where there was a gate, a hill, a forest. It was the best that could be done. Finding our three dogs, among them Macbeth's favorite hound Diarmid, a big gray wolfhound who was a son of Bodhe's dog Cu, I sent them toward Angus, who grabbed them by their leather collars and leashed them.

Then I saw Macbeth, who called orders to scores of men—some to remain and fight the fire, some to snatch weapons and armor and follow him. I ran toward him, and he took my arm.

"You and the others," he said brusquely, "go out through the back postern gate."

"What of you?" I took hold of his sleeve. "You must come with us—"

"I mean to put an end to this." He pushed me onward, but I turned back, suddenly terrified beyond all measure—not for myself, but for him. I put my arms around him, and we stood, tight and silent. Then he pushed me away. "Go, Rue."

I ran toward the relative coolness of the back palisade, and heard Macbeth shouting behind me. Feet pounded after me, and I turned to see Angus and Conn running, sent as our guard. The others—Lulach and Anselan and their men, Macbeth, Giric, Ruari, and all the rest, but for those who were fighting the fire—were gathering at the burning gate, ready to depart in pursuit of Malcolm Canmore and his war band, who had fled into the night.

Much of what followed is a blur to me now.

With Angus and Conn urging us forward to safety, we few escaped burning Kincardine O'Neil, and made our way in the dark down to the river at the ferry crossing. Crowding all of us onto the barge, along with the dogs, we were taken to Constantine mac Artair's fortress at Banchorrie. He was gone when we arrived, already summoned to Kincardine by a fast runner from among Macbeth's housecarls. Banchorrie's guards shepherded us inside, where we were met by Constantine's new wife, a woman younger than me. She provided food, blankets, a place to wash and to rest. That good woman even lent me one of her own tunic gowns and a veil for my head, for I was not dressed properly. I remember the tunic was brown, embroidered in black vines. Somber.

And so we waited through the morning, until we heard that our own riders were coming along the riverbank, while the ferryman's barge was following the track of the water with the wounded upon it. The men entered the gate subdued. I waited in the hall, twisting my fingers anxiously. Ingebjorg paced with her crying infant, Bethoc held Nechtan, and Constantine's wife stayed with us. We were mostly silent, mentioning only mundane things as necessary.

Sitting there, I realized the day was the Feast of the Assumption. Seventeen years ago, Macbeth had killed King Duncan to assume the kingship. "The attack was deliberately plotted for today," I told the others, breaking the quiet. "Malcolm planned his revenge and sought to ruin Macbeth and his family on the anniversary of his father's death." The women stared at me sadly and nodded.

Finally the curtain to the hall drew aside, and my heart filled with hope. Constantine strode across the room, greeted his wife with but a look, and came toward me. His face was lined and grim; Macbeth's uncle was past seventy then, though still a vigorous man. I stood as he approached.

"What news of Macbeth?" I asked.

"He is asking for you, Lady. Come with me. Bethoc," he called, turning. "Your skills are needed." She handed Nechtan to Constantine's wife and came with us. Dread whorled inside me as we hastened through the doorway.

My husband was not in the bailey, though I looked around. I recognized the men there, and they stopped what they were doing—tending to horses, wiping fire soot and blood from their faces. Some watched me in silence. I did not see Lulach, Ruari, or the others. I turned to Constantine, fighting panic, aware something was deeply wrong.

"Macbeth—" I began.

"On the barge, asking for you," he said, and we went out the gate and down a long slope to the riverbank. Through mist and rain, I saw a cluster of men on the barge, and one man seated at their center on the planked deck.

I hurried so fast to gain the barge that someone lifted me onto it before I tripped. Bethoc and Constantine boarded behind me, the vessel dipping slightly, water lapping.

My husband sat on a stool, with Lulach standing beside him, a hand on his shoulder, Ruari to the other side. I breathed out in relief, the burden of fear lifted, until I noticed how somber they all were. How pale and drawn Macbeth's face. Then I realized that Lulach and Ruari were holding him upright, while Finn stood close.

I sank to my knees in a flurry of skirts, and reached out. *"A Dhia!"* I uttered softly, seeing the cloth wrapped wide about his middle and his chest, deep stained with blood on the right side. His chain hauberk had been removed, and he sat now in a bloodied and torn tunic, a cloak over his shoulders. He was shivering, though it was not cold. *"A Dhia!"* I said again, and touched him, arm, shoulder. Face, rough-bearded jaw.

"Rue," he said. His breath was raspy, and both eyes drooped low, the injured eyelid lowest. "We must travel south—get your things. Get the children."

"Ingebjorg?" I glanced in confusion at Lulach, who nodded. "We cannot travel now. Come inside—bring him inside, why are you all waiting on this barge?" My voice rose, frantic. I came to my feet. "Lulach! Ruari—bring him inside, quickly!"

Finn turned. He had been speaking to Bethoc, who gathered her skirts and hastened back to the fortress, no doubt for medicines. "Rue," he said, and took my arm. "We want to bring him inside, but he refuses to be moved."

"Why? What happened?" I looked at Ruari, who had joined us, having given his post to one of the Norman knights, who now buttressed Macbeth where he sat. "Tell me!"

"We chased Malcolm and his men as far as Lanfinnan," Ruari said. "Malcolm brought only a war band to attack Kincardine. There was a skirmish. Macbeth and Malcolm fought. Your cousin MacDuff was there, too—he and Malcolm fought Macbeth, both against the one."

I set a hand to my chest. "What wound did he take?"

"Malcolm's dagger between the ribs," Finn said. "Deep."

"Oh, God." I faltered, but shook off Ruari's hand on my arm. "He is strong. He has survived other wounds, poisoning, too. And you were there to tend him, Finn."

"He took a bad stroke, but he gave as much to Malcolm, and wounded MacDuff sore as well. For a man nearly twice their age, and near blind in one eye now, it is a wonder he was not killed outright—" Finn stopped. "Well. Malcolm and your Fife cousin are wounded, too. They gathered what remained of their force and fled into the hills."

"We sent men after them, but no word as yet. When we headed back to Kincardine, or what is left of it," Ruari said, glancing at Finn, "Macbeth collapsed. Only then did we learn how severe his injury was. He did not admit to it at first."

"I cauterized, stitched, soon as I could," Finn went on. "But I cannot repair what is torn inside. A lung, I think, is damaged. Perhaps more. There is a chance he could heal. Always a chance." His voice, expression were flat; he did not think so.

My own breathing was too fast, too tight. "He can recover. Bring him inside."

"He refuses. He says we must all go south," Constantine said.

"Why? To pursue Malcolm? He is in no condition to—"

"Rue, listen." Finn took me a little aside. "Talk to him. Convince him to rest here. He will not last long if he stays on this barge. I am sorry to say it," he added.

I broke from his grasp, sank again to kneel by my husband. "Macbethad," I said gently, taking his hand. "We will travel when you are rested and well—"

"Do not argue," he said, sounding strong, firm. Had it not been for the blood, the rasp in his breath, I might have thought him only tired. "We go to Scone. Now. Quick."

"Why?" I asked softly. "You cannot pursue Malcolm now, not yet."

"Not that." He reached out to cup my head, pull me close, so that only we two could hear the other. Near enough to kiss, but we whispered fervent. "We must go to Scone, and crown Lulach there."

My fingers tightened on his wrist. "But—"

"Listen," he rasped. "You have the right as crowner. We must witness your son made king, tonight and in secret, before Malcolm can discover it."

I sobbed, shook my head, denying what was left unsaid: he had little time.

He pressed his brow to mine. "If I die in the north," he said, "and Lulach is not a crowned king, you both are in danger. You could be hunted and killed. Lulach's children could be slaughtered for their bloodline. Or Malcolm may force you to marry him, as victor, if he cannot eliminate you. . . ." He caught his breath, exhaled. "Tell the others for me. You are queen. See it done." He let me go and sat back, closed his eyes.

I stood. The others had glanced away to give us privacy—perhaps thinking we whispered the last parting words of a loving husband and wife, rather than a final scheming. I set a hand to my husband's shoulder, beside my son's hand.

"We go to Scone," I said firmly.

Constantine took charge quickly, organizing the journey, sending riders ahead to secure ships at the seacoast. Lulach sent his Norse guard with word for his father-in-law, Thorfin. We all knew Macbeth could not easily travel over land for any length of time. Water was the swiftest, kindest route for a man in such pain and difficulty. Bethoc, Finn, and I made him comfortable with a pallet and pillows, but he insisted on sitting up, leaned against some wooden chests. The ferryman skimmed his barge along the river, negotiating its winding turns and rocky stretches, and he and his poleman moved us efficiently enough.

Darkness fell early that day, given clouds and rain. By the time we reached deeper waters at the mouth of the river, we were enveloped in shadowing mists and gray light. A large and elegant longship awaited us, manned by twenty oarsmen from the loyal province of Buchan, and the new mormaer joined us, a young man who had fostered with Constantine. Assured of our friends, we soon picked up a swift wind and sailed south and west around the tip of Buchan and down toward the firth and mouth of the Tay.

The longship provided a fast, smooth transport, and Macbeth seemed to improve, sitting up, drinking a little wine. Though weak, he refused to lie down, said he could not breathe that way. I sat beside him on the pallet, legs tucked like a girl beneath me, and held his hand.

He did not speak often, for that, with impaired breathing, took effort. Before we left, Bethoc had obtained certain herbs from Constantine's wife, and she applied nettle poultices to the wound to stanch the bleeding—it seeped, would not stop, though we put pressure on it, though Bethoc and I both blessed it with charms of healing. She added willow and other herbs to his wine to help the pain, and we all shared the strong wine that Constantine had brought, needing a bolster of courage on that voyage.

Sallow and pale, he was, and quiet, and his eyes were too bright. "Straight to Scone," he told Constantine. "Pull into shore once along the coast of the Mearns to ask for riding messengers. Our old friend is dead who once led the Mearns, but his nephew is mormaer now, and a good man. Tell him the true king wants word taken to Scone to warn the priests of our arrival."

Whatsoever he asked, we did it. The journey was too long, and too brief. Though I did not want to leave his side, I had to speak to my son. Taking Lulach aside, away from the others, I told him the whole of what his stepfather wanted.

He said nothing, though I watched the path of his thoughts, the denying of it, as I had done, the reluctance—he did not want to be king, not at this cost—and finally a dawning acceptance. Nodding soberly, he went to sit with Macbeth. The two stayed alone, Lulach leaning forward, intent, while Macbeth spoke to him for a long while. Only they knew what was said then.

When Lulach left Macbeth's side to talk quietly with Ruari and the others, I went back to kneel beside my husband. He grimaced with pain and gave me a crooked smile.

"I should have put up my shield faster," he said.

"Hush you," I whispered. "Rest." He closed his eyes.

I went to stand in the prow of the boat, huddled in my cloak though I was not cold, and I watched the waves, felt the spray upon my hand where I set my fingers on the painted rim. Seabirds dipped overhead, and one sat on the high prow. I remembered a day when I had seen three ravens perched on a standing stone, and had felt a great dread of the future, in that very place. Lanfinnan, it was—where Macbeth finally met Malcolm.

And I thought back on my dreams and visions. All of them had pointed the way to this day—dreams of battles, of Macbeth facing a giant opponent, of Macbeth and our sons sailing west, as we did now, entering the firth. So it was in a way the final, mystical westward direction of the dreams.

Years before, I had seen a vision in a bowl of water on Enya's table. In that image, I stood with others in a longship that carried a dying king. We had taken Duncan's body by ship. But once again I rode a longship carrying a king who was wounded—dying, if I forced myself to see truth.

Looking at Lulach, my treasure, I caught my breath. When omens repeated, look for three, Enya had once told me. But Lulach—I could not bear to endure this a third time. My son took a great risk in agreeing to be crowned. We all did, in supporting Macbeth's scheme. The usurper would seek each one of us out with a vengeance. Retaliation is a dark and constant thread in the Celtic weave.

Watching the prow of the boat surge through lapping waves, I knew that I had protected Malcolm from retaliation. By honoring my promise to his mother and following my own heart as a mother, I had prevented his murder as a boy. And he had returned, just as the mormaers had warned. I had brought this tragedy about.

But if that chance came again, I could not order the deaths of children. A devil's bargain, that, to choose sin or grief. Closing my eyes,

I rested my face in my hands and struggled, overcame a weeping urge. What I had done had been most rightful, though it came with a hard price. It was the way of things.

As we entered the mouth of the Tay and swept over the water to Scone, I returned to Macbeth's side. I thought he was still sleeping, his breath raspy. Then he whispered my name. "Tell me that you understand why we must do this," he said.

I leaned toward him. "If you deem it necessary and it gives you peace, we will do it. Lulach will be crowned king as a precaution. Then you will rest, and recover." I would not speak of his death as a surety, though he seemed to accept it himself—and though I felt a knell of dread within. But I would not say so aloud.

"More than that," he said. "I will not die in the north, a wounded king with half a realm. I will die at Scone, rightful King of Scots."

I nodded. Pride and principle were always strong within him. He could not bear for his years of kingship to be diminished. I could not either. "I do understand."

"One thing more," he added. "I have the right to be buried at Iona with the kings who have gone before me. Malcolm will try to prevent it. Promise me you will see to it."

"I promise." That vow I would keep, be it days away, or years.

His fingers tightened over mine. We sat in silence, fingers clasped, with the lap of water and rushing wind around us, and our silent companions standing by.

I leaned down and kissed his brow, and rested my head against his own, and we rode to Scone nestled and silent, with the wind blowing us too fast.

Foggy darkness prevailed when we reached Scone, and we docked quietly, met by a group of monks summoned by fast riders from the Mearns. In stealth, we carried Macbeth on a litter up to the moot hill where he had sat so many times for courts, and for crowning.

Of that hour, I will say little. Some of what happened is for me alone.

Surrounded by that small and trusted company, Macbeth rested and watched as Lulach sat upon the *Lia-Fàil*. A priest set the red mantle upon his shoulders, and two more priests whispered furtive prayers in the misty dark. Then I lifted the gleaming crown over my son's golden hair and set it there to rest. *Power of wolf, power of raven, power of air, power of stone . . .*

I stepped back and turned.

Macbeth waited only to witness that. Just as I reached his side I heard it, the escape of the soul: a whisper, and gone.

Epilogue

I have missed morning prayers, as I sometimes do, having arrived at the great hall too late. Drostan is finishing the blessing, and now the others rise from knees to feet again. I suppose it is a sin to avoid group prayers, but God must know how fervently I pray, each day and often, to appeal for justice, remembrance, and peace for myself and the souls of the very dearly departed. And even some of the others.

A servant girl enters the room. "Lady," she says, hopping from one foot to the other, "the king and his party are arriving at the gates. King Lulach," she adds.

Quick, I run to the window, hearing shouts outside, and the peal of a ram's horn to announce an arrival. I throw open the shutter without waiting for a servant to do it for me. Tall as I am, I must stand on my toes to see over the sill. The winter air is sharp and cold, and I am smiling, waving. Visitors at last. No king's messenger this time, but a band of very welcome souls. I see my son, his sweet wife, their children, all bundled in furs on horseback.

Drostan and Bethoc are behind me as I run to the door and out, down the steps, gown lifting, veils flying, shoes slipping a little on hard-packed snow. Drostan takes my arm so I will not fall, and Bethoc stands to my other side. Ruari is with them, and he dismounts first, helping Lulach's consort from her horse. The king, my son, dismounts.

We are all stamping feet in the cold, arms crossed, frost with every breath. I hold out my arms for my grandson, the current mormaer of Moray. I kiss him and pull up his furry hood and scold him for letting it down in such cold. Nechtan scolds me in turn, laughing, for wearing no cloak myself. He is not even three years, and though he has the title of mormaer, he is interested only in the little wooden warriors that he keeps in a pouch and takes everywhere with him.

Then Ailsa, my granddaughter, so lovely at one year that she takes my breath away, a golden angel to rival any painted on a church wall. Her mother folds her into my arms, lightweight and snug in furs and wraps. Little Ailsa reaches for Lulach, and he takes her, then hands her to her nurse, a plain girl who has accompanied the royal family.

Ingebjorg comes to me, cloaked in red wool and fox fur, a handsome young woman, and we embrace with true warmth. The gift she brings to Scotland, the continued strength of the Orkney alliance, is very valuable to Lulach's reign. Fear of Vikings in ships helps keep Malcolm Canmore, the usurper king in the south, at bay.

We go to the hall quickly to escape the cold, the tips of our noses turning pink. We are laughing, and my family sits with me by the fire basket. The servant girls bring warmed spiced wine and baked apples, and hot milk with honey for the children. I am acting regent of Moray for my grandson Nechtan, and he likes to ask me how his province fares. It is a little game between us.

"Very well," I tell him. "Brimful of peace and plenty, and your people sing your praises. They say you are a wise and good leader." He smiles at that, though he does not understand.

I turn to our King Lulach, take his hand, and smile at his wife as well. The children play at our feet like little fairy folk. "Why have you come out in the cold to visit me here? Is there news from the south?"

"Not recently," Lulach says. "Malcolm Canmore has kept to his own business in the southern provinces, though I hear he is persistently after Macbeth's widow to marry him." He is frowning. "He sent word to me that if you act as peace weaver, we may negotiate a truce."

"Do not believe him," I warn. Lulach shakes his head. He does not.

"Let him pine after me and send gifts. He will thrash about when I refuse, but he will not come north so long as the winter weather holds."

"And by then," Lulach says, "I will have an army gathered. Despite the weather, my men have been traveling about, calling upon the loyalty of the provinces. Macbeth's memory is strong, Mother," he says. "They do not forget. They will follow my lead, and we will come against Malcolm once more, and finally, for the sake of Scotland."

My heart quails. I look away. Scotland will come to great change, and the young king may not prevail. I have seen something in water and flame, but I will say nothing of it, and pray that it will not be so.

Ruari enters the room, takes a seat, glances at Lulach. "Tell her," Lulach says.

"What is it?" I ask.

"It is done, Lady Rue, what you requested of us," Ruari says. "We returned just days ago from the west and Iona. Finn and I, with Giric and Mungo—Anselan, too. We made sure of it together."

I sit up, hands folded in my lap, fingers twisting. "He is at rest now?"

"On the brow of a hill beyond the chapel on Iona, interred with the other Scottish kings. You would be pleased with the peaceful spot chosen for him," Ruari says.

I draw a long, deep breath. "Thank you," I say. "In the spring, I want to visit."

"When spring comes, Mother," Lulach says, "I want you to move from Elgin to Craig Phadraig. It is farther north, and close to Inverness. We can better protect you there. Ingebjorg and the children will go there as well."

I nod, thoughtful. When spring comes, he will do the work of a king and ride against his enemy, the one who killed his stepfather. Lulach is not a vengeful soul, but he knows what is rightful, and what must be done. Even in his bright weave, there are dark threads.

"I will not go to Craig Phadraig with you," I say, deciding at last.

"Stay here at Elgin? I do not think it wise," my son the king says.

"I have had enough of moving from one household to another," I say. "I have had my fill of steel-games and gifts of silk and figs from usurpers and murderers. I am done with waiting, with fear and scheming, with wondering what the next messenger will say, and what must be the reply. And I do not want to endanger you further. I will leave."

"But where would you go?" Ingebjorg asks.

Macbeth's hound Diarmid sits at my feet, and I reach down to rub his head, thinking. Forming how to say what I must.

"There is a little house in a quiet cove on a northern shore," I say. "I will go there. You can find me whenever you like, but the usurper cannot. There is less danger to Ingebjorg and the children that way. You can send them into hiding at Craig Phadraig, or to Orkney for protection, without the risk of my presence."

"But, Mother—" Lulach begins.

"Canmore wants me. If he cannot marry me and link his blood to mine to strengthen his claim further, then he will have me killed, or harm those I love. For now, it is best if the dowager queen vanishes, while King Lulach tends to the enemy at the gates, as he must do."

They all watch me. I see comprehension dawning in their eyes. Lulach slowly nods. "Perhaps for a few months only, until we rout Malcolm Canmore once and for all, so that he can no longer worry Scotland."

"Of course," I say. "A few months." It will be far longer, I think, but I am a willing exile. There are some studies that I let go and wish to resume.

I am done with sorrow and intend to seek a little peace and magic. For now.

Lulach mac Gillcomgain Ardri Albain domarbhadh la
Maelcolaim meic Doncadh i Cath
(Lulach mac Gilcomgan, King of Scots, slain by
Malcolm mac Duncan in battle)

—*Annals of Ulster,* 17 March 1058

I n March 1058, Lulach mac Gilcomgan, the young King of Scots, perished in battle against Malcolm Canmore at Essie in Moray. The location indicates Malcolm's aggression in coming north; one of the
annals states "*do marbad . . . per dolum,*" or "slain with treachery." Later
sources refer to Lulach as "The Fool" or "The Simple"—epithets likely
attached during Malcolm Canmore's reign. At the time of his death,
Lulach was about twenty-six years old, and Macbeth had been dead
some seven months. Within days of Lulach's death, Malcolm Canmore
was crowned king. Soon after, he married an Ingebjorg, said to be
Norse, and perhaps either the widow or daughter of Jarl Thorfin of
Orkney. Possibly she was Lulach's own queen. Lulach's son, Malsnechtan, was relegated to a monastery; Lulach's daughter, whose name is
unknown, married a MacWilliam. She had a daughter named Gruaith,
or Gruadh. According to naming patterns common in early Scotland, it is
possible that this child was named for her maternal great-grandmother.

So little is known of Macbeth's queen that historians have drawn
conclusions based on the events and circumstances around her. A set of

documents from the Priory of Saint Andrews, charters of land donations between 1040 and 1057, provide her name and lineage: "Machbet filius Finlach . . . et Gruoch filia Bodhe, Rex et Regina Scotorum." Her father and therefore her royal line are identified, and she is accorded the title Queen of Scots here, in itself significant: she is full queen beside Macbeth, not consort.

While Lady Macbeth appears in one extant eleventh-century document, Macbeth is mentioned in several contemporary documents, mostly entries in annals written by Irish, Scottish, and Saxon monks. He is variously called Mac bethad mac Finlaech, Macbeth, Makbeth, Machbet, possibly even Magbjotr (in the *Orkneyinga Saga*), and "the king with the outlandish name," as one contemporary Saxon source refers to him. Spelling was a free-form art early on.

The name *Gruoch* is a bit of a puzzle. It appears in a single Latin document, and no Gaelic female name matches it. Possibly it was a cleric's phonetic attempt at a Gaelic original. Although historians have stuck with Gruoch, I wanted my fictional queen to have a more palatable version. Since Gruoch had a great-granddaughter named Gruaith or Gruadh, that settled the matter for me—it could have been the queen's own name, and perhaps even belonged to Lulach's daughter as well. Also, *Gruadh* has a precedent as a female name in Irish myth. Keeping the welfare of the reader in mind, I further shortened the name to "Rue."

Throughout the book, I did my best to simplify some challenging Celtic names wherever possible. Also, for consistency, I have usually used Scottish Gaelic in the text; in eleventh-century Scotland, Irish Gaelic was the norm, though even then it was transforming into the Scots version spoken today. Other languages that Scots could have encountered regularly in their own land included Latin, Norse dialects, and Saxon English. The verses that appear in the story are my own versions based on traditional Scottish verses, such as those collected by Alexander Carmichael in the late nineteenth century (*Carmina Gadelica*, Floris Books, Edinburgh, 1992).

Most of the major events in the novel are based on historical account, either events that definitely occurred, or could have occurred under the circumstances. Gruadh's first husband, Gilcomgan of Moray, died in 1032, trapped in a burning tower with fifty men at Burghead Sands. Perhaps the attack was orchestrated by the displaced Moray warlord Macbeth, about age twenty-seven then, acting alone or in cahoots with King Malcolm II, his maternal grandfather. Historians have assumed that Gruadh was probably married at about fifteen years old, placing her birth between 1015 and 1018. Lulach's birth in late 1032 to early 1033 implies that Gruadh married Macbeth following Gilcomgan's death, but before the birth. A victor immediately marrying his vanquished foe's widow was not uncommon in Celtic society; it gave protection for the widow and children, and instant kinship ties discouraged vengeful kinsmen from killing the groom.

Macbeth's marriage to Gruadh was clever and necessary. Her claim to the throne was the best in Scotland, yet her gender prevented her from ruling alone. Not long after their marriage, Bodhe and/or his son or grandson ("Mac mhic Bodhe" says the record, but the interpretation of the Irish differs) were murdered, possibly by order of King Malcolm II. Rather than destroying the line, this strengthened Gruadh's claim and that of her husband Macbeth, though after old Malcolm's death in a treacherous ambush, Duncan mac Crinan, another of his grandsons, became King of Scots according to primogeniture, a system still foreign to Scotland then. "King of Scots," as noted in the story, is the specific formal title, as is "Queen of Scots," for they were always considered rulers of people—not land.

Duncan was a warrior in his prime and something of a loose cannon. He took a foolish risk in going after the Orkney Vikings and Jarl Thorfin Sigurdsson. Even with capable Scottish ships, Duncan's forces were no match for dragon boats and Norse naval skills, and Jarl Thorfin was rumored by his contemporaries to possess magical knowledge; his description as dark, craggy, and tall in the *Orkneyinga Saga* is a common description given a wizard. Only a fool would have attacked that sea dragon repeatedly, enduring defeats and more than one saltwater dunking, yet Duncan came back for more. When he turned south to march on the Saxons, resulting in a horrifying defeat, his actions caught Scotland between two ferocious enemies. Scotland's warlords, including Macbeth, may have seen no choice but to stop their king.

Sources agree that Macbeth acted as a general for his cousin Duncan, and apocryphal tradition says that Duncan attempted to poison Macbeth, which is adapted in the novel. Medieval pharmacopoeia included the herb rue (*Ruta graveolens,* common rue, herb-of-grace), which was used as an antidote to poisons and herbal overdoses. It seemed fitting to produce that in the nick of time to save a warlord who must have survived all manner of dangers to reach the throne.

Macbeth and Duncan met in combat on Moray soil, whether it was battle or skirmish, in August 1040. Sources say Duncan was gravely wounded by Macbeth and taken to a nearby smithy at Pitgaveny—smiths were often the surgeons of their day—so it seemed logical that their fight would be hand-to-hand, and that Duncan would be surrounded in the smithy by a handful of comrades, including Macbeth and his warriors. Gruadh could easily have been there too, given the proximity of the field and the smithy to Elgin, Moray's main seat.

From a tiny bit of evidence, what can be surmised about Gruadh inghean Bodhe is fascinating. As a teenage girl raised in a warrior society, married to a great warlord, and destined to become queen if the men around her succeeded in their ambitions, and as a girl raised in a proud Celtic tradition that respected women's rights, she would have been tough, independent, and accorded some equality among males. Warrior women were common in Celtic myth and early society; eleventh-century Scotland was more Celtic and Dark Ages in its aspects than medieval. In fact, Scotland did not become truly medieval until Malcolm's queen, Margaret of England, influenced her adopted country with more European ways. In Macbeth's time, Scotland was still insular, provincial, and very Celtic. Gruadh would have been no stranger to weaponry and warrior practices, and only the tenets of the medieval Catholic Church—which still met resistance in the stubborn Celtic nature—would have prevented her from fighting.

She was a very young Lady of Moray and Queen of Scots, at first a teenager coping with enormous life issues, yet emotionally and physiologically still a developing girl. She became queen in her early twenties, and was around forty at the time of Macbeth's death. She was still alive in 1049 at the time of the land donations to the monastery at Loch Leven recorded in the Saint Andrews register, and likely she was alive in 1050 when Macbeth went on pilgrimage to Rome—the only medieval Scottish king to do so—where he reportedly scattered silver coins like seed, a magnanimous gesture on behalf of his small, fierce, proud country. Perhaps he wanted to curry papal favor, and perhaps he had personal sins to expunge—he may have killed two first cousins, Gilcomgan and Duncan, for the sake of his ambition, and for Scotland's sake.

That Macbeth and Gruadh never had heirs of their own may have given the king a need for a religious pilgrimage to have his sins forgiven. The question of Macbeth's children remains sadly unanswered; Gruadh had birthed one healthy son, at least. Some genealogies record a son, Fearchar, and another son born in the decade of the 1040s, but they apparently did not survive. A local tradition holds that "the sons of Macbeth" are buried near Kincardine O'Neil, although Lulach is buried on Iona. Macbeth appears to have given Lulach, his stepson and the son of his cousin and enemy, his blessing as heir to Moray; quite possibly, in a final act, he fostered Lulach's own kingship, as is suggested in the story.

Most striking and intriguing are the unspoken, unrecorded hints regarding Gruadh's marriage and relationship with Macbeth. The marriage was likely forced upon a young girl caught in brutal, tragic circumstances, yet the relationship seems to have been stable and respectful, at the least. Until the end of his life in August 1057, and over twenty-five years of a possibly childless marriage, Macbeth never set Gruadh aside in favor of a more fertile woman, as was often done when an heir was not produced. The mere fact that Macbeth left Scotland in 1050 for perhaps weeks or months indicates that Scotland was in capable and trusted hands; Gruadh would have acted as regent, with young Lulach and Macbeth's own war council supporting her. This suggests an atmosphere of peace and trust, not only in Scotland, but between Macbeth and his queen. The idea of Gruadh and others heading Malcolm Canmore off at a watery pass was my own, based on the possibilities.

Relative peace with the Vikings existed by then, and with Earl Siward of Northumberland and Crinan of Atholl defeated and deceased in the first part of Macbeth's reign, the only real threat was from young Malcolm Canmore and the Saxons who harbored and backed him. Malcolm's later foray into Scotland to claim his deceased father's throne was to end any halcyon years in Macbeth's Scotland. As for the seventeen years of Macbeth and Gruadh's reign, Scotland was described by an eleventh-century poet as "brimful east and west" with peace and prosperity.

Macbeth's death as depicted in the story differs from the long-standing historical record, which held that Macbeth and Malcolm Canmore met and clashed at least twice, first in 1054, when Macbeth forfeited part of Lowland Scotland to Canmore and retreated into Moray's mountain fastnesses, and again in August 1057—when Malcolm is said to have slain the king at Lumphanan, near Kincardine O'Neil, which I have called by its older name of Lanfinnan. Some accounts hold that Malcolm beheaded his longtime foe there to become rightful king himself. This discounts, above all, that Lulach reigned for seven short months.

The eleventh-century manuscript known as *The Prophecy of Berchán* gives a physical description of Macbeth, a rare gem in the historical record for any medieval king: "the tall, red, golden-haired one, he will be pleasant," it says of Macbeth. This long praise poem, written in Old Irish, is a chronicle disguised as prophecy. The verses were composed and written by more than one bard, cleric, and/or poet, each taking turns chronicling the Scottish kings while maintaining the "conceit" of a prophetic voice. Possibly the eleventh-century bard-scribe knew Macbeth personally, as the brief, intriguing reference to Macbeth's death implies an insider's knowledge of Macbeth's last day. Perhaps the bard was part of the king's household.

The Berchán poet says of Mac bethad mac Finlach: ". . . in the middle of Scone he will spew blood on the evening of a night after a duel." The theory that Malcolm killed Macbeth at Lumphanan is set a bit on its ear by this, and fascinating questions arise. If the lines are correct, then Malcolm would have wounded Macbeth at Lumphanan, with Macbeth surviving long enough to get away, and make it to Scone by the next day. What motivated such an effort, so that Macbeth met his death at Scone, rather than fifty-five miles north?

Benjamin Hudson, the translator of the Berchán poem and author of *Prophecy of Berchán: Irish and Scottish High-Kings of the Early Middle Ages* (Greenwood Press, 1996), suggests that Macbeth's motivation lay not only in his pride as High King of Scotland, but in the drive to do what was best for Scotland, while protecting his family. In part, the wounded, dying Macbeth strived to reach Scone so that Lulach could be rightfully crowned King of Scots on the Stone of Destiny itself, the stone being the king-maker. The right as crowners was held by the MacDuffs, as is known in later medieval history, such as the famous incident of the crowning of Robert Bruce by Isabella of Buchan. I merely assigned the first privilege to Gruadh, who was of that line through Bodhe.

Macbeth's further drive must have been to protect Queen Gruadh. Once he was gone—and he must have known he was dying to make such an effort—Gruadh would have been hunted by Malcolm Canmore, perhaps murdered for the value of the blood that had once placed her on the throne. Perhaps Macbeth knew that Canmore would have forced his vanquished foe's widow to marry him, as Macbeth had once done himself. The only way to keep her safe was to place her son on the throne as her king and protector. This also suggests that Macbeth felt sure that Lulach and Gruadh would have the backing of the warlords of Scotland. As his last act, Macbeth placed the welfare of Scotland, and the protection of each other, in the hands of his wife and stepson.

King Macbeth and King Lulach are buried in obscure graves on the island of Iona, where the rightful kings of Scots were laid to rest. Given Malcolm Canmore's vengeful nature, the existence of those graves is a remarkable testament to the loyalty of Macbeth's close followers.

The historical tale of Lady Macbeth and Macbeth, based on scholarly evidence, is a far cry from Shakespeare's wildly brilliant play. So it seems fitting to let Shakespeare have the last word: "For brave Macbeth—well he deserves that name . . ." (act 1, scene 1).

GLOSSARY

Pronunciation and Spelling: In Scottish Gaelic, "ch" is an aspirated sound, as in "loch;" "dh" is a soft "th" sound; and "bh," as in "dubh," is an "f" sound. Most of the Gaelic words given here are Scottish Gaelic; a few are Irish Gaelic, the language Lady Macbeth would have spoken.

Even today, Gaelic spelling can vary from one source to another; this is not a definitive list, but rather pertains to the novel. Also, for the purpose of fiction, some characters listed are invented, while the names and relationships of a few others have been slightly altered from their historical originals.

ROYALTY AND NOBILITY

Gruadh *(GROO-ath):* Full name is Gruadh inghean Bodhe mac Cineadh mhic Dubh ("Gruoch" in Latin documents); daughter of Bodhe mac Cineadh; wife first of Gilcomgan and then of Macbeth; mother of Lulach; and Queen of Scots. Born ca. 1015–1018, and crowned queen in 1040; later dates unknown.

Macbeth: Full name, Mac bethad mac Finlach; mother Donada, daughter of King Malcolm II; cousin of Gilcomgan and Thorfin; mormaer of Moray; served as military general for Malcolm II and later King Duncan; King of Scots from August 17, 1040, to August 17, 1057; born ca. 1006.

Bodhe *(BO-deh):* Bodhe mac Cineadh mhic Dubh (son of Kenneth III son of Duff); father of Gruadh; a prince of Scotland and mormaer of Fife; died ca. 1033.

Finlach mac Ruari *(FIN-lach mac Rohr-ree):* Macbeth's father; married Donada, daughter of Malcolm II; mormaer of Moray; died in 1020, killed by his Moray nephews.

Ailsa of Argyll: Gruadh's mother of Irish and Scottish descent; died in childbirth

Malcolm mac Farquhar mhic Bodhe: grandson of Bodhe; killed by order of King Malcolm II, 1033.

Malcolm II: Mael Coluim mac Cineadh (Kenneth II); cousin to Bodhe; grandfather to Macbeth and Duncan; called *Forranach,* the Destroyer; ruled Scotland from 1005 to November 1034, when he was ambushed by Scots.

Gilcomgan mac Malbríd *(Ghil-COM-gan mac MAHL-bree):* First husband of Gruadh; cousin to Macbeth; mormaer of Moray before Macbeth; in 1032, he burned to death with fifty of his men, trapped in a tower at Burghead Sands.

Lulach *(LOO-lach):* Son of Gruadh and Gilcomgan; born 1032 or 1033, he ruled as King of Scots after Macbeth, from August 1040 to March 1058; killed by Malcolm Canmore.

Crinan: Lay abbot of Dunkeld; mormaer of Atholl; father of Duncan and grandfather of Malcolm Canmore; died in battle against Macbeth ca. 1045.

Duncan mac Crinan: Son of Crinan and grandson of King Malcolm II; king of Cumbria and Strathclyde; King of Scots; died in combat against Macbeth on August 16 or 17, 1040.

Lady Sybilla: Anglo-Saxon wife of Duncan mac Crinan (later King Duncan); daughter of Siward of Northumberland; mother of Malcolm Canmore, Donald Bán, and two others.

Malcolm Canmore: Ceann Mór, "big head" or perhaps "great ruler"—son of King Duncan, grandson of Malcolm II, cousin of Macbeth; also called Malcolm mac Duncan; born ca. 1030 and ruled Scotland from 1058 to 1093.

Thorfin Sigurdsson: Son of Sigurd of Orkney; grandson of Norwegian king and of Malcolm of Moray; jarl of the Orkney Islands and Caithness; called Raven-Feeder, father of Ingebjorg; carried a raven-design banner said to be magical; died ca. 1064.

Ketill Brusisson: Thorfin's nephew.

Enya: Thorfin's grandmother; Eithne, the Irish princess who married Sigurd of Norway; mother of Sigurd of Orkney; famous for creating the raven banner whose magic protected both Sigurds and Thorfin in battle.

Ingebjorg *(INGA-byorga):* Daugher of Thorfin; wife of Lulach.

Nechtan *(NEK-tun):* Malsnechtan, son of Lulach, grandson of Gruadh; born ca. 1056, died a monk, 1085.

Farquhar *(FAR-kwar):* In Gaelic, the name is Fearchar; Gruadh's brother; also her deceased son.

HOUSEHOLD CIRCLES:
KINFOLK, RETAINERS, SERVANTS, AND OTHERS

Drostan: Childhood friend and monk; also Drostan mac Colum; descended of the "kin of Saint Columba"

Aella *(Ella):* Gruadh's Saxon maidservant; wife of Giric

Bethoc *(BETH-ock):* Gruadh's cousin and a healer in the household

Mairi *(MAH-ree):* Bethoc's mother and a healer

Maeve *(Mev):* Gruadh's nurse or "knee-woman"

Dolina: Bodhe's mistress and wife

Dermot mac Conall: Bard and astrologer in Moray

Father Anselm: Anglo-Saxon priest and member of Bodhe's household

Fergus mac Donal: Warrior at Abernethy, Bodhe's household; father of the warriors Ruari, Angus, Conn, and Brendan mac Fergus

Finn mac Nevin: Foster son of Bodhe; childhood friend of Gruadh; blacksmith at Pitgaveny; Macbeth's retainer

Ruari *(Rohr-ree)* **mac Fergus:** Son of Fergus, a warrior in Bodhe's house, and later one of Macbeth's elite guard

Angus mac Fergus: Redheaded son of Fergus; warrior under Bodhe, then Macbeth

Mungo mac Calum: One of Macbeth's retainers

Dubh mac Dubh: Known as Duff mac Duff, or Black Duff; Gruadh's cousin

Cu *(Coo):* A gray wolfhound

Constantine mac Artair: Thane of Banchorrie in Angus; uncle of Macbeth

Catriona of Kinlossie *(Kah-TREE-oh-na):* Widow, healing woman; cousin and mistress of Macbeth

TERMS

Abernethy: In Fife, the home of Bodhe and Gruadh

A Dhia *(Ah Je-ah):* Expression, "Oh God"

Aqua vitae: Water of life (see "uisge beatha")

Ard Rí Alban *(Ard Ree AL-bhan)*: High King of Scots ("Alba" is an ancient term for Scotland.)

cuaran *(kwar-AN)*: Soft leather shoe

ban-rí *(ban-REE)*: Queen

ban-sìth *(ban-SHEE)*: Fairy woman

Brigid *(BRI-jid)*: Celtic goddess of healing, childbirth, creative work; also Brigid

cailleach *(KAY-leach)*: Old woman

Celt, Celtic *(KEL-tic)*: The ancient term for Irish and Scots as a group (in some contexts this includes Welsh, Cornish, Breton, etc.); in Ireland and Scotland, also "Gaels"

Céli Dé *(KEL-eh-DAY)*: Known as the Culdees or Keledi; the monks of the Celtic Church

Da Shealladh *(da SHEE-lah)*: Means "two sights," as in Second Sight

deiseil *(dee-SEAL)*: A pattern of walking in a sunwise circle, from left to right

dun: A fortress, as in Dun Elgin, Dun Abernethy

dux bellorum: A general, later a "grand duke"

Elgin *(EL-ghin)*: Main fortress of the mormaers of Moray

fathach *(FATH-ach)*: A prophet

Gabhran *(GAHV-run)* and **Lorne** *(LORN)*: The ruling branches in Celtic Scotland

hauberk: Chain mail garment, like a mail tunic

housecarl: From the Norse *hus-karl,* house man or house guard; bodyguard

garron: Small, tough Highland pony

ghillie *(GHILL-ee)*: Servant

Lia-Fàil *(lee-ah FA-eel)*: Stone of Destiny

Lanfinnan: Ancient name for Lumphanan, Scotland; site of Macbeth's combat with Malcolm Canmore

lux mundi: Latin for "light of the world"

Rí a Moreb *(Ree ah MOR-ayv)*: King of Moray

Samhain *(sa-VAHN)*: All Saints' Eve or Halloween

Sassenach *(SAHS-un-ach)*: Saxon or English

Scathach *(SKY-ach)*: In Celtic myth, a princess who ran a school of martial arts

seanchaidh *(SHEN-key)*: Storyteller and keeper of wisdom

seanchaidhean *(Shen-KEY-en)*: Plural form of *seanchaidh*

Sgian *(SKEE-an)*: Small blade, also the original name for the town of Scone

Sìtheach *(SHEE-ach)*: Fairy ilk

Slàinte *(SLAHN-chuh)*: "To your health" or "cheers"

Taibhsear *(tay-sher)*: A seer or psychic

Tanáise: "Tanist" in English. An appointed royal heir, rather than a lineal descent heir

Tír na n'Óg *(Teer-na-NOG)*: Legendary paradise in Irish myth

uisge beatha *(OOSH-ke-vah)*: Water of life (later became whisky)